MW00830279

A PILE OF BODIES, A PILE OF HEADS

Let the Bodies Hit the Floor Volume 2

PRESENTED BY SINISTER SMILE PRESS

A PILE OF BODIES, A PILE OF HEADS

Let the Bodies Hit the Floor Volume 2

PRESENTED BY SINISTER SMILE PRESS

EDITED BY R.E. SARGENT, STEVEN PAJAK, & BRIDGETT NELSON

A Pile of Bodies, A Pile of Heads
Let the Bodies Hit the Floor Volume 2

Edited by R.E. Sargent, Steven Pajak, & Bridgett Nelson

Published by Sinister Smile Press
P.O. Box 637
Newberg, OR 97132

Trade Paperback ISBN – 978-1-953112-16-3

www.sinistersmilepress.com

"I've lived in darkness a long time. Over the years, my eyes adjusted until the dark became my world and I could see."

-Dexter Morgan

CONTENTS

FINDING GOD

LP Hernandez

OST DEAD BOYS DON'T GIVE MUCH consideration to how they're going to die. They plummet headfirst toward catastrophe, smiling with the wind in their face. Elementary schools are thick with dead boys, usually one or two each grade. The boys with chewed pencils and perpetual thousand-yard stares. They daydream of digging holes, of cemeteries, and tall trees with hefty branches. Scabby-kneed and always out of breath, they run hard, but not fast, toward their caskets.

Some dead boys are led to their deaths by a taller, faster, reckless friend, the aforementioned scabby-kneed type. Often, dead boys come in pairs. One is brutish and loud, the other meek and shy, prone to collapsing on himself, after years of being poked in the belly, or jabbed in the ribs, at the tail-end of a joke at his expense. They run together, one following in the shadow of the other, both racing toward the same destination.

Daryl and Jake established their roles early in life. Born two months apart and three houses away from one another, their friendship was inevitable. Settling into their roles took a little longer to figure out. Jake gravitated toward books as Daryl invaded emergency rooms and urgent care clinics almost monthly, byproducts of his lust for high places. Without Jake, Daryl would likely have been dead before his tenth birthday. Without Daryl, Jake would have fallen into one of his books and never emerged.

It was early July in central Alabama, a part of the state no one ever moves to on purpose. Between Montgomery and Birmingham, it's mostly pine trees, gas stations, and peach-themed restaurants. The summer between elementary and junior high didn't feel much different than any other summer. Jake, sweat stinging his eyes and skin sizzling like bacon on a skillet, pedaled with the devil at his heels. Daryl maintained a ten-foot distance in front of his friend without ever looking over his shoulder, as if the front tire of Jake's bike, and the back tire of Daryl's, were magnets with the same poles. No matter how hard his legs pumped, Jake came no closer.

"How…far…is…" Jake huffed, unable to complete the question.

"Not far," Daryl said, again, as he had ten minutes before.

Jake swallowed his next words and then spat onto the clay. His lazy Wednesday had been interrupted by a panting Daryl slapping his bedroom window.

"What?! What is it?" Jake asked.

"You've gotta come, bro!" Daryl yelled, and he would say no more.

Jake, legs numb from sitting, stumbled out of his house like a groundhog crawling from the earth, the sun shrinking his eyes to slits. Daryl was already pedaling down the street, and Jake, with needles in his toes, mounted his bike to play his part in the ritual.

The path was unfamiliar but looked no different than the dozens of other logging roads crisscrossing the county. Jake wondered what dead animal Daryl found. It would have to be big, bigger than a deer, to make Daryl so giddy. Maybe an alligator. That would be cool, but it was a bit too dry in that part of Alabama for alligators.

Daryl skidded to a stop, throwing a spray of clay and pebbles ahead of him. A paved road carved through swaths of pine trees, still a few years from the paper mill. Jake pulled up next to Daryl and frowned at the broken asphalt.

"Where does it go?" Jake asked.

"My dad told me about this place. He said it was big news a few years back. We were probably in diapers then."

"But what is it?"

"Come on. I haven't seen it yet. I wanted to save it for you."

They rode side-by-side, the sweat on their brows like melted ice cream in the shade of the trees.

"Dad said it was supposed to be a place for rich folks. They were gonna build golf courses and make a lake big enough for boats," Daryl said.

"Yeah?"

"But everything went to shit when the market crashed, whatever that means, and they stopped building."

"Why would they build out here? There's nothing to do."

"Dad said it would mostly be part-timers. Folks who come down in the winter to get away from the cold. From here to the airport is only like thirty minutes. They were even gonna build a road to the interstate, but…"

The boys crested a hill, and then the trees fell away, and their bikes crunched to a stop in unison.

"Alabaster Estates…" Jake said, squinting at the sun-bleached sign.

"Grand opening 2010," Daryl added with a chuckle.

There was a guard shack in a median dividing inbound and outbound traffic. Two concrete barriers blocked the lanes, seemingly as an afterthought, both slightly askew and not centered.

"Not much good without fencing," Daryl said, nodding toward the barriers.

"Yeah…" Jake said, his eyes scanning tire-wide strips of flattened grass circumventing them.

"Let's check it out!" Daryl said, rousing the magnets in their bikes as he hopped the curb.

"Wait!"

The asphalt was broken into irregular pixels by encroaching foliage, cracks widening to tire-snatching culverts. Knee-high anthills, quivering with vicious black and red bodies, straddled the road. Other than the boys, the ants seemed to be the only life in the immediate vicinity. There were no grating insects, just an occasional bird song that could have come from fifty feet, or five miles, away.

"Look at that!" Daryl said, slowing.

"Wow, they just left it all, huh?" Jake said.

They pedaled slowly then, their gazes directed at a dozen mini-mansions in various stages of completion or destruction. Red brick and white columns were the dominant aesthetic among the finished houses. Nature and the elements had begun the slow process of disassembly years prior, spotting the white columns with mold, fragmenting the mortar with black capillaries. Some houses were wooden skeletons, one thunderstorm away from collapse.

"There's still glass!" Daryl said and tossed his bike to the asphalt as if it was on fire.

He sprinted for the nearest rock, which burned his palm, though he hardly noticed. He grunted as he threw, but the missile missed its mark, bouncing harmlessly off the red brick. Jake looked toward the guard shack, which was hidden from view by the rise in the landscape.

"Are you sure?" he asked.

"Bro, there's no one here. This place is abandoned."

Daryl hunted for another rock as Jake propped his bike on its kickstand. He recalled the flattened grass bypassing the concrete barriers, wondering if Daryl had seen it or even cared. Probably, it was nothing. Just someone being curious. He jammed his hands into his pockets so they wouldn't pick up a rock of their own accord and walked away from Daryl, whose second throw missed a window by a couple of feet.

"Rats!" Daryl yelled.

Jake sauntered up the brittle driveway to a skeleton house. Its concrete slab was furry with grass, the wood blistered by the sun. He jolted at the sound of glass shattering, which was punctuated by a shout of *fuck, yeah!* Jake paused, lips twisted to one side of his face, as he considered the house next door. It appeared to be complete, at least the façade. Like the other houses, time and weather had taken a toll, but this one *felt* different. Jake could not have labeled it if he tried, but the feeling was far more interesting than the collection of beams to his left.

PING!

Jake flinched again as he crossed the grass of what would have been a sizeable yard, half an acre at least. There was a restaurant in town, Jim's, which closed its doors after about forty years in business. It was a town institution, but institutions need money to function, and there wasn't enough of it flowing through Jim's, with an increasing number of its clientele dependent on Social Security. Jake noticed how quickly the building appeared abandoned. Almost as if the mere presence of people kept the inevitable at bay. Within a week, one of its charming green shutters was partially dislodged. The bushes beneath the windows grew wild almost instantly. After a month, it was difficult to recall the parking lot ever being full.

Jake stood at the front door, his hands liberated but bunched into fists. The house didn't feel abandoned the way Jim's did. It felt different than every other house on the street, regardless of the state of construction.

"What is it?" Daryl asked, smearing sweat and dirt across his brow. He tossed the rock in his hand over his shoulder.

"I don't know. Something about this house. It's like someone's actual house, you know? Like someone's living here, or was."

Daryl viewed the house with different eyes. The front door was enticing. He had always wanted to kick a door down like they did in the movies. The porch lights would be good substitute practice for milk bottles when the fair came through town. He retreated a step as if preparing to run, but the door squealed open.

"Whoa!" Jake said. "I didn't think it would be unlocked."

Daryl barreled past his friend. "Let me see!"

The air inside felt hotter than outside, likely due to the lack of circulation. The smell of paint and sawdust burned away over time, leaving only a faint chemical odor, which tickled the nostrils. There was a dining room to the immediate left and a living room at the end of the foyer. Instead of light fixtures, cords sprouted from the ceiling.

"Damn, there's no lights," Daryl muttered.

Jake took the left and found nothing more interesting than dangling cords in the dining room. He stopped when he crossed the threshold into the kitchen, his breakfast cereal surging to the back of his throat.

"Daryl!" he whisper-shouted.

Daryl entered the kitchen through the living room. He followed Jake's gaze to the can of Mountain Dew resting on the kitchen island.

"Psshh. It's nothing. Just something left behind by the builders."

Jake nodded and entered the room. He approached the can while Daryl searched for things to destroy. A toilet handle rattled in an adjacent room followed by the sound of ceramic scraping.

"Gross!" Daryl said.

Jake lowered his ear, so that it hovered just above the mouth of the can. Then he gasped and backed away, as if

7

there was a cottonmouth inside.

"D-Daryl…"

Ceramic scraped, once again, in the bathroom and Daryl emerged, dusting off his hands.

"What?"

Jake pointed, unable to speak.

"What, the can? Probably builders, like I said."

Jake shook his head. "No. It's still fizzy. You can hear it."

Daryl frowned and grabbed the can.

"Oh yeah," he said.

"Don't you know what that means?"

Daryl's face went blank.

"Someone was just here. Mountain Dew goes flat pretty quick."

Daryl nodded and scratched the peach fuzz outlining the approximate area of a future beard.

"Let's look around. See what else we can find."

Jake's lips puckered like a fish on land, but he followed Daryl out of the kitchen into the living room.

"What's that?" Daryl said, jogging to the sliding glass door leading into the backyard.

Jake stood beside him and said, "A generator."

"Hmm…"

Daryl unlocked the sliding glass door and opened it. The searing breeze was a respite from the stagnant, swamp air of the house. Daryl walked to the generator, then picked up the electrical cord and followed its length, coming to a stop at a small window mostly hidden by grass.

"Goes to the basement," Daryl said, dropping the cord and angling for the door.

"Wait...we're not..."

"You don't have to come if you don't want to."

Jake massaged his hands, eyes fixed on the darkened basement window. It always came to moments like this. Sometimes, he successfully led Daryl away from the precipice. Other times, he simply followed and did his best to mitigate the damage.

"Wait!" Jake said.

"IT'S DIFFERENT THAN the others," Daryl said, tapping the doorknob.

Jake glanced at a nearby closet door, which had an ornate knob the color of old pennies. So did the bathroom.

"Like it was added later," Jake said.

"And a deadbolt. Why would you need a deadbolt for a basement?" Daryl said.

"No good reason I can think of. Can we leave?"

Daryl slid the deadbolt and turned the doorknob. The door screamed open, and both boys backpedaled from the stench.

"Jesus!" Jake said, hiding his nose inside of his shirt.

"Ugh! Something rotten down there. Maybe a possum got in," Daryl added.

The stairs disappeared into shadow, but there was murky light at the base.

"Daryl, I think we should leave. Someone's been here, and that smell is awful."

"So?"

"So, whoever it is wasn't bothered by it, or maybe they caused it!"

"You don't have to come."

Daryl took a step into the basement, his nose buried in the crook of his elbow. It was sauna-damp, but cooler. His body rippled with goosebumps as he grasped the banister, which was so wet he could not guess its composition. Light sounds from the basement rose above the level of his breathing. He pictured glistening rats fleeing for holes chewed through walls.

"Daryl!"

Jake took a step toward the front door, meaning to lock it, but he stopped at the sound of Daryl coughing.

"Daryl, wait!"

Jake closed the basement door as he walked through it. Beyond the gray haze at the bottom of the stairs, he was blind. He grasped the slippery banister, the back of his tongue tasting like sweetened milk.

"Daryl? What is it?" Jake said, responding to the noise from the basement floor. It sounded as if Daryl was stepping on a tarp.

"I don't know. Can't see. Hold on, the window's across the way."

Daryl took exaggerated steps to avoid crimps and lumps in whatever material was beneath his feet. He winced, hip-checking the corner of something hidden in darkness, and stood beneath the window. One jump. Two jumps. He grabbed the cardboard wedged in the rectangular space and plucked it free. Jake reached the basement floor as Daryl turned around to see what the light revealed.

For a moment, neither understood what he saw. The tarp was actually opaque plastic sheeting running all the way up the walls. There were buckets and tools around, and shelves, in ghost silhouette form, behind the plastic.

"What...is...that?" Jake said, pressing his back to the nearest wall, plastic crinkling as he did.

While Jake was repelled, Daryl was drawn to...it.

"Jesus Christ," Daryl said, placing a hand on his belly.

There was a dead man on the table in the center of the room. Both of his arms ended in stumps, as did one of his two legs. The crude stitch-work revealed these were not birth defects but recent, deliberate wounds. He was naked, the area around his crotch mostly shadowed, but Daryl saw enough to guess what might have happened there. His stomach rebelled at the thought, the sight, and the stench leaking from infected wounds, the yellow pulp bubbling through the shoddy stitching.

"It's a f-f-uckin-n dead guy," Jake said, inching toward the stairs.

Daryl crossed the few feet to the table, eyes watering. It wasn't like he thought it would be, seeing a dead body for the first time. There was nothing *cool* about what happened to this man. It was vile and violent. And worse upon inspection.

Two vacant sockets aimed at the ceiling, forever unblinking as the eyelids were also missing. Above and below the concavities, the skin was blotched with black crust. The same film coated the lips and chin of the dead man, the inky void of his mouth indicating this was a consequence of missing teeth. A spiny worm probed the dead man's bottom lip and then retreated into the mouth.

11

Daryl screamed, realizing it was not a worm but a blunted tongue, and the spines were more poor stitching.

"He's alive!"

The man, who was not dead, twitched and turned his head to the side, revealing a clogged ear canal. Too dark in the room to guess the material. Could have been glue or candle wax.

"Fuck, he's alive!" Daryl said, two hands then pressed to his stomach.

"We gotta call the cops. We can't stay here," Jake said, and though he felt like running, his shoes were melted to the plastic beneath them.

Jake scanned the rest of the room, eyes slowly adjusting to the darkness. There were shapes behind the plastic, instruments mounted to the wall. Shelves with jars and toolboxes. He looked to his friend, hoping to see his terror mirrored. Although there was concern on Daryl's face, there was no terror. Dead boys don't give much consideration to how they're going to die. The possibility a high, thin branch might snap under his bouncing weight. The consequences are far removed from the action, but at that moment, the consequences of some unknown action quivered on a table, in the basement of an abandoned house, far from any comfort.

"Can you hear me?" Daryl said softly.

The man on the table breathed in shallow gasps.

"Can you——"

Daryl's question was cut off as the man moaned, and blood and piss sprayed from the blackened ruins between his legs. It issued as both a stream and a mist, pitter-pattering on the plastic. The odor was like rusty nails in a bucket of seawater. The man writhed, wincing, chest filled with dry rags. Shackles hanging from the table rattled from his movement.

"We have to go!" Jake said.

He did not have the courage to come any closer, to drag Daryl up the stairs, could not will his legs to do anything more than keep his body upright. Daryl nodded but took no action. He licked his lips and stared at the squirming figure, but there was no instinct to pursue, no thought to chase.

"Why is he here?" Daryl asked.

"What do you mean? What does it matter?! We have to go!" Tears spilled, silver ladybugs tracing the cherubic swells of Jake's cheeks. The stench, the sound of the man's agony, was too much. His childhood innocence collected in a poisonous puddle in the plastic around the table.

"You want to leave him?" Daryl said, finally tearing his gaze away.

Jake threw up his hands.

"I want to get away from here! We can call for help from home. What if whoever did this to—"

The man on the table wiggled the stumps of his arms and moaned from deep in his chest. His mouth opened and closed, the lips forming letters he did not speak. He might have been praying, and Jake could think of only one prayer a man in his condition would want realized.

"He's afraid," Daryl said.

"Wouldn't you be?" Jake cried, hand grasping the banister.

Daryl shook his head. "No, it—it's different."

There was a rumble, like a thunderstorm, too far

away to matter. Jake's eyes shot to the door as Daryl cocked his head to the side. The man on the table mewled, maybe feeling the vibrations. The sound of the car door slamming might as well have been a knife through Jake's heart. His knees loosened, pulled to the floor in opposite directions. His grip on the banister prevented him from collapsing, but his perspective shrank to a pinhole, sounds muffled as if he was underwater.

"S-someone's c-coming back," Jake said, the words like cotton balls in his mouth.

Daryl dashed fifteen feet across the room and grabbed Jake by the shoulders.

"Hide! You need to hide! We can't hide together. He'll find us. Get behind the plastic!" Daryl hissed.

The front door opened.

Jake allowed himself to be led through a seam in the sheeting. He crouched between two shelves, and Daryl tucked the plastic around him, and then crossed the room to find his own hiding place. The front door of the house screeched open. The sound of boots on tile was suddenly the loudest thing either boy had ever heard.

Whistling followed and then a husky voice ad-libbing forgotten lyrics to a hymn.

Meet you in the mornin'...da da bright riverside,
Da da da da
Standin' at the portal da da gates open wide,
At th' close of life's long, weary day...

The door to the basement opened, and the singing turned to humming. Jake pressed his back against the warm, slick masonry, willing his body to pass through it to the outside. Across from him, Daryl gripped a broken brick, the closest thing to a weapon he could find.

Meet you in the mornin'…

The stairs popped, and the man on the table mewled again.

…bright riverside…

The plastic sheeting growled, and both boys gnashed their molars together, their bodies like tightly wound guitar strings.

"Two bicycles in the middle of the road, huh? How strange, out here where no one should be. What do you make of that, Mr. Fred?"

The woman was the approximate size of a refrigerator, with squared shoulders and a tree trunk of a neck, wider than the head it supported. Daryl had not expected a woman's voice, weathered or otherwise. Despite his fear, he strained for a better look. Out of her line of sight for the moment, he peeked through the tiniest gap in the sheeting but saw only the toes of her boots.

"Two bicycles and no little boys to accompany."

She walked farther into the room, eyes shifting left to right. The lack of light muted the color of her blouse, the yellow rulers and red apples turned gray.

"Imagine if they found you. They might have some questions, I bet. Probably think I'm a nut, huh? Leaving you like this. It isn't pretty. But it's only part of the process. You get that. Don't you, Mr. Fred?"

She stood in a puddle of his waste, eyes still shifting left to right. A textbook-sized hand gripped the man's thigh, just above the wound, and squeezed. The skin bulged at the seams of the stitching, thick blood and puss erupting like soft cheese through a grater. The man rocked like a beetle on its back, the pain concentrated in his throat as a high-pitched whistle. She strutted around the table to the man's head. He shrank away from her touch as she stroked his steel wool hair.

"What do you see, Mr. Fred? I wonder if it's the same thing I saw. What do you hear? Maybe you can't see or hear it yet. Maybe we need to dull the senses some more. I think the generator's low on fuel, and I ain't dressed for it, but we could make do. Think there's a saw on the shelf right over there," she said, looking to her left, where Jake crouched behind the sheeting.

From his perspective, she was a hulking silhouette, backlit by the small window. Her only recognizable feature was a pile of faintly glowing curls. Jake thought she must have heard his heart. It was beating so fast, there was no way she did not hear it. Sweat speckled his brow and tickled his nose. Would she hear if it fell?

Daryl slowly passed the brick to his dominant hand. It felt like baseball, when he was waiting for the pitch. No thoughts in his mind. Just anticipating the muscle memory.

She took a step toward Jake but stopped and turned back to the man on the table.

"I bet they could see! Oh, yes, I bet they could. I was only eight when I saw God the first time, when He spoke to me. What a gift it was! What an absolute gift, Mr. Fred!"

Her hand clamped over his mouth and nose. He lifted his arm stumps to defend himself, thrashed his head with the little energy he could muster. Daryl licked his lips but stayed hidden. The brick was light in his hand, but smothering the man to death would have been a mercy, and he did not wish to interfere. After a minute, she removed her hand and the man, Fred, gasped.

"Daddy used to do that to me sometimes. Then I'd wake up in the closet with new hurts. Like this one." She passed her left hand into the shaft of light from the window. The pinkie was broken in a forty-five-degree angle. Her voice was childlike, eyes cloudy with memory.

She shook her head and dabbed at a tear in her eyes. "It took years before I met God, though. That's why I put you on the *accelerated* program, Mr. Fred. This isn't about your body. It's about your soul. Your body...it-it just roots you to this place. The noise and distractions. You can't hear God with all that noise, Mr. Fred. I learned that in the closet, in the dark. That's where I met God. Daddy roughed me up pretty good, think my arm was broken that time. Kept falling asleep and waking up. Felt like I was stuck on a merry-go-round. Couldn't catch a roach to eat with my arm broke, and that was about all the food I had in the closet. Think I was *just* on this side of death when God spoke to me. It's all I ever needed, Mr. Fred. I-I've been so lucky to bring God to so many people."

She surveyed the room again and then loomed over the torso, frowning.

"How could you not believe in God, Mr. Fred? How could you not believe me when I told you I *heard* Him! I heard Him! I've seen Him! Where did all of this come from, if not from God?" she asked, gesturing to various points in the room, while indicating the world beyond it.

She clamped a hand around the thin, sagging skin of his belly. "Why, it makes me just want to rip you apart, you know that? I-I don't want to cause you pain, Mr. Fred, but it's part of the process. How else will you seek Him, if not to escape the pain?"

She squeezed, and Fred whimpered, blood and spit gurgling in his throat.

"I've done it before, you know. I've ripped someone apart with just my hands. She didn't cry out to God at the end, couldn't really, but I know she found Him. I know she went to the Lord with a willing heart."

The woman stood on tiptoe and shifted all of her weight to the heel of her palm, pressing until she felt the ridges of his spine. Fred cried and coughed, and then the room filled with worse smells.

"Do you hear Him, Fred? C-can you see Him now? He's on the other side of the pain you're feeling. Just on the other side of it. You just gotta call to Him, Mr. Fred! It's easy. Like peeling a banana."

The whimper trickled through Jake's lips before he realized it was coming. He gritted his teeth, heartbeat like machine-gun fire in his ears. He heard only his heart, nothing else, nothing in the room, nothing outside of his own skull. The giantess released the pressure on Fred's belly. She smiled on one side of her face showing ragged, gray teeth, like a handful of pulverized concrete. Jake shrank into as small a shape as he could manage, willing her to overlook him.

Instead, she leaned over, hands resting on her knees, and peered through the plastic. "You must be the boy with the missing bike, huh? Where's your friend? Do you boys believe in God?"

Jake snapped his eyes shut and held his breath.

"You *do* believe in God, don't you?" she asked, voice hovering between concern and anger.

She came closer, her breath fogging the plastic, suddenly excited. "I can sh-show Him to you. If you don't believe, that is. I'm real good at it."

Slaver leaked out the side of her mouth, and she licked her lips. She pawed the plastic, searching for the seam.

"I'll start with your pinkie. How 'bout that? Just a pinkie like Daddy did?"

Her plump, blunted fingers appeared above Jake's head.

"Just a pinkie for God? That's a fair deal, huh? Maybe both pinkies, a couple of fingers."

She groped blindly, nearly grazing the crown of his head.

"Then you can live a full life like me. It's such a gift to know God so young. Unlike poor Mr. Fred. He's got all these years behind him, years of lies. Been a tough nut to crack."

Her fingers briefly grasped his hair.

"But, sometimes, tough nuts have the sweetest meat inside."

Jake shrieked as a handful of hair was ripped from his head, like weeds from soft earth. The woman stood erect and slapped at the small of her back where the brick struck. Daryl was already on the hunt for something bigger to throw. He tore down plastic sheeting and rifled through the items on the shelf.

"Paint brushes, paint brushes, fuck!" he hissed.

Daryl found a hammer, but it had a rubber head and,

considering the size of the woman, might have annoyed, rather than incapacitated, her. He heard plastic shifting behind and knew time was running out. He grasped the handle of a can of paint and hoisted it.

"You little devil!" she screamed, hands turned to claws.

Daryl hurled the can toward her stomach, but the rusted handle snapped, and the can sailed harmlessly across the room. She seethed, spittle sparking off her lips. Between the rumpled, denim columns of her legs, Daryl saw Jake emerge from the plastic. He had that look he got when he was in over his head. Daryl knew his friend was on autopilot, that he was no longer a wingman but an anchor. He also knew Jake would not have come if not invited, would have left the abandoned house if given the option, and would never have entered the basement. Her terrible, powerful hands trembled, eyes burning white through shadows.

"Run, Jake!"

He did not act, barely seemed to hear the words directed at him. The man on the table rolled his head to the side. Had his eyes not been removed, he would have been staring at Jake. Black pudding purled from his lips.

"Run, Jake! You have to run!"

To glance over her shoulder required the woman to shift her entire body. Between the two boys, Jake was easy prey. Daryl knew this. Foxes take the weakest chickens first. It minimizes risk. Predators understand this innately. The quivering wall of her back was presented to him fully. Jake was somewhere on the other side of that wall and might as well have been staked to the floor.

Daryl was in centerfield, with a runner rounding third. He preferred centerfield because it gave him the most room. He reared back, with the only weapon he had available, a rusted hook too degraded to support the weight of the paint can. Then he threw it to home, missing the cutoff man at shortstop, putting everything he had into this final act.

Her knees buckled from the pain, and the impact, as the metal pierced the skin just above her hip bone. Jake darted away from her toppling body, taking a step toward the stairs without realizing it. A meaty arm smacked the table, jolting the nearly dead man, who lifted his arm stumps a few inches.

"Run! Run, Jake!"

Daryl darted toward the stairs, his arm a windmill beckoning Jake.

"We gotta go! Jake!"

Jake blinked a few times, looking at the torso before him and the woman now rising to her feet.

"Now!"

Daryl rushed back to Jake and hooked a finger inside the collar of his shirt. He yanked him forward with everything he could muster, and Jake's instincts took over from there. He stumbled to the stairs and grasped the banister.

"Go!"

Jake scaled the first step.

CLINK

The metal around Daryl's wrist felt like a cold snake. He pulled the chain taut, and the table shifted half an inch. Jake froze on the stairs, eyes like a jackrabbit caught in a snare.

"Daryl…" he said.

Her hands were on his shoulders then, and she spoke without unclenching her teeth.

"You got the Devil in you, boy. I can smell it. I got to—to get it out of you."

Daryl's elbow ricocheted off her stomach. She squeezed tighter. His next elbow missed its mark, and he crumpled like a puppet whose strings were cut.

"Daryl…"

He lifted his head. "Go Jake. You have to…"

"No, not him. H-he's next. He got the Devil in him, too."

She released Daryl, who dangled at the end of the shackle.

"Two boys, mmmhmmm. Two boys full of the Devil."

"RUUUUUN!!!" Daryl screamed, loud enough to make her stop half a second, loud enough to penetrate the blocked ear canals of the man dying on the table, and Jake, as he always did eventually, obeyed.

He took the steps two at a time, his consciousness disconnected from the actions of his body. He careened down the hallway, like a puppy loosed from its crate, and barreled through the front door into sunlight.

She gave chase, but only for a moment. By the time she reached the front door, Jake was mounting his bike, face shiny with tears and snot. She pressed a hand to the wet spot on her back. It was probably worth a visit to the hospital, but that might not be possible since the boy got away and would no doubt alert the police. She returned to the basement and stood at the head of the stairs. The other boy was crying softly down there, kind of like she used to in the closet. But he wasn't crying to God, no.

That would have to change, and she had the perfect place in mind.

Meet you in the mornin'…

SIX MONTHS LATER

FOR THE FIRST week, Jake slept at the foot of his parents' bed. He associated his own room with Daryl, sleepovers, and quiet afternoons reading comics. More than an hour passed before the first police officers arrived at the abandoned house. The truck was gone, and so was Daryl. No effort was made to hide the evidence of crimes committed in that basement. Fred succumbed to the torture and died with a throatful of vomit he did not have the energy to expel. Based on the evidence collected, he was not the first.

She was a woman named Debra Cain. Her fingerprints tied her to petty crimes throughout the country, mostly resisting arrest, related to proselytizing at busy intersections and bus stations.

In August, a battered truck was found parked beside a hunter's deer feeder in Tennessee. The next vehicle stolen was a car, a car with a large trunk. And then nothing. Debra Cain was a ghost, fodder for true crime podcasts.

In January, a few stray snowflakes danced on a light breeze in central Alabama. Most melted before they touched earth or concrete. A few lingered for a moment on the lip of a Mountain Dew can, still frosty from the cold soda within. Beneath it was a note, the letters written with a clumsy hand too big for the pen, the paper wrinkled from condensation.

Jake saw it from the street, placed just in front of the entrance mat. His stomach had only recently untied itself from the collection of knots it had become since the summer. He cradled himself, the strength seeping from his legs, like the ichor from Mr. Fred's mouth. There were no cars on the road, just the rumble of the departing school bus and the laughter of children on other streets he could not see.

He patted the cell phone in his pocket but did not withdraw it. His mother insisted he carry one at all times. She said women like Debra Cain aren't as visible as other women. Older and unattractive. She could be anywhere. Jake inhaled sharply, the crisp air shriveling his lungs. Buried within his gnarled organs was a flicker of something, hope maybe. Daryl was not found, alive or dead. And, so, the possibility existed for the former.

Jake tugged the note free.

He found God, by the end.

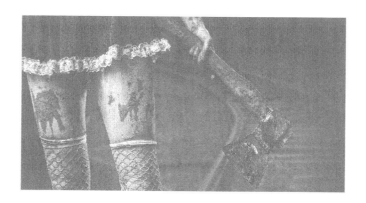

THE GAME

Sarah Jane Huntington

'D LIKE TO TELL YOU MY STORY, ALTHOUGH it isn't finished—not by a long shot. I guess this would be Chapter One in a large, fat, and dusty book. I'd also like to point out that this won't be a pleasant tale. Or maybe it will. I guess that all depends on your personal perspective. My work should be praised. I am, after all, giving order to the chaos.

Let me start by attempting to give you insight into people like myself.

You might see us portrayed on the silver screen, posting severed heads in boxes or leaving coded clues for weary old detectives, in an ancient game of cat and mouse. You might see us chaining people to old pipes and setting up elaborate traps or games.

We are often pictured with dramatic, gruesome, or

quite gory flair, and for us, there can be none of the redemption you normally see screen characters undertake. People like us cannot change, and if we tell you that we can, we are lying. We are highly skilled liars.

You might feel unsettled after you leave the movies. On your dark walk alone to your car, you may even breathe a heavy sigh of relief and tell yourself, "It's only a movie."

You go home to sleep in your soft bed, with your meaningless dreams, untouched, and untroubled.

To you, people like us are one-in-a-million rare.

So rare, in fact, that you comfort yourself with the warm and toasty lie that you'll never, in your life, meet one of us.

I'd like to tell you how wrong you are. We serve you in your favorite coffee shop, we teach your children how to read, we sleep in the bed next to you, and we tell you that we love you. We are very convincing. We have to be.

We act. We hide in plain sight.

Each of us wears a metaphorical, or yes, a sometimes literal, human mask, which our survival instinct makes us inclined to do.

On occasion, someone's mask inevitably slips down, or falls off, entirely. What lies beneath is a horror most people refuse to comprehend, and it nearly always ends in a bloodbath, lethal injection, and a long, endless book by a popular profiler.

Those dark souls make a study of us, a profile. They make intricate lists, indicators, risks, strategy, capture. They say there are signs in childhood. They say there are treatments.

The last one makes me smile. As if treatment could ever exist for people like me. I don't know how to be anything else. I was born superior.

Being a killer is hardwired into my genetic code, my DNA, and my very cells. It is everything I am. I am the next level of evolution, and you are nothing but my failed predecessor. It is my nature to kill, not my nurture.

I guess I should really start with a little of my background. I was never a bedwetter, and never once have I hurt an animal. I'm actually quite fond of animals. I even had a cat once. I admired how she'd catch mice, even though she wasn't hungry and had no intention of eating them. She only caught them as a source of brutish amusement. All sharp claws and savage cruelty. I understood her need completely.

I do not have a type of victim or a preference in choosing who I kill, although, to some, it may look that way.

I do not have mother or father issues and didn't have an abusive childhood. It was actually very dull and normal.

My parents were good people. They raised us well. My elder brother was difficult, yes. He was born with a grudge against the world and was graced with a deep resentment and jealousy of anything that didn't revolve around him.

I was born three years after my brother and was named Anna. Yes, I'm a woman. You may find that surprising, but there are many of us, I assure you. It's my own personal belief that we are smarter than our male counterparts and, therefore, lesser known. We don't make testosterone-fuelled mistakes.

By age five, my parents began to notice my lack of emotion. I was rarely sad, but clever and quiet. I liked learning about the insides of people, the essential parts that made them tick.

By age seven, I was smarter. I watched the people around me. I studied expressions, unconscious gestures, tones of voices, and mannerisms. Eventually, I became the perfect mimic.

I prided myself on being able to copy and being the ultimate trickster. Deep down inside, a grim, almost desperate, darkness grew.

That darkness was my true nature and, for me, it was a guiding light that others wouldn't, and couldn't, understand. I knew my path, and I felt happy there. Blessed even.

At age twelve, I pushed my brother out of our attic window. He plummeted to the ground like an old rag doll. He died, twisted up in a tangle of limbs, while, in those very same moments, I was reborn.

Local rumor of a terrible accident soon settled into fact, in the small town I'd been born in.

My parents cried endlessly, particularly my mother. I watched her, I made soothing noises, and I filed her reactions away for later use. She called me "her rock."

At age fifteen, I made a mistake, one I have never let myself repeat: speaking without first thinking through my words.

A philosophical question was posed to our class at school. Our gray-haired teacher asked us, "If a hospital needed three organs for three dying people, and a very bad prisoner from death row came in for treatment, would it be right or wrong to take that prisoner's life, harvest the organs, and save three?" He pointed straight at me to answer.

"Kill the prisoner," I said. To me, it was a mathematical question. It was simple.

"All life has value, Anna," our teacher chastised me, as my class gasped and turned wide-eyed.

"No, it doesn't. Lives have different values. I'd kill the prisoner, even if the person wasn't a prisoner at all."

"How would that make you feel?" he asked.

"Good."

After that minor incident, my parents sent me to therapy.

My mask almost slipped a few times during that period. My therapist was a small, delicate woman with extremely high intelligence, and I almost came undone. She made me feel as if she could see past the layers I'd constructed to hide my true self. I was far too exposed in her office. I led her to believe I was traumatized by the accidental death of my brother, and that was my problem.

At night, if I couldn't sleep, I'd fantasize about killing her in a thousand different ways. It always relaxed me so much, I could finally sleep. I began studying books and articles related to famous serial killers. I wanted to know their mistakes, particularly the ones that led to them being caught. I refused to make the same errors.

After I was released from therapy, I felt untouchable. I began to crave the control that had filled me following my brother's death, the power and the ultimate life or death decision, which I held only in my hands.

I toyed with the idea of becoming a doctor, but I had

no desire to help others. Besides, killer doctors are always caught. I remained undecided about my future.

I was just eighteen when I happened upon *The Game.*

I'd been on the dark web for a while. As I mentioned, I'm smart. Nothing seemed out of reach for me, and if it was, I simply tried harder.

Failure is an unknown word to people like me.

I found a fairly large group of like-minded individuals, all in competition with each other. They even had categories.

Best kills. Most original kills. Reenactment kills (which meant either copying from historical cases or from movie scenes). And, finally, untraceable kills.

Anyone was considered prey, with the exception of children and pregnant women.

I was more than happy with those rules. I never regarded childkillers as one of my own. To me, they were the epitome of evil, as were rapists. They were below regular humans on the ethical scale.

A point system was already in place, and there were three top killers. Each one had press cuttings of their victims, and the details of the murders, uploaded for proof. Sometimes, even crime scene photographs too, prior to police investigations.

I decided, then, that I would outdo them all. One by one.

Once I had an idea in my head, I always stuck with it. It never mattered to me how long it took, only that I achieved my goal.

The number eight ranked serial killer caught my eye.

A vicious kind, a coward, one who liked to strangle and then dump the body. He only went after women who were alone. He called himself Mr. Darkness. I loathed him so much, it made my skin itch.

Once I had that kind of hate, it grew into a fury all on its own. I am not at all capable of love, but hate and me? We were old, and comfortable, friends.

The tendrils of bitterness and loathing wrapped around me and held on tight. One rainy and scene-setting night, while lying on my bed, I decided to kill him.

Now, my life, then, was a permanent juggling act, but not once did I falter in my crazy circus world, although it was exhausting. I attended school and did extremely well. I had friends, empty-headed, stupid ones who I despised, but friends all the same. I needed them, as part of my act, to fit in. There was anonymity in a crowd.

I made my parents proud. I acted and played at being smart, popular, and pretty. I was hidden in plain sight.

The red-hot, burning need I felt inside me needed to cool.

A friend of mine had a date, one Friday night, with an equally moronic high school soccer player. He had a reputation for pressuring girls into sex, and I knew what would happen before he ever even hit upon the idea himself.

They'd planned on going to the movies, then taking a drive up to Overlook Pass—the place in town where bored, or horny, teenagers drank beer and made out. The whole idea was a cliche.

I snuck out that night, dressed in black, and armed to the hilt. I favored knives early on, that cool, smooth metal I liked to sharpen and hold. I enjoyed caressing the edges too, almost in an erotic sense.

I cut through the woods, and sure enough, there was his car, steamy windows…all very predictable.

I stopped and enjoyed the scents of the night—pine trees and damp soil. The moon illuminated the scene, as if I'd been given my own private spotlight. My blood sang, my heart quickened. My fingers and toes tingled. Inside my belly, great fluttering birds took flight.

The only sounds were the thudding of dull music from the car and the odd groan of pleasure.

I dropped and crawled across the damp grass, in a hunched-down position, trying my hardest to be silent. Theirs was the only car, and I briefly thought of the Zodiac killer. He was someone I'd admired, even with his foolish cipher games.

My intention had been to kill the soccer boy, and only him. I figured she'd run, and I intended to let her go.

I hadn't taken into account my bloodlust, my genetic need for destruction.

I rapped hard on the window and listened with delight to their cries of alarm.

"It's Anna!" I fake cried. "I was jogging. A strange man tried to grab me. Help! I'm scared."

I didn't quite manage to mimic terror in my voice. I was trying to be the hapless female, running around alone.

I counted two beats of worrying silence before I heard the frantic zipping up of clothing. I raced around to the driver's side and arranged my face into the best expression of hurt I could manage. The car door flew open.

"Help!" I sobbed.

"Are you okay? Where is he?" his shocked face hissed. He towered over me but was far too busy scanning the treeline to see the danger standing directly in front of him.

I stabbed him in the heart. That's actually harder to do than you might think. But I assure you, it's wonderfully satisfying. The crack and tear, the rip, the warmth.

A burst of air left his lips as he crumpled, much quicker than I expected. Blood poured from his chest and mouth, as his wide eyes blinked rapidly. I shoved him off me as his friend screamed and grabbed at her door handle. I'd wanted her to run, but her panic had set in far too fast.

I stabbed her in the back multiple times. I tried to count, but a hot fever had taken hold of me. After her whimpering stopped, I carried on stabbing. I was, after all, practicing.

It felt delicious. Otherworldly, a primal rage.

The power. The thrill. The pressure I hadn't even realized was squeezing my mind lifted.

I felt glorious. Absolute bliss for the first time in my life. I wanted to run through the woods, to be free and wild, as I felt the power surge inside me.

I was untouchable and hooked on the element-of-surprise technique. It was thrilling.

I walked home humming to myself and left them both where they lay, crumpled. I hid my clothes, took a shower, and climbed back into my bed. I had the best night's sleep I've ever had.

By the next afternoon, the news had spread all over town. Friends called and parents cried, police held a press conference, curfews were set, and adults were outraged.

No one, not one person, suspected me. My smile had

been hard to hide, so I took to placing a hand across my mouth to fake my shock.

"Who would do such a thing?" I repeated to whomever I spoke to. "It's an act of evil."

It was far too easy.

Their murders remain unsolved. It was, and still is, assumed that a drifter, or passing psychopath, came across them and wreaked havoc. They were both spoken about more highly in death than they ever were in life. By now, I'm guessing an entire urban legend has been conceived in their honor.

My own mother, even after commenting that her new knives were dull, never had any clue that a killer lived under her roof.

So, that made a total of three kills. And three kills made me a serial killer. I craved more. I needed it. I yearned for that moment of euphoria.

I wanted Mr. Darkness.

On the dark web, people are untraceable. However, there are ways to find their approximate location. With him, there was no need to go to any great lengths. The arrogant fool believed he was safe among his own kind, and he'd made a comment about an "unrelated to him" murder, which occurred in his small town.

A simple search of the internet revealed the town. Easy.

I waited two months. By that time, I felt frantic to kill again. I kept my mask firmly in place and managed to get through each day by sheer force of will.

"Road trip," I told my parents. Half of me wanted to kill them, but I am nothing if not resourceful. My home might provide the safehouse I'd need in the future, so I made sure I left on good terms.

I picked up one hitchhiker on my way to seek out my prey. I didn't kill her.

I wanted to, and I'd planned to. But after only ten miles together, she'd told me she was pregnant and, therefore, she was off-limits.

I left her at the station, when I stopped to fill up with gas.

I drove for two days. One night, I stayed in a cheap roadside motel. The kind of place you can imagine the real Norman Bates might hang out. I slept on cheap, stained sheets with a knife under my pillow, itching for someone to try and get to me.

No such luck.

The next day, I arrived in the small town where Mr. Darkness lived and booked myself into the one and only bed and breakfast.

I went for a walk. I noticed a few stares. I was, after all, a new girl in town—a pretty, smiley, harmless new girl. I visited every store; I wandered the town park. I acted friendly to every person I came across. I looked for eyes like mine.

We can fake our expressions, but our own eyes betray us. Dead eyes, I call them. No hope lives in our orbs, no fear, and certainly no love. My eyes are my one weakness. They will not lie.

I found the one bar in town, sat, and flirted. I sipped at the one beer I ordered. I batted my eyelashes, and I waited.

People judge. They can't help it. Human brains sub-consciously assess a threat level each time they meet some-one new. Either their defenses go up or drop down, de-pending on how a person looks and how they are per-ceived.

I know how people see me. They see an attractive, but not beautiful, young woman. Next, they make the as-sumption that I'm not very bright. They judge that I'm pleasant, kind, a good-time girl, and harmless. They sup-pose that I can be manipulated, persuaded, and that I'm not the least bit threatening. I wear shorts and thin-strapped tops. I wear boots for better concealment of weapons. I wear make-up and lots of it. Also, push-up bras. Every woman, with a mind to kill, needs a good push-up bra. Trade secret.

I work hard on my mask, my persona. Everyone I meet comes to the same conclusions, because that's what I need them to believe and see.

I studied every man who walked through the bar doors. Mechanic, nope. Butcher, hmmm, nope. I was waiting for my instinct to alert me and point him out, my honed skill, an advanced instinct that defined me above most humans. I searched inside myself for that pull, the one I felt sure I'd feel as soon as I met one of my own kind.

Two police officers came in. Both seemed like regu-lars to the bar, and one of them sent my hackles up and my blood pulsing in my ears. A lawman, I should've guessed.

I was certain I'd found him.

He glanced over and saw me looking, grinned, and judged me exactly as I needed him to.

He wasn't bad looking. He had the kind of charm that made me understand how some might find him attractive.

I smiled back, and he came strolling over. Too confident. I could tell he felt invincible and full of power. Killing does that to a person.

"Little lady," he said and tipped his hat. "New in town?"

"I am, passing through," I told him, and straight away I knew my mistake.

"To where?"

"Next state."

"For?"

I should have had my script straightened out in my mind, a childish error.

"Am I under arrest, officer?" I laughed and turned on the charm. I threw my hair back over my bare shoulder and reached down for my bag to give him an eyeful of my chest.

"Course not." He laughed. " Can I buy you a drink?"

"I need to sleep. I'm exhausted and sweaty. Maybe later? Will you be around tonight?"

"Will be if you are."

"Then it's a date." I winked. "I'm looking forward to it."

I saw his sly smile. I knew he'd dropped his guard. Me, the weak, stupid female. I'd given him an opportunity he didn't want to miss.

I went to the B&B and logged onto the game. I waited for him to post. I paced and waited for so long, I figured I had the wrong guy after all. But, sure enough, two hours later, Mr. Darkness started boasting about the kill he's going to make, and record, that same night.

It was too easy. The hunter had no idea he had become the hunted.

I thought carefully. I had plenty of knives. They were, after all, my weapon of choice. I tucked one down my boot, one up my sleeve. I holstered one to my thigh and placed the best one I owned in my bag, along with a few others. I already knew he liked to choke and strangle, but I guessed that being an officer of the law, he'd have a gun on his person too.

I headed back to the bar. My blood thrummed with excitement and anticipation. I enjoyed the feeling. I welcomed it.

I had to sit and wait for an hour before he showed up. In that time, I passed on several drink offers. My heart picked up speed as soon as he walked in. He hitched up his trousers and came straight for me.

"So, stranger. What's your name?" he drawled.

"Jane," I lied.

He, Mr. Darkness, told me his name was Tom. I can drink a fair amount of alcohol without it affecting me. It was a skill I'd worked hard on back in high school. We drank a couple of beers and downed a few shots before I leaned over and made a suggestion.

"You got somewhere private we can go to, Officer?"

At that point, I was fully aware that the townspeople had seen us together. I was also fully aware that folk might have clocked my license plates. Both those thoughts tumbled around in the back of my mind. Each one tried to push its way to the front. I discarded them. All I could do was focus on him.

"Your folks know you're in this town?" He grinned, and I shook my head.

"Nobody knows. Why?"

The leer on his face told me everything. He took my hand inside his damp one and led me out of the bar, as if he were a gentleman. I very convincingly pretended to be a little drunk and leaned in toward him. His body odor repulsed me.

"Let's go somewhere remote, outside," he suggested.

I clutched my bag and giggled.

The drive itself was straightforward. I made a log, in my head, of every direction and corner we took. He played country music, and that made me despise him even more. He put his greasy hand on my leg. I didn't flinch. Instead, I grinned and placed my own hand on top of his.

He stopped near the tree line of the woods, on the edge of town, and turned to me. "Backseat or al fresco?"

"Outside," I whispered.

He climbed out, chuckling. No doubt, he was thinking how easy everything was going to be for him. He had a dashcam, and I noticed the green light blinking away.

I climbed out and made a show of being unsteady on my feet, as he stood leaning against the front of the hood. He patted it and raised an eyebrow.

My skin was tingling, and I felt on fire all the way into the marrow of my bones.

"Be gentle now," I sang. I stumbled over, and as he caught me, I stuck a knife into his belly and yanked it straight up.

I felt the warmth and stickiness of his blood pour out

over my hands. The expression that crossed his face amused me. First, an almost comedic surprise, followed by agony. He clamped a hand across his belly, trying to hold his intestines in. They flopped out like sausages.

I stabbed him again, and again.

My mind switched to fury as he fell, and a red fog descended. One that crept in and settled heavily. He was lying on the ground, still, but gurgling, as I sat across him. I reached down and undid my belt. I wrapped it around his neck and pulled it hard.

"Karma, you fucking scum," I told him. "You got taken down by a girl."

I hope those were the last words he ever heard, but in all honesty, I think he was already dead by that point. And he pissed himself, too. The big, old, scary Mr. Darkness pissed his pants and cried for his momma.

I hoped the majority of my attack was caught on his dashcam, so I took it. I do like memorabilia—a trophy, my prize.

I opened my phone and took a quick picture. It had already crossed my mind that he might be a rapist, along with being a killer. He'd certainly seemed the type, and he definitely tried to take advantage of a woman he believed was drunk.

I have my special knives and a few ordinary cooking knives, the kind you can pick up in most stores. I took one from the bottom of my bag, cleaned it of prints, and then stabbed him straight in his balls. I intentionally left the knife sticking up dramatically, and took another photo. I felt happy, gloriously, deliciously happy.

Getting back to town was easy. I took his keys and

drove his car. After changing my clothes in the backseat, I left it in the parking lot of the bar. Then I climbed into my own car. Since I'd left nothing at the bed and breakfast, I drove fifty or so miles and then logged into *The Game*.

My name, I wrote, *is Vigilante. Your boy, Mr. Darkness, is dead. He died begging and screaming for his momma, as I killed him. I believe I'm owed ten points, at least. Here is an image for your enjoyment.*

I logged out, deleted the photos from my phone, and drove some more.

In the next state, I stopped at another dive motel. I had a long, hot shower and took a two-hour nap. I ventured out for food and also picked up some hair color. I ruined several cheap, tacky towels and dyed my hair a pretty shade of red.

I searched the internet for news. Sure enough, Mr. Darkness's body had been found by a dog walker. Why is it always dog walkers who happen to stumble upon bodies? One might think they go looking.

I logged back into *The Game* and added the town's local news link.

Within five minutes, there was a flurry of activity. A few were angry, mostly over how I'd found him in the first place, and worried over their own safety.

I had, however, received ten points.

An alert on the top of the forum reassured its members of the site's security. A note added underneath welcomed me as the newest, active member.

A new thread had been created: "*What's next for Vigilante?*"

I scrolled through feeling curious. They at least seemed to know I was a woman. That fact had shocked a few of them. I was currently ranked eighth.

The seventh-ranked killer was a man called "The Hidden Dragon." A guy in the San Francisco area with a knack for breaking and entering and killing wealthy, older couples as they slept.

"What's next" is that I aim to be number one in The Game, I wrote.

How? came the immediate reply. *We've built our kill list up over years, sweetheart.*

Now, they say serial killers are smart with high IQs. Not one member of the group seemed to have figured out the obvious.

I'm not your sweetheart, I typed back. *And how? Easy. I eliminate the competition. See you all very soon xx*

I closed my laptop and smiled. I wasn't at all sure how I'd find any of them, but surprisingly, I'm a big believer in fate. I know that in life, nothing is impossible if you try hard enough.

These people likely had marriages, jobs to hold, a mortgage to pay, all as part of their disguises. I had no anchors or chains. I had no relationships I wouldn't think twice about severing. I had no one I'd miss. I knew how to steal. I knew how to hotwire cars. I knew how to live unseen, and I knew how to thrive. No remorse.

The killers in *The Game* made errors, simple tiny errors, purely out of arrogance. They each believed they were in a group of like-minded individuals. That made them lax, and it caused them to make mistakes.

They all knew I'd be coming for them, and that

would make them do one of two things. They would either make more mistakes, and then I'd find them, or they'd stop altogether, and I'd climb up the leaderboard.

Win-win.

People like me, we aren't defined by a list some FBI profiler put together. We don't fit into a box of characteristics, a checklist of certain traits. A particular upbringing cannot create what already lives inside. We are born this way.

We are the next step of evolution.

A bear doesn't worry about who it hurts. An alligator won't be upset if it snaps off your leg. A mighty lion doesn't stop to consider the feelings of its prey. They are hardwired to catch, just as they are hardwired to kill. Like me. I appreciate that animals kill to eat. Some of us do that too. Not me. I'm feeding a different hunger, but it's a hunger all the same.

Next time you happen to see a pretty female, think twice before you judge her. We hide in plain sight, and you might find yourself looking into my dead eyes. You might actually believe I'm harmless.

You might even find me, or someone like me, in your bed. Or, at least, underneath it.

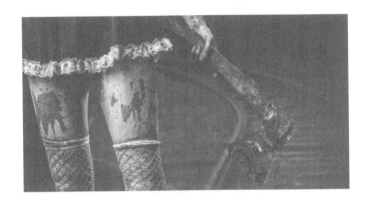

REUNITED

R.E. Sargent

CHAPTER ONE

"**O**NE HUNDRED–DOLLAR BID, NOW one-fifty, now one-fifty, who will give me one-fifty? One-fifty bid, now two. Now two hundred…two hundred, who will give me two hundred…"

"One seventy-five!"

"I have one seventy-five, one seventy-five. Who'll give me two hundred…two hundred…I have one seventy-five going once… twice…and SOLD to the little lady in the purple shirt!"

"YES!" Carly yelled as the other hopefuls gave her varied looks from indignance to daggers. Although only her second time attending storage locker auctions, she had learned from her mistakes during her first time and scored three different lockers this time. With the third locker being the last auction of the day, she paid up, placed her own lock on the final unit, and jumped in her truck to grab lunch.

As she parked her rig and went in to order at a nearby fast food restaurant, Carly planned the triage of her three units. It was late afternoon, and she only had forty-eight hours to clean out all three lockers, so she would need to get going. While she could easily come back the next day and pick up where she left off if she ran out of time—or steam—she preferred to get everything cleaned out all at once.

Not one to waste time, Carly ate on the way back and pulled her twenty-eight-foot enclosed cargo trailer up past the first unit.

Taking the lock off, she slid open the door and remembered why she had wanted this unit so badly. While she had no idea what was in the boxes and totes, she noticed how organized and uniform they were. All the boxes were the same size, were all stacked neatly, and were all turned the same direction. Someone gave a shit about the contents of this unit, and for whatever reason, they abandoned it and stopped paying the bill. Now it was hers.

Rather than start opening boxes now, and potentially put herself in a position that she would not get the units all emptied today, she grabbed her utility dolly out of the trailer, slid it under the first stack, and tilted it back, pulling the heavy stack up the ramp of the trailer and depositing it in the front. Methodically, she emptied out the first unit, her willpower beating out her curiosity.

As she worked, she thought about how her life had changed so much two years ago. One single event and her life would never be the same again. One event that started a cataclysmic waterfall of the end of life as she knew it. A ten-year career gone up in flames. Her husband of eight years gone—just walked out the door and never came back.

For over a year, she lived in one of the darkest holes she could never have imagined existed. The grip of depression held her so tight that she didn't know how to escape its grasp. She contemplated doing the unthinkable. Then, one morning, everything changed. When she opened her eyes to the sun filtering through the leaf-patterned curtains, she felt a spark. Like the fight in her had been re-engaged. Like suddenly, the life that had almost taken hers pushed her to fight again. To live again. To be happy again.

Within a week, she had cleaned up the modest three-bedroom home that had turned into a shithole during her depression. She washed the piles of dirty clothes and dishes. She got her hair done and even started wearing makeup again.

A cursory look at her bank account left her surprised that she still had around forty-eight thousand dollars left—more than she thought she would have after more than a year of not bothering to check the balance and not caring what happened to her. The only good news around her husband walking out was that he left everything behind, except a suitcase full of clothes and the five thousand dollars in an envelope they kept hidden in the bottom of the dresser drawer for emergencies.

As she swept out the first unit and slid the door shut, she smiled. She loved what she did, and it allowed her the flexibility to work when she wanted at a pace that worked for her. Although she was trying to get her life back to something that resembled normal, many days, the pain crept back in and she had to spend a day or two fighting to pull herself back up out of the emotional mire that consumed her.

Buying the contents of storage lockers at auction and selling the items for profit wasn't something she had experience in, when her life had been more traditional. It was during her dark days, where she laid in bed all day long with her blackout curtains pulled tight, that she began to binge watch episodes of *Storage Wars*, both old and new. There was something about what the stars of the show did that intrigued her. It was like a treasure hunt to her. It was when she chose to pull herself out of her fog and go on with life that she decided she would try her hand at it rather than go back to a traditional job. She took a huge chunk of the money that was left and bought a cargo trailer to pull behind the Dodge Ram she already owned. It wasn't long before she bought her first two storage lockers and made an agreement with a local secondhand store that would buy the sellable items from her for half of what they felt they could sell them for. Of course, anything of higher value, she would sell herself.

She pulled up to the second and third units, which happened to be almost across from each other. After removing the locks, she rolled up both doors and started the process of loading the items into the trailer. She thought about the measly three hundred dollars she had made for the first two units she had purchased before. She had paid way too much for the units, and she knew it before she even went through the locker's contents, but she had gotten caught up in the excitement. This time, she was more observant and felt confident she would turn a decent profit.

As Carly loaded the last boxes in the trailer, she noticed the sun was sitting low in the sky. She swept both units out, slid down the metal doors, secured the trailer, and slid behind the wheel of her truck. She would just make it home by dusk. Sorting through the contents would have to wait until the next day—something she was anxiously anticipating.

CHAPTER TWO

CARLY CARRIED A box of trash to the dumpster that she kept on the side of her house. After the first two units she had purchased, she learned quickly that one man's treasure is another man's—or woman's—trash. She estimated that a quarter of everything she pulled out of those units had not been sellable, so she had ordered the dumpster as a permanent addition to her home and business.

This time was no exception. Carly had unloaded and sorted a quarter of the contents of the trailer, and so far, she had dumped six boxes of crap: a dented toaster, a stained set of bedsheets, a portable commode that was obviously used. All things that exactly no one would be lining up to buy.

Still, for all the crap she found, the treasures outweighed those items significantly. Her biggest scores, so far, had been an expensive set of golf clubs, seven boxes of old comic books that appeared to be mint and in protective sleeves, and a five-gallon glass water dispenser bottle full of coins that she estimated might be worth the amount she had paid for all three lockers combined. With plenty more items to go through, she knew that she would come out way ahead on these units.

Methodically, Carly brought one box at a time off the trailer, placed it on one of the sorting tables she had set up in her garage, and worked through them. Clothes were placed in plastic bins with other clothes. Small appliances were placed on shelves over in the corner. Bigger items were staged along the far wall. She brought a bulkier box off the trailer, set it on the table, and opened it. Clothes.

Finding boxes of clothes was the last thing Carly hoped for when she went through her newly acquired items. They really held little to no value, and she would typically sell them to the store for a few dollars per box. Even then, she still had to sort through them and make sure they were sellable. She certainly didn't want to put her arrangement with the secondhand store at risk.

She started pulling out the clothing, one item at a time. Little girl's clothing. Possibly for a two-year-old. Carly froze. Memories came flooding back, and she shoved the items back in the box, closing the flaps as quickly as she could. Tears flooded her face, and she had to walk away and go inside the house. She sat on the couch and bawled, until there were no more tears left in her.

In the kitchen, Carly made a cup of tea and tried to calm down. She thought she was moving on with her life, but there was no way to move on when the pain was still so fresh.

Back in the garage, she tentatively stared at the box. She could dump it in one of the clothes bins without going through it, toss it in the dumpster, or face her demons and open the box. It seemed like an hour before she finally made up her mind. She approached it, opened the flaps, and dumped the contents on the table.

Small pairs of pants in different colors and different patterns. An array of shoes, sandals, and little boots. Carly sniffled and dug through the contents. A patterned dress with flowers and butterflies. Her breath caught in her throat. The dress was exactly like one Gracie used to have. A lump formed in her throat as she remembered her beautiful, bubbly, two-year-old daughter.

CHAPTER THREE

GRACIE WAS EVERYTHING to Carly and her husband, Brian. After years of being told she would not be able to have children and against all odds, Gracie was conceived. When she was born, she was perfect and healthy in every way.

As a baby, Gracie was happy and rarely fussy. Brian and Carly had multiple conversations about how they had lucked out—how God had been looking out for them and had saved the most special one just for them. As Gracie started crawling, and then walking, the smile never left her face, and Carly could honestly say that she had never known a love as true as the love she held for that little girl.

Now, Carly stared at the dress that reminded her of their little angel. Tears welled up in her eyes as she tried to hold it together. Gracie would have been four in a couple of months.

The memories hit Carly like a freight train. Her getting up in the morning to get ready for work. Checking in on their little girl before the nanny arrived. Opening the curtains to allow the morning light to slowly wake Gracie up, so they could get her ready for the nanny. Then the blood. Obscene amounts of it soaked the bedsheets and blankets. Carly frantically yanking the covers back to get to Gracie. Her lifeless form. The pajama top sliced to ribbons, the color unrecognizable.

Carly slumped to the ground, holding the dress. Her mind took her back through the slew of memories. Events that destroyed her life. Her screams. The police showing up. The coroner taking Gracie away, covered by a sheet. The millions of questions. The invitation down to the station, where the interview turned into an interrogation. They had separated Brian and Carly in different rooms and had drilled them about what they had done to their daughter. Eventually, they cleared both of them. No other suspects were identified, but they did find signs of entry through Gracie's bedroom window as well as boot prints in the flowerbed below.

At first, Brian tried to console her—to be her rock. But he wasn't prepared for the dark place that she went to hide. After months of trying to help her, and his efforts being rebuked by a torrential tirade of screaming and profanities, Brian couldn't take it anymore. Soon after, he left, and life for Carly was never the same. It was then she sank into an abyss darker than any she had ever experienced before.

Carly snapped back to the dress. Carefully folding it, she carried it into the house and tucked it into the closet of Gracie's old room. She would keep the dress as a reminder of Gracie. All the other possessions belonging to her had been purged from the house by Brian—his way of trying to make it easier for Carly. Instead, he had only made her hysteria worse.

Back out in the garage, Carly numbly started working through the boxes again. She came across several more boxes of clothes, some fairly cheap jewelry, and some other little knickknacks.

The boxes that were all the same size and neatly stacked were all books, and from the way they were all protected and packaged, she had a feeling they were worth some money as well, so she set them aside with the comic books to take to an expert and possibly sell on consignment.

As she was cleaning out the last of the trailer, she noticed a small black duffle bag she had set to the side of the ramp when she was unloading the boxes. She rubbed her temples with her thumbs, then brought the bag over to the table. She was almost done for the day and would wait until tomorrow before she started figuring out what to do with her bounty.

She pulled open the zipper and peeled back the sides of the bag. On top was a piece of clothing. She pulled out a pair of coveralls, dirty and stained. Someone's work bag, evidently. A couple of pairs of gloves followed. In the bottom was a roll of something that looked like black nylon.

She scooped it out, noticing its considerable weight. Laying it down on the table, she untied the two strips that were entwined in a bow and unrolled the nylon onto the table. Her breath caught, and an audible gasp left her lips. The roll consisted of ten individual plastic sleeves. Slid into each pouch was a tool: mostly knives, a couple of hand saws, and a sharpener. It reminded her of the summer she had worked at the local grocery store as a teenager, where she had to take out the trash throughout the store as one of her duties. One of the meatcutters—he called himself a floater and worked in different stores daily—had a kit similar to this, but there were a lot less knives. And what were the hand saws about? To her recollection, anything that needed cut with a saw was cut on a big band saw in the back of the prep room.

She knew that knives were expensive and that this kit would be valuable, so she decided she would research it later and try to sell it herself. There was no way it was going to the secondhand store. Rolling the pouch back up, she tied it closed and set the roll on the bottom shelf of the storage racks. She would get to it later, after the books and comic books had been sorted out. And of course, after the big jar of coins—which she needed her utility dolly to move—was carted down to the coin-counting machine that hid out in the lobby of the grocery store a mile away.

Cleaning up the last of the garbage, she slid the black duffle bag, the coveralls, and the gloves into the box and went and dumped the last of it into the dumpster. After a shower and a change of clothes, she decided her night would consist of a stiff drink and a binge watch of a new Netflix series she had her eyes on.

CHAPTER FOUR

OVER THE NEXT several weeks, Carly attended two more auctions and brought home the contents of four more lockers. Her prior lockers had turned a hefty profit, and she had found buyers for the collections.

She had just finished processing the last of the boxes out of the trailer for her most recent run, and turned to place an electric can opener on the shelving units, when she spotted it. The nylon roll of knives tucked into the back of the shelf. She had forgotten it was there. She slid it out and unrolled it on the table again, running her pointer finger over each handle, wondering what material they were made out of. They certainly weren't cheap plastic. Each one had an inlay. Could it be ivory? She had no idea where she could take the set to have it analyzed. Although it wouldn't make her rich, she had a feeling that she could make a few hundred off the kit. She decided she would research it the next morning.

The next day, after she ate a quick breakfast of apple cinnamon oatmeal and toast, she went to the garage to grab the knife set. It wasn't on the table where she thought she had left it. She returned to the shelving unit she had stored it on earlier. It wasn't there either. Methodically, she poked her way through every part of the garage to find it. An hour later, she still could not locate it. She checked the side door to the garage, and it was still locked and showed no signs of forced entry. She had slid the switch the night before to lock out any remotes from opening the large rollup door, so she knew no one got in that way either.

I'm losing my damn mind.

Unsure of where she left them, Carly went inside the house and got on her computer, looking for a place that might be able to buy them from her, or at the very least help her ascertain their value. Only one place looked like it fit the bill, but it was two hours away. Perhaps the next time she was in the area for an auction, she could swing by and get the set checked out. That is if she could figure out what she did with them.

That night, Carly got ready for bed and settled on the couch to watch a show. The television was the only company she had, and it never caused her pain.

A loud noise coming from the television woke her up, and she sat upright. She hadn't even remembered falling asleep. She grabbed her phone from the arm of the couch. Three thirty-two a.m. Definitely time for her to drag her ass to bed.

She turned off the TV and shuffled to her room, her eyes still half closed. Pulling back the covers, she climbed into bed, pulled the sheet up to her chin, and shifted her body to get comfortable. Her pillow felt lumpy. She tried pushing it down and laid her head back on it, but it still felt off. As she reached under it to scoop it up, her hand knocked against something. Reaching in the dark, she felt something foreign under her pillow. At the edges of her consciousness, she felt like she knew exactly what it was, but she could not identify it for sure in the dark.

Jumping out from under the covers, Carly turned on the overhead light and returned to the side of the bed she slept on. Apprehensively, she moved the pillow, wondering what could be under it as she lifted it. The rolled-up nylon knife case stared back at her.

What the fuck?

Although the mystery of where the case went was solved, she knew damn well she hadn't put it there, so how did it get there? If someone had been in her house, there'd be other signs of it. Was she losing her mind?

Rubbing the base of her neck, Carly scooped up the set and took it out to the kitchen, laying it on the counter. She was tired and could not process what was happening, but she was sure she would think of a logical answer in the morning when she was more alert. Maybe she had simply been absentminded and moved it there without paying attention. Slipping back into bed, she closed her eyes, and sleep took over almost immediately.

IN THE MORNING, Carly awoke to the trash truck outside. Rubbing her eyes, she stumbled into the bathroom, turned on the shower, peeled off her pajamas, and climbed inside. As the hot water cascaded over her head, she pumped shampoo into her open hand and started washing her hair. The stinging of her right palm caught her attention, and she rinsed the suds out of her eyes and off her hand to investigate. An angry, two-inch cut adorned the surface. It wasn't deep, nor was it actively bleeding, but it was definitely fresh. She searched her memory for anything that could have caused the wound and once again came up empty.

When she was out of the shower, she dried off and

gingerly patted a clean towel against her palm. Pouring peroxide on it, she watched it bubble a bit and when it looked like it was done, she rinsed it again, dried it, and wrapped some gauze around it to keep it clean. Back in the bedroom, a cursory search of the bed provided no clues, however she did note that she bled on the sheets and pillowcase. After pre-treating the blood and throwing the sheets in the washing machine, she went out to the kitchen to make something to eat. She stopped short at the entry-way.

Spread out across the kitchen floor were all the knives from the pouch that had been on the counter, the empty holder strewn across the floor nearby. Each of the knives, as well as the saws—*Are those bone saws?*—were haphazardly scattered, a skinny bladed–knife with drops of blood on and around it over by the refrigerator.

Now I know how I got the cut, but was I sleepwalking?

Confusion welled up into Carly's brain and overtook her emotions. She was definitely losing it. She had never sleepwalked before, to her knowledge, but that might explain the strange happenings of the knife set being moved around without her being aware of it.

Carefully, she placed the knives back in the pouch and rolled it up, tying the strings that kept it in place. Placing the kit on the far end of the counter, she opened the refrigerator to grab something for breakfast. Yellow material peeked out at her from the back behind the milk. Carly moved the gallon jug and it hit her. Flowers and butterflies. The dress. The one that was just like Gracie's. What was it doing in the fridge when she had placed it in

Gracie's closet?

Carefully, Carly reached for the material and pulled it out. The splotches of blood dotting the fabric immediately caught her eye. Apparently, she had been handling the dress after she cut herself. Despair stemmed through her as she thought about Gracie and all the blood. Then a thought cascaded over her and she fell to her knees, sobbing. What if she had killed Gracie after all? What if she had gotten up during her sleep, grabbed a knife, and stabbed her, going back to bed unknowingly immediately after? Could she really rule that out, knowing what she did now? But...surely, she would have had blood on her hands or her nightgown if that was the case, wouldn't she have? Then there were the boot prints and the evidence of window tampering. No, it couldn't have been her. It wasn't possible, but as she battled with herself, she wasn't so sure.

CHAPTER FIVE

CARLY WOKE UP screaming, the dream still vivid in her mind. Every detail of the nightmare was etched into her brain, and being awake brought little relief from the horrors that were conjured up in her head while she slept. Little Gracie. In the dream, Carly had stood over her bed, watching her sleep. The soft light of the moon filtered through the curtains, casting a glow across Gracie's face. She bent down and kissed the little girl's forehead, and then she plunged the knife through her heart. Little Gracie did not even have a chance to scream. Her eyes shot open, she gurgled for a few seconds, and then a vacant look seeped in. Seconds later, she stopped moving.

Carly snapped on the bedside light and sat shivering, the images wreaking havoc with her thoughts. It was all too much...losing Gracie, then her marriage, and then...the weird happenings, possible sleepwalking, and now this. Her thoughts turned to the times that she felt like offing herself...maybe she should have already answered that call loud and clear.

She sat and rocked for about half an hour before finally calming down from the dream. It was all too real. She wondered again if it had any basis on reality.

Switching off the light, finally, she laid her head back on the pillow and burrowed in. A familiar feeling took over, and she reached under her pillow, hoping she was wrong, but her hand latched onto the nylon case anyway. The knives were back under her pillow.

Knowing she needed to get rid of the knives—strange things were happening ever since she acquired them—Carly grabbed her truck keys off of the dresser, ducked outside in her bare feet, and locked them in the backseat of the cab. She would deal with them in the morning.

IT FELT LATE when Carly finally opened her eyes. She looked at her phone and saw it was after one p.m. A groan escaped her lips, and she thought back to the nightmare from earlier that morning, about the knives. She pulled herself out of bed and climbed in the shower to wake herself up. When she had toweled off, she pulled on a pair of blue jeans and a t-shirt.

In the kitchen, she paused in front of the refrigerator, contemplating making something to eat. Instead, she grabbed her keys and headed out to the truck. The sooner she got rid of those knives, the sooner she hoped life would return to normal. And then it registered with her—what she should have known all along, but was either too ignorant, or too innocent to figure it out—those knives didn't belong to a meat cutter at all. They belonged to a killer. Carly had bought a storage locker that belonged to a fucking murderer and the knives were part of his kill kit. Had the clothing and jewelry belonged to his victims?

The realization caused her to retch, and she tried to hold back, but whatever still remained in her stomach from her last meal found its way out, splattering on the ground by her rear driver's side tire. She wiped her mouth on her arm, took a few deep breaths, steadied herself and opened the door to the truck, peering inside to verify the knife set was still in the back seat. It wasn't. She dug through the contents of the entire truck but could not find it. Shaking, she returned to the house and searched room by room before tearing apart the garage as well. The kill kit wasn't anywhere. It had disappeared, along with another portion of her sanity.

Determined to take her mind off things, Carly tried to process some of the items in the garage, but she couldn't focus. She found herself back in her living room, pulling shut the blackout blinds, pulling her knees up under her chin on the couch, then rocking back and forth. Helpless,

Carly felt the darkness creeping back in, deep inside of her—the darkness that she had lived with for so long after losing everything.

Day turned to night and night to day. The world faded out around her, and she stared, blank faced, at the television while the twenty-four-hour programming continued to cater to an inattentive audience. She was unaware of the dishes and trash piling up around her. She had no awareness of eating or using the bathroom. The lights were on, but no one was home.

CARLY STOOD AT the foot of the bed. The little girl was dressed in a set of Eeyore pajamas, her blond hair cascading over the pillow. Carly could make out the rise and fall of the girl's chest. She did not recognize the child, but she estimated her to be Gracie's age—at least the age she was when she had been killed.

Not understanding what she was doing in this child's room, she walked closer to the bed. Maybe she would recognize her up close. Carly leaned over and took a better look. The girl was not familiar to her. Still, Carly felt a connection, but in an ominous way. As she watched, it seemed as if the rise and fall of her little chest stopped for a moment, and then the girl's eyes flicked wide open. Before Carly even knew what was happening, she plunged the blade she hadn't even realized she'd been holding directly into the heart of the now-awake child. Just like in her dream, the scream never escaped, and the child's life faded from her eyes quickly.

Carly tried to scream but couldn't. She had no control over her body or her movements. She wondered if she had actually done what she just thought she did. Looking closely in the dim light, she saw the red blooms of blood saturating the pajama top.

Panicked, she looked around the room and spotted the open window. It beckoned to her, telling her to get out of there, and she did. Leaving the scene was a blur, her emotions in a hyper-sensitive state. Before, she had thought she might be going crazy, but this. THIS! How had it happened? How had she even gotten into the child's room and who was she?

Did it really happen? Did I kill her?

Carly found herself back at her house and quickly curled up on the couch, holding her head, deep sobs racking her body. The room was pitch black, and she kept it that way, hiding from the world and herself. Eventually, she cried herself out and fell asleep.

CARLY OPENED HER eyes. Light filtered into the room from various places in the house, casting shadows across the floor. The events from the night before immediately entered her brain. She tried to process everything, and then it hit her.

It was a dream, just like the other night.

Breathing a sigh of relief, she sat up on the couch. While she still might be going insane, at least she hadn't killed anybody. She stood up to go to her bathroom to take a shower. The feel of the rubber soles on the bottoms of her shoes stopped her. They felt strange. She looked down. Not shoes at all—boots. But not a pair of the feminine ones she kept in her closet. These were work boots. And they were too big on her—men's boots. Her eyes squinted as she tried to remember where she had seen them before. Then it became clear…the boots were in one of the storage lockers she had purchased, and because they were well worn, she had thrown them in the dumpster. So how had she come to be wearing them? More importantly, why?

Carly fumbled with the laces and pulled the boots off of her feet, opened the front door, and threw them out on the porch. The morning sunlight was bright, and she stopped in her tracks, holding out her hands. *Blood.* She checked her clothes. There was blood on her shirt as well.

Panicked, she rushed back in the house and looked around. The living room appeared to be normal, but it was in the kitchen that she found what she was hoping she wouldn't. In the sink sat a knife, blood coating the blade. She recognized the knife as one from the kill kit. It wasn't a dream. It was real. Someone died at her hand. A child even.

Her thoughts turned to Gracie. The little girl she killed was about the same age. Then she remembered the boot prints outside Gracie's window. Had it been Carly after all? Had she been crazy way back then and hadn't realized it? Was she the fucking monster that took her own daughter's life? A numbness settled over her as she tried to make sense of everything. She picked up the knife and examined it, imagining what it would feel like if she plunged it deep within her own chest.

A thought hit her, and suddenly, she found herself running towards Gracie's bedroom. The dress was in the closet where she had left it. She took it out and held it up. The dress reminded her of Gracie, because Gracie had one just like it, but what if…what if the dress was the actual one Gracie had owned?

Carly turned the dress around and looked at the zipper. The dress had come with a nylon one that had broken. Carly could still remember the tears that slid down Gracie's cheeks when the zipper had come apart. It was her favorite dress. After calming her down, Carly promised to fix it. She remembered that Gracie had made her pinky-promise. And so the next day, Carly had stopped by the fabric store and bought a new zipper. A metal one, in gold. She stayed up late that night, ripping out the stitches holding the old zipper in and then sewing the new one into place. She surprised Gracie the next morning with it, and Gracie had worn it to school that day. Carly was not one to break a pinkie-promise.

Carly ran her pointer finger over the gold metal zipper. This dress wasn't *like* Gracie's. It *was* Gracie's. How did a stranger end up with it when Carly knew for a fact that it was missing when Gracie was killed? She knew, because she looked for it. She wanted Gracie to be cremated in that dress, but it was nowhere to be found.

The dress. The knives.

Just like a jigsaw puzzle piece that finally fell into

place, Carly connected the dots. The owner of the storage locker was the one. The bastard that had killed Gracie. The person that was responsible for destroying her entire life. She had to go to the police. Surely, they could find out who owned the locker, right?

While you are at it, maybe you can explain how one of those knives ended up in the chest of a two-year-old. That should be fun.

Defeated, she slumped down to the floor of Gracie's closet and cried.

CHAPTER SIX

CARLY SAT ON an old wooden chair in her garage, the knife roll laid out at her feet. She turned the boning knife over and over in her hands. She pressed her right pointer finger against the tip, and a bright red drop of crimson pushed out of her finger and dripped onto the floor.

For the past three weeks, she found herself mired in that place again. The one where she could no longer go on. If she wasn't sleeping, she was plotting, planning. She had concocted thirty-seven different ways to leave the world behind, many of them horrible ways to die. She even came close to trying a couple of them. In the end, she chicken-shitted out. She didn't have the guts to do the only thing that seemed to make sense in a world that had torn her soul to shreds.

Her child was dead. Her husband was gone. And she was just as bad as the fucker that had killed Carly. She had killed a little girl, and two more in the past three weeks. The scenario was always the same. She became aware that she was in each room—most of them adorned with toys, dolls, and a multitude of pink—and then she stabbed. The last two times, when she saw the precious little girls lying in the bed, asleep, she knew. She knew what she was about to do even before she did it. And she tried to stop. Both times, she willed herself to leave, drop the knife, something. Anything that would have saved them—either of them. It's like she was powerless to control her actions. The knives—she knew it was the fucking knives. Somehow, they manipulated her. She wondered how that could even be possible, but she had the blood of three innocent victims on her hands—all little girls—and four, if she was responsible for taking Gracie's life. She couldn't live with herself...was too broken to even try, but too afraid to die.

She screamed, a guttural yell, and threw the knife at the garage door. The handle bounced off, and the knife went skittering across the concrete floor. Unable to go through with what she had planned, she abandoned the knives where they lay and went into the house.

Inside, Carly went to the kitchen and opened the refrigerator door. She hadn't eaten in two days and was starving, but each time she thought about doing so, her stomach churned. She eyed the two plates of food in the sink—her attempts at eating that didn't go as planned. Inhaling sharply, Carly shut the refrigerator door, went into the bedroom, crawled under the covers and closed her eyes.

THE GLOW FROM the Little Mermaid nightlight partially illuminated the room but did not quite reach the dark shadows in the corner. Carly stood, watching, as the little girl, who was laying on her stomach, slept. She didn't have to look—she knew the knife would be clenched in her right hand. While distraught and frantic on the inside, she was calm and collected on the outside.

She thought about some of the news stories she had recently watched about the murders. The authorities felt the killings were tied back to a string of other child murders years before—murders that had never been solved. Child victims. Including Gracie.

They think I'm him.

Then another thought hit her.

Or maybe he is me.

Could she have been the one this entire time? Was she simply continuing on with what she has started years earlier?

She tried to reason with herself. *The tools. The dress. They were in someone else's storage locker.*

The little girl mumbled and flipped over on her back. Carly glanced at the open window, the printed images of Ariel dancing from the slight breeze. She willed herself to walk to the window—to climb through it and just leave. Her feet disobeyed her, and she stood rooted to the floor. She knew what was to happen next. History would repeat itself. She would finally move...and she would stab, exactly once. And the blade would penetrate the precise location it needed to.

Involuntarily, her right foot moved one step forward, and her left followed. She felt her right arm start to rise, and then she saw it, the knife, where she knew it would be.

At the side of the bed, she took in the girl's innocence. An innocence that would be shattered by violence. Carly pulled the knife back over her head, poised, ready to slam it down into the chest of her victim.

Brilliant light flooded the room.

"What the fuck are you doing?" a man standing inside the open door screamed.

Oh shit. Her father.

"Get away from her," he yelled, eyeing the knife. He was frozen in place, unsure of what to do.

Carly tried to speak and couldn't, her body a mere pawn.

"Put the knife down and leave the way you came. You don't want to do this."

She tried to talk again. This time, she almost succeeded. "I—d-d-d..."

"Who are you?" he demanded. "Why are you here?"

She shook her head. "D-don't k-k-k-now."

He held out his hand. "Give me the knife."

Carly paused, unsure of what to do. She actually felt like she could control her movements for the first time since standing in the room. If she surrendered, then one life would be saved, but her soul would still forever be damned. Then there was the fact she'd rot in jail. She'd rather be dead.

"C'mon. Hand it over. I can't let you hurt Jessie." His tone softened and became luring. Carly hesitated, then held the knife out in front of her, handle first. The man froze, his mouth open, his eyes wide.

"Where did you get that knife?"

"D-does it matter?"

"Yes. It matters. The ivory inlay on the handle is unique. In fact, I have only ever seen that design once before."

The strange circumstances that surrounded the knives—the ones that threw her life into complete chaos ever since she had them in her possession—came crashing down upon her. Before she could react, the man lunged forward and grabbed the knife out of her hand, slicing her fingers in the process.

"Where?" she demanded. "Where have you seen it before?"

The man paused, contemplating his answer. Finally, he spoke.

"I designed this handle and had it custom made."

The past two years' events came ripping through Carly's head like a freight train. Memory after memory flooded her thoughts, like a news highlight reel. Dots started connecting, and she was on the verge of a realization she knew she wasn't ready for, but she had to be sure.

"You designed this knife?"

"Yes."

"Just one?"

"No. An entire set. Where did you get it?" he repeated.

"I think you know," she whispered, menacingly.

"Where is the rest of my stuff? That locker was mine. You had no right to touch my things."

The little girl started stirring in her bed.

"One hundred seventy-five dollars says that the contents are no longer yours. They belong to me now. Including that knife. Give it back."

Carly stared at him, surprised at what she saw. He was thin and small in stature. He wore wire-rimmed glasses on his round face, and his head was balding on top.

The man ignored her request. "Is it you? Are you the one responsible for all the killings on the news?" He looked confused.

"Apparently," she responded.

"How? Why?"

"I was hoping you could answer that question for me."

If she caught him off guard, it was only evident in his expression for a millisecond. He quickly resumed his role as victim.

"Are you a copy-cat killer?"

The little girl mumbled and turned over again.

"Copy-cat? Copying who?"

The realization finally smacked her in the head so ferociously that her knees buckled and she sank to the ground. Images of Gracie's dress filled her head. The dress that was missing after Gracie was murdered. The dress that she found in a storage locker she purchased. A storage locker owned by a serial killer.

He didn't answer her. He didn't need to.

"I think it's time we call the police," he said.

Carly paused, contemplating the situation. "You think that's a good idea?"

"You broke into my fucking house. You were about to kill my daughter, for Christ's sake. Yes, I think it's a wonderful idea." He reached into his robe pocket and pulled out his phone.

A dark smile settled on Carly's lips. "What are you going to tell them?"

"The truth."

"All of it?"

"Yes, all of it."

"Are you going to tell them who killed the other girls, before me?"

"What do you mean?"

"I think they will find it interesting that the knives in the set I now own will most likely match up with the stab wounds for all the little girls that died before I got involved."

"As they should. It's your set, so you must have killed them."

"But I can prove when I bought the locker contents."

"I don't recall ever having knives in my storage locker. Prove otherwise."

"I'm sure the company that created the inlays will be able to identify the knives as yours." She glanced at the boots strapped to her feet. "I'm sure these boots have your DNA on them as well."

He frowned. "You're not being very smart about this. You should have left well enough alone."

Flipping the knife around in his hand, he inched toward Carly, ready to strike. As Carly watched, the man brought the knife back, his intentions displayed upon his face.

"Daddy?"

Both their heads whipped around toward the bed. The little girl was sitting up, looking back and forth between them.

"Daddy, what are you doing? Who is that?" She pointed toward Carly.

In a split-second reaction, Carly dove for the knife. The man lost his grip on it, and it bounced on the carpet. Carly dove on it, and the man jumped on her back, trying to get at the weapon before she did. The little girl screamed from her bed, cowering in the corner. The pair tussled on the ground, each one getting a little bit of an advantage and then losing it again. While the man had a slight weight advantage, pure adrenaline was driving Carly's basic will to survive, which—as she scrambled for the knife—surprised her, considering the suicidal state she had resided in for longer than she could care to remember.

As Carly's hand grabbed the handle of the knife, the man slammed his fist down on her wrist. Fireworks exploded in her brain as intense pain shot up her arm. The knife fell from her grasp, and the man picked it up and thrust it toward her heart. The knife blade sunk halfway into Carly's flesh, but it missed its mark as she turned at the last second and caught the cold steel in her shoulder. A howl escaped her lips as the pain flared through her body. She landed a kick to the man's testicles, and he went down, groaning.

"Fucking bitch," he gasped.

Carly looked at the knife that was still sticking out of

her shoulder. She knew pulling it out wasn't necessarily a great idea, but she needed it. With a grimace on her face, she grabbed it and yanked. Tears ran down her face as she tried to hold back her screams. The man rolled onto his knees and started to get up. With everything she had, she dropped her entire body weight down as she drove the blade between his shoulder blades and smashed his face into the floor. In the dim light, she watched the blood soak through his pajama top as he moaned into the carpet.

Carly looked over at the little girl who had stopped screaming and had her knees tucked up under her chin, her lips trembling. Carly grabbed the knife with both hands, her right one pulsating with pain, and yanked. With her foot, she flipped the man over, face up. He glared at her, the hatred evident in his face. He didn't move. Carly wondered if she had paralyzed him.

To the little girl, she said, "Close your eyes and cover your ears." When the girl complied, she turned her attention back to the monster before her.

"Do I have your attention now?" she asked. He continued to glare at her. "We all know what you are," she continued. "I just didn't know *who* you were until tonight. And me being here is either one hell of a coincidence or one big twist of fate. Either way, I'll take it. I've waited a long time to meet you."

"Who are you?" he asked again.

"You don't know me. But you were acquainted with my daughter."

"Your daughter?"

"Yes. Cute, blond. She was two when you stabbed her in the heart and ended her life. I think she might have been your last victim."

"Her? You're her…" His voice tapered off.

"I'm her trainwreck of a mother. When you took her life, you took everything from me."

"How…"

Carly shook her head. "I'm asking the questions. And I need to know why. Why did you kill Gracie? And for that matter, the other girls?"

He blinked, his chest rapidly rising and falling. Carly could see resolve starting to kick in. She glanced over at the little girl who still had her face buried against her knees and her ears covered. She made the sound of an injured animal as she rocked.

Carly's tone deepened and she spoke slowly "Maybe…you… didn't…fucking…hear…me. WHY?"

He looked at her and shook his head. "You wouldn't understand."

"Try me."

"It sounds weird saying it. I'm not a monster. At least I don't think of myself as one. It was simply the one true love I had in my life. I got a taste when I accidentally killed my little sister, who was around the same age. I was so scared…afraid they were going to send me away. But they thought it was some freaky accident, and no one blamed me. I was too innocent in their eyes. I loved her, and I regret what happened, but the surreal power of taking a life and getting away with it was more than I could control. I had the hunger. I fought it for years, but as I became an adult and moved out of my parents' house, I could not keep the beast at bay any longer. It had to feed. It claimed a new victim every time I lost control of it."

"So, my d…daughter. There was no rhyme or reason for it? You just had an urge to quench?"

"It's more than that. It's hard to control. And I never knew when it was going to rear its ugly head."

Carly's face went pale, and she spoke through clenched teeth. "So…why did you stop?"

The man's eyes shifted toward the girl on the bed. "My wife got pregnant and Jessie was born. Suddenly, I had a new love in my life. She grounded me. She made me better. I haven't killed since."

"Touching, but you never paid for your sins."

"Apparently. That time is now, I imagine."

"Apparently. You'll never know how many lives you fucked up. You'll never know how badly you destroyed everything I had. All I've wanted since was a bullet to the brain. Until tonight."

Peace settled across the man's face. "Do what you have to do. Just don't hurt Jessie. She's innocent and shouldn't have to pay for my bullshit."

"You foolish man," Carly sneered. "Do you think I'm going to spare her because you asked me to? After what you did to Gracie, you deserve to watch her die. There's a special place in hell for you. I'll see you there."

Carly grabbed the man by the hair and tilted his head back, gliding the knife across the bare flesh of his neck. His eyes shot open wide as a crimson necklace appeared. His mouth fell open and his lips started to move, but only a gurgle came out.

As the life started to drain out of him, Carly made sure he watched her as she wiped the knife off on the leg of her jeans, repositioned it in her hand, and approached

Jessie, the knife raised in the air. That image was the final one burned into his brain when the last of his life leaked out of him.

EPILOGUE

CARLY FLIPPED THE pancakes over on the griddle, admiring the almost perfect roundness of the fluffy circles. They would be a great start to the day, which already was looking promising based upon the weather forecast that morning. The cotton-candy clouds billowed sparsely across the brilliant blue sky, and she had noticed a slight breeze earlier when she had been outside loading up the truck.

When that batch of pancakes was golden brown on both sides, Carly used the spatula to add them to the plate where the first two batches sat waiting.

Carly looked down at Barley, a Golden Retriever that had won over her heart and whose hair took over the house.

"How many are you good for this morning?" she asked as Barley eyed the pancakes.

"All of them? Don't be greedy. Save some for the humans."

Carly set the plate of food on the table and took the tray of bacon out of the oven that had been warming there. She put the bacon on a plate and added it to the feast before making sure that the three different kinds of syrup were all waiting to drown the flapjacks. Filling a glass with orange juice, she set it on the table and poured a cup of coffee. She was just adding her vanilla creamer when Barley jumped up and ran to the edge of the room.

Carly glanced over at Barley giving kisses and receiving muzzle rubs.

"Good morning, sweetie. How did you sleep?"

"Really good!"

"Did Barley sleep with you again?"

"Yep! But he's a bed hog."

"He just loves his little girl."

"Thank you for getting him for me, Mommy."

"Of course, honey."

Jessie saw the plate of pancakes, and her eyes opened wide. "Are those blueberry?"

"Your favorite!"

"You're a good mommy."

"And you're a good daughter!"

Carly kneeled down and scooped Jessie up in her arms. Jessie was getting so tall. At four years old, she had changed so much in the two years that they had been together.

The first few months had been rough. Jessie had pushed back on everything and constantly asked about her father. It was through many conversations that Carly learned that the mother had died after childbirth. Carly wondered if it had been from natural causes. Eventually, Jessie got to know Carly and grew to like her, and after six months, she confided in Carly. Her father scared her and was not a nice person. As Carly and Jessie grew close, eventually, Jessie stopped talking about her father, and one day, she asked Carly the ultimate question. *Can I call you Mommy?*

The need to kill drained out of her as Jessie's father's blood drained out of him. At that point, Jessie was never in any danger, but it sure made her feel better knowing that the last thing he saw as he died was her hovering over his daughter with a knife.

A new house, in a rural town, in a new state, was just what they had needed. It gave both of them the time and space they needed to heal. And although Carly missed every little thing about Gracie, she knew that Gracie would want this. Would want for her mommy to be whole again. And aside from the special place Carly kept in her heart that was reserved only for the memories of a little blond girl who she adored, the rest belonged to Jessie, and she would always know how loved she was.

TAKE A RIDE WITH ME
TO THE PIGGY FARM

Robb T. White

T HAD TAKEN MONTHS, AND MOST OF HER
savings, to get everything assembled, just as it had
taken years to get to this point in the practice, where
she was solidly established in Northtown's community of
professionals. Thanks to the gaping maw of the internet,
she not only knew all the symptoms to be wary of display-
ing in public, but also the dirty little secrets of her victims.
Men unused to the touch of another man's hands on their
flesh would tense up; a woman's fingers kneading their
skin, however, seemed to release those inhibitions instan-
taneously. She'd been propositioned more than once, by
seemingly straight-arrow husbands, who'd come to her
clinic for back-spasm treatment.

Jerry, the pig, had made his move on the first visit...
Since her acquisition of the slaughterhouse, in the

middle of Amish country, she thought of them as her very own "piggies." One old farmer, with knotted, arthritic fingers, had given her the proverb, which unintentionally fit the joke behind his saying: "Pigs got fed, but hogs got butchered."

Her sly joke, because they all got slaughtered—those she selected, those who came to her, hat in hand, begging for it.

She reveled in the term *sociopath*. The *DSM*-5, and its double-jointed language, was less realistic than Grimm's *Fairy Tales*. She even preferred those thundering biblical prophets, who twisted themselves into knots, groveling before Him. The only value those pinhead academics provided was her subscription journals, like *Abnormal Psychology* and *Psychology Today*. They kept her cognizant of the red flags that marked "a deviance from baseline normal," as one article on "the widespread prevalence of sociopaths among us" put it.

For years, ever since puberty, she'd trained herself to fit in. For example, she never harmed animals—first and best sign of a budding serial killer—and she avoided being caught miming facial expressions in the mirror. Looking at her parents in distress taught her how to mimic the right facial expressions. Pity was as alien to her genetic makeup as the color blue was to a blind person. Her parents were surprised she didn't elect veterinary school as a career choice, so accustomed were they to thinking her an animal lover. Growing into adolescence, she fought the urges to allow her true nature to run free into the world. Like Shakespeare's Prince Hal, she knew how to bide time until it was safe to rise above the "base clouds" of these lesser beings, none of whom breathed her rarified air.

The news crawl that morning claimed two hundred forty souls had gone into the drink when an overfilled ferry capsized on Lake Victoria. "God's grace is as scarce as life jackets," she mumbled to the TV as she headed outside, on her way to the office. Compared to His murderous wrath, she was a piker. "A minimalist with perfectionist tendencies," she once described herself on an online dating site.

Neurologists weren't any better, she reasoned, for they wanted to locate everything back to electrochemical mutations of the genome. *Have a migraine headache, do you? Must be something wrong with your Notch 3 gene of chromosome 19.* She was content to be exactly who she was.

Beams of sunlight streamed through the windows of the old slaughterhouse on the back lot of her property. They were filled with swirling columns of dust motes and gnats. From her platform, she beheld the metal and machinery occupying the floor: shackles, trolleys, hooks. The skinning cradle and hide pulling equipment, the saws, hand-held stunners, hydraulic knives, and accessories for skinning and tanning. One instrument dazzled in the midst of the rest, its chrome exterior shining in the sunlight—a surgical brain saw, the newest catalog model—an impulse buy.

Wearing trail-hiking boots, she patrolled the boundaries of her two acres of land, with its crumbling, twin cement-block structures that came with the purchase. They were built by a local Mennonite family named Erb. Some unknown Erb ancestor had established the small slaughterhouse, for sheep and pigs, at the turn of the last century. The Erbs had done well for themselves and had found more genteel professions to pursue in the following decades. Their tiny Mennonite community sat isolated in the midst of the much larger Amish community that settled in Ohio and Pennsylvania. The same names on the mailboxes, for the last five miles on the ride out, testified to how closed these two communities were—incestuously so, she mused—but another plus to her designs, as her foremost criterion was privacy. No passersby, no pedestrians, no hunters or hikers—no foot or motor traffic, of any kind, out here to disturb the peace. The only sound she'd heard, since she sealed the deal, was the comforting *chirring* of crickets in the overgrown fields. There was nothing around for miles but stunted trees and abandoned fields, where the cicadas were coming out of their burrows after their years-long slumber beneath the sod.

This aura of tranquility extended into the drab building interiors, where once squealing pigs and bleating sheep were led through chutes to the killing floor. The red reek was long gone. The second building, where sheep were led up a steep ramp and driven over the edge, causing them to break leg bones, making them more docile for slaughtering, was the sole reminder of the true purpose of these forgotten buildings.

Water stains covered the ceiling, where orb weavers worked away. Some faint stains could be seen around the scuppers in the corners. An overhead bank of fluorescent lights came on with a sizzle after she hit the switch. Fortunately, the Erbs kept the utilities on in both buildings. The whole *ambience* reminded her of this tiny community's prayerful celebrations of baptisms and wakes, the humble gatherings to celebrate harvests. All of it tickled with delicious irony; she was reactivating an honorable historical tradition—the only difference being the animals weren't animals.

Watching Farmer Erb drive off with his check, a warm flush invaded her cheeks. A staccato series of caws from the abandoned orchard across the highway, where the branches of apple trees grew into one another, signified nature's own appreciation.

She'd researched each piggy to find that vulnerable spot. If a transient or a junkie disappeared, a weak investigation followed. No suspects meant a cold case—ho-hum, forgotten on some dusty shelf in a precinct basement. But let a member of the city council or of Northtown's gated community disappear, and—voilà, headlines in large type, follow-up articles, pressure on the police, gossip on social media, and radio updates. Cops bragged they worked a prostitute's murder as hard as an upstanding citizen's, but the truth was obviously different. A murdered whore was a beneficial population adjustment; a missing citizen was trouble. She lived for the challenge.

Piggy *numero uno* down there in the cage, for example. A big-shot financial consultant from Boise lands in Cleveland. But Mr. Jerry Persig—to name the chosen swine—had girlfriend problems galore. He knocked up a dancer at a sleazy titty bar and nearly killed her with an abortion pill he'd slipped into her drink. This respected family man was also a "person of interest" in the case of a colleague's missing teenaged daughter. One of the last people to see her alive, he claimed he'd given her a ride to her job at a fast-food restaurant. But he told detectives that was "a mistake"; he meant to say the day prior, because she never clocked in the day she disappeared. His sloppiness offended the perfectionist in her.

Jerry was due for his appointment at her Northtown clinic in forty-five minutes. He'd checked out of the Radisson and was dropping in for his appointment before heading back to Cleveland-Hopkins airport for his flight to Idaho. He wasn't shy about letting her know—he expected this meeting to result in sex, especially since he was leaving on the next flight.

She'd have to step on it. Looking around, she nodded in satisfaction that all her preparations were complete. She was ready and waiting for him. She smiled at the FBI's pathetic profiles of "organized" and "disorganized" serial killers. *Why not have it both ways?*

"Time's up, Jerry," she said to the blank walls. She patted the syringe in her blouse pocket. Frustrating weeks of experimenting with varying dosages of succinylcholine, Rohypnol, and ketamine had finally created the perfect cocktail. The goal wasn't to drop them like a horse but to get them to shuffle, in a drugged daze, out the back door to her specially adapted van, where she immobilized them for the ride south to her pig farm.

TAKE A RIDE WITH ME TO THE PIGGY FARM |
Robb T. White

"WHAAA—UMMMPH—UMMM—uhm—meeuh?"

"I'm sorry," she said, hearing him mumble incoherently again, while she ratcheted a stuck valve, "did you *oink* something, Jerry?"

She dropped the big crescent to the floor, stepping over to his squat, metal-ribbed dog cage. Opening the latch, she ripped away the gag. The duct tape left a white rectangle over his mouth.

"Why…"—pausing to suck air into his heaving lungs—"why are you…doing this?"

"Why am I doing this?" She paused, as if to give the question serious pondering. "I'm doing it because I have an obligation to maintain my credentials in the American Society of Sociopaths." She quickly replaced the tape. His eyes popped.

"Suffice it to say, Mister Persig, I have a hunger equivalent to that of a heroin addict's urges. And I'm not talking about cracking backs in my office."

She inspected the hinges, braces, and fasteners for the final stage and ignored the muffled cries behind the tape. She was past explaining now.

Her family background was a far cry from that image of the state-raised, violent, psycho-killer of pulp literature. She was never abused and had never abused anyone in her life—discounting her current work. Her intelligence taught her to roll with life's punches, never to provoke, never to be center stage—even when she clearly surpassed her peers intellectually and could have gone to medical school instead of opening a clinic in shabby Northtown. Becoming a medical doctor meant a busy practice, a too-big investment of time—and *time* was the crucial factor. She wanted only to be busy with her life's true calling. Supernaturally patient, never impulsive like the low-browed killers of crime shows, who draw attention and show reckless disregard for avoiding detection. She laughed at the nitwits who yammered away on their cell phones at murder scenes and splashed bleach around, thinking cops would never know.

Patients called her "Doctor," paid good money for massages and the gobbledygook she soothingly spewed out, such as "vertebral subluxation" and "Cox flexion-distraction technique." They deserved to be hoodwinked. Her chunky office manager, Sheila Pinnady, whom she privately called "Pinhead," flaunted her Vo-Ed diploma behind her desk out front, managed the books, and kept track of her appointments. The rest of her time was reserved for her passion.

Looking down from the elevated platform, Jerry stared upward, his eyes bulging from his cramped cage. "Let me help you," she said.

She'd plucked him right out of the parking lot of a strip club in Mayfield Heights, a Cleveland bedroom suburb. The folded printout of the itinerary in his suitcoat established he'd landed in Cleveland-Hopkins two days earlier—perfect. Never troll for piggies among the locals— that was her first rule. Jerry's business card had the texture of a silk pillow and touted a bulleted list of his expertise in various enterprises, such as cloud computing and integrated financial reporting systems.

"Odd place for consulting, Jerry. I'll bet those strippers were impressed to have an expert, like you, available to unburden themselves of their financial woes."

She bent the card with a fingernail and thumb and then flicked it into the air. Jerry's big eyes followed its flight over the cement floor, watching it sail on a draft, like a child watching a butterfly.

Though bound at the ankles and wrists with nylon cuffs, the piggy could still surprise her, so she kept a fish billy club tucked inside her khaki work pants and never relaxed vigilance. She was wary of dosages, too. Unable to purchase drugs without a medical license, she had to purchase off the dark web. Buying locally was too risky even though Northtown, a rust-belt Midwestern town, had the kind of opioid problem where even grandparents nodded off in cars or fell off park benches from fentanyl-laced heroin.

"I'll let you go soon," she said. "I just want to take some bondage photos for a magazine."

"Uh-huh."

"We're going to walk to it. Try anything stupid, and I'll hit you with this stunner."

She waved the stun gun in front of his face.

Helped to his feet, Jerry was a load. She kept the weapon in her other arm free to swing at him if needed. His hairy belly wobbled over his belt with every step. She took his weight but kept out of reach of his bound hands.

"What chair?"

"See the one where I'm pointing?"

"That's no chair—what are you—I'm not—"

She jammed the stun gun under his turkey wattle and watched the sizzling blue arc disappear into the fat folds.

His whole body jerked, and he almost took her down to the floor with him.

Lugging his dead weight across the floor to the machine took several long minutes and quite a few breaks, despite her devotion to power yoga. It would be a terrible irony if she threw her own back out doing this. *Mental note: Purchase one of those carts, with wheels, that mechanics use to work under cars.* Jerry's bulk was a curious bonus—more skin meant more spectacle.

She attached chains to Jerry's ankles and hands, while the man was prone, moaning, his head half-hidden beneath the machine's braces. Bought at an auction in Southfield, she also purchased a power hose to clean it, knowing flies would be drawn to the miniscule bits soldered into the chain links. Although bovine and slaughter chickens were run upside down on the rail, she wanted piggy's head to be upright. *One needed to see the moment scored across the face, a forever imprint like a Hallmark greeting card for the neocortex...*

Human skin, unlike cattle hide, slips and tears easily. The average adult possesses ten pounds of flesh, which covers about twenty-two feet. Pig skin, on the other hand, bears similarities in texture to human skin. This is the obvious reason pharmaceutical and cosmetic companies order their white-coated minions to torture pigs. *Auschwitz for animals goes on and on*, she thought.

She'd purchased euthanized hogs from a farmer in the next county, who offered to run them through his singeing machine first. When she felt confident of the right places for the initial skinning cuts, she was ready to harvest her first. Only the *crème de la merde* would do:

those smug, condescending, *respectable* types like Jerry would be chosen. Her fantasy was to have some Silicon Valley whiz kid fall into her hands—a billionaire who developed apps for gossipy teens, but who acted as if he'd found the cure for cancer. She'd make every effort to draw him to her.

The machine itself resembled a do-it-yourself guillotine. Hydraulically powered, it came with a joystick control. She modified the contact points to avoid "shredding" and adapted integrated trigger grips in the incisions attached to the chains.

I should patent this, she thought, *sell it online.*

She placed a three-legged stool ten feet from Jerry and set the control on his lap, waiting. At last, her piggy stirred, woke, and blinked stupidly at her. Then he shook his head like a dog.

He can't assemble in his mind what's going to happen.

A light touch on the joystick kick-started the chains spooling, at a controlled pace, into the stainless-steel drum. Jerry's arms slowly lifted him to a sitting position. Another touch on the joystick and he swung around on his haunches, as the lower chains wound toward the stainless-steel drum attached to a pulley in the crossbeam overhead.

She was pleased to see the incisions hold. Some new blood flowed over the first streaks, made from the incisions she'd cut with a surgeon's scalpel—an obsidian sharper than any razor made. Jerry's chest and belly were crisscrossed with rusty blood that disappeared into the folds beneath his vast stomach. Jerry's penis, like a tiny woodland creature sensing danger, disappeared into his ginger pubic tuft.

She set the joystick on a towel lying on the stool and hopped lightly forward, doing a Fred Astaire shuffle. Piggy's eyes begged her.

"Can't breathe with that thing over your mouth?"

She pulled the tape from Jerry's face, revealing a deeper rectangle of blanched skin. Jerry's body was filmed in greasy sweat; he exuded a ferocious body odor.

"Sort of a clown mouth in reverse," she said, musing.

Jerry's gaze drifted to his powder-blue suit, which, like the matching tie, was neatly folded and laid across a pipe rail. The dark-blue sneakers placed below.

"You'd like to put those expensive Tiziano sneakers on and run out of here, wouldn't you, Jerry?"

Vigorous nodding of the head, his voice a rusty croak.

"Sorry, that sounded like a cough."

"Go...home...won't say—"

"—won't say a word to anyone, huh?"

The clichéd TV dialogue offended her sensibilities. She wanted—*what? Something far grander, more honest.* Nonchalantly returning to the stool, she donned the white disposable suit with hood, mask, booties, and latex gloves. Then, unfolding the towel to expose the electric knife wrapped in it, she showed Jerry the joystick and wagged it at him.

"Sorry, about the bondage ruse. I don't think you're svelte enough for the magazines, Jer."

She thumbed the levers into action. A rumble of

chains stirred in the drum. Jerry's mouth opened in an operatic O of surprise. The chains yanked him to his feet. The wires attached to his skin tautened. She thumbed the levers to medium speed; the network of wires began pulling downward. A cry that began in Jerry's throat as a scream climbed the scale to a soprano's piercing warble.

"Sumi Jo couldn't hit that note! Let's do that again."

She thumbed the lever controlling the wires.

Her eyes bored into his. She pushed the chain controls to maximum, until Jerry was stretched out a foot above the floor, arms extended upward at the pulley shackled to the steel crossbeam above his head. His eyes acquired the glazed look of a dying bird. She didn't want to waste the moment, so she took a final sip of the man's pain.

Big strips of flesh began parting from Jerry's torso; the hide-pulling wires lifted wide ribbons of flesh. She had to get in there fast with her electric knife to prevent tearing and cut directly behind the wires as the skin began to stretch. It wasn't perfect—capillaries burst, and one trigger guard failed and dangled with a four-inch square of flesh in its grip. Her grim-set face was a mere foot from his. He bucked against the chains stretching him, but it only resulted in more tearing.

He stopped wiggling, frozen, as her busy knife seared away flesh behind the wires embedded in his skin. He could not comprehend, even at the moment he died, the spinning black hole of pain he had entered.

Beautiful, just beautiful...

She stepped back, the knife falling from her hand, in

time to see Jerry's face become a wobbling red orb, with ropy drool flowing out of his mouth, followed by an eruption of frothy mucus, and a regurgitated spume of yellow bile.

Jerry's torso looked as if someone had stuck buttered popcorn all over it. Globules of fat dotted the red where his flesh had been. His skin hung all around him, while she played the joystick, easing tension so that they flapped. The contrast between Jerry's white face and the red gristle of his torso was…*exhilarating.*

"You're a tubby Maypole," she said. "Your lap dancers could skip around you like corrupt maidens."

Blood streamed over the incisions; drool leaked from the corners of his mouth.

She stuck a knife into his heart, although the coup de grâce was unneeded. Jerry was long gone. As if on cue, his bowels voided noisily with a hideous stench.

"Thank you," she whispered. "I do mean that sincerely."

Her hands trembled. She set the joystick on the stool. Her legs wobbled from the delirium of sensations cascading over her.

What a rush—

Staggering back to the stool, a narcotic fuzziness enveloped her. Dispassionately, she regarded Jerry, hoping for an involuntary muscle spasm, a lifeless marionette. The fixed stare and dilated pupils affirmed he had no more to give her.

Still, sated, pleased with this first effort, she glanced toward the bench where the saws and knives were assembled in a precise array on a chamois cloth. The fifty-five-gallon barrels of styrene in the corner were the final phase.

Waves of giddiness passing, she set to work on the finale. She looked at the row of glittering knives assembled on the cloth and selected one, a carbon skinning knife, regarding it like a doting parent and a favorite child.

TWO MONTHS LATER

THE SECOND PIGGY, an insurance executive from Florida, lived in a gated community. His secret took real gumshoe work: He had a common-law wife, besides his coiffed and cultured legal wife in Land O Lakes. A slattern, half his age, whom he must have forgotten to divorce when his career took off. Like Persig, he couldn't resist an attractive woman fawning over him, when she casually encountered him in a coffee shop over a latte. What started as a request for directions to a Cleveland boutique on East Ninth ended in an impromptu visit to her clinic before his flight home.

The bigamist's wife lived in a seedy trailer park, beyond the Liberty City township, overrun with feral cats and squalling children, the byblows of the roving baby daddies who put in work for the neighborhood gangs by selling drugs and boosting anything not nailed down. Sexual gluttony struck her as more nefarious, a darker sin, than alcoholism or drug addiction. It would serve to deflect an aggressive investigation once this piggy disappeared.

Trolling professionals had an advantage, she realized: they liked their perks, especially those expensive jaunts to conferences they could write off, always scheduled in warm places during cold winter months. Her chiropractic conferences were ghastly affairs, done solely to obtain the certificates to polish her image in Northtown. Pinhead certainly seemed awed by them as, one after another, she framed and mounted them in the reception area along the "vanity wall."

It was all she could do to keep awake, listening to pseudoscientific drivel the speakers waxed enthusiastic over.

Charlie O'Day, however, had no intention of listening to some buttoned-down speaker maundering on about international mixed asset mutual funds. She followed him around Miami's South Beach, watching O'Day meet with a dark, exotic-looking woman, after his conference. He couldn't wait to wrap a lawless leg around his secret woman.

Her motel off Flagler served as a base of operations for "the grab"—the tricky part. Both room and rental car were listed under false names. Her sugar daddy took an Uber to and from the woman's trailer. O'Day's dash up the rickety iron steps was as much public exposure as he allowed himself outside the conference.

Cheap bastard, she scoffed. *You could have set her up in a decent place.*

Her most expensive research databases revealed the man's six-figure income and intimated a fat stock portfolio. O'Day used every lever he could pull to avoid paying a single dollar in taxes over what he could get away with.

For surveillance, she chose a touristy ensemble picked off the Goodwill racks and affected a slow, aimless gait—

another gawking snowbird who gathered in Miami's winter, like toadstools after a shower.

Her field glasses kept Charlie's rental Navigator in view. The SUV had been parked in a Rite-Aid lot for the last three hours. The spy camera she'd set up the day she'd discovered O'Day's mistress' lodgings involved a big risk. She planted the camera in a gap between the wooden frame and the window-box air conditioner. Retrieving the video on her first recon proved her suspicions correct: Piggy Two wasn't exactly a Don Juan in bed. He lay atop his slag, a couple shivers of his buttocks and he was done. The time stamp showed two more hours passed before he was ready for another foray. Even then, the poor woman was forced to work her jaws for twenty minutes before he achieved erection. Allowing him to play stud once a month was okay with the woman, as long as he left a wad of bills on the table beside the door.

She pulled up beside the Navigator as soon as the Uber driver dropped her off in the pharmacy lot. She sat patiently while Piggy Two started the vehicle and took off. Her backup surveillance outfit was a pair of khaki work pants and a denim shirt with the name *Josephine* stitched across the pocket. A worn ballcap, hair in a practical bun, eyes behind sunglasses, and face covered by the brim. She worried about the outside CCTV cameras.

Putting herself a few cars behind, she trailed him, confident he was heading back to his hotel for the morning seminar. That giant Idaho potato bought at a supermarket had been peeled at her motel, cut in half, and was now jammed deep into the SUV's tailpipe. Twenty minutes' driving time, however, and dark smoke emitted from the exhaust in separate black puffs, like Indian smoke signals.

Charlie's Navigator made the turn for Doral Boulevard.

Come on, hurry up, she urged, worried her plan might fail.

There! Got you, Second Piggy—

The SUV sputtered, slowed, jerked forward, and almost stopped in the middle of the road. Horns blared, impatient drivers swung around the Navigator. She put the emergency lights on and stayed on the Navigator's tail as it wheeled over to the shoulder doing fifteen miles per hour. She pulled up behind the stalled SUV, rolling down the window. Taking a deep breath, smile at the ready, she stepped out of the vehicle like any Good Samaritan about to help a motorist in trouble.

Tapping on Piggy's window, she smiled brighter and leaned in.

Let him see the reassuring Josephine stitching riding the tops of her tits.

Window glare made Piggy's expression invisible until his window descended. She suppressed a laugh at O'Day's blood-suffused, angry face.

Don't have a heart attack on me now, she prayed. *Save that purple face for later…*

Unsurprisingly, O'Day showed little gratitude for being bailed out of his dilemma; he almost ordered her to take him to his Ramada Inn.

"What about your car, sir?"

"Fucking piece of shit!"

TAKE A RIDE WITH ME TO THE PIGGY FARM |
Robb T. White

Her piggy was blowing a fuse.

As she turned into the parking lot, she couldn't resist.

"Say, Mister, do you think I might have a couple bucks for the gas money? I got me a sick kid at home," she whined, overplaying the part.

"Je-sus frigging Christ," O'Day fumed. "I should have known this would happen!"

As he stuck a hand inside his suitcoat to draw out a wallet, she hit him under the jaw with the stun gun set to maximum. The juice made O'Day's head slam backward against the seat and bounce forward so hard he slammed into the dashboard.

A double knockout—nice!

She sat back, head on a swivel, looking to see if anyone noticed. *Everyone too busy with their own oinking, pathetic lives—*

Fun waited back in Ohio. She pushed Charlie over to the passenger's side. He looked simply like a man slumbering if anyone in a big rig bothered to look down in passing. Hiding in plain sight was another favorite operational principle. Her van, prepared before leaving Northtown, awaited. Ringbolts welded to the floorboard and side panels had taken less than an hour. Strapping him in for the long ride home had to wait until dark. She'd chosen both the motel and her room for their obscured locales. Hiding her tracks in Florida took a few hours. She had to wipe down the room, return the rental, and toss her disguises and the spy camera into a dumpster on the interstate.

She was less concerned about Farmer Erb snooping

around the abattoir while she was away "on vacation." Worst case, if he snooped around, he'd see nothing amiss, even if he pried the lids off the acid barrels. The flesh and organs of Piggy One were long gone, a sludgy mess of bones at the bottom. She used a "piranha solution" with sulfuric acid, adding great dollops of hydrogen peroxide to supercharge the combustion power of the acid, and rigged a ventilation ductwork to off-gas the resultant steam and sulfur dioxide.

On the ride home, she found a classical music station playing Barber's *Adagio for Strings*, always good for up-lifting the mind. She thought of the Piggy back there, breathing shallowly, snorting behind the mask, while the miles steadily ticked off beneath the chassis. Like any good professional, she mentally conducted a post-mortem. All challenges met, she vowed to keep striving for perfection.

A comforting image, as ever, passed the time: Jerry's skin exploding from his body—a peeled cantaloupe, a droopy face collapsing into incredulity—*well, a mixed success all in all,* she thought.

How to prolong it? Refine, refine—that was key.

The next composition filled the van with its silver notes, the chords of a familiar arpeggio. It took her mind in another direction: Where were Piggies Three, Four, Five, *ad infinitum* right now? Going about their mundane lives, oblivious of the horror that would come for them one day, in those nondescript brick buildings amid the cornfields.

Slaughterhouse, abattoir, knackery, meat processing factory, rendering plant...

All with their unique shades of meaning. She drove

through the black night listening to the soft opening violins that gave way to the lower strings two beats after the violins. The hesitation in the melody was a magnificent stroke, she considered, like a despondent man reluctantly climbing the stairs.

Nothing pretentious or extraordinary about it. *Just like me, your average, professional chiropractor waiting for you in the office, smiling…always smiling as she looks at you approach for your scheduled treatment.*

THE DEAD OF NIGHT

Ricki Whatley

THE AIR WAS FRIGID THAT NIGHT. Crowds of pedestrians milled along the sidewalk, scurrying from one pub to the next, the icy wind biting at their rosy cheeks. Three days had passed since Bonfire Night, but the acrid smell of black powder still hung over the cobbled streets. Compared to the usual reek of decay and horse shit, it was actually somewhat pleasant. On the dark, gas-lit sidewalks, unfortunates stood clutching their thin shawls. Occasionally, they lifted their petticoats to flash a potential customer a glimpse of tantalizing flesh. The women eyed their patrons warily. Each man who approached raised the question that all of England was asking: *is he the one?*

On the corner of Commercial Street, the doors of a certain friendly pub stood open. The inviting warmth from the glowing lamps and raucous laughter of the clientele beckoned to the passersby.

Come inside. I'm waiting for you, it seemed to say.

One such person, a young woman of lower class, stepped out of the darkness and into the cozy bar. She took a deep breath and gave the barkeep a familiar smile. For her, *any* night was a good night to drink, but tonight, she needed an *especially* stiff tipple.

Mary had been dating Joseph Barnett for almost a year. He was a kind man, if not exactly hardworking. He had been out of a job for nearly six of their eight months together. For all that time, it had fallen to Mary to earn enough money for food, rent, and, of course, drink. It was a constant merry-go-round fight they had. Joe never had enough money to support them, so Mary would inevitably turn to the streets. When she returned from a night spent peddling her only marketable skill, Joe would fly into a rage. He would berate her for her condemnable lifestyle and threaten to leave her. She had finally called his bluff two weeks ago. After a particularly intense argument, Mary threw him out and took in a more reliable, female roommate to help cover the bills. Still, Mary was forgiving, and her heart was sympathetic to all fellow urchins. She allowed Joe to remain a friend, and occasional lover, since his expulsion.

Until tonight.

Tonight, he had come to tell her he would not be coming around anymore. His *wife* had caught wind of his marital dalliance with Mary. Seeing as his wife was the breadwinner in their relationship too, she was not about to tolerate his perfidy. Joe arrived at her door, tail between his legs, to end his affair with Mary—once and for all. His marriage came as a complete shock. Humiliated, Mary wandered to the nearest watering hole, The Ten Bells, to drown her sorrows.

Approaching the sticky wooden bar, she called, "Give us a whiskey, would you, Harold?"

"Sure thing, Mary. Celebratin', are we?"

Mary scoffed and tossed her head disdainfully. "Celebrating the loss of that twelve stone, good-for-nothing layabout from around me neck!"

"Well," Harold replied, sliding a cloudy glass toward her, "not to worry. Plenty more where he come from." He sniggered at his own joke.

Mary gave a sarcastic, sideways grin, by way of a reply, and took a drink of lukewarm booze. She turned in her seat to survey the crowd. The men were rowdy and half-drunk, a bad combination. That meant by the time they were ready to take Mary home, their dicks would be limp, and their tempers would flair. She could almost guarantee the night was going to end with a black eye. As her head swiveled, analyzing her options, her gaze fell upon a woman she had never seen before. She looked to be around thirty, and most of her teeth appeared to be intact. Her hair was piled in a frizzy blond nest on the top of her head. At the time she bought her corset, it probably had been nice. Now it looked grimy, and Mary could see a brown swatch of fabric under one armpit where she had repaired a tear. Clearly, a working girl. However, this must have been her day off. She seemed completely disinterested in the men around her. Instead, she focused her attention on a small, dog-eared penny dreadful. A still-full pint stood forgotten on her table. Every now and then, she thoughtfully licked a finger and turned a page. Mary was never one to share her territory with rival prostitutes, regardless of whether they preferred books to business. She slid off her bar stool and sauntered toward the stranger, sizing her up. The other woman raised her head, finally taking notice of Mary's approach. She politely closed her book and tilted her head toward the other chair at her tiny, circular table.

"Mind if I sit?" Mary asked, almost managing to sound friendly.

"Help yourself," replied the stranger. She took a sip from her beer and smiled wanly. Clearly, she was also appraising her competition. Mary tugged self-consciously at her tattered shawl and tucked a loose strand of red hair behind her ear.

"Haven't seen you around," she offered blandly.

"Is that right?" the stranger retorted. "Been looking a long time, have you?"

Haughty bitch, thought Mary, forcing an acidic smile.

"Girls know this is *my* corner. They tend to stay away, lest they want their hair snatched out."

The stranger raised her eyebrows at the threat, feigning shock. Her voice was level when she said, "Oh my! No need to stop being a lady. Who says I'm working tonight, anyway?" The woman shrugged and waved her booklet innocently. "Just having a pint and a read in a warm place on a cold night. Nothing wrong with that, is there?"

Mary settled into her chair and finished her whiskey,

weighing her next words carefully. Before she could continue their verbal dance, the stranger interrupted her chain of thought.

"Why don't you join me for a spell? I'll buy you a drink as a symbol of good will." The stranger stood and waltzed to the bar without waiting for an answer. Mary cast a glance over her shoulder at the peculiar other woman.

What could it hurt? Mary supposed. *Better to have a free drink with her than earn one on me knees with one of these heavy-handed Toms.*

The woman had left her book behind on the table. Mary picked up the worn paperback and examined the cover. Stamped in black ink, a man in a butcher's apron loomed, wielding a knife, above the cowering form of a terrified woman. Presumably, the tableau depicted a scene from the featured story of the week. Its title was scrawled across the page in theatrical, melting letters: *The Dead of Night.* Mary rolled her eyes and tossed the book carelessly on the opposite side of the table. As she did, her new friend returned with a fresh drink. She placed the offering deferentially before her companion and took her seat. Mary eagerly grabbed the glass before the other woman could change her mind. From the height of the liquor, it looked as though the newcomer had paid for a double, and Mary was not about to let it go to waste. Bringing the glass to her lips, she observed a strange film around the inner edge of the cup. Old Harold had really been letting his housekeeping skills slip in the last year. Mary would have to reprimand him for it later. With that, she tossed back half of the drink in one satisfied gulp. The alcohol coursed down her throat with a satiating burn, spreading a delightful fuzziness throughout her belly and limbs. Mary set the precious libation on the table, wrapping her hands around it protectively. Her inhibitions considerably lowered, she got comfortable and prepared to interrogate this useful friend.

"I didn't catch your name," she started.

"Emmeline. Emmeline Bar—Barker."

"Pleasure, Emmeline. I'm Mary Kelly."

Emmeline nodded and took a casual drink from her beer. "All right, Mary."

"So, if you ain't working, why are you down here at this hour?" Mary inquired. Her words were already beginning to slur.

"I told you. I just wanted a place to have a read and a drink. I don't need to be down here for no work. I have a *respectable* job. I'm a midwife."

"A midwife? That's a secure position. Babies are born every day, ain't they?" Mary chuckled and took another drink. "If you don't mind the mess, I suppose!" Both women let loose peals of harsh laughter.

"The mess don't bother me none," Emmeline replied quietly. "A bit of blood never hurt no one." She grinned ominously. Mary felt a chill creep up her spine. She finished her drink to calm herself and bring the warmth back into her face.

"Yeah, well, I imagine you don't want to be lurking on any dark streets after reading that." Mary flicked her chin in the direction of Emmeline's tattered book.

"You frightened of the penny dreadfuls?" Emmeline asked with a dubious sneer. "They ain't nothing but a bit of fun."

"Well, you can keep that fun, far as I'm concerned," answered Mary. She lifted her glass with a shaky hand. She slurped at the remnant dregs of whiskey, but the scant droplets did little to steady her nerves. "There's enough killing going on around here. I don't need to waste me money on no book to read about *more*."

"Do tell," said Emmeline, tittering mischievously. She seemed to be oblivious to Mary's distress.

"You haven't heard about the Whitechapel Ripper murders?" Mary screeched. A few of the male regulars in the bar turned a glaring eye on the two loud whores. "They've been all over the papers, they have. Since the summer, girls have been turning up gutted like pigs!"

"Well, I do love a good murder," Emmeline cackled. Her maniacal laughter garnered a few more irritated glances from the crowd around them. She caught Harold's eye and motioned for another round. The woman bowed her head conspiratorially and leaned forward on the little table. She stared up at Mary from under dark, lowered eyelids. "Go on, then. Tell me what you know."

The hair on the back of Mary's neck stood up. Emmeline had a sinister glitter in her eyes that hinted at something more than just a morbid curiosity. Mary scanned the room for an excuse to step away from the table, but as she did, a skinny barmaid arrived with another whiskey. Mary greedily traded glasses with the homely waitress and took a long pull from the cup. This one, at least, was cleaner. There did not seem to be any more of that greasy residue.

"Keep 'em coming, love," Emmeline hollered. "We've much to discuss, me and my new friend." She smiled at the girl, but her expression was all wrong. Emmeline's lips stretched just a little too far; she exposed a few too many teeth. It looked more like a hungry growl. A terrifying leer that was anything but friendly. The girl nodded and then hurried back to the safety of the bar.

"Right. It all started back in August," Mary began. "There was two women killed that month, but the coppers think only the last one was the Ripper. He cut her throat *ear to ear.*" Mary drug her index finger sideways across her own neck for emphasis. She lowered her voice and glanced furtively around the room. By now, no one was giving the women a second thought.

Emmeline licked her bottom lip and pressed her weight further into the table. "I remember hearing about that," she said excitedly. "I thought there was one before that, though."

"I already told you, you deaf cow," Mary chided impatiently, "there was *two* birds killed but only *one* was done by the Ripper."

"How can they be sure of that?" asked Emmeline, tilting her head inquisitively. Her tongue idly searched the corner of her mouth. Mary stifled a shudder. To her, Emmeline looked like a cat, working out how to open the canary cage. "Maybe the first one was practice," the strange woman persisted. "You know, people don't die right away when you stab them. They fight and they scream. Slitting the throat silences them. But the *first* time you kill someone, you don't know that, do you?"

Mary took a slug of whiskey. *Did I tell her that the first victim didn't have her throat cut?* she thought vaguely. As reticent as she was to turn down a free drink, her new companion's unnerving disposition was starting to outweigh the benefits of her company. Mary raised her glass to drain the contents and take her leave.

Suddenly, Harold appeared at her side. He clapped a meaty palm on her shoulder and jovially exclaimed, "I won't have no problems with you two ladies tonight, will I?"

Mary shrugged and chuckled sheepishly. "I don't reckon you will, Harold. I'm actually just about to head back out, so…" Mary tried to stand, but Harold pressed her firmly back into her chair.

"Oh no, you're not!" he bellowed happily. "This friend of yours has paid for more of your drinks than you *ever* have! Making a fine profit off her, I am." Harold tipped his head and offered Emmeline a gentlemanly smile. "You stay as long as you like, missus! Keep our little Mary well hydrated, all right?" Harold laughed heartily. He reached across Mary's chest and filled her glass for the fourth time in less than thirty minutes. With a wink, he plunked the bottle down on the table, then turned and strode back to his post at the bar.

"There we are then," Emmeline chirped. "Tell me more about this *mad killer* the papers is on about."

Mary stammered and nervously smoothed the front of her dress. This lady was really starting to give her the creeps. "Eh, that kind of thing scares me, love. Why don't we talk about something else for a bit? Something chipper. Tell me about yourself; you married?"

Emmeline curled her lip contemptuously and spat on the rough-hewn floorboards. "Thought you wanted to talk about something chipper? Yeah, I'm married, all right.

He's a worthless gal-sneaker, I don't mind telling you! Couldn't give me no children. Always out of work. Stays out all night chasing tails, brings home all manner of filth to our marriage bed. Why do you think I'm here alone? I'm better off without the likes of him hanging around, can actually relax."

Mary nodded. She knew the betrayals of the opposite sex better than this stranger might have guessed. With one failed marriage already behind her and the blood from Joe's recent betrayal not yet dried, she could certainly relate. "Don't get me started on the heartache that is the male condition. They're a bunch of scoundrels, the lot of 'em."

"You have a husband?" Emmeline seemed truly surprised. "I didn't think men would waste their time trying to make an honest woman out of a whore."

"Oh, piss off!" Mary crowed with harsh laughter. Ribbing of this variety was common in the rough alleys of Whitechapel. Life was tough in the slums. Even the humor would cut you. "I got myself a man. Had. He's a married rat, as it turns out. Been playing me the crooked cross for almost a year now."

Emmeline's eye twitched unconsciously at the mention of infidelity. "A whole *year* you say?" The tendons in her throat flexed tight as piano wires. "Suppose we've got that sort of masculine treachery in common then. I keep telling meself that every affair will be me husband's last. Every time he steps out the door, I think, *Today is the day he'll change.* But he never does. And a woman does have her limits. There is only so far a man can push a woman, until she finally breaks." Emmeline clung to the last sylla-ble, dragging the *s* into a long, drawn-out hiss.

Mary bobbed her head in slack agreement. As she poured herself another drink, her foggy thoughts began to swirl and take the shape of her own profound, drunken philosophy.

"Come to think of it," Mary mumbled loosely, "it ain't just the men. We're better off without women friends, too. They're just as likely to stab you in the back."

"Done false by your own kind too, Mary?" Emmeline inquired with saccharine innocence.

"Aye! But the bitch got her comeuppance I'd say! Murdered by the Ripper one month past!"

"No," exclaimed Emmeline, blinking rapidly. She took a dainty sip from her beer. "You lie!"

"Hand to God! He killed two birds that night, and one of 'em was that lying roller, Catherine Eddowes!"

"What did *she* do to *you*, Mary?" The raspy concern in Emmeline's voice made the question sound grossly un-natural.

"The night before, she gets nibbed for disrupting the peace, right? Drunk as usual, squawking like a siren, mak-ing a right fool of herself! So the coppers bring her down and lock her up so she could dry out. When they ask her for her name, what do you think that old coward told 'em?" Mary stared expectantly at Emmeline before saying, "MARY ANN KELLY! She gave 'em *my* name! Tried to pin the charges on me, that slag! Too daft to get away with it, though, bloody cow. *My* middle name's Jane! You ask me? She got what she deserved."

Emmeline clenched the edges of her shawl and pulled

it tightly around her elbows. She seemed to tremble, despite the warmth of the crowded pub. "But she only had her throat cut, right? If I wanted revenge on someone, seems I'd do a lot more than *that*." A feral smile spread across her face. Her words rumbled toward Mary as low and menacing as an avalanche.

Mary failed to notice. Worry tugged at her for only the briefest second. *For someone who says she doesn't know the Ripper, she knows a lot of details without me telling her*, she pondered. Unfortunately, the concern left her just as quickly as it came. The alcohol coursing through her system had painted the world a happy, rosy pink. In her pickled mind, she was simply enjoying a cozy drink—and some scintillating gossip—with an old pal.

"Oh no," she contradicted Emmeline, "that was Long Liz. Poor thing. Papers say she was spared the worst of it because ol' Jacky was interrupted. He surely took his time with Catherine, though. Tore her up proper. Sliced off her nose, her ears, took her womb as a trophy, even cut her bloody eyes out!"

"Lids."

"Aye?"

"The eyes weren't cut *out*," Emmeline corrected her. "The lids was just split open."

Silence hung over the table like a circling vulture. Emmeline took a small drink from her glass; Mary took a large one from hers.

"How do you know *that*?" Mary dared to ask. There was no skepticism in her slurry voice. Only genuine, intoxicated fascination. Emmeline ignored the question. She continued talking as if she had not heard Mary speak at all.

With a faraway look in her eye, Emmeline said, "You know, ol' girl? I'd be very careful if I was you. Seems to me, if someone using *your* name is butchered, could be *you're* the one the killer is looking for."

"No," Mary quickly responded. She spoke with all the bravado of someone who just finished her sixth whiskey. "No, because there was three girls killed before that."

"Four," Emmeline interjected.

"Right, four then," Mary agreed carelessly. "And *they* wasn't named Mary Kelly. He wasn't looking for no one with a certain name. He's just killing any old whore. Ain't no target on me," she concluded assertively.

Emmeline considered her response before slowly answering, "Maybe you're right. Maybe you're wrong."

"How do you figure?" Mary asked, grabbing the bottle off the table.

"Maybe the first four didn't matter. Could be this killer, this *Ripper*, never killed no one before. If you want to kill someone, a specific person, for a special reason, you've got to plan it. What would be the most satisfying revenge you could get from them? You think of the worst way to take her life. A lingering fate that would torture that person *and everyone* who ever loved her."

Mary wobbled in her chair and fought to keep her head straight. Emmeline's words were starting to bleed together in one long, unintelligible hum. She chatted on, heedless of the other woman's confusion.

"You wouldn't want the object of your malice to be your first kill. You would need to practice first. Start slow. Maybe you stab the first one, and that's how you learn it takes dozens of punctures to finally put her down. So you try slitting the next one's throat, thinking that will be quicker and will silence the bitch so's you don't have to hear her mouth the whole time. But a throat is hard to cut through. Much harder than you think it's going to be. And the blood spurts absolutely *everywhere* and makes a real fucking mess. So, the next time, you're prepared for that. You know how much pressure it's going to take and that you have to stand behind 'em to keep the mess off yourself. That's when you start to practice the *good part*. Opening up those nasty cunts and taking away all the parts that make them a woman."

Mary nodded dumbly. The bottle was starting to feel light in her hand. *I hope Harold brings us another whiskey before she finishes her story,* she thought optimistically.

"Because a whore really isn't a woman, is it, Mary?" Emmeline asked. Her voice was barely more than a husky whisper. Mary strained to hear her over the rowdy din of the bar.

"A whore is just a disease-riddled creature who preys on good men and deprives honest women of their husbands. Isn't it, *Mary*?"

Mary wagged her head sloppily. It was becoming impossible to follow Emmeline's reasoning. Mary could no longer tell whether she was supposed to be agreeing or disagreeing with her. *Whiskey sure is strong tonight, Harold,* she thought merrily.

"Whores don't deserve to have the same anatomy as real women. That's why the killer takes their organs. Sh— He's removing their womanhood."

Emmeline's words, at last, struck a chord with Mary,

and she perked up excitedly. "Yeah! That's what they've been saying in the papers! He has to be a doctor of some kind, because he knew where all the organs was. They say the womb and kidneys is hard to find. Doctors would be the only ones who knew that kind of thing."

"Or a midwife."

"Yeah," agreed Mary, "a midwife would surely know." She had a friend who was a midwife, but at the moment, she could not for the life of her remember who it was…

"How are you feeling, Mary?" Emmeline asked sweetly.

"I feel great," she yelled drunkenly. "I've had a right fine time, I have. Think I'll go home. Supposed to be meeting up with a friend later."

"*Joe* will be wondering where you are." Emmeline's words dripped acid. Her body quivered with anticipation and rage.

Mary laughed derisively. "Joe! I don't even remember telling you his name…you know him? That worthless old sod."

Emmeline clenched her jaw. Under the table, her fingernails bit into the tense flesh of her thighs. Within the folds of her petticoats, deep, red crescents marred her white flesh. Her muscles twitched with anger; they writhed under her skin like electric eels.

"Is that your man's name? What a coincidence," Emmeline droned monotonously. "That's my husband's name." *It's almost time*, she thought with gleeful hatred. *It's going to be rather difficult for her to suck my hus-*

band's cock with no face. "Wait right here, love," she instructed Mary. Emmeline stared unblinking at her quarry.
Her most coveted prize. The object of her wicked desire.
She had hunted her for so long; she could not bear to let
her out of her sight for even a second. "I'm just going to
pay our bill. I'll be right back to walk you home."

"Oh, you're a dear thing," Mary blubbered thankfully. "I only live across the way, off Dorset Street. You
really needn't do all that for me."

"I insist, Mary," Emmeline replied. "It would be my
most gratifying pleasure." She pushed her warm beer to
the side and grabbed her penny dreadful off the table, *The
Dead of Night.* Emmeline bent to retrieve the soft leather
bag at her feet. She opened the top clasp and dropped her
book into the depths of the purse. Beside it, the metal
blade of an eight-inch surgical knife winked up at her.
Come, my friend, thought Emmeline. *Tonight's the
night. This is what we've been practicing for.*

THE NEXT MORNING was crisp and clear. By early
November, the sun in England was lazy. It rose slowly over
London, stretching its thin orange light over the sleeping
buildings with a lethargic yawn. Emmeline slipped quietly
out of 13 Miller's Court and into the dim glow of the emerg-
ing day. She breathed in deeply. The chilly air was invigorat-
ing. She began her leisurely stroll back home, reveling in the
previous night's accomplishments. To anyone viewing her

from behind, she appeared an image of serenity. Nothing more than a woman with a happy spring in her step.

From the front, she was a horror show of gore.

Crimson stained the sleeves and bodice of her dress. Two large, saturated ovals on each knee revealed where she had spent extended lengths of time kneeling in some deep, bloody puddle. Black, dried blood caked all ten of her nail beds. Flecks of skin and tissue clung to her face and décolletage. Arterial spray from Mary's severed neck had misted Emmeline's hair a glistening, delicate red.

Joe always did like redheads, she thought with foul delight. *Won't I be a sight for his sore eyes when I get home?*

Despite her heinous appearance, Emmeline waltzed without a care. She practically glided on the post-dawn air. A docile smile graced her lips, and she swung her leather valise at her side, as a schoolgirl might swing her lunch pail. Less than two blocks into her journey, a voice broke her tranquility.

"Stop!" yelled a policeman, jogging across the street. Emmeline froze in place, casually watching him approach. The cop was still holding his night shift lantern in one hand and shone the flickering light over Emmeline's form like a magician wielding a wand. "What the devil happened to you, missus?" the cop gaped. His brow shone under the brim of his cap, covered with beads of anxious perspiration.

"I'm just on my way home," Emmeline answered placidly. She spoke with the sweet calm of a woman perusing vegetables at the market.

"Where on earth are you coming from looking like

that? Are you hurt? Has someone hurt you?" The policeman continued to scan Emmeline's body, undoubtedly looking for signs of an injury severe enough to explain her gruesome appearance.

"Hurt *me?*" she repeated the question with no sign of comprehension.

"Missus, look at the state of you!" The cop was nearly hysterical. This poor woman was almost certainly in shock and in need of assistance. He retrieved his whistle from a chain in his breast pocket and began lifting it to his already pursed lips.

But Emmeline gently placed her gummy hand over his and lowered the tiny metal instrument back to his side. "There'll be no need for all of that, now," she comforted the young officer with motherly reproach. "You see, I'm a midwife," she said truthfully. "I've just come from a job. Paid a woman a visit over the night," she said, *also* truthfully.

"Midwife?" the cop replied, reassessing Emmeline's dress with a completely new perspective.

"Aye, sir. A midwife." She gestured helplessly at her ruined dress. "Sometimes, our greatest moment in life isn't as pretty as we'd like to think."

The cop pulled his hand away with a grimace. If this woman was a midwife, then that meant the blood all over her was from a woman's…*Oh God*, he was going to be sick.

"Take my customer last night for example. I had to slice her open from her cunny, all the way up to her—"

"Oy!" the cop interjected, recoiling in disgust. He wagged his finger angrily in Emmeline's face, scolding her like a child. "Don't you say another word! I don't need to be knowing the indecent particulars of your business, madam." His concern had vanished. In its place was unconcealed revulsion. "If you ain't the victim of no violence, then you need to get yourself home and into a clean frock. Polite society is going to be waking up and we don't need them seeing you walking about like a bloody Ripper victim!" Inexplicably, at the mention of the Ripper, the strange woman erupted in peals of hysterical laughter.

"You're right about that, Gov'nor! I sure don't want to be mixed up with him!" Emmeline doubled over and clutched her belly, wheezing with amusement.

"You think that's funny, do you?" The young man lowered his voice, trying to sound authoritative. He could not help but feel that this odd stranger was somehow mocking him. "The whole city on alert for a deranged lunatic and all you can do is laugh?"

Emmeline straightened up. She sniffed back a fresh batch of chuckles and managed to put on a semi-serious face. "Nothing funny, old cock. That Jacky has been an *awfully* naughty boy. I do hope you and your comrades catch him soon." Emmeline leered like a Cheshire cat. The uneasy patrolman took an involuntary backwards step.

"I'm sure we will, missus," he answered uneasily. This lady was really starting to give him the creeps.

"Keep your eyes and ears open, my son. The alleyways are dark and perilous. All manner of evil lurks within these Whitechapel shadows. Ain't like the killer is just going to walk right up and shake your hand, is it?" With that, Emmeline's composure crumbled, and she covered her mouth in a weak attempt to dampen the giggles simmering in her throat.

The cop looked warily around the street. He was still alone with the eerie woman. Sunshine was starting to creep between the glowering buildings in long pink tendrils. He stepped into the gutter and began retreating toward the safety of the expanding sunlight.

"Right," he said, clearing his throat. "Well, you'll be on your way then."

"Oh, I certainly will." Emmeline smirked. She raised her hand at the cop's retreating physique and wiggled her fingers in a demure wave. Once he was out of sight, she turned and sedately continued on her way.

I will say this for womanhood, thought Emmeline. *For all the injustices, the beatings, the tribulations…all the plight that comes from being born of the fairer sex, there is one indisputable advantage: our anonymity. We live our lives cloaked in underestimation. Our gender is a mask we wear, and it shields even our most egregious misdeeds from scrutiny.* Emmeline smiled broadly, savoring the irony. *That young rookie hasn't the faintest inkling he just come face to face with Jack the Ripper. I doubt if he'll even tell anyone about our little exchange. There will be no report of our meeting. My sins will haunt the world for decades. Yet, when they look back on this place, at this moment, no one will remember me at all. History will swallow my name forever.*

With the sun rising behind her, Emmeline walked westward. Her profile grew smaller as she marched into the gaping maw of the ravenous city. If anyone had bothered to notice her, they could have watched the narrow streets devour her alive.

But no one did.

THE SNIPPER

Ben Gamblin

AUGIE AND I HAD A BAD FEELING about *Puget Sludge Report* from the start. Everyone at Tacoma Violent Crimes did. A website like that was bound to stir a few pots, maybe even get someone hurt. Murders, though? I don't think anyone could have predicted that.

Puget Sludge Report was a platform for exposing residents of the Seattle-Tacoma area who had abused, harassed, or mistreated women in some way. Lewd jokes at work, touching without asking, slapping, shoving, not taking no for an answer. The whole garbage spectrum. These sites are common nowadays, but it was a novel concept back in April '06, when social media was in its infancy and #MeToo was still a decade out. The idea caught like a bad flu. *PDX Offender Alert* launched in Portland later that spring, followed by similar sites based in L.A. and the

Bay Area. By Memorial Day, the entire West Coast was under surveillance.

The site's founder was Claire Westby, a former high school counselor from Tacoma's North End neighborhood. I caught her interview in the paper after the site went live. Westby said her inspiration was a sophomore at her school named Marjorie Blake. Earlier in the school year, Marjorie began showing up to class with bruises on her neck, on her wrists, and around her eyes, nose, and lips. Teachers approached her, the principal sat her down, and she eventually found herself in Mrs. Westby's office. Even then, the girl downplayed her situation. *I tripped down the stairs. I bumped into a doorknob. I can be so clumsy.*

Westby knew Marjorie was covering, so she asked protective services to visit the girl's house as soon as possible. It must have been a busy week for shitty parents on the north end, because CPS didn't stop by for a few days, and only after Marjorie missed her morning classes. A cop tagged along for good measure. They found the girl lying on her bedroom floor with a fractured skull, clinging to a pulse but fading from blood loss. Her father was passed out in the backyard. After the cop woke him up, the guy spent several minutes pretending he didn't know what had happened to Marjorie before he broke down sobbing on the lawn. Or maybe that was just when he remembered. It's hard to tell with drunks sometimes.

Marjorie never woke up. The D.A. waited until she was off life support to file a second-degree murder charge. Her father pled not guilty. "It was the whiskey," he said. "Without that devil sauce, I'd have never hurt my sweet girl." The jury disagreed, as did the judge who sentenced him to twenty years. The devil sauce defense can be a dice-roll that way.

Meanwhile, Claire Westby had seen enough.

"I wanted to create a safe place where women could openly discuss their abusers and their experiences," she told the reporter. "A sanctuary that affords them privacy, dignity, and safety."

She took night courses in computer programming and web design, bought a domain, and developed the site in her spare time. *Puget Sludge Report*—great name, I'll admit—launched over spring break.

The site was simple, easy to use. Anyone could write and submit posts anonymously, and each entry included a comment section where other readers could chime in and, in many cases, corroborate the accusations. The homepage featured a current ranking of creeps who'd earned the most "red flag votes," indicating offenses readers found especially egregious, along with contact information for shelters, helplines, and other emergency services.

Puget Sludge Report collected a few dozen posts on its first day and exploded from there. Westby's superintendent was far from thrilled when he learned about his counselor's little side hustle, especially since she'd done nothing to conceal her, or her employer's, identity. He told her to ditch the website or clean out her office. She asked him where the boxes were. From there, Westby transitioned to outing local scumbags on a full-time basis.

I won't lie, I performed a few self-searches. I wouldn't call myself sleazy or unchivalrous, even in my younger days, but curiosity won out. Did Brenda have anything to say? We'd split up two years ago, but the wounds were still raw. What about ex-girlfriends or former colleagues? Had I slipped up somewhere and never realized? Thankfully, these searches yielded zero results, but I'm glad I checked the site when I did. Otherwise, I might have missed the post about Richard Riggs near the top of the red-flag pile.

Riggs owned a burger joint in North Tacoma. According to the post, published by a "former employee," Riggs had a penchant for drugging his waitresses with Rohypnol. He'd mix them a drink after closing time, drive them home, help them to their door—you get the idea. Several commenters backed up the initial post, some with claims going back more than a decade. There were potentially dozens of victims.

Chief Mooney had given us strict orders *not* to investigate activities reported on *Puget Sludge Report*, no matter how heinous, unless we had physical evidence or witness testimony to back them up. A waste of resources otherwise, he said. He wasn't the only one—every top badge from Olympia to Bellingham had issued similar commands—but the post about Riggs was particularly hard to digest. Ignoring such depravity went against every instinct I had as a detective.

My hunch proved accurate, but for entirely different reasons. One week after the Riggs post appeared, a man's body washed up on Titlow Beach. Augie and I caught the case. The corpse was banged-up beyond immediate identification, but we found a soggy wallet in his trouser pocket. The driver's license belonged to none other than Richard Riggs, disgraced local restaurateur.

"I'll be damned," I said.

"You know him?" Augie asked.

"Of him. I read about him on that *Sludge* website."

"What were *you* doing on that site?"

"Right, like you haven't checked it out."

Riggs was full of saltwater, but the official cause of death was a stab wound to the gut. Someone worked him over first. In addition to the fatal gouge, he had nicks and scratches on his face, chest, and back, all inflicted pre-mortem. The time of death was roughly two days earlier. He'd probably bobbed around the sound for at least thirty-six hours before drifting ashore.

Oh, and, uh, one more thing: his cock was missing. Not fish nibbled, either. Sliced clean off at the base. The wound had been cauterized before Riggs died, judging by the tissue damage. A hot knife or pair of scissors was our best guess.

Now, assuming the allegations against him were true, I didn't exactly weep over the grisly fate of Richard Riggs. Bastard had it coming. But I'd sworn an oath to uphold law and order, and all that, so when Augie and I began our investigation, I had to at least pretend to care. First, we met with Riggs' wife. She was a gem.

"Those horrible girls and their accusations," she wailed. "My Richard would never...now someone has killed him for it!"

His staff felt differently. Two female servers immediately came forward as drugging victims, and a few former employees revealed themselves in the days that followed. We checked them out as they trickled in, but each one had a solid alibi for the night of the murder, which wasn't a shocker—killers don't give themselves up so easily, unless they want to get caught.

The crime scene didn't help. Riggs' car was left at the restaurant overnight, but the building was locked up, suggesting he was ambushed in the parking lot. Since there was no physical evidence on the premises, we figured he'd been taken to a different location before he was killed. That's all we had to go on. He'd closed up alone that night, and the building's security cameras had more blind spots than a Braille academy. Suicide occurred to us, some sort of self-flagellation to atone for his sins, but without a note, that theory was hard to pin down.

Augie and I spun our wheels for a couple of weeks. We were about to suspend the investigation when a construction manager named Terry Hollenbeck washed up on the rocks not far from the first crime scene. Waterlogged, perforated, and completely cockless. Augie and I pulled down his jeans to see for ourselves and then sped back to the office to check the computer. These were the pre-smartphone days, mind you.

Hollenbeck's post on *Puget Sludge Report* came from a "former houseguest" and friend of his daughter's who claimed he'd forced himself on her years earlier during a slumber party while the other girls were asleep. She was twelve. The post's timestamp was eight days prior. Since it had been published, two more former houseguests had leveled similar accusations in the comment section. More than enough to send Hollenbeck to the top of the red-flag ranks.

"Fuck me," Augie said.

I nodded. Fuck us, indeed.

AUGIE STILL DRANK in those days. He had two boys and a perpetually tired wife at home, while I'd been living alone since Brenda left. On working nights, we'd pick up a half-rack of Olympia and review case files in my living room. We'd usually watch the Mariners or the Sonics while we worked, but on the evening after we found Terry Hollenbeck, the TV stayed off, and we barely touched our beers. It wasn't just the murders that troubled us, but also the dearth of evidence. Someone had kidnapped two local men, tortured and killed them, and dumped their bodies in the sound. Yet we had no eyewitnesses, no video footage, no DNA. Not even a single cock to show for it.

"You think it's a woman?" Augie asked after a couple hours had passed. "Feels like a woman to me."

"Could be," I said, "but these were big guys. Unless she's a weightlifter, she had help."

"Or a wheelbarrow."

"Probably keeps it in the toolshed next to the pruning shears."

We reached one firm conclusion that night: we needed to meet with Claire Westby as soon as possible. Augie called her first thing the next morning and arranged to meet that afternoon at her home office. Westby's demeanor was gentler than I'd imagined, but she had a tight handshake and unwavering eyes that told us she was no pushover. She offered us coffee and ushered us into her modestly furnished workspace.

"Nice setup," I said. "One-woman operation?"

"I pay a couple of college kids to moderate during my off hours." She flashed a cool smile. "The rest is all me."

Augie did most of the talking. He told Westby we believed the killer was picking his (or her) victims based on *Puget Sludge Report* posts. Two men were already dead, and whether or not they deserved to die, whoever was responsible would be prosecuted to the fullest extent. She sat with her shoulders straight and her hands folded in her lap, nodding patiently while Augie made his arguments. Once he was done, she presented hers.

"I find it interesting," she said, "that the police are unwilling to investigate reports of rape, assault, and sexual harassment, but when the alleged perpetrators of these crimes end up dead, you can't locate the guilty party fast enough."

"We need evidence or testimony to bring charges," Augie replied. "No matter the offense. We can't arrest people because the internet says they're guilty."

"Perhaps victims believe going to the authorities would be a waste of time."

"Perhaps. That still doesn't change the legal parameters of our investigation."

She sipped her coffee. "What would you like *me* to do, detective?"

"Handing over information for the site's users would be a start."

"You're serious? Even if I could disclose that information—which I wouldn't willingly—I can't for a very simple reason: personal details aren't required to submit posts. Not even an email address. It's the only way to ensure complete anonymity."

"We could still get IP addresses. Everything is traceable with computers nowadays."

"In that case," she said softly, "you'll need a warrant."

"Look, ma'am...I understand what you're doing with this website, why you're doing it. But people are dying as a result. Doesn't that concern you?"

Westby considered her answer for a moment.

"Two men accused of unspeakable acts have died," she said. "Deaths, yes, but hardly tragedies. Imagine how many women won't face a lifetime of horror because Richard Riggs and Terry Hollenbeck have been removed from society."

Augie nodded and pulled a manila folder out of his coat. Westby arched an eyebrow but otherwise didn't budge when he tossed it onto the table.

"What's in there?"

"Autopsy photos," he said. "Pretty graphic, I should warn you."

"Why would I—?"

"So you can see where we're coming from."

She took a deep breath and flipped open the folder. The first photo of Riggs showed him naked, lying on the coroner's slab with a stump where his manhood used to dangle. She didn't even flinch, and the sight of Hollenbeck's body got the same non-reaction. If Augie expected her to crack, his plan failed remarkably.

"Their wives and children have my sympathies," she said, closing the folder.

"You'll cooperate?"

"Of course. Bring me a warrant, and I'll share whatever you need. Until then, detectives, please give me a bit more notice if you plan to visit again. I'd like my lawyer to join us next time."

The drive back to the station was less than upbeat. Upon returning, I found a copy of the day's paper on my desk. "No Leads in Gruesome Killings," the headline mocked, but the opening paragraph was what grabbed me.

"...but police believe the motives of the killer, dubbed 'The Snipper,' may be linked to..."

The Snipper. People actually get paid to come up with that shit.

OUR WARRANT FOR *Puget Sludge Report* was shot down. Lack of reliable information showing probable cause, the judge said, since anyone could have accessed the site's posts, regardless of who published them.

When no other leads turned up in the Riggs-Hollenbeck murders, Augie and I started grasping at whatever we could. We decided to question homeowners with waterfront property in the vicinity of Titlow Beach. The bodies had been dumped close to shore—otherwise, they wouldn't have washed up on dry land so quickly, based on time of death. A strong heave-ho off a dock during high tide could have done the trick. And given the lack of eyewitnesses, a private residence with water access could have been the launch point.

Augie and I went door-to-door. The day was fairly uneventful until we arrived at Jeannie Lepschatz's house. She answered the door wearing a bathrobe and a loosely knotted headscarf. Mid-fifties, mostly grey from the hair we could see, with sunken cheeks and deep lines around her lips.

"How can I help you?" she asked, lighting a Pall Mall as she stepped onto the front porch.

We showed our badges.

"We're investigating two murders that occurred in this area," I told her.

"You mean those fellas who washed up on Titlow?" She took a long drag. "Well, maybe *fellas* isn't the right word."

"Do you know anything about them?"

"Only what I've read in the papers. Sounds like they had it coming."

She struck me as overly confident, like she'd been rehearsing her lines in anticipation of detectives showing up on her doorstep. Augie noticed too.

"The victims may have been taken to a house with direct water access," he added. "Seen anything suspicious lately? People on the docks late at night, that sort of thing."

"I wouldn't call that suspicious around here. But to answer your question…no, I don't get out much these days."

"Does anyone else live here?"

"I live alone. Have for years."

Augie handed her his card. "Before we go, could I get your name?"

"Jeannie. Lepschatz."

"Spell your last name for me."

"It's on the mailbox."

The door squeaked shut.

We must have rung three dozen doorbells by day's end, but Jeannie was the only person who struck us as vaguely suspicious. Augie and I huddled around my desk that night, combing local news archives for "Jeannie Lepschatz." That name didn't pop up, but we got a hit on "Jeannie Sanderson," complete with a photo in one. It was her, right down to the wrinkles.

The article was from December '97. Jeannie Sanderson and her then-husband, Earl, had a teenage daughter named Hailey. Hailey's boyfriend, Leonard Wales, assaulted her in the backseat of his Nissan one night when she refused to put out. He scratched her face and took a bite out of her shoulder before she got away. The judge gave him two years, citing his age and lack of priors. Two goddamn years.

Next, we found Hailey's obituary from November '99. It was brief and vaguely written, only a mention of her "sudden passing" and details about her memorial service. Her coroner's report was more helpful. Suicide, it said. Pills. A whole handful. Augie and I planned to pay another visit to Jeannie Sanderson/Lepschatz first thing the next morning. Only the next morning didn't come the way we'd planned.

The third vic was Ignaty Christoff, a real estate agent down in University Place. It's funny, the shit you learn about homicide victims during an investigation. We eventually figured out Ignaty had a nice little racket. Foreigners, mostly from the Soviet bloc, arrived at Sea-Tac International, with suitcases full of cash, looking for a place to buy. Ignaty would take them to some shithole he'd already picked out, convince them to skip the inspection in order to close quickly, and then escort them to the lender's office, where he'd "translate" the terms of the loan for his clients. When they couldn't afford their mortgage payments, and Ignaty stopped answering their calls, they were forced to foreclose—and the slimy bastard usually had a new buyer lined up for the property. Most returned to their home countries, and none bothered reporting anything to the stateside police. For all they knew, a crime hadn't taken place. Ignaty got away with this shit for years and made a small fortune in the process.

But we didn't know any of this on that drizzly morning at Chambers Bay, a few miles from Titlow. All we knew was that Ignaty was dead, ballooned with saltwater, and missing one key extremity. He'd been dead longer than the others, about four days judging by the level of bloat. A cursory search on *Puget Sludge Report* found a post about him—his violent sexual tendencies, in particular. Choking women until they couldn't breathe, much like he choked immigrants out of their hard-earned rubles. The guy had a pattern. Interestingly, Ignaty's post wasn't in the red-flag pile. We had to do a bit of searching. The Snipper, by all appearances, was now pulling from the bottom of the deck.

Chief Mooney threatened to reassign us if the Snipper claimed anymore victims. Augie and I decided to pay Jeannie one more visit. We returned to her place a couple days later. She answered the door with a wry, sideways look, like she was wondering what had taken us so long.

"Hello, Ms. Lepschatz," Augie said. "Or is it Mrs. Sanderson?"

"Was," she replied. "Haven't gone by Sanderson since me and Earl split up. Did you come all—"

"What were the reasons for your separation?"

She reached into the pocket of her robe, removed her pack of Pall Malls, and lit one.

"If you know my married name, I take it you know about Hailey."

Augie nodded. "I'm sorry for your loss."

"Well, *Detective*, there's your reason. Earl and I got along fine, but we didn't have that glue that holds people together when bad shit comes along. After Hailey passed, we didn't bother faking it anymore." She released a long, wheezy gust. "Does that answer your question?"

"Was your daughter's suicide related to what Leonard Wales did to her?"

She smiled. "You know what? You can—"

Whatever she said next was lost in the slam of the door, but we got the gist.

YOU KNOW HOW detectives in movies hammer homicide suspects until they confess? Complete horseshit. You have to finesse them, make them feel comfortable, back off if they get defensive. Otherwise, they might ditch town or take another life just to spite you. Best-case scenario, they lawyer up. Now you can't get them alone when they're most vulnerable.

Augie and I liked Jeannie for the killings. If she wasn't the Snipper, then she at least knew more than we did, but we couldn't bring her in without evidence. Rather than taking the bulldog approach, we decided to have a word with her daughter's attacker. Leonard Wales had changed his name—smart move, given his pedigree—but as a matter of public record, that information was easy to obtain. "Jared Murphy" came outside to meet us when we drove up to his house.

"What's this about?" he growled.

"We're here about Hailey Sanderson," I said, flashing my badge. "You remember her, don't you, Leonard?"

"I served my time for that. That ain't my name, either."

"Relax. We just have a few questions."

"Maybe I don't have time for questions."

"Maybe I call your boss. Tell 'em about Hailey."

It was a bluff on my part. I didn't know his boss—didn't even know if he had a job—but it worked.

"Fine," Leonard muttered. "What do you need to know?"

Without mentioning the Snipper, I explained we were investigating a crime related to Hailey's death. I asked him why she'd taken her own life. Leonard couldn't say. He'd written her a few apology notes while he was locked up, part of his rehabilitation, but he never mailed them, on account of the restraining order. He had no intention of contacting Hailey on the outside. But then he disclosed a curious detail: Jeannie had called him a few days after he was released.

"What did she say?" Augie asked.

"'Stay away from Hailey.' I told her I planned to."

"How'd she take it?"

"Didn't believe me. Threatened me."

"What'd she say?"

His eyes drifted to the asphalt. "Look...I didn't report this at the time. With everything I put them through it seemed like she was just—"

"Tell us, Leonard."

He sighed. "She said, 'Come near my daughter again, and I'll cut your fuckin' dick off.'"

Augie and I exchanged a glance for the ages. Leonard's eyes lit up.

"Hang on, does this have—?"

"Thanks for your time, Leonard. We'll be in touch. I'd watch your back if I were you."

We returned to the station that afternoon to find we had visitors: Holden Powell, publishing tycoon turned philanthropist, and his attorney, a stout little man with a horseshoe of grey hair.

Spring '06 hadn't been kind to Powell. Nine women had posted about him since *Puget Sludge Report* went live. How he'd hired them out of college, groomed them, promoted them, and then made his move, once they were comfortable. First came the flirting, followed by private dinners and hotel room nightcaps. Those who refused his advances found themselves promptly unemployed, their reputations in tatters. Now Powell could relate—he'd already been booted from two boards, and more ousters were likely to follow—but professional standing wasn't his top concern.

"Given the recent killings," Powell's attorney said, "my client believes he might be a target."

"Has anyone made threats against you, Mr. Powell?" Augie asked.

"Not *yet*," the old man grumbled.

"Then there's nothing we can do. Frankly, I don't think you need to worry. The killer seems to target men whose behavior goes a bit further than what you've been accused of." Augie paused. "Unless more serious allegations are coming."

Powell squirmed in his chair. "These lying sluts are out to ruin me. Who knows what they'll say next?"

"Sounds like you might have *some* idea."

"Detective," the lawyer cut in, "I don't see how interrogating my client is productive."

Augie shrugged. "We can help him if he goes on record about everything before it comes out. But without a statement, he's on his own."

Confess and receive protection or maintain innocence and potentially face the Snipper. Quite the dilemma. In the end, Holden Powell chose a third option. He, and his attorney, stormed out of the station that afternoon, and the next morning, his maid found him swinging by the neck from a closet rack. The note read, "I'm sorry." Nothing more. One can only speculate.

THE BACKLASH AGAINST *Puget Sludge Report* was brewing. Elected officials and police union mouthpieces lambasted the site for circumventing the justice system and inciting vigilantism. Then there were the various locals claiming they'd been falsely accused of horrific crimes. Westby remained defiant. "I stand behind this online community," she said, "and there is much more work to do."

Augie and I had plenty of work ourselves. We assigned a squad car to keep an eye on Leonard Wales, in case the Snipper paid him a visit. As for Jeannie, Augie and I handled her personally. Three straight nights we surveilled her. We wanted to keep eyes on her place during nocturnal tide, so we parked down the street from her house in the early evening and stayed put until early morning. By the third night, we were loopy and ill-tempered, but we powered through the boredom and the fatigue, hoping to catch a break. Then we caught a big one.

I awoke around eight in the morning to Augie tapping my shoulder, and we both watched a small shuttle bus pull into the driveway. Jeannie hobbled outside a moment later, coughing vigorously, and stepped into the vehicle. We tailed them across town to a small clinic near the hospital that bore the name TACOMA CANCER CARE CENTER. Jeannie deboarded and shuffled inside the building, still coughing to high hell.

"There's our fuckin' motive," Augie said, once she

was out of view. "Nothing to lose. She can't touch Leonard without us connecting her to it, so she scratches the itch by killing a couple of random scumbags on her way out."

"Or maybe she killed the other guys as a way of getting to Leonard without being a suspect. Make it look like a serial killing instead of a personal vendetta."

"Maybe."

"That's assuming she's terminal, though. She could be getting a checkup for all we know."

"C'mon, you saw how she was hacking."

I had to admit, the theory wasn't bad, but it still had a major hole: how could a frail, cancer-stricken woman subdue grown men, transport them to the waterfront, and dispose of their bodies? Augie and I resolved to stay in the overflow lot until Jeannie left the clinic. Only she didn't. We watched that entrance all damn day, and there was no sign of her.

We were both half-dozing and bleary-eyed when the call from dispatch came around ten. An elderly widow who lived in a townhome near the Narrows Bridge had woken to frantic scratching at her front door. Thinking it was her cat, she opened the door and found a young man lying face-up on the doormat, whimpering and begging for help. Both of his hands were bound with rope and the zipper of his chinos was open, revealing some sort of bloody wound. She phoned 911 and, in her panic, decided to inspect the injury before the paramedics arrived. The kid's cock had been snipped. Not all the way, though. It still clung by a thin ribbon of tissue.

He was semi-conscious when the ambulance arrived,

ghostly pale, and mumbling incoherently. One of the medics dug out his wallet and contacted dispatch with the name. Jesse Bergman. A junior in college, according to his student ID. Augie asked dispatch to plug his name into *Puget Sludge Report* and check for hits. Nothing. Conveniently for us, Bergman was transported to Tacoma General. We sat in the waiting room for several hours, sleeping in shifts, while he underwent emergency reattachment surgery. Just before sunrise, the receptionist told us we could see him. The kid was trembling, his eyes darting across the room. He had a stitched-up laceration on his left cheek and a thick bandage wrapped around his crotch like a diaper. We introduced ourselves. That didn't seem to alleviate his anxiety.

"I know it's difficult," Augie said, "but we need you to tell us everything you remember."

"That isn't much," he rasped, pointing to a yellowish bruise around his neck. "I was bringing in groceries. All of a sudden, I felt something around my neck, and I couldn't breathe."

"Did you see your attacker?"

"No." He paused. "Attackers."

"How many?"

"Three, at least."

"What were their voices like?"

"Women. All of them." He swallowed hard. "They pulled me down, dragged me across the sidewalk, put me in a car. Then I passed out."

The kid said he woke up in a dark room, bound with rope at the wrists and ankles. Two women held him down, one on each side, while a third stood before him—with the lights out, their faces were nothing but silhouettes.

"Do you know why you're here?" the third woman asked him.

Bergman shook his head, and she sliced his cheek with a straight razor. She repeated the question several times, cutting him in a different place every time he gave the same answer. Then she left the room and returned holding a pair of scissors, both points burning red in the darkness. "Don't worry," she told him, unzipping his chinos. "We remember."

She started snipping, and Bergman nearly passed out from the pain—not to mention the smell—but before the blades snipped through, he managed to push back his assailants, wriggle his feet free, and bolt for the door. He couldn't be sure if they gave chase, but he ran anyway, zig-zagging through backyards and alleyways. At least a mile, by his estimation. The pain was excruciating, he said. When he couldn't push any further, he collapsed onto the nearest doorstep he saw—the widow's place.

"This place they took you," Augie said, "where was it?"

"Couldn't tell you, I didn't look back. Near the water. That's all I know."

"I need to ask, Jesse…have you ever been accused of mistreating women?"

The kid's eyes narrowed. "The hell does that have to do with anything?"

"It could help us find who did this."

"I'm the victim here." Tears began to brim. "*They* attacked *me*."

"Sure, but—"

"Do you have any fucking idea what they did to me? You wanna see it?"

He started sobbing. We were about to take our leave when he sat up with a start.

"Mitch was," he said with a sniffle.

"Mitch?" I asked.

"Mitch Kemper. My roommate. His ex-girlfriend ratted him out on that *Sludge* website."

"Bad stuff?"

Bergman nodded. "He won't even leave the house now. Makes me run all the errands."

Augie flashed me a look.

"Jesse," he said, "do you own a car?"

"No."

"You take Mitch's car to get groceries?"

"Yeah," Bergman said. "Why?"

Augie and I left the kid's room and walked straight to the cancer clinic. We breezed past the receptionist and headed down the hallway. A nurse stopped us immediately. Augie demanded to know which room belonged to Jeannie. The nurse refused to say. Jeannie was quite ill, she told us, and could not receive any visitors. Augie told her he'd pound on doors until he found her. She threatened to call security, and he flashed his badge. That smartened her up.

"You're disgraceful," she said, pointing to a door at the end of the hall.

Jeannie was barely awake when we entered her room. Without the headscarf, we could see how thin and patchy her hair was.

"Who did it?" Augie asked.

Jeannie lifted her head off the pillow, squinting at the lights. "Sorry?"

"You were here all night. So who attacked the guy? We know there are others."

"Others?"

"You let them use your house, is that it?"

"I have no idea what you're—"

"Don't bullshit me, Jeannie. I've got a kid downstairs with his pecker hanging off, and you know who's responsible."

She eyed me. "What's with *him*?"

Augie was about to erupt. I stepped in.

"The nurse said you're sick."

"First, it was just my lungs. Now the shit's in my stomach too. Doctor says I've probably got a couple weeks. Maybe a month, if I'm lucky. That's what he said. If I'm *lucky*."

"Then tell us who else is involved while you still have time. Save other people from getting hurt."

She cocked her head. "Let's say you're right, that I am part of all this. Tell me, detective, why would I care about helping any of these bastards?"

"Jeannie, the victim tonight was driving his roommate's car. He's an innocent man. The wrong guy got attacked."

"Innocent man, huh?" She closed her eyes and leaned back onto her pillow. "He tell you that?"

Augie stormed over to the bed, inches from her face. "I don't care if you've got a week to live. I'll make sure you spend your final days in a fucking cell. You and your accomplices. Understand me?"

No response.

"Do you—?"

It was no use. She was totally conked.

JEANNIE LEFT THE clinic later that day and returned home, now with a hospice nurse to keep her company. She died eleven days later. Not so lucky after all.

Augie and I hounded Chief Mooney to bring charges against her up to the end. He refused. Her connection to the murders was tenuous at best—and if we were wrong, we'd be accused of harassing a dying woman instead of finding the actual killers. Once the Bergman kid could walk, we drove him to her house, in fresh daylight, to help jog his memory. Still nothing. Jeannie Lepschatz went to the grave with a spotless record. She must have had a good chuckle on the way out.

A few weeks after Jeannie's death, Holden Powell's family filed a lawsuit against *Puget Sludge Report*. "Baseless, libelous accusations," his attorney stated, "caused Mr. Powell to lose his job, his reputation, and ultimately to spiral into a deep depression." The widows, Riggs and Hollenbeck, quickly hopped aboard the gravy train. A class-action suit soon took shape, involving twenty-two "innocent men" who'd endured various hardships after being accused on the site.

Claire Westby didn't flinch then either, though

maybe she should have. She was sharp enough to understand the dilemma. If she hoped to emerge victorious in court, the site's contributors would need to come forward and accept subpoenas—and asking them to reveal their identities went against everything she'd promised about anonymity and safety. She vowed to see the case reach a courtroom, and the proceedings sounded the death knell for *Puget Sludge Report.* The judge ruled in favor of the plaintiffs, and amid the bad press, the company that hosted the website cancelled Westby's subscription. She couldn't find any other takers. After the dust settled, she held a press conference and bid a tearful farewell to her supporters. "Never stop fighting for justice," she told them. "Never think you're alone."

Westby turned out all right in the end. Not long after *Sludge Report* went dark, she co-founded a nonprofit called Marjorie House. Her focus, once again, was abused women. Job and interview training, home loans, affordable healthcare. The first shelter went up a short time later, and others followed. I believe there are seven or eight now, scattered throughout the greater Tacoma area, and she's still the director. These women are lucky to have someone as tenacious as Claire Westby fighting in their corner. The world needs more people like her.

As for Jeannie, she took the names of her accomplices to the great beyond. Assuming the women who snipped Jesse Bergman were actually accomplices and not half-assed copycats, which had also occurred to us. Maybe they got spooked after botching the Bergman job. Maybe they thought four victims—five if you count Holden Powell—was a sufficient benchmark. Augie and I spent the next few months rushing to the morgue every time a guy washed up on one of the local beaches, just to check their hardware. But as far as I know, the Snipper(s) never snipped again. Not in the South Sound, anyway.

Of all the homicides Augie and I worked on, this was the case that finally broke him. Once we'd filed it away, he told me he either needed to quit drinking or stop investigating murders. In the end, he opted for both. He transferred to the Pierce County Juvenile Justice Division in February '07 and has been sober going on twelve years. We don't communicate much, aside from Christmas cards and the occasional email. Our line of work doesn't really lend itself to fond reminiscing.

I get to thinking quite a bit now that I'm retired. I can live with my failures, professional and personal, but the Snipper case still stings me. Too many lingering questions about the perpetrators, the killing locations, the body dumps. But most of all, I just want to know: what in God's name happened to all those cocks?

Then again, maybe every question doesn't need an answer.

AS DARLA SPINS

Nikki R. Leigh

BEN KNEW THAT HE WAS IN HIS HOME, but his home felt foreign to him in that moment. Purple sheets lined the walls and floor, creating a velvety mirage. All traces of such feminine colors had been erased when his wife left him, and he shivered as he remembered her smell, while the room came into focus.

He couldn't move, his wrists bound by zip ties, his feet tied together with a thick rope. The varied sensations of burning from the rope and cutting from the ties sent his mind into a frenzy. He felt warm from head to toe, but especially around his midsection, where urine had soaked through his sweatpants moments ago. He was embarrassed by this display of incontinence, although he was alone. Moments passed, and then he saw her face. Brown hair and brown eyes—as inconspicuous as could be.

His ears buzzed, and he thought he was hearing static

before he realized she was humming over him, a monotonous sound. The sound crept into his skull, wrapped around his brain, disoriented him further. She wore a mask, surgical in nature, which caught droplets from her mouth and nose as she breathed heavily above him.

He struggled, weak attempts to remove the vices from the ends of his limbs, attempts that proved futile in his drugged state. The poison burning inside his veins was enough to subdue him, but it didn't stop the sharp fire that erupted in his stomach, as she took her first pound of flesh. She cut from him, removed skin, in thick layers, from his abdomen, and revealed the musculature underneath. He was always proud of his physique, wearing muscle tank tops with armholes open enough to showcase his finely toned body. But right now, he damned the way his body spasmed once his insides were exposed to air. Those six-pack abs were certainly less impressive without warm skin stretched over them.

Ben wanted to pass out, but he couldn't find solace as she continued that soft, single-toned hum under her breath, removing strips of skin and placing them on what looked like a grocery store scale, weighing them for reasons he couldn't understand. She was on her seventh sliver of skin before she focused on other areas of his body. She snipped some hair, sandy yellow and tinged with sweat. A stray piece fell into Ben's open eyes, bright blue, pained, crazed. She must have sensed his discomfort from the hair in his eye, though it was barely a blip compared to the torrential devastation to his stomach. She took the eye next.

With his sight completely gone on the left, he saw her

form hover over him once more. The rest of his vision finally waned as his mind gave up attempting to comprehend his dilemma. The pain subsided, the room distorted, and the last thing he heard was a soft voice whispering.

"For you, Darla."

I WAS A slave to Darla. Her sleek body was everything mine wasn't: smooth with a penetrative glare—a beacon. Where she pointed, I went. And where I went, death followed.

Darla lived in a leather sheath around my waist, tucked underneath my shirt, barely noticeable against my stiff denim jeans. I took her everywhere with me. I always listened carefully to her song, a gentle hum that brooked peace in my soul, knowing that she was near and ready to use me.

Darla was in her usual place, secured on my belt near my right hand, while I scanned the fourth gallon of milk being purchased by the same pencil-mustached man at the register. I smiled at him, wondering why a man needed four gallons of milk and why he bought those four gallons of milk twice a week. He shopped at the Stop N' Go frequently enough that his strange dairy pattern had been seared in my mind. One gallon of fat free, two gallons with extra Vitamin D, and one gallon of whole fat milk.

"Variety," he stuttered out, short of breath.

"Excuse me?" I responded, wearing the best fake cashier smile plastered across my face. I continued scanning the rest of his items: a T-bone steak, a bag of golden potatoes, rosemary, butter, cereal (but certainly not enough for that quantity of milk), and a jar of pickles.

"The milk. It's better with variety." He grinned back, a man looking much too confident, considering the amount of dairy he was purchasing. "Most days it's Vitamin D," he continued. "But sometimes I crave the thickness of the whole fat, and some days I need respite from the heaviness."

I nodded slowly, beginning to package his items after prompting the register to process his payment—$48.91—for this man's hearty meal and milk. I was feeling a bit uneasy with his sudden share, and I wondered if Darla was passing along a message.

The man took out his credit card and inserted it into the reader. I checked his license, noted the too-cheery smile in his photo, scanned his loyalty card, and continued bagging.

"What are your plans after work?" he asked, seemingly trying to change the subject from his dairy diary.

"Just gunna put my feet up, probably," I replied. "Maybe watch a little TV or read a book. Gotta get to work early again tomorrow, so tonight won't be too crazy," I elaborated, trying to keep up my buoyant appearance. "What about you, sir?"

He smiled at my interest. "Probably a little gaming with my friends. We have some rivalries to settle online tonight and a little wager going on regarding who can get the most headshots per session. Winner takes all. Best prize ever." He trailed off, urging me to ask.

"What's the prize?"

"The tallest glass of milk money can buy," he answered, straight faced as ever. I kept my own expression as steady as I could but was saved by him bursting into laughter. "I'm sorry," he said after he finished laughing. "I couldn't resist. Just wanted to make sure you knew me forever as 'that weird milk guy.'"

I laughed. "Wouldn't want that to happen," I said sarcastically, a smile on my face.

"No," he replied. "I'd rather you know me as Jean." He reached out, and I gave him my hand. He shook it and then headed towards his bag of groceries. "Have a good night now, Tricia." I almost blanched before realizing I was wearing a name tag (funny how easy it is to forget that.)

"Good night, Jean," I sounded after him. He picked up his bags, straining a bit at the effort, before tipping his head and making a funny face with his arms jutting out.

"Strong man take food to car now," he said in a silly caveman voice. As he left the store, my last customer for the day, I couldn't help but hope that Darla didn't choose him.

ONCE JEAN LEFT, I closed up shop. I managed the small grocery store owned by a hands-off businessman, who knew little of the operations I oversaw. I'd worked there as a teenager, never leaving, because I enjoyed the interactions with people and was eventually offered the position to manage the store. We had a handful of other employees: stockers, a couple cashiers, and janitorial. I worked most days, over-seeing the day-to-day business, usually picked up a cashier shift every couple of days, managed books and inventory during other days.

My job was perfect for Darla. I found plenty of potentials for her, especially on the days I worked the cash register. She hummed on my side when she sensed a worthy candidate, and I would fold a corner down on our copy of the customer receipt for her consideration later. Since I handled all the books and accounting, my access to receipts was never questioned. This meant I could lay everything out in my office for Darla to choose when she was ready. The thrumming on my thigh suggested she was.

I opened the register and grabbed the bundled stack of receipts. The drawer opened with a *bing*, coins rattling inside. I took the money too, along with the cash envelope, in order to prepare our deposit for tomorrow. With my hands full, I walked to the office.

After going through the business motions and logging data, sales, inventory, and completing other managerial tasks, I removed the dog-eared receipts and combined them with the small stack of those already collected earlier in the month. There were fifteen receipts total, marked by their tiny down-turned corners. My hands shook as I arranged them in a circle on the hardwood floor, approximately a yard in diameter.

Once in place, I unsheathed Darla from my side, feeling her energy move through my fingertips and up my arms. I placed her in the center of the circle, closed my eyes, and sent a silent prayer to whatever was out there to spare the customers who did not deserve Darla's touch. I pictured each of their fifteen faces, holding them in my mind as I reached forward and placed my hand on Darla's center—where her sharp blade met her sturdy, leather-wrapped hilt. I pinched the sides, gently snapped my hand, and sent Darla into a spin.

She spun quickly at first, dizzying in her smooth windmill, but slowed as friction decreased her momentum. I closed my eyes again, hearing the screams of the chosen in my head. When I opened them once more, Darla had stopped. The tip of her blade, cleaned of the blood from her past victims, had settled on the second of this month's sequence. Jean was spared for now, it seemed, as the knife pointed to Mark Jensen. Mark, I remembered, had fingers filled with shining rings. I knew that was what Darla would want to keep under my floorboards, in remembrance of him.

I picked up the remaining receipts, placed them in the filing cabinet with the other paperwork, and took Mark's receipt to the computer in my office. I downloaded his details—provided by his loyalty card sign-up—and marked his address in my notebook, which lived in my pocket. Like Darla, it was always by my side.

Once Darla chooses, I have to act fast, so it's a good thing I'm as efficient as I am at doing the awful things I do. I found directions to Mark's residence, locked the shop, and went hunting.

AS DARLA SPINS | *Nikki R. Leigh*

MANY OF THE homes in Ragwood were strewn about the woods, separated by dense thickets of trees and streams. I knew not to drive up the long roads until dark and to do so with my lights off. My generic tires surely wouldn't give me away, and I've long since worn shoes with the tread worn down, a few sizes too big for my feet, and different styles from what I usually wear—just in case.

Mark's house was small, modest for these parts, and just as secluded as the ten other houses I'd been to before. I always completed my tasks soundlessly, surreptitiously, and without an ounce of suspicion thrown my way. If anyone had traced the bodies to the Stop N' Go, it wasn't public knowledge, and I haven't had so much as a rent-a-cop in my store since I began. In fact, none of the bodies had yet been found, as I had an excellent storage space for them. I was confident I could keep killing for Darla.

My blood began to heat up as I approached Mark's dwelling. It was well past midnight, and his lights were off. A single car sat in his driveway, and I thought back to his grocery purchases—frozen dinners, beer, and protein powder—the habits of a man who lived alone. I walked the perimeter of his house, peering in windows, and finally located him in his bedroom, sound asleep. I went to the backyard, picked the spring lock on the back door, and let myself in.

As I approached the bedroom, I removed the rag and

chloroform from my fanny pack, soaked the rag, and tip-toed to his bed. In one swift motion, I placed the rag over his mouth. If he tried to scream, the rag stifled it. Within moments, he was out. I bound his limbs: ropes for his ankles and zip ties for his wrists. I made several trips back and forth to my car, grabbing the sheets, the tools, the containers, and the grocery store scale I'd taken with me from the Stop N' Go months earlier. I inventoried the appliance as broken before purchasing a new one for the store.

I set my things up in Mark's bedroom and waited for him to awaken.

MARK'S EYES SHOT open, and he appeared more co-herent than the last few I'd dealt with. I'd get the flesh I owed Darla from him, but we'd both have some fun at his expense first. He mumbled something from behind the cloth covering his mouth. I had no interest in what he had to say. I hummed low, mimicking the sound I felt Darla make by my side each day.

I started with his fingers, as I knew she'd want those rings. He wore them to bed, his fingers too chunky to slip them off each day. There were four of them, so I snipped each finger off, weaseling my sharp shears between the webbing of his hands. He moaned each time—low, deep, animalistic—but he could do nothing about his lost digits. The blood trickled out of each stump at a ferocious pace.

I placed each piece of him I removed on the scale, weighing out the several pounds I wanted to harvest, all part of my instructions from Darla.

I hesitated for a moment, wondering just how much of this Darla had, in fact, demanded from me. During my first few killings, I was conflicted in my intent. The urge to take lives had sprung up suddenly, and the voice haunted me each day. I attributed it to the knife, calling to me from the bedroom. At first, I thought there was no possible way I was hearing what I thought I was, but she was persistent. It was all so clear then, what I had to do, and for whom. But now…I was having trouble remembering if I was doing this for Darla or for…me.

I shook myself out of my thoughts. I didn't want a cloudy head while I prepared Mark to become a husk of the person he once was. I wrapped the meat, placed the other goods in a small leather pouch, and assessed my work.

When I was finally satisfied with the amount of his flesh I'd be keeping, I started cleaning up. He passed out long ago, his breathing becoming more and more shallow, the color of his skin matching the ichor of diseased flesh. He'd be dead soon, from blood loss, a heart attack, or the final stab of Darla, my partner, into his chest. I packed the sheets into bags, leaving one last piece of purple cloth beneath him. Just one more thing to do before I hoisted the sheet holding his body throughout the house.

I woke him with gentle pats to his cheeks while continuing the single-note hum and dragged Darla down his chest before plunging her deep within the cavity.

His body tightened, as did mine, and I could feel

Darla's release within my own chest, satisfaction, relief blooming across my body. In these moments, I questioned, again, who was truly calling the shots.

LAST NIGHT'S HUNT had been successful, and I had new fleshy parts within my large freezer. I'd disposed of Mark's body in the private lake on my property, my home in the hills, one of the few good things my parents left me. I'd always been thankful for a town that minded its own business.

Preparing for work—I'd picked up another cashier shift at the Stop N' Go—I contemplated my monthly decisions so far. I had fourteen prospects left, unless a new one was added today.

I'd carried out this plan the four previous months, gathering potentials throughout the weeks that passed. Some days produced several new choices, though most yielded nothing.

It was always up to Darla, and Darla's decisions were mine.

I'd already taken Ben and partitioned his remains for safekeeping. The fleshy strips inside the basement freezer were for me, the non-rotten parts were housed in a locked box under the floorboards of my bed, and the rest of the body went into the lake outside my home. Ben had been easy, just like the others. Single, alone, unmissed by those around him. He may have been the most physically attractive one so far, but like the others, most found his personality repugnant. Mark was the second of the three men I'd take this month, the third and final body yet to be determined. Getting ready for work, I placed Darla in her sheath on my waist, remembering, as I often did, the times she found me.

I'd first met Darla when I was nine years old. She stabbed me. Who stabs a kid, right? Well, it turns out that when your mother is in the throes of a psychiatric meltdown, she might. I remember how the knife felt sliding into my shoulder. My mother had turned, expecting a demon or some other menacing form she hallucinated without her meds. Instead, she found her daughter, wet and shivering from the tub she'd been left in, trying to get her mother to calm down. I remember wondering how something could feel so sharp and so blunt at the same time. People always describe a stab like something moving through butter, and while a knife may part the skin, it parts muscle and tissue and tendons with much less gliding.

The knife was lost when my mother went into a tailspin after realizing what she'd done. I was removed from her custody. As I gathered my belongings, before I headed off to live with my dad (they'd divorced even earlier in my life), I found Darla in a pile of my clothes, and I took her. She had been inside of me, a part of me, and she was all I had left of my mother. I couldn't help but wonder if, someday, I'd have another part of her—the ugly parts that made that terrible night happen.

I had Darla with me throughout every part of my life,

but she never featured prominently until a few years ago. I took her with me, apartment to apartment, in my older years and finally back to the home I inherited from my father. All at once, in my early thirties, she called to me. She found me again, and this time, she had plans.

Plans that I needed to finish carrying out tonight.

THE DAY MOVED slowly at the Stop N' Go. I twiddled my thumbs, counted receipts, and waited for the hum that signaled a possible prospect. Nothing, it seemed, until Jean walked into the shop, grabbed his milk, beer, fresh chicken, vegetables, and chips, and sauntered up the aisle, a smile on his face.

"Hey, Tricia," he said. "How's it hanging?" He blushed. "Or you know, how are...you?"

I grinned, finding his awkward behavior charming. "Doing fine, Jean," I replied as Darla hummed. I noted his chips and beer. "Big plans tonight?" I asked.

"Weekly game night with the guys. Beer to be consumed, asses to be kicked."

"Sounds like a rager."

"Wanna come?" he asked, finding a burst of confidence.

Only if Darla says it's okay, I thought darkly. "I'm no good at games," I answered. "Wouldn't want to ruin the fun."

"Oh, nonsense," he responded, waving his hand.

"But I won't press. Maybe dinner sometime?" Bold, this one was.

I chuckled. "Only if milk isn't on the menu." He laughed. I finished bagging his groceries, trying hard to ignore the hum of Darla's insistence. Or was it my own? I wanted him, I felt, but in what way?

"Next time, I'll come prepared with a plan." He winked, smiling wide. He grabbed his groceries and exited the store. I closed up, went to my office, and prayed Darla would choose someone other than him.

Receipts in a circle, fourteen now, I spun Darla around and around. She stopped. I sighed. *Sorry, Jean.*

"MY MAN, JEAN," Bobby, started. Jean rolled his eyes, already knowing where this was going. "You bag that grocery chick yet?" And in three, two, one…Bobby was sure to point out his joke. "You see what I did there? 'Bag'?"

Jean stared at Bobby, one of his oldest friends, though for reasons he couldn't quite remember at the moment. "I asked her out. Tricia. She didn't say no…"

"…yet," Bobby finished.

"We'll see, man. We'll see," Jean muttered. He grabbed a beer from the table. "All right, Paul should be here soon, but you want to squeeze a few rounds in? Get warmed up?"

"You bet, *Mr. A Pair of Pants.*" The two men set up the game they were going to play that night. Jean logged into his gaming system. His gamertag, *apairofpants*, flashed on the screen as the game booted up. Jean hated his name. Bobby and his other grade school pals had teased him mercilessly for years, calling him "denim," "wet pants," "corduroy boy," and other variations of his name. In his later years, he embraced it, like one does with so many of the things that haunt you early in life.

His friends also made fun of his strange milk habit before learning he was consuming copious amounts of the high-calcium liquid to try and stave off osteoporosis. He and his friends all watched his mom suffer, just as she watched her mother suffer before her. Realistically, Jean knew it probably wouldn't help, but he, at least, felt like he was doing something instead of waiting for his own inevitable diagnosis.

The boys played for a few minutes before hearing a knock at the door.

"Come on in!" Jean shouted, and the door opened shortly afterward.

"What's up, my dudes?" Paul's booming voice sounded from the hallway. "I brought tortilla chips and dip!" He came into the room, grocery bags crinkling.

"Just be careful," Jean admonished. "One of you wrecked my last controller with some soy sauce."

"My bad," Paul said. "I didn't even know I had any on my fingers."

The friends gamed for hours, zoning out, yelling occasionally, consuming all of the chips and dip, and then pausing for a break, clinking a few beers together.

"One more?" Jean asked. "I'm feeling jazzed and ready to kick your ass again."

"Fine, fine," Bobby responded.

"Let's go!" Paul screamed, hyping himself up.

The match started up once more, and the three were focused, eyes narrowed in concentration.

Rustle, rustle.

"Did you hear that?" Jean asked. He turned his head to quickly gaze behind him and then whipped it back toward the television, not wanting to miss the action.

"Nah, dude. I just hear the sounds of your imminent death," Bobby said, slamming his thumbs into the buttons.

Rustle, rustle, rustle.

"It's coming from the front window. I wish this game had a pause," Jean sighed. He desperately wanted to get up and check out what might be causing that soft scratching sound at the window. It sounded like wet leaves being crushed beneath large feet.

Oh well, he thought. *If I die, I die.* The game continued on.

TONIGHT WOULD NOT be the night. If I decided to proceed, it would be much more harrowing than the original plan. Jean really did have friends over, and at two o'clock in the morning, they were still in his home. Crumbs adorned their laps, and their eyes were red from staring at the television screen for hours. That much I could see from my perch by the window.

Jean looked away from his game, as if he noticed me at least once, but he never fully pulled himself away from the screen. I was in the clear for tonight. I'd come back tomorrow. Or...maybe I'd just stay.

I could entertain myself during the time it would take Jean's friends to leave. It had to be soon, right? I was lost in my thoughts, trying to remember my life before Darla commanded blood be spilled. I was happy, content enough. No friends, no partner, no real family left, but I had my job and my customers and, at home, the gentle lake, a soft vinyl record playing from inside the house, and a shelf full of books. It was easy to get buried in the tales and pretend to live a life very different from my own. Open the cover, become someone else, close the cover, and enjoy a life free of the characters' traumas. Yes, that spot by the lake, book in hand, traveling to far-off places for hours at a time was certainly one of the finer parts of my life.

Because of Darla, that lake was now filled with bodies. Each told their own story, their own journey...up until the point their story met my story, anyway. For some, death was certainly unfortunate, but for others—they would at least be remembered now, by me.

I transported myself there in my mind, waiting for Jean's rowdy friends to depart so I could finally feed Darla and give her what she wanted. I was beside the lake, legs outstretched on the canvas-cushioned chair, a book in hand. I heard the gentle lapping of the waves as the water reached the shore. The waves were never large enough to disrupt the view at the bottom. What once was a lake floor filled with rocks, a few scavenging fish, dirt, and algae was now landscaped with black plastic bags. They were relatively inconspicuous, especially as sediment and flora began to sprout between the folds and then on the flat surfaces. I was their master, the only person who knew they were there, except, perhaps, the fish that nibbled at the bags occasionally, trying to find the flesh within.

I, once again, pondered my relationship with Darla. She came to me, crawling from my past such a short time ago. I wondered, sometimes, if I was afflicted with the same psychosis as my mother: triggering hallucinatory personas, urging me to learn a new life. I hated the thought that I was broken, that I had inside me what she had inside her—that awful thing that made her stab her own child with Darla's less-than-soft kiss. But, perhaps, in that moment, she had planted in me something that would lay dormant for years, only to awaken when I needed it most. These thoughts, these doubts, that Darla was nothing more than a product of my own mind, were fleeting though. I wasn't brave enough to entertain them.

Car doors slamming broke me from my reverie, and instead of envisioning wet, bloated bodies, I could see nubile, youthful men climbing into their cars. Their drinking buzzes gone, they were ready to make the trek home before heading to work in a few short hours. Friends who had, unknowingly, just seen one of their oldest peer kinships for the last time. Perhaps, if they had, they would have refrained from calling him "Wet Jeans" in quick, mumbled goodbyes.

At any rate, Jean was alone. But he wouldn't be for long. I ran my fingers from Darla's leathered grip to her sheathed point and prepared my entry.

AT THIS POINT, I wanted to disregard Darla's ritual. I felt my earlier thoughts nagging, lingering. Was this for Darla? Was this for me? I knew I wanted Jean, and I knew Darla wanted Jean, but who wanted him more?

I busted through his door, and his shocked face stirred within me something I had not felt at first, not at all, in fact, since I began spilling blood for Darla. I knew, in that moment, that no matter who won out, Jean would die by *my* hand.

I charged forward, grabbing a superhero statue he owned, and slugged him across the head. He crumpled to the floor, unconscious, as my heart raced. For me? For Darla? *It doesn't matter. It doesn't matter. It doesn't matter*, I rambled in my head. Darla was a part of me and had been for a long time, so it would always be for both.

I dragged Jean's body to his bedroom. He would be out for a while; I could tell from the steady stream of blood winding its way down his chubby face. He was a handsome man, though not traditionally so. I found him even more attractive with his scarlet crown, crafted from my touch. I bound his hands with zip ties, his feet with rope, and rolled him onto his side on the bed.

I could feel, in that moment, that this kill would be my undoing. Jean had friends. They may have seen my car on the way out, as I hadn't followed my usual precautions. I acted under Darla's insistence that he be the one, but I wanted him on my terms too, and that would no doubt get me caught. I didn't know if Darla was a sickness inside my head or an excuse to do the things I desired to do, but Darla was the guidance I needed to keep myself safe. Who would have thought that as we became one, I would become less?

Due to my haste, there would be no purple sheets to line the room. No scale to measure my pound of flesh. Just me, Jean, and Darla. But this time, rather than Darla calling the shots, she would merely be a vessel. My terms. My death.

I slapped Jean awake. He stirred, eyes unfocused, scrambling to understand his predicament.

"Tricia?" he asked, his voice low and weak, as he continued to adjust to his immobile state. There were none of the usual drugs in his system, so I hoped he would remain as subdued as the others.

"I'm sorry," was all I could say. I wanted Jean, but in my heart, I knew he was as good as dead. He didn't deserve what came to him. Most didn't. But I wanted that feeling. I *needed* to feel it one last time for Darla, for myself.

"What's happening? Why?" he continued to question, his eyes widening in terror as he became more aware of what was about to befall him.

"You're just...the answer," I responded, struggling against the hum at my side, the hum in my throat, the hum in my hand, as I began to wrap my hands around Darla.

"The answer to what?" he squawked. "The answer to what?"

I held Darla firmly, choking her, as she had once

choked the life out of me. Her sharp presence in my shoulder took my breath as a child, breathed in new life that would shape me, and shape me, and shape me. Now I was shaping her. I choked her; I raised her up.

"To me," I said, heat in my hand, fire in my eyes.

Darla plunged down, as I commanded. Jean squealed, a sound as far away from pleasure as one could imagine, fear and stress twisting his vocal cords. The knife entered his stomach. Darla ripped downward through his intestines, spilling Jean's insides onto his bed sheets. He groaned, gargled, and then threw up a mass of chips, dip, and beer in his wild pain.

A smell struck my nose, so rancid I almost threw up myself. It wasn't just his own wet regurgitations that wafted to my nose, but the smell of his gut, perforated, digesting gallons of milk and the food consumed the last couple of days. I gagged at the smell of rotten dairy. I thought of my soul. It, too, was rancid from sitting and waiting to truly become…something.

Jean died quickly, unlike his predecessors. Those were my terms. Darla enjoyed the suffering; I enjoyed the release. With Jean, a sweet man, dead, I knew my time was short. I left him there, innards and all. I took no tokens for myself, except the blood drying on Darla's silver, metallic skin.

I drove home.

My thoughts were everywhere and nowhere. There was nothing to grab on to, just random voices whispering in my head. Voices I had once attributed to Darla, discernible by her sullen hum, telling me to do her bidding. The voices had multiplied now, but they all told me the same thing.

This was my undoing. As I untangled my life from Darla, as I removed my mind from her demands, I began questioning my sanity, my inability to accept that I needed help. I was long past help, after what I'd done. There was only one thing left to do.

Like always, I knelt on the ground. I removed Darla from her sheath on my hip. She left my side for what I imagined was the last time. I placed her on the ground, pinched her sides with my fingertips, and heaved her into a spinning circle, waiting for her guidance. There was only one potential victim tonight.

She spun for what felt like hours. But when she stopped, my path was clear. She confirmed what I already knew. Where she pointed, I went. And where I went, death followed. Darla, with her sleek, blood-stained body, was pointed at me.

FRIENDS OF FOWLER

Peter Molnar

I'M FINDING MY RAGE IS BECOMING MORE cumbersome as the days roll on. I nearly vault the counter to wrap my hands around the punk-looking cashier as she smirks at me with her arms crossed.

"So, you won't take it down?" I ask, heat rising up my neck. "I just told you who I am."

The big-boned girl, in a black lace tutu, pink and blue knee-high stockings, and a white Bowie shirt, shakes her head with all the smugness of a spoiled child. "No can do, ma'am," she says, leering with a smile of misapplied black lipstick. "It's not my decision to make. If you're feeling triggered, then my advice would be for you to leave the store."

"That's not the point," I say. "That...*thing*...nearly killed me. He's no icon. And you put him on a goddam shirt?"

It seems, for a split second, that I've penetrated the girl's pale, pudgy exterior. The cashier, whose nametag identifies her as **BAILEE**, right under the words *Pogo's Rock Store*, in its sinewy font, drops her arms to her sides and casts a wide glance all around. Then she takes a step towards me until she is almost leaning over the glass display case. "*You* don't even *look* like *her*. Does this get you off somehow? Walking around telling people *you're* Rebecca Murphy?"

"But...I *am* R-Rebecca Murphy."

"Really?"

"You...little—"

"*You're* Fowler's Final Girl?"

"Bitch." I spit out the insult like a bit of chicken bone, but the sound itself bears no venom. It's barely a whisper. My therapist, Dr. Bantham, has explained to me this is all part of the crippling PTSD I've developed following my narrow escape from that *thing's* fallout shelter five years ago. She calls it *diminished personality*. I tried Googling it to find out more about this symptom I thought sounded made-up. There is no such thing, and if there is, it has escaped detection by the trillions of special-interest groups, around the globe, who write about everything from the mating habits of snails to the hundred-and-one life hack uses for ear wax. Dr. Bantham must have coined the phrase. For some reason, that did not sit well with me. I haven't been back to see her since.

That was three months and two days ago.

Behind me, a soccer mom snapping bubble gum between her tanned, rolling jowls reminds me and the cashier (Bailee) there's a line nearly out the store. "Could you at least open the other register if you two are gonna need more time to sort this out?"

"No, ma'am," Bailee says in a sweet and sing-song voice that contrasts profoundly with the one she seemed to have saved just for me. "This customer was just leaving." Bailee looks me in the eyes and says, "Pogo's doesn't tolerate foul or abusive language."

"Are you kidding me?" Before I realize what I'm doing, my hands have seized her by the low-cut V of her shirt and hauled Bowie's likeness almost all the way up, past the heft of the girl's belly. My head jerks around, and I jab a free thumb at the wall of rock and pop culture t-shirts adorning the entire south wall of Pogo's Rock and Roll Store. "There's literally a shirt hanging up that just says '*FUCK!*' on it! You see it?"

The girl's hands grab for my wrist, just as I free her and offer Bailee an added little shove that tips her over, somewhat, onto the display case behind her.

My body is shaking like a leaf.

I've never put my hands on anyone before in my life.

And yet the action itself had come as natural to me as swatting a gnat that won't quit dive-bombing at my eyes.

"*GET! OUT!*" Bailee tells me, already reaching for the landline phone at her elbow. "I'm calling the—"

"Police, yeah. You do that."

I thread my way through the trees of hanging shirts and pants. I hold my head high as I rush past the line of moms and their tween daughters, who are staring outright at the unhinged woman with a smile spreading across her face.

IT ISN'T SO much the shirts with the silk-screen likeness of Henry Marshall Fowler on them, although lately I've seen them on more and more celebrities than I could have ever anticipated in my wildest nightmares. The lead singer of the alt-grunge band Grifters Anonymous wore a Fowler shirt to the Grammy Awards this past February, and one of the E! News people, standing on the red carpet, went so far as to stop him just so they could ask about his choice of clothing. They actually seemed to admire the little prick's choice in pairing a black Fowler tee with maroon leather pants tight enough to show the cucumber he, no doubt, had stashed down his crotch. But no, that wasn't what prompted the mini-tour of all the Pogo stores in my hometown of Detroit, Michigan, for the sole purpose of shaming their employees into taking down their Fowler tee displays.

Daisy Wilson, a YouTube influencer, wears a Fowler tee regularly when she posts her "life-hack" videos. Stupid little tidbits of moronic advice that go viral before the little nitwit is even finished filming.

It is prominently featured in the rapper Yawn Boy's video for the song "Murder Iz My Bidness." He plucks at it every time the camera zooms in for a closeup, drawing further attention to Fowler's dervish-of-a-face emblazoned across the kid's chest. It's about as real for him, what Fowler did, as an urban myth. Asshole. I fantasize about taking that little fucker by the scruff of his neck and rubbing his nose in the deep, curlicue scars in my belly where Fowler carved the number of the beast and then went over it again for good measure.

He's just a kid. They're all ignorant. Sheep, I remind myself.

Sometimes it helps.

Then it's something else.

Hell, it wasn't even the fucking manifesto Fowler somehow managed to get published a year into his life sentence. Apparently, he'd written it over the course of the three years he escaped detection while brutally raping and disemboweling fourteen women across three of the eight fly-over states. In it, Fowler railed against everyone from his nursery school teacher to Senator Lindsay Graham. He put forth ideologies regarding how world events were dictated by lunar cycles and the coming apocalypse would not wipe out all of humanity, as much as it would effect a "much-needed" cleansing of the religious that "plague the planet." Fowler's book, *In All Manners of Speaking,* spent seventy weeks on the *New York Times* Bestseller List, and there's talk of a documentary getting the greenlight by Netflix executives to start shooting next November.

After the incident with Bailee at Pogo's, I manage to talk through my sudden blinding embrace of violence with my therapist. Apparently, I was projecting my learned helplessness onto Bailee, so I could see that same brand of fear in someone else's eyes other than my own every time I look in the mirror. Dr. Bantham sends me home with an adult coloring book, along with a slew of worksheets addressing everything from mindfulness to proper diet to exercise regimens. She even sneaks in a flier for a kickboxing class that convenes every Thursday night at Rollin' Joe's Martial Arts Center.

Fair enough.

Later that night. Everything changes.

MY KIDNAPPING AND subsequent attack rendered me something of a homebody. There is no boyfriend, and there hasn't been in years. I suppose I can't blame what happened to me for that. I still managed to hold on to my job as a waitress at a greasy spoon diner called Opie's Inn. I never once fell short of rent or any other bills. Not even when my roommate, Sarah, broke the news to me a couple months after the police found me, dehydrated and cut up, in a drainage culvert a mile from my apartment. Her long-time boyfriend had asked her to move in with him, and I'd either have to swing everything on my own or downgrade or...

Like Depeche Mode says, "enjoy the silence" of being alone. I did, until I didn't. Between my racing thoughts and the steady onslaught of various alternative scenarios by which I did not make it out alive from Fowler's fallout shelter, I made it a practice, by degrees, to turn on all the televisions in the apartment. When I went into one room, I'd turn up the sound and turn it down again when I left.

I did this in every room, all day. Not healthy for my electric bill, but I was lonely and had to make do somehow. My best friends became Rachael Ray by day and the cast of *Modern Family* by night. I fell asleep to *I Love Lucy* episodes on Hallmark and woke up to *The Golden Girls* and another day peppered with laugh tracks that did not match up to the desolateness of the life I'd managed to salvage.

So it wasn't as if I'd set my DVR for Sergio Suarez's much-publicized interview with the object of my waking nightmares, Henry Marshall Fowler, live from the Federal Correctional Institute, Milan. It was the first live special on a premium cable network that did not center on a sporting event. I was channel surfing, and before I knew what I was seeing, my breathing turned ragged. I sat down hard in front of the television in my living room, hesitated, then slowly turned up the sound on the set. The lights were off, and as much as I wanted to get up and switch on the nearest lamp, I couldn't move.

Honestly, I was about to go to bed.

I hadn't laid eyes on him in three years, not since the trial.

My stomach lurched. Somersaults. I squeezed my eyes shut, staving off tears of terror and rage. But they would come.

Why did I leave it on?

Sometimes, we bludgeon ourselves just to feel alive, don't we?

The interview took place in a sterile white room with a steel footstool set up between Fowler and Suarez. Two bottled waters waited in the event Fowler felt parched, which was a small atrocity in and of itself. Henry Marshall Fowler was unusually tall, but his frame was spidery and all sinewy, shrunken muscle. He swam in his khaki jumpsuit. He did not so much sit in the folding chair as he perched on its edge. He was shoe-horn bald when I sat across from him in court and gave my testimony in such a small voice both the prosecutor and defense attorney had to ask me to lean in closer to the microphone. But this Fowler's head is shaved, and a thick gray handlebar mustache framed his non-existent upper lip. The same straggly, long white beard jutted out of the bottom of his chin, like an icepick.

State's evidence revealed he was a heavy crystal meth user and had been under its influence throughout his most active years. They even tried to blame his addiction for the things he'd done. But even through the plexiglass he sat behind the entire trial, I could see they had drugged him so he would not make any outbursts or incriminate himself in any way.

For the interview, Henry Marshall Fowler's little gray eyes were bright and lucid. He rubbed his hands together every couple of seconds, like a child waiting to tear open a stack of birthday presents.

Sergio Suarez, "reporter at large," according to the title at the bottom of the screen, was mid-sentence when I managed to refocus my eyes on him.

"… she started writing to you. What did you think of that?"

"Thought she sounded like a nice lady," Fowler said. "Her first letter, she talked a lot about her faith. Maisy's a Wiccan. I dunno I woulda' hit it off with her if she told me she was Christian. I don't go for that garbage. There ain't no resurrection. Ain't no judging of the living and the dead. People judge each other, and they're the ones make the judgment. Every damn day. In a way, it's all of us doing God's work. Every day. Handing down that good ol' Old Testament justice." He fell silent, then slapped his right knee with his left hand and realized he had more to add. "A nice enough lady, yeah."

Suarez shrugged, his legs crossed and hands folded on them with papers pinched between his fingers. He adjusted himself in his seat, cleared his throat. "You don't believe in the justice system?"

"What? The *U.S. justice* system?"

"You prefer a brand of street justice?"

"I don't remember using those words, exactly. You wanna answer your own questions or jumble what I'm saying all around to fit your narrative, hell, I'll just get to stepping. Maisy and I got things to do, as you know. Mister *Suarez*—"

"That's not at all what I'm doing here, Henry."

"Goddammit, you call me Mister Fowler. Just like I been doing with you. This whole interview."

"Why does that bother you? We're twenty minutes in?"

"What's that?"

"I'm asking you *why* it bothers you whether I use your surname or not?"

"All right," Fowler said, straightening in his seat. "Let's see about this." My chest tightened. My bowels loosened, and I reached for the remote to switch off the TV. I remembered how he used to set up a brown folding

chair across the fallout shelter where he kept me chained
to shackles hammered into the damp brick wall. How he
liked to try and talk philosophy, or his lazy and rambling
version of it, with me. And I was so tired. I was bleeding
internally from the three closed-fist hits to my side. I'd
bitten into my tongue almost clear through. He wanted
Aristotle, not a terrified and dying woman bound in
chains. I couldn't give him that. So he lost his temper
when I wouldn't play along. When I couldn't. One minute he was leaning forward in his chair, just like during
the interview on TV, and the next he pounced on me
and...

Just as I snatched up the remote and located the
power button to depress it once and for all, Suarez held his
hands up in some form of supplication or peace-making
gesture. It didn't work at first, but Fowler eventually reas-
sumed his previous position. He leaned forward once
more, though he was still bothered. "How about I call you
Fuckface Wetback? You *cool* with that?"

"Okay, let's...just...can we? All right."

Fowler grunted. His eyes wandered off screen, and
something curious and unsettling happened.

The sonofabitch smiled.

Suarez took his cue from Fowler's unlikely ghost of a
smile that disappeared as quickly as it appeared. Suarez
craned around, said something indecipherable to somebody, nodded stiffly, and beckoned for someone off-cam-
era to join them. The camera frame widened to accommo-
date another chair set up a few feet away from Fowler.

I watched his eyes as they followed whomever it was
around until a slightly built blond woman with a feathered

Stevie Nicks hairstyle claimed the empty chair.

The woman smiled so widely, I thought her jaw was going to unhinge.

Sergio Suarez returned the smile, but with a far more reserved one. "Hello, Maisy!"

Maisy gave a feeble little wave and cast an idolatrous glance at Fowler, who returned the gaze of admiration. "What do you think about this, huh?" Fowler said. "Ain't the world a remarkable place?"

Sergio Suarez offered a small nod, more of an acknowledgement of the vile matchmaking that had brought these two monsters together. I was certain this Maisy person must be as much a ghoul as Fowler. How else could the two of them have found the common ground to come together? Had I been there front and center, I knew in my heart I would have torn the flesh from their bones. I would have devoured the both of them on camera for all the voyeuristic viewing world to see.

My black well within bubbled and spilled over its sides. Putrid. Fetid. Intoxicating.

It spoiled all the goodness I have ever nurtured within my mind and heart, like crude oil drenching a field of yellow, waving wheat. Murdering every stalk and bending them over. Something snapped, a brittle webwork of nettles on a forest floor trampled underfoot. I could have sworn something *popped* deep inside my brain, neurons sizzling and dying. Whole neural pathways succumbing to extinction. On my hands and knees, I crawled towards the television. I splayed my hands across the glowing screen and watched through the openings between my fingers as Suarez stood and backed out of the frame to make room for someone else. I started to cry, and then I was laughing. Pleasure and pain came together as Fowler and Maisy were about to do by the bonds of marriage.

Televised.

They stood at their places and turned to one another. Maisy took one of Fowler's shackled hands. A tall man in black denim jeans and a puffy white shirt stood behind the two of them. A thick, blond ponytailed mane was draped over his left shoulder, and a clipped, manicured beard framed his soft jaw. They didn't wire him for sound, and his words were faint and indecipherable. Fowler and Maisy spoke softly to each other, heads bowed. Then they arranged their arms, side-by-side, with one another. The ponytailed minister produced a pair of red and black scarves, and he wound them around their arms, conjoining them.

I scraped my nails down the flat screen of the television, leaving luminescent purple trails in their wake.

Maisy giggled and wiggled in place, like an antsy child.

Married.

With a little push, I tipped the television over backward and remembered very little after that. Only the sparks. The black screen. And a sea of Smirnoff vodka.

LET ME TELL you something, motherfucker!

I'm *no* final girl.

And this is the sequel. My Part Two. Right here and now, parked across the street from the VFW, where six women who call themselves "Friends of Fowler" meet every third Thursday of the month. No doubt to swoon and wet themselves over press photos of their favorite serial killer, especially the one that made it on to t-shirts and adorns many of the true-crime books written about "the strange case of the Custodian Killer." Fowler swept the floors, mopped up puke, and wiped down soiled toilets at a local elementary school, just outside Dayton. In one of the many interviews he gave, Fowler was even quoted as saying, "I'm like the *Good Will Hunting* guy on the campus of MIT, a genius trailing a soap bucket behind him, and nobody knows just how smart I am the whole goddam time, until they realize I done the impossible behind their backs!"

And I have it on good intel that Maisy Watson, newlywed to the fiend himself in what turned out to be the most-watched special since Netflix's *Tiger King*, is the moderator and founder of this group, "Friends of Fowler."

Of course, my invitation must have gotten lost in the mail.

No bother, though.

This blond bob wig itches, and when I go to scratch at the hairline, it shifts. I tried it on in the Halloween store because I didn't want to get home only to find one size does *not* fit all, as the label states. These pop-up stores are a godsend, and I'm thankful it's October. Otherwise, I would have had to order something online. God knows what sort of product would have shown up in my mailbox. Some misshapen, matted rodent pelt I couldn't comb out.

I must say, I have never looked better than with these green-colored contacts. My eyeballs sit inside the sockets like deep-set emeralds rounded in shadow, borne of the five sleepless nights leading up to this moment of truth.

Six fifty-six p.m.

The meeting starts at seven p.m. sharp, according to their website. I happened upon it after falling down a rabbit hole that started by Googling Maisy's name.

Needless to say, the bitch was trending at the time.

Wonder whose name will be trending by the time the sun comes up tomorrow morning.

I don't know where I read it or if I heard it during what I've come to call my *lost week*.

"To be the man, you gotta beat the man."

I adjusted the gender tags in this quotable quote and then spray-painted it all over the walls of my apartment.

To be the woman, you gotta beat the man!

LOST WEEK.

Leading up to this, my moment of truth.

Five days of drinking and isolation. A poisonous mushroom growing in the dark of my apartment over time. Work blew up my cell phone for the first twenty-four hours, wondering whether or not I'd show up to take the orders of their truck drivers and geriatric clientele ever again. Once the calls stopped, I imagined they had accepted my unspoken resignation.

By degrees, all the people and places and things that had functioned like an umbilical cord connecting me to the Mother World outside my apartment building rotted and fell away. I became a lonely fetus floating in the darkness of the womb. An astronaut come untethered from their lunar module. Waiting to hit the great blinding white nothing or to birth myself into whatever circumstance I'd molded. I took a lot of baths in the dark, awoken only by the water gone ice cold and the faint traces of another bland morning limping back into my life.

Six fifty-nine p.m.

How do you *beat the man*?

I step out of my car into the crisp autumn evening with a swirling in my gut. With my handbag slung over my shoulder and a box of coffee from Ragamuffin Donuts hanging at my side, I start towards the house. A year ago, I would have chalked this up to nerves. Anxiety that I'd shed like a second skin in the cold water all those nights as the last remaining moments of my life ticked away. Now, the stirring in my belly is something different as I cross the street. It is my black well bubbling over again. I stand there for a moment before walking up the broken concrete pathway to the humble blue rancher with a slew of cheap Halloween decorations staked in the front yard and a weak lightbulb shining down onto the entryway.

A TALL, SKINNY woman with snaggle-teeth answers

the door to Maisy's home. She wears a brown turtleneck, and unwashed brown hair, parted down the middle, hangs shoulder length. The ends are as frayed and fuzzy as the fabric of her shirt. Lines crinkle her high brow as she takes me in. She looks to my left and right, as if expecting someone else. She takes note of the box of coffee hanging from my left hand. Then her eyes settle on me, and she smiles thinly. "Can I help you?"

"I hope I'm not too late," I say. "I'm here for the Friends of Fowler meeting."

"Uh-huh," she says. "Let me get the lady of the house."

The woman moves to shut the door on me. My hand shoots out, and I grasp the edge of it, propping it open. "Maisy's here? This is *her* house?"

"Yeah…of course. Can I ask…how did you find out about—"

"The club? Oh, well, I've been a penpal of Henry's for the last two years. He's, y'know, *so* nice. Just so *humble*. And he turned me on to Maisy's website. I visited it, and there's a listing there for your group. I know I probably should have phoned first, but I didn't think it'd be a problem." I laugh a self-deprecating laugh, slap my forehead, and back away from the door. "I always do this. I'm sorry to have bothered you. I'll call Maisy and—"

"Fawn!" a voice calls from within, touched by that same midwestern drawl I remember from the Fowler interview special. "Who is it?"

Fawn turns towards the sound of the voice. "They—er—there's a woman here who wants to, y'know, join up." She swivels her head back in my direction, the sharpness of her expression softening somewhat. "I'm sorry—what was your name, hon?"

"Kristen," I say. "Kristen Noble."

"Her name is Kristen No—"

My chest tightens, and a cold finger fans up the buttons of my spine, like a wooden mallet across a xylophone.

Maisy Watson-Fowler crowds Fawn out of the way and fills the doorway, wearing a long black velvet afghan swept around her upper body and beige yoga pants. She raises a hand in greeting, her wrist ringleted in a dizzying array of bracelets that ring out sharply against one another. Her feathered hair is sprayed up, and her makeup is not nearly as well applied as it had been for the cable special. Her green eyes are boastful. "Oh, sweetie, you come right in." She reaches for my hand and guides me inside, much to the chagrin of Fawn, the Self-Appointed Sentry of the home.

"Oh, I just *love* your hair!" Maisy's words trail behind her as I am led from the cramped foyer through a kitchen that is a straight-shot, with no room for a table and chairs.

"Thanks," I say. "I...wanted to look my best for tonight."

"And you brought coffee!" Maisy laughs. "How'd you know that's your ticket in?"

"Lucky guess."

The tile floor is sticky, and my sneakers catch on it with every footfall. It smells of fried fish inside the house. The countertop to my right is wrought with stacks upon stacks of unwashed silverware, plates, and Tupperware bins, still holding food inside that has gone to spoil. The sink is a Jenga conglomeration of precariously piled pots and pans that, I swear, give a slight shudder as I file past them, with Maisy drawing me into the living room and Fawn bringing up the rear.

Passing an off-white refrigerator beside the sink, I am immediately dizzy and euphoric at the sight of what is a veritable collage of good and evil pinned to the front of the appliance by countless magnets. Black and white photographs of what looks like a lumberjack-type man smoking a pipe and wearing baggy overalls and billowing flannel. A color photograph of a woman who looks like she could be Maisy's older sister, only slimmer and bored-looking. She is frozen in time with a half-opened Christmas present balanced in her lap. A feather tickles my nausea at the sudden striking appearance of a slew of wedding photographs snapped by someone during the televised wedding. The happy, twisted couple standing there with their dumb fucking arms bound together, staring wholesomely into one another's eyes, as if Fowler were a decent man rather than an unhinged predator.

Then I notice the crude crayon drawings of a child mixed in with the rest of the clippings. This draws my eye to the school photograph of a little boy with small, birdlike shoulders and a smiling mouth, full of empty spaces and crowded baby teeth. The boy has Maisy's thin, hooked nose and splash of blond, unruly hair.

Shit. No.

Before I realize what I'm saying, I ask, "You have a son?"

Just as Maisy leads me into a dimly lit living room, her answer both unnerves and relieves me at the same time. "Yes. His name's Paul. I'd introduce you, but he's sleeping over at a friend's house."

I worry that Maisy senses the way my hand turns clammy all at once, and I withdraw it from hers as cleanly as I can. "Some other time then."

"Ladies," Maisy says, waving me all the way in when, at that moment, I would much rather have faded into the wood paneling on the walls. "I'd like you all to meet our newest member. Go ahead," she says, beaming over at me. "Introduce yourself, babe."

I offer a small, stiff wave. "Nice to meet you all. I'm Kristen."

Behind me, Fawn completes the sentence I had already finished. "Noble. That's her last name."

Maisy crosses in front of me. "And she brought us something to warm our bellies to boot!" She motions for me to set it down on the oval coffee table.

The living room is an extension of the slovenliness and squalor of the kitchen, spread across more square footage and stamped into the battered furniture and secondhand coffee table in the center of everything, like a nicked, scratched, wooden buoy bobbing in the center of rough seas. Little Paul Watson's Batman Big Wheel is parked right next to the entertainment center, and both are held together by swatches of duct tape. The dark mauve sofa and shit-brown recliner fade into the rich, profoundly outdated wood paneling that seems to compress the room like that giant trash compactor in *Star Wars*. Two mismatched lamps cast a weak glow a meager foot and a half outward. So, of course, when I notice the floral banner hanging over the sofa, just above the heads of three of the women crammed into the sinking plushness of the upholstery, and I read the ornate pink words that run across it, I am thrown by how much it clashes with the squalor and what the words reveal:

HERE COMES THE BRIDE!

This is a wedding shower. A belated fucking wedding shower.

"Kristen?" Maisy calls to me. "You okay, hon?"

I snap to and quickly set the coffee box down on the table as instructed. Any doubts I had been harboring up until that moment have evaporated, and there is only a cold, steely determination to carry on.

Maisy has claimed the recliner. Beside it, a pile of bright, gleeful wrapping paper, covered in wedding bell patterns, lays in a haphazard pile. The unwrapped white boxes are stacked waist high next to that. "Hey, Fawn?" Maisy says. "You know where the mugs are? Grab some. Carton of cream's in the fridge, and the Sweet N' Low's in the cupboard over the stove in a little plastic container."

Without a sound, Fawn disappears back into the bomb of a kitchen.

"Sit anywhere, Kristen," Maisy tells me.

For a wedding shower, the attendees, consisting of seven women scattered about the room on the sofa, the rug, and a wingback chair, seem glum and sullen. Even in the deep pockets of shadow that pervade the room, I can tell these are women who were born in the wrong decade. High hair, heavily sprayed. Kinky curls cut into bowl shapes. Caked-on, blotted eyeliner. Red lips that seem to glow in the dark, like I'd stumbled across a vampire coven. Oversized, patterned sweaters. Grandma cardigans. Mom jeans that ride halfway up their bellies.

Maisy introduces each of them by name. I make no effort to listen to her.

What would be the point?

"Terry? Karen? Scooch so Kristen can sit down."

Terry and Karen smile sheepishly and slide towards opposite ends of the sofa. I cram myself in between them. Above the television set, one of those *Live, Laugh, Love* wooden ornaments hangs on the wall. My eyes snag on it, and I am surprised at the effort it takes to tear them away when one of the women, sitting on the floor, starts talking to me.

"You from, er, Kristen, is it?"

"Oh," I say, smoothing the hem of my black skirt down, "Wichita. Not much of a drive. I was so happy to find you're local. I don't know that my little Subaru would have been able to trek outside of Kansas without blowing a gasket or something."

Maisy waves at the banner over the sofa, the wrapping paper, and the present boxes. Her tone is almost embarrassed. "They threw me a little something to celebrate."

From the depths of my soul, I summon the demon sitting inside my gut. It grants me the power to deceive with the utmost grandiosity. "The wedding! Yes! *Yes!* I saw it! You are *such* a lucky devil! I was, literally, eating my heart out watching the two of you say your vows to each other!" I add this for good measure: "Blessed be!"

"You're Wiccan, Kristen?" Maisy asks, jerking forward in her recliner.

"I am," I lie.

"Well," she cries, the smile spreading across her face like a lengthening wound, "you and I are going to have to have us a nice long conversation. But…later. We wouldn't want to alienate the other ladies. We've got some Christians in the house. Gwen's an agnostic. And Jody's Jewish. We welcome all faiths, of course. And, on a side note, that comes straight from Henry himself. I asked him to guide me in putting together the Friends of Fowler Club, and that was one of the things he insisted on. And this coming from a man whose stepfather used to beat him bloody with a Bible if he dared get a verse wrong at Sunday school. Henry is a forgiving, decent man."

Forgiving.

Decent.

It's all I can do to keep myself from launching myself at her. Tearing her throat out.

But I will wait, because there is much worse to come.

Maisy opens her fat, wet trap to say something else when Fawn re-enters holding a tray with mugs, a cup of cream, and sugar balanced on it. "Let's drink to that," Fawn says. "The smell of the coffee is making me crazy!"

A wave of muttering works its way around the room as the women help themselves, one-by-one, to coffee just the way they like it. I take mine black and set it down on the coffee table. After a few minutes, the Friends of Fowler have all settled back into their respective spots in the living room, and the only sound is that of lips slurping and a smattering of *Aaahs* as the warmth unfurls itself in the pit of each of their bellies.

Then I step into the silence and begin:

"So, Maisy, I wanted to ask you. How does Henry feel about his celebrity status?"

"How do you mean?"

"Well, he had to have noticed or someone made him aware of the fact that they sell t-shirts with his face on them. Famous people wear them. Rock stars. Actors. He's a bestselling author. And I read somewhere the interview, and your wedding, was watched by close to five million viewers."

"Oh, *that*," Maisy says, waving it off and blowing on her coffee. I notice her body tilt to the right the slightest bit as if she's off balance, but it is not overt enough for anyone else to take note of. "There's been some talk about it. His lawyer wanted him to copyright his likeness, so his mother could cash in on the whole thing. Maybe it'd help her get into a new house or pay off her debts. Honestly, Henry hated it at first. Now, he's working with the lawyer to get any Henry Fowler merchandise officially licensed. It's only fair he get something out of it, don't you think?"

"What about signing all the proceeds over to his last surviving victim?"

I see Maisy stare across the rim of her mug at me with a flicker of annoyance. From the corner of my eye, I see Fawn has taken to leaning against the wall, gripping the threshold leading into the kitchen. She is holding herself up. Maisy clears her throat as her eyes lower into slits and then snap open wide. She straightens up like a shot.

Futile, you bitch. So so futile.

"Funny story, Kristen," Maisy says. Her words are drawn out. Slurred. "Did you know that crazy woman actually called the cable network's offices? Threatening to sue them over the interview. And when they refused...get this. She told a receptionist she was going to drive to their headquarters, and I think she said 'show you how serious

I really am.' I mean, the woman is damaged. She doesn't understand Henry was heavily into drugs when he did the things he did. He didn't know what he was doing. The man was sick. He tried so hard to get clean. He wanted to enter a rehab program, but he didn't have any insurance. He couldn't pay out of pocket. His mother has leukemia. This is a man who has paid for his ills."

"His ills?"

"In spades, Kristen. Henry has paid his dues. And he is a good man. I know I'm preaching to the choir...and...you know...that's a pretty...strange thing...to ask."

Honestly, I don't even remember calling the cable network, but I must have. I laugh out loud, say, "Just so I'm clear, you think Henry Marshall Fowler deserves to be famous? Iconic? A part of pop culture?"

A blur of motion in my periphery as Fawn slides down the wall and collapses in a heap.

The mug in Maisy's hand drops to the floor with a dull thud.

The woman to my right on the sofa grabs me by my shirt sleeve, tugs weakly on it. Her bleary, distant eyes try in vain to fasten themselves to me. "You...you did something."

I shrug her off violently and rise off the sofa as the hands of the women on either side of me make graceless swipes at my legs. I manage to skirt the coffee table when one of them manages to grab hold of my ankle. I kick out and feel the tip of my black stiletto heel puncture the woman's cheek. Her hand falls away from my leg. Freed, I cross the room and make my way into the kitchen.

The sounds coming from the living room are a cacophony of profanities, sleepy groans, and incomprehensible admonishments. Fawn's head is poking out from around the threshold on the floor. I take a running kick at it. Her skull remains intact, but she screams so loudly, I am forced to stomp on her head until my legs are on fire, and I have left a bloody, oozing mess of whites and grays and reds pooled inside an open cross-section of a brain beneath my heel.

"What's that?" I say, crouching down over her. Listening intently. "I can't hear you, Fawn! I can't *fucking hear you anymore!*"

Black spots dance before my eyes, and I feel dizzy. The adrenaline has made me tipsy, spilling over as the black well overflows inside my poor brain. A slow, churning burr sound rips its way out of my throat.

From the other room, I hear Maisy.

I find her crawling across the crusty rug, her progress negligible and sluggish. Her fingers close around the tufts of the rug, but she cannot pull herself forward any longer.

"What'd you say, Maisy?"

Her words are a warbly mess of hard consonants and droning syllables that amount to nothing.

I seize the back of her hair, wrench her face up, and bend over to look her in eyes that cannot see. Her mouth works, but there is no sound.

"Sleep for now," I tell her. "You're the last in line. I'll wake you when it's your turn."

IT DOESN'T TAKE me long to wake Maisy Watson-Fowler, but she is extremely groggy. I have left a bloody handprint on her cheek and thought of wiping it off. The mark suits her, like a scarlet letter of sorts.

"It's your turn, Mrs. Fowler," I tell her as her eyelids flutter and Maisy's head lolls to and fro. "I've dealt with all the other friends."

Her husband marked me with the number of the beast, and I've had to live with the ghostly residual scars of those three pinwheeling sixes around my navel for the last five years of my life. The way I see it, Fowler's new wife can live with her bloody mark. She'll be spending far less time with it than I've had to with my mark. And ultimately, I have come to understand that the moment Henry Marshall Fowler carved those sixes into my soft flesh, I was doomed to this endpoint. Yes, I believe he put me on the trajectory to this night. This finale. A part of me suspects Fowler possesses some form of extra-sensory, clairvoyant ability that foresaw this night in October. Wichita, Kansas.

Still, I don't believe he was privy to this scene in its entirety.

That would mean he knew, full well, he was marrying a dead woman walking, so to speak.

No, he only knew in advance he'd doomed me to embrace my inner, newly broken sociopath. The one he had sculpted within my mind and etched into my body by slow, excruciating degrees of torment, over the course of two months' captivity. That I would kill as he had killed. That he had *let* me live.

To take what he'd done and provided it some continuity.

To outdo him.

To beat the man.

The dopey moron can't steady her head and remains on this swivel that frustrates me. So I seize her by the chin and watch her eyes bulge. Maisy screams into the duct tape I've wound round and round her head, over her mouth. Her cries of protest are muted and neutered. At first, she offers my hand resistance, but I break her will with a jerk of my wrist. She has no choice but to view the monstrous display I'd put together while she slept her deep, Rohypnol-induced coma. The coffee. Ragamuffin Donuts makes one helluva bitter cup, and I counted on that. Dissolving the twenty pills into the box o' joe, bitter pills at that, would not affect the taste.

"See? They were your friends. Look at them now, Maisy. In a way, you got all of them killed. Because you're such a sick, twisted bitch."

The sight of it breaks something inside of Maisy. I swear I hear it, a crisp, audible fracturing of an already compromised and diseased mind. I hear it in the heightened, raggedy pitch of her scream behind the duct tape.

I reach underneath the bottom hem of my turtleneck. Rub at the three sixes dimpling the skin around my navel. Like a worry stone. Drawing strength from it. There is no worry in this equation.

It was a nasty business. That I cannot deny. With

some of the women, I had to saw at their necks with the hacksaw for ten minutes before the eventual squelch and snap, signaling their head had separated from their body. All of them awoke, to some degree, the moment the hacksaw's teeth bit into their throats and the inevitable cascade of blood rushed out of them to saturate the already filthy rug. I had gone about my nasty business without a word, stacking the heads into a pyramid on the coffee table. I wound the wedding banner around the arrangement, an afterthought that aided in binding them together. A happy accident. Then I set each of the headless bodies in the places they'd occupied when I'd first come in. I had slit open each of their bellies and run out their intestines, like one lets out a hose to water the lawn. They were slippery and slimy as sausage links, and I had to keep wiping off my hands on the front of my shirt. Eventually, I completed the second step and stepped back to admire my handiwork. *Friends of Fowler. Behold, this unbreakable fucking bond of the sisterhood.* Joined by their own innards and knotted together in such a way that where one of their intestinal ropes ended, another began.

Just as I'd imagined it. Conjured in my mind's eye during those five lost days of cold baths and vodka straight from the bottle and the bashing of my own head against all the walls in my apartment. The sinister, at times overwhelming, moments by which I contemplated suicide. Of warming the cold bath water with warm blood, tapped from a pair of opened wrists. *That is not how you beat the man, Rebecca! That is how you feed yourself to the man in one swallow. This is the only way! And don't you feel satiated?*

In all the excitement, I'd forgotten to remove my wig and pop my contact lenses out.

It hangs askew on my head. I must look a sight!

Maisy does not have the energy to fight the restraints. She is tied to a small desk chair from her son's room. Duct tape around her arms and legs bind her to its steel frame. For a woman who just tied the knot with one of America's most notorious serial killers in the name of love, she does not have the stomach for the new nightmare adornments in her living room. Maisy lowers her head. I lay a hand on her shoulder like a consoling friend. "I know you know who I am," I say. "And you let me in. Now you tell me, Maisy, do I deserve a t-shirt for what I've done? A televised wedding? A book deal? Cult status? You fucking tell me. This is your hard lesson! This is your tough love!"

Of course, she can't answer. I leave the duct tape over her mouth, ensuring she doesn't misunderstand the questions to be anything other than rhetorical.

"As you can see, I've gone to…well, I went to a *lot* of trouble to prove my point."

When Maisy's nose starts to twitch and she casts a feverish, twitchy glance all about, I realize she smells the gasoline.

Let's just say the fish smell has been taken care of. Masked.

I take hold of her chin and force her face upward so she has no choice but to gaze into my eyes. There is no fight left in her.

"Maisy," I say in a flat and patronizing tone, "there's one last thing I need you to do for me. Now, I'm going to remove the tape from your mouth so you can talk. If you try to scream, I'm going to pin your eyes open, and then I'm going to dissect you. Do you understand?"

Maisy's eyes bulge. Her eyeliner has run down her cheeks, and she looks very Alice Cooper.

I produce a cheap flip phone from my back pocket. "Is this yours? I found it in your purse."

There is hesitation, but she nods in the affirmative.

"Once…right off," I say and tear the tape away in one quick swipe.

Somehow, she holds true to her word and stifles any scream of pain. Her heavy lipstick is smeared beyond the boundary of her mouth. Maisy Watson-Fowler looks like the low-rent clown she has, no doubt, played the part her entire life.

The cellphone is locked and requires a password. With little goading, Maisy reveals the four-digit code: 1007. October seventh. "How lovely," I mock. It's the date of her wedding to Fowler.

I thumb open her contacts list, scroll down to his name.

Press the dial button.

"Will he be able to take the call?"

Maisy gasps, coughs violently. "Y-yes."

I tell Maisy what to say when she is connected with Henry Marshall Fowler. "Don't stray from the script either. No ad libs."

"But I…d-d-don't understand."

"You don't have to. He *will* understand."

It wasn't all that long ago a certain quote had me baffled as to its origin. Yet the answer had been staring me in the face all along. My poor brain had buried it deep, along with all the torture, and the mindfuckery, and the hope-lessness, and the prayers for a quick death. A period at the end of my life's sentence. But the memory of its origin bubbled up to the surface of my memory, a black bubble. In the cold bath, it came to me.

Henry James Fowler's final words to me before he pronounced what would have been my death sentence had I not escaped that fallout shelter in a moment of God's grace.

To be the man, you gotta beat the man.

"Is he on the line?" I ask Maisy.

"Y-y-yes…Henry? *H-Henry…*"

"Don't forget your lines."

On the other end of the cell, I can hear the man who had promised to *dissect me* barking into the phone. The powerlessness in his voice, even somewhat muted, is pal-pable. So satisfying.

"Say it!" I bark.

"R-Rebecca…Murphy's here. And…sh-she wanted me to tell you sh-she…"

"Go on."

"…she-*she beat the man after all!*"

"Good girl," I tell her. I fish deep down in my jeans pocket for the book of matches, strike one, and light the entire thing.

Toss it down at Maisy Watson-Fowler's feet. Burn her from the feet up like an infidel.

Maisy goes up like a dried-out Christmas tree. In the building warmth of the fire beside me, I punch in 911. I walk outside with her cell phone and lay it down on the front stoop, where I will wait for help to come too late.

SCARS

Bridgett Nelson

"Emotional scars have a tendency to bleed...again and again."

— *Tahsin (A Badist)*

PROLOGUE

BART

Facebook
Bart Christensen

January 1, 2020 at 8:16 PM
Hello, everyone, and Happy New Year! Any of you ready for some exciting news after a long, crazy holiday season?

I know I am. Writing for my next novel has commenced, and to show my appreciation, I'm going to select THREE of my fans as characters in this upcoming psychological thriller. Just leave a comment below, and I'll randomly choose the winners on Sunday. Those selected will also receive a signed copy of the book when it's released next year. Good luck, and let's have some fun!

I SAT BACK, RE-READ THE PARAGRAPH, AND without further contemplation clicked *post*. Within seconds, I heard dozens of pings signifying incoming comments. I left my iPad lying on the taupe-colored leather sofa and went to the kitchen. Opening the fridge, I grabbed a Bud Light, popped the tab, and took a long draw from the can. I leafed through the bin sitting on the counter—the one where I threw all my mail and correspondence. It stayed there, unmolested, until I had time to go through the pile, which meant I never had to worry about misplacing anything important. Sifting through the stack, I found bills, advertisements, and magazines I'd never subscribed to in the first place. Bored, and feeling oddly antsy, I took another swig of my beer, traversed the hallway back to the library, and reached for my iPad.

Adele Murray
January 1, 2020 at 8:19 PM
Pick me, Bart! Pick me!
Harry Samuel
January 1, 2020 at 8:19 PM
That's mighty kind of you, Bart. I hope you'll consider my name. I'd be honored.

Whitney Galloway
January 1, 2020 at 8:20 PM
Haha, bitches! This has my name written all over it.
Literally! Bart, you handsome devil, you know you
want me.

I read a few of the brainless comments and sighed.
Turning off the Apple device, I rested my head on the back
of the couch and closed my eyes. It would happen…I just
had to be patient. Didn't good things come to those who
wait?

ONE YEAR LATER

FARRAH

"WHAT HAVE YOU got for me, Dr. De Biasi?" questioned Detective Javier Perez.

The petite blond physician took off her gloves, removed her face shield, pulled the mask down over her
chin, and gave a sympathetic smile to the decidedly green-
hued detective standing in the autopsy suite of the Cook
County Medical Examiner's office, located in Chicago's
west side. Even the toughest, most hardened long-time
cops often had a difficult time in Farrah's domain. The
sights, the sounds, and *especially* the smells would frequently send them running for the toilet. Hell, this particular autopsy had affected even her—the woman's suffering
had been horrific.

"Not a lot, Detective Perez, but head to my office,
and I'll be right in to give you the lowdown," she said as

she carefully threw her gown, shoe covers, and hair covers in the red biohazard bin near the door. "First door on the right—and please make yourself comfortable while I wash up," she instructed, standing serenely in her light blue scrubs and the pair of white, easy-to-clean sneakers she used specifically for autopsies. Detective Perez mumbled his thanks and gratefully exited the autopsy pit, but Dr. Farrah De Biasi was already distracted by the process of disinfecting her hands and arms and failed to respond. She scrubbed her skin carefully in the industrial, stainless steel sink, where Betadine soap reigned supreme.

Several minutes later, Farrah strolled confidently into her office, a characterless space with no windows, bare gray walls, and—aside from a few color-coded case files stacked in a precise central pile—an empty, uncluttered desk surface. She sank stiffly into her black leather chair and shuffled through the multi-colored folders before her. Detective Perez shifted impatiently within the confines of his chair. He couldn't help but admire how strong this tiny woman was, having just watched her maneuver the dead weight of a corpse all by herself. Pushing the files aside, Farrah reluctantly focused on the detective.

"As you already know, because we worked this crime scene together, the body is that of a sixty-three-year-old female named LaRue Kingston. She was found by her cleaning lady, as she had no local family and wasn't married. Ms. Kingston was a psychiatrist who lived and worked in Wicker Park, tending to the mental health of the well-to-do. Good at her job, from what I understand, and her patients paid a pretty penny for her skills." Farrah paused, delicately cleared her throat, and then walked to a small mini-fridge sitting in the corner of the room. "Can I offer you a drink? I have bottled water and a variety of fruit juices. No coffee. Sorry…can't stand the stuff."

Swallowing back the bile rising in his throat, which threatened to evacuate his body every time he thought about what he'd seen during the autopsy, Perez nodded gratefully. "Water would be great, thanks." Farrah grabbed two eleven-ounce bottles of Evian and hustled back to her desk, handing one to the handsome and fit detective. She unscrewed the bottle cap, took a long drink, and sat back down. Letting out a tired sigh, she got right to the point.

"I know this is all review material for you, but it helps me to lay everything out in an orderly timeline, and I also feel like it puts us on the same page." Javi nodded in understanding.

Farrah continued, "According to her maid, the victim was a loner. Rarely went out unless it was job related. She was found in the master suite of her home, tied to the bed. Cause of death was asphyxiation. Duct tape was placed over both nostrils. Her tongue was severed and shoved deep into her throat cavity. While she was gasping and struggling for air, her lower abdomen was crudely sliced open, the uterus was excised, and a plastic Mardi Gras baby was inserted into a deep incision on the lower anterior portion of the organ." Farrah looked down at her desk, obviously distressed by the suffering the poor woman had endured. "That's the area where Caesarean section incisions are typically made."

Rubbing her temples in a circular motion, trying to ward off an impending headache, she pushed her blond hair behind her left ear and went on. "The uterus was then placed on Ms. Kingston's chest, over her heart, and skewered with a letter opener carved with the victim's initials. The maid identified it as the victim's and reported it was normally kept in her office. The letter opener managed to penetrate her chest cavity. While she was still alive, though likely not conscious, a large butcher knife—taken from the knife block in her kitchen—was plunged into her mouth, stabbing entirely through the severed tongue blocking her throat and wedging itself into her cervical spine. Basically, the takeaway is this, Detective—Ms. Kingston suffered a long, excruciating, and terrifying death."

Perez's focus was on one peculiar piece of information. "A Mardi Gras baby? Like the kind baked into a King cake?"

"That's exactly what it was…a naked, plastic baby, a little over an inch long, with tiny black eyes and bright red lips," Farrah answered.

"Jesus, that's fucked up. I saw you pull something out of her uterus during the autopsy, but I couldn't tell what it was. So, since this is something we just learned, I obviously haven't had time to research…do you know anything about Mardi Gras babies? Are they exclusive to specific stores?" he questioned, hope edging into his voice.

"They're on Amazon and not at all hard to find. I've even seen them on store shelves all over the city. Sorry, Detective." She coughed, took another drink from her water bottle, and went on. "My apologies…my throat always gets terribly dry while I'm in the pit." As if to prove this, she once again cleared her throat. "There were no signs of sexual assault. No bruising or indications of a struggle. I sent her nail clippings for testing, on the off chance there might be some DNA lingering, but at this point, I don't have high hopes. Her body was very clean." She leaned back in her chair and stared at the detective sadly. "I suspect she was asleep when she was attacked and never really had a chance to fight. Unfortunately, I don't have much in the way of forensics for you, Detective Perez. This homicide—it seemed very personal—and meticulously planned."

"Indeed, it did. And please, call me Javi," he responded, hiding his disappointment regarding the lack of usable evidence. Standing, Javi handed the doctor his card and walked slowly toward the door. Stopping, he turned and asked, "You'll call me with the test results?"

"Of course, Detec…of course, Javi." She gave a small grin.

"Thanks, Dr. De Biasi. I appreciate your help." He turned and walked forcefully down the gray hallway, leaving the chief medical examiner staring blankly at her bleak, gray office wall.

JAVIER

JAVIER EYED THE purple shadows swaying gently across his ceiling, the leafless branches of the maple tree outside his window looking vaguely sinister when reflected upon the drywall—like skeletal appendages reaching for his vulnerable, sleeping body. Not that he was actually sleeping. He lazily turned his head to the right and peered at the bright crimson numbers on his digital alarm clock—2:53 a.m. Insomnia had become a constant companion.

SCARS | Bridgett Nelson

His mind refused to stop processing the brutal murder of LaRue Kingston. A week had passed since her autopsy, yet he was no closer to finding her killer. Dr. De Biasi had informed him yesterday evening that no DNA was found under the victim's nails. He felt as though he was running in circles. Nothing about this case made sense, and at this point, he'd exhausted all potential leads. Javi could only hope that some crucial piece of information would come to light...and soon.

The sudden blaring of Lady Gaga's "Telephone" from his cell caused his body to startle and jump. Calls in the middle of the night never brought good news. He rolled over and grabbed the phone. "Yeah?" he snapped, not looking forward to what he was about to hear.

"We've got ourselves a cold one. Meet me at the intersection of 63rd and Wallace in West Englewood. You'll see a tan brick building, three stories. Don't fuck around, Javi. I'll see you in twenty." With that, Detective Sergeant Reynolds clicked off without waiting for a response. Cursing under his breath and ashamed to feel a thread of excitement trickle through his veins, Javier quickly pulled on the same suit he'd worn yesterday, grabbed his badge and gun, and ran to his car.

JAVI PULLED HIS brand new black Jeep Grand Cherokee onto a side street, one block from the multitude of

207

strobing red and blue lights. He hated to leave it unattended in this neighborhood—one of the worst in Chicago. Giving his SUV one final, longing look, hoping it would still be in one piece when he'd finished up, he hustled toward the derelict-looking apartment building. Ducking beneath the crime scene tape, he noted the extensive graffiti covering the light tan brick...and the missing front door.

Javi flashed his badge at the rookie guarding the entrance and asked, "Where's Reynolds?"

Stiffening his spine, the newbie cop, who appeared no older than sixteen, looked directly into Javi's eyes and, in his best grown-up voice, said, "Three-oh-four, sir. Second door on the left when you exit the stairwell."

Javi, after glancing at the man's name tag, responded, "Much obliged, Officer Morgan." Smiling to himself at the look of pride that spread across Morgan's face, Javi entered the building—which reeked of pot, boiled cabbage, and urine—and climbed the filthy stairs to the third floor. Littered with feces-filled diapers, empty syringes, and even an abandoned, cum-covered teddy bear, Javi tried his hardest not to breathe as he ascended through the stairwell. He'd need a fucking STD test after leaving this shit hole.

As he stepped onto the third floor, he was immediately assaulted by the putrid smell of human decomposition. The closer he got to apartment three-oh-four, the stronger, and more offensive, the odor became. He, once again, flashed his badge at the officer standing outside the door and reluctantly entered the squalid residence. Waves of heat hit his face, and his eyes immediately found the source of the stench—a large man, Javi placed him around six feet four inches tall and around two hundred fifty pounds, whose purple-tinted, bloated body was sprawled across the living room floor.

"Detective Perez, hold your breath and come on in," his boss yelled out gaily. "It's a goddamned party up in here!" Watching where he stepped, as there was barely any walking room in the cluttered space, Javi slowly made his way toward Reynolds. "Who do we have here, Sarge?" he asked, smelling the rancid sweat coming off the superior officer in waves. It was stifling in the small apartment. "And what's up with this heat?"

"We're guessing whoever killed this dude cranked the heat way up before he left to confuse the time of death...and it sure didn't help the smell either." Sergeant Reynolds coughed, appearing put-out by the temperature and pungent scents surrounding them. Underneath the human rot, Javi could also detect the scent of rat droppings, spoiled food, and days-old garbage. Between the heat and the suffocating aromas, he already felt sick. "The vic is Ben Rodgers, a thirty-nine-year-old bouncer at the titty bar up the street. He didn't show up to work his two scheduled shifts Monday and Tuesday night." The sweat droplets covering Reynold's upper lip glistened in the dim light and caught Javi's attention as his boss continued talking. "A coworker found him. They'd made plans to go to the casino together late Wednesday night. Now, here we are, smelling this reeking body *way* too early on Thursday morning," he complained, fanning his face in an attempt to relieve the offensive odor. "But what I really want to fucking know is how nobody in this dump thought to investigate this infernal stench. What in the Sam hell is wrong with people?" He huffed out a loud sigh. "How much you want to bet none of them saw anything either?" he asked, rolling his eyes.

Not responding, but nodding his head in agreement—he had no doubt Reynolds was right...folks in these parts were rarely willing to help cops—Javi bent down and examined the corpse. The man was flat on his back. He wore a black Nine Inch Nails t-shirt and was nude from the waist down. What had once been a muscular physique had gone to flab. Draped over his chest, like that of a corpse in a coffin, were his two mitt-sized hands...one placed primly over the other. His legs were obscenely splayed. Rigor mortis had long since come and gone, and his skin now looked like melted wax, slowly oozing away from the skeleton. Javi noticed the reddish-purple skin on the undersides of the man's arms and legs. The body's lividity, or the pooling of his blood into the dependent tissues due to gravity, told Javi the vic likely hadn't been moved after he'd died.

Javi's eyes scanned upward toward the man's head. His hair was salt and pepper—still mostly pepper—and cut into a shaggy mullet. His face, though somewhat bloated with decomposition, still displayed certain features—the remnants of a strong jaw and chiseled cheek bones, and a straight, Roman nose—features which indicated he was once a very handsome guy. Sticking out of his left eye, the brown iris now clouded and gray, was what appeared to be a fondue skewer. Cringing, Javi's gaze traveled to the man's exposed genitalia. The shaft of his penis was purple, swollen, and oddly distorted. Blood, now brown and coagulated, had dripped from the urethral opening and pooled on the dirty, mustard-colored carpet. His scrotum was MIA. As far as Javi could tell, poor ol' Ben hadn't put up much of a fight when losing the family jewels. He could discern no defensive wounds.

Hearing a new voice at the apartment's front door, Javi looked up and saw Dr. De Biasi making her way toward him with a serious look on her face. "So we meet again, Detective Perez," she intoned, her eyes taking in the squalor of the victim's domicile. She grimaced. "Though I wish it could have been in a more hospitable environment, it's still nice to see you."

Javi laughed out loud and said, "What? You don't like Ben's pad?"

Ignoring him, she focused entirely on the body while instructing the crime scene photographer on specific shots. Taking her not-so-subtle hint, Javi got out of her way and began discussing the case with Reynolds at the apartment's front door. Within seconds, they heard a shocked gasp, and both men turned to look at Farrah.

"Everything okay in there, Dr. De Biasi?" Sergeant Reynolds looked worried.

Her voice was robotic and without affect when she responded, "Come here, please...both of you." Heeding her request, the two men moved closer and noticed she was holding something round and black in her gloved hand.

"What have you got there?" asked Reynolds, genuine curiosity in his voice.

Clearly uncomfortable, Dr. De Biasi responded,

"What I have is Mr. Rodgers' scrotum and testicles. They were lying on his chest, tucked under his hands. There appears to be fresh stitches on one side." Further palpating the hairy, Jell-O like mass, her expression went rapidly from calm to curious. "There's something inside."

"Lead me to your medical bag, and I'll get whatever you need to open it up," Javi offered, his anticipation and curiosity causing a temporary cessation of any and all common sense.

Farrah looked at him coolly. "You know I can't do that, Javi. I'll examine it in the pit when I autopsy the rest of his body."

"You're right, of course." Javi looked embarrassed. "Please pardon my overabundance of enthusiasm."

"There's nothing to apologize for." She gave him a small grin.

Wiping the sweat off his forehead with the sleeve of his shirt, he asked, "How much do you think this heat affected the decomposition process? Any guesses at all as to time of death?"

"Significantly, I'd say. The humidity is high, and any kind of moisture breaks down a body more quickly, especially when combined with the sweltering heat. I can't give you an accurate time frame, but based on the amount of decomposition, while also considering external factors like the heat, my best guess is *at least* forty-eight hours, give or take twenty-four hours." Farrah looked down at the corpse. "Somebody really didn't like this guy."

Staring at the mushy black scrotum sitting in a collection jar beside the man's desecrated body, Javi muttered, "Ain't that the truth…"

FARRAH

FARRAH PICKED UP her cell phone, stared at the St. Bernard case she'd purchased to honor her favorite childhood pet, and then pushed the button that would connect her to Detective Perez.

"Perez," he bellowed, obviously annoyed by the interruption.

"Javi, Doctor De Biasi…er…Farrah here. I had a few things I wanted to discuss about the Rodgers case. Do you have a couple minutes to speak with me?"

"Hey, doc! Of course I do. Give me just a second to find a quiet room." Farrah could hear phones ringing and a multitude of voices in the background, which led her to believe he was currently at the police station. "Okay, go ahead," he encouraged as the ear-shattering sound of a door slamming shut emerged through her cell phone's speaker. The distracting background noise immediately ceased.

"I wanted to wait until I had the results of his blood work back before I called, and those arrived just this morning. This is the first chance I've had to glance at the findings, and they're…surprising, to say the least." She paused, and Javi could hear her typing on her keyboard. "Okay," she resumed speaking. "Ben Rodgers had a very large amount of flunitrazepam in his bloodstream. We're talking enough to knock out an elephant. He would have been completely incapacitated, which explains how the physical torture happened without any signs of a struggle."

"Flunitrazepam? That's Rohypnol, right?"

"Yes, it is. Have you traced his whereabouts in the

days leading up to his death? When was the last time he was seen alive?"

"He went to the corner market around nine o'clock on Monday morning to buy cigarettes and a case of Miller Light and then walked right home again. That's the last time the street cameras captured him prior to his death," Javi responded. "As you know, we responded to the scene in the early hours of Thursday morning. He was supposed to have worked at the strip club on Monday and Tuesday but never showed up."

"That actually fits pretty well with my time-of-death appraisal. I suspect he was killed sometime Monday afternoon or early evening," she informed him and then continued. "What about people going into his building? Did you see anything that stood out to you?"

"Not really. We had the landlord, if you can call that filthy old geezer by that title, look at all the people who came and went those three days on the video footage…he was able to identify everyone. Not that it matters much. There's a back entrance, via the alleyway, and not a single camera in the vicinity. That's likely the door the perp used." When he began speaking again, his voice held a tinge of hope. "We did notice something interesting though. Officer Morgan, the same cop who was guarding the entryway to the building on the morning of the homicide, drove by that very apartment building no fewer than four times on the day before the murder in his squad car. We're looking into his background now."

"That's…something, I guess," Farrah commiserated, not sounding hopeful. "But, Javi, there's something else you need to know. Mr. Rodgers had a wire pipe brush forced into his urethra. That's why his penis looked so misshapen and bizarre. It was pushed completely inside…about eight inches of stainless steel covered in nylon bristles and as wide as my ring finger. It was pushed in so far it penetrated one side of his bladder and exited right through the other. The pain would have been unbearable, though I'm guessing he was already unconscious when it happened. This murder, it was also personal. Very personal, I'd say."

"Yeah, I picked that up. Most men don't lose their balls for just any reason." He paused and then asked, "What actually killed him?"

"His official cause of death was cerebrovascular accident secondary to traumatic brain injury. The fondue skewer punctured the ophthalmic artery and caused a hemorrhagic stroke. Likely, this guy drank a little too much Rohypnol-spiked beer, fell asleep, and journeyed right on over to the other side without ever waking up."

"So, how long are you going to keep me waiting? What the hell was in Ben's scrotum?"

"Well, that's an interesting question, Javi."

"Interesting how?"

"Interesting in that it ties our two homicides together, and that is why I saved this information for last. Ben had a Mardi Gras baby in his scrotum—completely identical to the one found inside Kingston's uterus."

"You have *got* to be fucking kidding me."

"Do I seem like the kind of person who would joke about a case, Javi?"

"That's a negative, De Biasi. But it's wonderful we have actual physical evidence tying them together, because believe it or not, I actually have some news for you, too—some rather big news. We were finally able to find another connection between Kingston and Rodgers."

Farrah, her interest piqued, responded, "You have my attention. I literally cannot imagine two victims with less in common than Ms. Kingston and Mr. Rodgers."

Javier chuckled. "Right? It's like yin and yang. So, get this—apparently, they're book nerds. They both entered a contest on Bart Christensen's Facebook page last January. From what I understand, he's a pretty well-known author who lives in the Chicagoland area. I've never personally heard of hi…" Javi stopped chattering when Farrah's muffled gasp came through his cell's speaker. "What's wrong? Are you okay?"

When she responded, her voice was shaky. "What contest, Javi?"

Her obvious distress sent chills down Javi's spine. He struggled to reorganize his flustered thoughts. "Okay. Give me a minute. It…uh… this guy, Bart, had a contest to choose characters' names for his next book. I think there were three. I haven't had time to read the book yet, but when I typed those two names into a search engine, his Facebook post popped up. The book just debuted three weeks ago, and it's already a *New York Times* bestseller. I sent one of my team members to buy me a copy."

His phone remained silent. Several seconds passed.

"Farrah, are you there? Hello?"

A breathy whisper reached his ear. "Javi, I entered that contest, too." He heard a muffled sob. "I was one of the winners."

JAVIER

JAVI STARED STOICALLY at the body, trying not to let this death get to him. Both arms had been disarticulated—severed at the shoulder, elbow, and wrist joints. The multiple pieces were displayed perpendicular to the body, as though the corpse was using her arms to try and balance on a high wire. A large puddle of arterial blood, dried to a deep maroon, surrounded the body. Flies buzzed around the lifeless face. Encircling the woman's remains—their tiny, plastic bodies stuck within the syrupy, burgundy goo—were dozens of Mardi Gras babies. Babies identical to those found at two previous homicide scenes.

What the hell is going on with this fucking case?

Javi had read Bart Christensen's novel, *Scars*, over the past week. The crime scenes of both LaRue Kingston and Ben Rodgers were identical to their characters' deaths in the story, though the settings varied. In the book, LaRue was killed in her office and Ben in his bedroom; the manner of death, however, was the same. Javi had tried contacting the writer, both by phone and by unexpectedly dropping by his condo in Forest Glen, but he had yet to hear from the man. When he'd contacted Christensen's agent, he was told Bart was in the midst of a promotional tour for his book and that Javi's message would be passed along. Javi was desperate to talk to him. Bart might be able to give him some insight as to what the bloody hell was going on. Officer Morgan had been cleared of any wrongdoing, and right now, a crazed fan acting out Bart's fictional scenes was Javi's best guess as to the perpetrator of these crimes.

"What have we got here, Detective?" Sergeant Reynolds' unexpected voice was harsh in the church-like quiet of the Wrigleyville apartment.

Not wasting any time, Javi began reciting the facts as he knew them. "Our vic is Nancy Peet. She was a fifty-one-year-old social worker for the Illinois Department of Human Services. Divorced. One child. Her daughter, Jade, found the body. When momma Nancy didn't show up for their weekly lunch date at Blackbird, in the West Loop, and then failed to respond to any texts, Jade came looking for her."

"Is the daughter still here?" Sarge asked.

"No, I interviewed her and got her contact information. She had no idea who could have killed her mom—said Nancy was well-loved by everyone, even her ex-husband, went to church, volunteered at the local soup kitchen, yada, yada..." Javi answered. Reluctant to bring it up, but knowing he had to, he looked at his superior's pock-scarred face. "But, Sarge?"

"Hmmm?" Reynolds replied, his mind obviously elsewhere.

"Nancy Peet wasn't a character in Bart Christensen's book, yet she's obviously connected. Look at all these fucking dolls." He growled in frustration. "We've got a psychiatrist, a drunken deadbeat accused of sexual assault, a social worker, and possibly, a medical examiner. How does it all fit? And what the fuck do these dolls have to do with anything at all?"

"Rodgers has a criminal history? I wasn't aware."

"Sorry, Sarge. I just found out earlier today...haven't had a chance to fill you in." Javi ran his fingers through his hair, his frustration obvious, and continued. "So, yeah, Rodgers was accused of raping a sixteen-year-old girl four years ago, but it never went anywhere. The alleged victim ended up backtracking and refused to testify."

"Have you interviewed her?"

"Not yet. I tried to get in touch this morning, but she's currently living in Morgantown, West Virginia. She's a junior at West Virginia University, on the dance team there, and she didn't answer her phone. Her father, who as far as I can tell was her only living relative, died in a car accident last year."

"So, basically another dead-end. Great. I hate to even say this, but we have ourselves a serial killer, Perez. If we don't get this solved, like yesterday, the FBI is going to descend and be all up our asses."

Javi countered, "Would that be such a bad thing? It's been weeks since Kingston died, and we're no closer to finding her killer. I've been working my ass off every day for weeks, but I may as well be twiddling my thumbs. Nothing about this case makes sense, and now we know Dr. De Biasi is a target. She's part of our team, Sarge. We *need* help."

"Speaking of, do we have a cop on Dr. De Biasi?"

"Yeah, Jones is with her now."

"Good. As for the FBI, we do not want them swooping in, taking our very high-profile case, solving it, and making us look like a bunch of Goddamned chumps. Hell, no! Are you fucking insane, Perez?"

"I understand, Sarge." Javi's shoulders slumped.

"Remind me again, how was the good doctor killed in the book?"

"She was decapitated, a Mardi Gras baby forced into the severed, dripping tissues of her neck," Javier answered despondently.

Sensing Perez's attachment to De Biasi, Reynold's ordered, "You're on De Biasi duty tonight, Detective. I can't think of a person on our team who could protect her any better. Take tomorrow off and get some rest. I'll expect you back on duty, fresh as a fuckin' spring daisy, on Thursday morning."

FARRAH

SLIDING HER FEET into the slip-on shoes she left beside her front door, Farrah wrapped her winter coat tightly around her body and shuffled down the sidewalk, her face lowered against the frigid wind blowing off Lake Michigan. Glancing both ways, though traffic was rarely an issue in her gated community, she crossed the street, heading toward the black Jeep parked in front of her house. When she was just a few steps away, Javi rolled down his window—a genuine smile lighting up his handsome features, quickly followed by a look of concern.

"Everything okay, Farrah?"

"Oh. Yes, everything is fine." She realized her mistake. "Sorry to worry you. I just, well, I made a huge pot of corn chowder, way too much for just me, so I thought I'd invite you to join me for dinner," she said, a faint blush creeping over her cheeks.

"Hmmm," Javi pretended to think. "I guess my answer would depend on whether or not you have strong black coffee and some good dipping bread."

"Does Starbucks' dark roast and perfectly crispy crostini slices strike your fancy?"

"Affirmative." He nodded and rolled his window back up. Stepping out of his SUV and locking the doors behind him, he placed his hand lightly on her lower back and politely ushered her toward the large, colonial-style home.

Stepping through the front door, Javi immediately felt his body warming up and relaxing, the soft lighting and appetizing aromas coming from the kitchen creating a cozy tableau. He took in his surroundings, noticing the light, airy feel of Farrah's home; the pale blue walls, minimalistic artwork, multiple weathered-gray shelves filled to the brim with hardcover books, the gently burning gas fireplace, and plush, inviting sofas covered in throw pillows, which were various shades of blues, purples, and greens. It all came beautifully together and fostered an incredibly comfortable space.

"This is beautiful, Farrah," he complimented as he walked with her toward her kitchen.

Grabbing two deep, ceramic bowls from a cabinet and then walking toward the simmering soup sitting on the stovetop, she replied, "Thanks, Javi. I decorated it myself. I basically wanted the exact opposite of the dungeon-like pit I work in every day."

Javi watched her ladle the cream-colored soup into both bowls and then sprinkle the top with diced, roasted red peppers and feta cheese. Farrah placed two pieces of crostini into each bowl—the golden, buttery crust protruding from the depths of the soup causing his stomach to grumble—and grabbed a couple spoons from the drawer. She placed the dishes side-by-side on the marble island, along with cloth napkins and the salt and pepper grinders. "Would you like anything besides coffee to drink?"

"Just the coffee is fine." He inhaled the enticing scent of the soup. "I thought you didn't drink coffee? And for the record, this smells amazing, Farrah."

"I don't, but I keep it around for guests. As for the soup, I think it turned out well this time. I'm not always so lucky. My cooking abilities are subpar, at best." She grinned, setting a thick coffee mug beside his bowl. She grabbed herself a strawberry Kombucha from the enormous stainless steel fridge and then took her seat next to him. The only sound in the house for the next few minutes was the soft hissing of their breath as they blew on the hot soup to cool it down and a gentle crunching as they each bit into the crispy, flaky bread.

"Man, this totally hit the spot on a cold winter's day. Thanks so much for inviting me to dinner." Javi patted his stomach, a look of contentment spread across his features. He stepped down off the stool and slipped his arms into his coat.

"Where are you going? You can't leave yet...there's dessert. I made apple strudel," Farrah informed him, a tinge of anxiety creeping into her voice.

Sensing her unease, Javi took off his coat and returned it to the back of the chair. "Well, I can't possibly miss that now, can I?" He walked into her kitchen and said, "Tell me where your plates are, and I'll get us each a piece. It's the least I can do."

Directing him to the correct cabinet, Farrah replied,

"I guess you can tell I'm pretty tense?"

"It's understandable, Farrah. There's a crazed luna-tic—one who has a distinctly odd obsession with a Mardi Gras toy—walking the streets of Chicago. And as far as we know, you're next in his fucked-up line of sight," he stated matter-of-factly as he placed the strudel, topped with a perfectly round scoop of French vanilla ice cream he'd found in the freezer, in front of his friend. "So please don't be ashamed of being scared. It would be more unusual if you weren't."

Farrah sighed. "I know. I've just prided myself on be-ing strong and in control. It's a vow I made to myself as a teenager, when absolutely nothing in my life seemed to be within my control. I hate this insecurity and fear that's slowly seeping its way back into my consciousness." She took a bite of cinnamon-and-brown-sugar-covered apple, swallowed hard, and asked the question she'd been trying to get out throughout the entirety of their meal. "Would you spend the night here, Javi? I have a guest bedroom and spare toiletries. I even have some sweats you can borrow. I...I'm more anxious about this situation than I thought I'd be. I'd feel much more comfortable knowing you were in the next room and not all the way across the street."

Javi debated for only a second, wondering how Reyn-olds would feel about him sleeping in the chief medical examiner's home. But hell, who said he needed to know? He and Farrah had become friends over the past few weeks, and if having him stay inside the house helped her feel more secure, he was happy to oblige. "Of course I will. We can even watch a movie after we finish eating—a com-edy, to take your mind off things."

Grinning, Farrah responded, "You have yourself a deal, Detective."

JAVIER

THIS GUY COULD be a model, Javi thought to himself as the well-known author opened the door to his penthouse apartment. Bart Christensen was masculine, rugged, and stylish all at once. Javi estimated he was six feet, two inches tall. Slender, but muscular, he showed off his physique in light-blue, slim-fit jeans, an untucked V-neck white t-shirt, and a medium gray two-button jacket with rolled-up sleeves, left casually open. On his feet was a pair of stark-white Adidas sneakers, worn without socks. A solid black cross, about six inches long, was tattooed on his left inner forearm, neighboring a black Rolex watch. He gazed at Javi from warm, toffee brown eyes. Black hair—cut shorter on the sides and left longer on top—set off his tan skin and strong jawline, which was covered in neatly groomed scruff. Javi had no doubt that this was the dude women fantasized about when they pulled those trusty vibrators from the drawer of their bedside tables.

"Detective Perez?" Bart inquired in a soft, pleasant voice.

Nodding, Javi flashed his badge at the man and said, "Bart Christensen, I presume?" He already knew to whom he was speaking...he'd seen his photos all over the internet, but he wasn't keen on Christensen knowing that information. At least not yet.

"Indeed, I am," he replied as he opened the door and motioned Javi inside. "Please come in."

Javi was immediately struck by the unlived-in look of the man's home. It reminded him of a college pad: nothing on the walls, no personal items or décor to make the place homier...just an expensive-looking sectional leather sofa, a stainless steel floor lamp in the corner, and the biggest television Javi had ever seen mounted to the wall.

"I'm afraid I haven't been home for long and don't have much in the fridge, but I do have a few cans of soda or bottled water," Bart offered.

"No, thank you. I'm fine."

"Well then, please have a seat," Bart responded, motioning to the sofa.

Javi sat down on the shorter end of the L-shaped couch, while Bart sat across from him, on the far edge of the long end.

"Mr. Christensen, I have a few questions for you regarding multiple homicides which have occurred over the past month."

"I'm happy to answer anything, Detective, but please, call me Bart. And let me preface this line of questioning by saying this—I've been out of town for several weeks, so I know nothing of these crimes. I'm not sure I understand how these people's deaths have anything to do with me."

Javi gave Bart a grim smile and responded, "Two of the people who have died are the character contest winners used in your book *Scars*...LaRue Kingston and Ben Rodgers. Not only were they both characters in your novel, but they were killed using the same methodology you created."

He watched Bart's tanned skin slowly fade to a sickly white as the man digested Javi's words.

"Oh my God! Ben and LaRue? They're long-time

fans of mine. I've met them both multiple times at local book signings. How awful," Bart said, swallowing hard.

Javi proceeded with his questioning. "Mr. Christensen, do you know a social worker named Nancy Peet?"

Staring out his front window at the Chicago skyline, Bart took his time thinking about the name. Finally, he replied, "The name doesn't sound familiar, but I'm better with faces than names. Do you happen to have a photo? I see and speak to so many fans each day, it would be very easy for me to forget a name."

Javi obliged and pulled up Nancy's morgue photo on his phone, a close-up image of her face only. He showed it to Bart, without any forewarning, wanting to see how the man responded to the macabre nature of the image. Gazing at the translucent white skin, marbled with threads of decomposing veins, and the cloudy, staring eyes of Ms. Peet, Bart's hand flew to his mouth, as though trying to prevent himself from upchucking. For all Javi knew, maybe that's exactly what he was doing—but shouldn't a guy who thought up gruesome murders for a living have a stronger stomach?

"I'm sorry, Detective. I don't know that woman. Can you please get that horrible photo away from me?" He gasped for air and mumbled, "Jesus."

Javi retrieved his phone and responded staunchly, "Just a couple more questions, then I'll get out of your hair."

Bart, looking haunted, simply nodded his head.

"Do you know of anybody who would want to hurt you or your fans?"

Staring straight into Javi's eyes, Bart replied, "No. I

absolutely do not. I have a great relationship with my fans and have never really had any worrisome incidents throughout my career. Sure, all authors attract some crazies, but the ones I've dealt with were relatively benign." He let out a raspy breath and went on, "I honestly can't think of anyone."

"Okay. Final question—do you know Farrah De Biasi?"

Bart shook his head and said, "Only as a character in my story, Detective."

Javi stood up and began walking toward the front door. "Thanks for your time, Mr. Christensen. I appreciate it. Please, if you think of anything that might be pertinent to this investigation, give me a call," he said, handing the author his card.

"I absolutely will," Bart said. "This is so sickening. I feel like it's my fault."

Refusing to assuage Bart's guilt, the two men shook hands, and Javi walked toward the elevator. Bart had denied knowing Farrah, but just before the man had responded to his question, Javi had seen something in the man's eyes he didn't like. Not even a little bit.

FARRAH

AS THE CLOSING credits of *American Pie 2* rolled across her screen, Javi grinned at Farrah and said, "Not a serial killer anywhere to be seen." After a brief pause, he mimicked a scene in the movie and said, "It's a good news day!"

Without breaking stride, Farrah finished with Eugene Levy's infamous quote, "Don't forget your penis cream!" They both grinned.

Farrah languidly stretched her toned body and said, "I think I'm going to hit the shower before bed. I haven't even brushed my hair today. I'm disgusting. Make yourself at home, and help yourself to anything in the fridge."

"Oh, you know I will. I've gotta keep up my strength for that smelly lady I'm forced to guard."

"Laying it on a bit thick, aren't you?" Farrah replied, rolling her eyes. During the past month, they'd developed a fun-loving friendship, but neither was interested in taking it further. She laughed light-heartedly and walked up her grand, curved staircase. Entering the master suite, she smiled to herself thinking of Javi's crazy antics.

He was nothing like his father.

JAVIER

OPENING THE FRIDGE door, Javi evaluated the contents: Greek yogurt, several varieties of expensive cheeses, olives, homemade hummus and guacamole, fresh veggies and fruit, and leftover Thai food from the previous night. Although they'd just eaten pizza a couple hours ago, Javi's stomach was growling. Grabbing the leftover Thai cartons and a glass bottle of some exotic fruit juice, he shut the door with his foot and carried his goodies to the island. He'd debated having one of the many Bud Light cans in Farrah's fridge, but since he needed to be alert and focused, he figured beer probably wasn't the best idea. Opening the juice, he took a long swig and set it back on the marble countertop. Smacking his lips, he decided whatever that sugary shit was, it wasn't half bad. Planning to eat his snack cold, he grabbed a fork from Farrah's silverware drawer and quickly turned back around, clumsily knocking the pink juice all over her hardwood floors. Shattered glass, in a multitude of sparkling sizes, littered the floor.

"Fuck!" He jumped back to protect his socked feet. Anxious to get the mess cleaned up before anybody got a glass shard stuck in their foot, and before the fluid warped the expensive hardwood, Javi ran to the linen closet located just outside Farrah's lower level guest room. Grabbing several thick, plush towels, Javi heard something clatter as it hit the floor. Anxious to replace whatever he'd dislodged and get back to his mess, he squatted down to search for the fallen object.

Shifting several boxes and storage containers around, he glanced into the back corner...and froze.

Lying propped against the wall, its black, unseeing eyes staring straight into Javi's soul, was a plastic Mardi Gras baby—one which perfectly matched those found at his homicide scenes.

FARRAH

FRESHLY BATHED AND super comfy in a white thermal, long-sleeve shirt that read "Cozy Chic" in teal across her breasts, a pair of worn, distressed jeans, and some white fuzzy socks, Farrah walked sedately downstairs, feeling relaxed and mellow. Until she saw Javi sitting at the kitchen island, a pile of glass covering the floor near his feet, that is. "Are you okay?" she gasped, running toward him. She stopped abruptly when she saw the bag of plastic dolls gripped within his hands. A tense silence filled the air.

"Where did you find those?" Farrah asked finally, her voice calm and resolute.

When he spoke, his voice was gravelly and full of tension. "I was getting towels out of your linen closet to clean up the mess on the floor, and one of these little dudes decided to make an appearance." For the first time since she came downstairs, he looked directly at her. "Why do you have these, Farrah?"

Staring him directly in the eye, she stated, "People in Chicago have Mardi Gras parties too, Javi."

"Of course, that's true. When did you have a party, Farrah?"

"I didn't, but a friend did, and I volunteered to bake the king cake."

"Oh, yeah? What friend?" Javi tried to make his voice sound lighthearted, but internally, his heart felt as if it would soon catapult out of his chest. "And I thought you said your cooking and baking skills were 'subpar, at best?'"

"You don't know this woman. I went to medical school with her… and why do you care anyway? Just because I'm not a great baker doesn't mean I can't put together a simple cake. This is completely circumstantial evidence, and you know it, Javier. Probably half the homes in America have one of these plastic Mardi Gras babies inside them." She swallowed hard. "You *know* me. Do you honestly think I'm capable of these horrific crimes?"

Javi's gaze dropped from hers, no longer able to meet

her pleading eyes. "No. No, I don't. But I *do* think it's a pretty big coincidence that I found these dolls—dolls that are an exact replica of those at our crime scenes, I might add. And I'm not gonna lie, Farrah. I do find your current demeanor suspicious. There is a sheen of sweat covering your face, and your hands are shaking." Javi stopped talking, the anger in the pit of his stomach growing. He knew where this conversation was headed, and the betrayal was already eating away at his gut. "So, let's do this—I'm going to ask you one more time, and I want an honest answer. Why do you have these dolls, Farrah?"

Letting out a huge sigh, Farrah slumped onto the bar stool beside Javi. "Why do you think I have them?"

"I mean, no...there's no way...you wouldn't..." he stammered, trying to wrap his mind around this information. Despite knowing what she was going to say, actually hearing her admission was like being hit in the face with a brick. "You're not a killer, Farrah." She stared at him without saying anything. "No, I don't accept that." He stood and began pacing the kitchen. Stopping, he turned to look at her and demanded, "Jesus Christ, Farrah. What the fuck is happening here?"

"It's a very long story."

"I *need* to hear this, Farrah."

"Please sit down first, Javi. Your pacing is making me anxious."

"Do you think I give a flying fuck that you're feeling anxious right now? Dammit, Farrah! You just blew my entire world apart, yet you expect me to sit calmly? You know what? Fuck you." Javi threw his arms in the air and continued his overwrought march around the kitchen.

Farrah stood and shuffled hesitantly toward him, her hands held palm out, at shoulder level. When she reached him, she gently put her hand on his shoulder. His body recoiled at her touch. "Javi, please. I want to explain myself, but, Christ—I'm begging you—please sit down with me while I share my story. It's not an easy one to tell on the best of days, but trust me, it is far worse when also confessing to serial murders. And though I realize I don't deserve it, I need your support to get through."

He said nothing, just stared sightlessly at the floor. Finally, his body reluctantly followed her back to the barstools. Instead of sitting beside her, however, he picked his chair up and carried it to the opposite side of the island. He had no desire to be anywhere near her cold, dreadfully clammy hands. "Okay, I'm sitting." He looked at her expectantly.

Farrah stared blankly at her lavish kitchen, her mind elsewhere. Just when Javi thought he was going to have to push her to speak, she began.

"When I was sixteen years old, our school planned a spring trip to New Orleans for the juniors and seniors. I was so excited about that trip, Javi. I grew up with very strict, religious parents, and at that point in my life, I had never even left Chicago. I helped with bake sales, and car washes, and all sorts of fundraisers to pay my way. My parents were not keen on the idea, convinced New Orleans was a sinful city full of voodoo and false Gods. Nevertheless, for whatever reason, they decided to let me go." Farrah grinned, thinking back to her distant victory.

"The trip was only scheduled for three days and two nights; one day was planned to get there and another to get back. We reserved one of those huge Greyhound buses with the bathrooms and comfy seats. We all just *knew* it was going to be the greatest trip of our lives. It was around an eighteen-hour journey, with breaks and food stops included, so we left at three o'clock in the morning. When we finally arrived at our hotel, some cheap Holiday Inn nowhere near Bourbon Street, the chaperones got us all tucked into our rooms, and that's where we spent the rest of the night. The next day was brilliant. We went to the National World War II Museum that morning, had lunch on Bourbon Street, toured the Voodoo Museum in the afternoon, and then went to a nice restaurant for dinner. Looking back, that was probably one of the happiest days of my life."

Farrah's face glowed with pleasure as her memories engulfed her. "Later that night, my roommate, who was also my best friend, decided she was going to sneak to her boyfriend's room. So they'd have privacy, she was going to send his roommate back to our room. I wasn't thrilled, as I didn't really know the guy. He was a year older than me and, frankly, didn't have the best reputation."

She looked at Javi and asked, "Are you still with me?"

"Yes. Not that I want to be. Just get to the fucking point, Farrah."

Stunned by his coldness, she faltered briefly, and then continued. "Shortly after she left, there was a knock on my door. It was him. For a while, we sat and watched TV, made small talk, and attempted to lessen an incredibly awkward situation. We even discovered we were both avid readers who favored psychological thrillers. But then, without any warning, he moved to my bed and sat down, acting as though I had invited him. I hadn't, Javi. I didn't want him anywhere near me. He was very good-looking and a really popular football star, but something about him unnerved me. Before long, his hand was on my leg, kneading and rubbing. I kept shoving it off, but he'd come back, more aggressive each time. Before I knew what was happening, he had me flat on my back with my arms pinned above my head. I was wearing leggings, but he easily managed to get those off, despite my struggles. I was biting and screaming and kicking my legs, but I'm so damn petite, Javi. I wasn't as strong back then as I am now. I weighed *maybe* a hundred ten pounds soaking wet. It was like a mouse trying to take down a cat."

Javi noticed that as Farrah's story progressed, her breathing became more and more rapid, her pupils dilated, and the sheen of sweat had reappeared on her forehead.

"He hurt me so much, Javi. When he'd finished, he said, 'Thanks for letting me tap that tight little pussy, Franny,' and then walked out of the room. He didn't even know my fucking name. I'll never forget the smug smile he gave me as he left. I wanted to kill him. I was a virgin before that awful night. Instead, I showered and put on clean clothes, then pretended to be asleep when my friend came back. The rest of that trip was a blur. I honestly don't remember anything else that happened. When we arrived home, my parents asked if I'd had a good time. I told them I had. What else could I possibly say? I tried so hard to just put it all behind me and move on with my life."

Tears ran down Farrah's face. Javi, his demeanor softening after hearing how horribly she was violated, went to the fridge, got her a bottle of water, and set it beside her on the counter. Nodding her head in thanks, she took a drink and then continued.

"Two months passed. My friends began ghosting me. I'd become zombie-girl and nobody understood why, not that any of them cared enough to try and find out. Every time I'd pass my rapist in the hallway, he'd leer at me—sometimes suggestively licking his lips or winking. It sent chills down my spine, Javi. Then one morning I woke up and was violently sick. I puked for hours. Mom, assuming I had a stomach bug, let me stay home from school. I spent the day in bed, watching game shows. She loaded me up with ice cold Ginger Ale and lime Jell-O. After a while, I grew bored with Bob Barker and pulled out my diary. I'd been writing about my feelings several days a week, attempting my own version of therapy. Turning to a new page, I jotted down the date and completely froze. It had suddenly occurred to me that my period was very, very late. I hadn't menstruated since before the trip to New Orleans."

Farrah was sobbing now, her jagged breath coming in hiccups as she struggled to regain control. "I was pregnant with my rapist's baby, Javi. At first, it made me absolutely sick. I wanted nothing more than to vanquish that *thing* from my womb. The thought of my genetic material mixed with his was utterly repulsive to me. But as the days passed, this tiny little human managed to capture my heart. I began thinking of him or her as mine only—no rapist genes to be found. I wanted the baby. I wanted to be a mother. I wanted to raise this little person to be better than his father."

She stared at her feet as she wiped her sweaty palms on her jeans. "When I finally found the nerve to tell my parents, as expected, all hell broke loose. They demanded I have an abortion and called me a jezebel." She laughed. "A jezebel, for fuck's sake—like I was some sort of ancient, defiled biblical character. My mom made an appointment for me at a Planned Parenthood clinic, and when I refused to go, they forced me to see a therapist who was paid handsomely and explicitly instructed to push me toward terminating my pregnancy. She tried like hell to convince me that looking at my rapist's baby would be detrimental to my mental and emotional health, every single day, for the rest of my life. It didn't work, but my parents definitely got their money's worth with that one. She was vile.

"Fortunately, I had waited so long to tell anyone, I was already well into my fourth month, and second trimester abortions were illegal. That's when my parents decided to pull me from school and begin a homeschooling curriculum. They couldn't have their harlot daughter tarnishing their holier-than-thou name. They'd resigned themselves to the fact I was having this baby but refused to entertain the thought of me actually keeping it. They went behind my back and found an infertile couple who was willing to adopt my bastard child. I was never told and didn't realize they'd forged my name on the paperwork. Long before I gave birth, and completely without my knowledge or consent, my baby was already lost to me."

Farrah paused in her storytelling and blew her nose. Javi watched her intently from across the island.

"On February 14, 2001, I gave birth to an absolutely beautiful baby girl, via Caesarean section. Every time I would bear down and push, her heartrate would decelerate, so they decided to take her via an urgent C-section. I couldn't stop staring at her—my gorgeous little Valentine.

"She had silky blond hair and big blue eyes in a cherub face. It was like looking at my own baby picture, Javi. I just knew she was all mine, and this proved it. The sperm donor had dark hair and eyes…so you'd think those dominant genes would have expressed themselves in our child, but no. She was my mini, and I convinced myself he'd had no part in her creation. I was so in love with my little angel."

Her face suddenly flushed.

"About an hour after she was born, I was still cuddling my daughter. She hadn't left my arms. I had even attempted to breastfeed her. Then some random woman, accompanied by a police officer, came parading into my room without knocking. She informed me she was the social worker who was there to take my baby to her new parents. I felt like I'd been gut-punched. 'What are you talking about?' I asked. 'She's not being adopted. I know nothing about this.' Without even listening to what I was saying, she attempted to grab the baby from my arms. I instinctively protected Angelina, which is the name I'd given my baby girl, and pushed that annoying fuckwit away. She fell to the floor, let out this loud *oooff* sound, and sort of bounced on her lard ass. I giggled…couldn't help myself. The cop helped her up, then came over and physically restrained my arms so that woman could snatch the baby. I tried to get out of bed to give chase, but the cop held me down. When I wouldn't stop yelling, the fucker slapped me. He pushed the bedside call button to summon my nurse. I swear she was standing just outside the door, waiting to play her role on what was, without a doubt, the worst day of my life. That bitch was there within seconds, probably another of my parents' paid minions. While I struggled and screamed, she injected something into my IV. I don't remember anything after that. When I woke up, it was dark, and my baby was long gone. In the days that followed, my milk came in...but I had no baby to nourish."

As Farrah told her story, her voice grew louder and louder. Her face was infused with blood, and ropey veins protruded from her neck and forehead.

"Rather than live with my traitorous parents, I moved into a group home for teenagers until I graduated. I suppose the assholes felt guilty, because they still paid for my undergraduate degree, and I let them. It was the least they could fucking do. I spent all my free time trying to find my daughter, and when that failed, I instead focused on punishing those responsible for stealing her."

Farrah paused, relishing her big reveal.

"My therapist was LaRue Kingston, and I made sure to shut her vitriol-spewing mouth permanently; my rapist, Ben Rodgers, was penetrated without his permission...with a wire brush; and the bitchy social worker was Nancy Peet, who no longer has arms to carry babies away from their mothers. Next on my list was the cop. Unfortunately, he did my job for me. He died in 2005 during a shoot-out in Garfield Park."

Javi stared at her, his face registering the shock churning in his gut. He stood and backed away from her.

Farrah laughed. "Yes, Javi, it was your dad who restrained and slapped a post-partum teenager whose baby was being kidnapped. Not his finest moment, was it?" She reached behind her, pulled out the Glock 9mm pistol, complete with silencer, which had been secured in the waistband of her jeans, and aimed it at Javi. "But how convenient for me...he has a son on the police force. So, what do you say? Do you want to square things up for your old man? His son for my daughter? Seems fair to me."

Without warning, she pulled the trigger, and Javi's left knee exploded in a spray of blood and bone.

As he writhed on her floor, screaming in pain, Farrah kept the gun pointed at his chest and continued her story. "I've been meticulously planning all this for years now. How silly of me to let something like a package of cheap, plastic dolls bring down this tower of cards." Farrah shook her head in disgust. "Such a stupid oversight...but then again, it's not like I left them lying in plain sight. They were tucked behind piles of towels in a linen closet that is never used," she grumbled. "The good news? I'm not done yet. The nurse, Melissa Goodwin, still needs to be dealt with. I have a very grisly death planned for her. She chemically restrained me during the kidnapping of my precious daughter, so I was thinking Drano in an IV line would be an appropriate comeuppance. What say you, Detective?"

Gripping his knee and attempting to slide as far from Farrah as he could, his words came in bursts of guttural pants. "How could you possibly have been planning this for so long, Farrah? The deaths match Bart Christensen's book perfectly. You couldn't have known what he was going to write."

Farrah threw back her head and laughed. "You haven't figured it out yet? Just what kind of detective are you, anyway? I thought for sure it would become clear as I told you my story."

He stared at her, confusion and pain clouding his eyes.

"Oh, for Christ's sake—*I'm* Bart Christensen, Javi. It's my pen name. Jaxon Dufresne is a struggling actor I hired to be the face of the infamous Bart, and his apartment is there for appearances only. I purchased it with the inheritance I received following my parents' deaths, though according to the records, it's owned exclusively by a Mr. Bartholomew Rupert Christensen. As far as the government is concerned, Bart is a real person...with a social security number and a credit rating. He even pays taxes. I went all out, spent a small fortune getting all the paperwork on the dark web. Before each of my books publish, I give Jax all my notes and the final draft, which he studies meticulously, so he can answer any questions our fans may ask. Or cops." She smirked. "For the record, he knew nothing of my plans to kill these people."

Javi gaped at her revelation.

"I originally started writing as a hobby, but I never wanted the fame. It came unexpectedly and with great aplomb. It wasn't until I noticed Ben and LaRue were fans of Bart on social media that I realized I could use this so-called hobby to my advantage. It took several years, but I had it all perfectly planned out. There was no way any of this could come back to me. I even inserted myself as a potential victim, in an effort to throw you even further off my trail. I'm so angry at myself. You're getting off way too easily, Javi. Consider it a gift, as I'd originally planned to dunk your face into acid and erode those chiseled cheeks of yours, a bit of payback for the stinging, reddened cheek your daddy-dearest blessed upon me."

Smiling, she pulled the gun's trigger two times, both bullets impaling Javi's torso. She watched calmly as his respirations slowed and finally ceased. "Not nearly enough suffering, in my opinion," Farrah mumbled to herself. She opened the back door, letting the cold winter wind quickly fill the cozy kitchen, picked up the bag of dolls, and ran upstairs to the master suite. Grabbing her cell phone from the charger on her night stand, she ran into her walk-in closet, leaving the door open behind her. Sliding open the secret compartment she had installed, she placed the dolls inside, silently berating herself for not placing them there to begin with.

Cursing her own stupidity, she took a deep breath and, not letting herself think too deeply about what she was doing, shot the meaty part of her inner thigh. Screaming at the intense burning pain, she nevertheless geared herself up for round two. It had to be done. Pointing the gun toward her abdomen, she aimed for the lower right quadrant...less likely to hit anything crucial there. She pulled the trigger. The impact of the bullet penetrating her intestines caused her body to fall to the floor. Bleeding profusely and in intense pain, she made sure there was no blood on her hands and struggled back to her feet. Hiding the gun in the concealed space, she closed the door, which blended seamlessly into the wall, and pulled shoe boxes back in front. Dizziness overtook her and she fell back to the floor. She managed to dial 911 on her phone just before her world faded to black.

FARRAH

FARRAH'S EYES BLINKED open and then quickly closed again against bright sunlight streaming through the room's only window. A faint beeping sound could be heard just to the right of her head, and a medicinal smell permeated the air. She should probably feel disoriented, but Farrah knew exactly where she was—the hospital. She remembered everything, and now it was time to see just how well she'd played her part.

"Hello, Dr. De Biasi. So glad to see you're awake."

The deep voice, one she recognized, came from her left, near the door. She squinted, trying to see her visitor while allowing her eyes to adjust to the obscenely obnoxious light in this room.

"Sergeant Rey—" Her throat was sore and her voice raspy. She cleared it as best as she could and went on. "Sergeant Reynolds, where am I?"

"You're at Rush University Medical Center. You were shot during a home invasion. You had emergency surgery and have been sedated for nearly forty-eight hours." His eyes peered intently into Farrah's. "Please, Doc, I know you are probably feeling pretty rough, but if you can, tell me anything you can remember. Anything at all."

She tried to sit up, but the pain in her abdomen was intense. Reynolds stepped forward and pushed the button to raise the head of her bed.

"Thank you," she said, placing her hand over the bandage that covered a large portion of her torso. "I'll tell you everything I remember, but first, will you please tell me how Javi is?"

Reynolds hesitated as an internal battle was waged. He finally made a decision. "Detective Perez passed away, Farrah. He was found in your kitchen by the paramedics. Nothing could be done."

Tears streamed down Farrah's cheeks.

"I'm so sorry, Sergeant Reynolds. His death is my fault. If he hadn't been protecting me, he'd still be alive today," she cried.

Allowing her a few moments to collect herself, Reynolds once again asked her to share with him everything she remembered. "We had pizza for dinner and then watched a movie," she began. "After that, I went upstairs to get a shower and told Javi to help himself to anything in the fridge. I was gone maybe twenty minutes. When I came back downstairs, I found Javi lying on the floor with several bullet wounds. I turned and started running upstairs to get my cell, which I'd left in my bedroom. I wanted to call nine-one-one and then get started on resuscitation," she explained, her hands clutching the sheet in a death grip. "When I was halfway up the stairs, I heard footsteps behind me and saw a large figure wearing a balaclava. I don't know for sure if it was a male or not, but the build was more masculine—broad shoulders, narrow hips, a bit of a gut where men typically carry weight."

Farrah sniffled. "I'm sorry, but would you mind handing me a tissue?"

Reynolds patiently obliged and handed her the white

Kleenex. After she wiped her tears and blew her nose, she continued. "I ran into my bedroom, hoping I could get to my phone. I grabbed it and headed for my walk-in closet, which locks from the inside. I desperately wanted to get inside, secure the lock, and call for help, but the intruder was too damn fast. Before I could get the door fully closed, he out-muscled me and shoved it open. I'd say he was well over six feet tall and probably weighed around two-fifteen. Before I could do anything, he shot me—I don't even know how many times—and left me for dead. I remember trying to call nine-one-one before I passed out, but I can't remember actually succeeding. I guess I must have since I'm here now, alive and well." She gave a bitter grin.

Farrah stared despondently out the window while Reynolds made some notes in a small notebook he kept in his jacket pocket. His pencil was worn down to nothing but a nub. "I don't mean to dismiss you, Sergeant, and I'll help in any way I can with this investigation, but would you mind getting my doctor or nurse? I'm in quite a bit of pain, and I'd like to know what's happened to me, medically speaking."

"Of course I will," Reynolds said, standing and preparing to leave. "Take good care, Farrah."

That could not have gone better, Farrah thought as she watched the man walk out of her room and turn left into the busy hallway.

TWO WEEKS LATER

FARRAH

Dearest Madison,

It's hard to even know where to begin, but I'm just going to get this out of the way quickly and, hopefully, painlessly. My name is Farrah De Biasi, and I am your biological mother. I gave birth to you at age seventeen, in Chicago, Illinois. Unbeknownst to me at the time, my parents had found a childless couple yearning for a baby and then forged all the adoption paperwork. Shortly after your birth, you were stolen from my arms, and being a minor with limited means, there was absolutely nothing I could do. I have spent every day of my life looking for you, wondering how you were, and longing to have a relationship with my only child. I hope you can find it in your heart to forgive me for all those unbelievable and dire circumstances. I would do anything to begin building a relationship with you. You cannot imagine all that has happened in my life to get me to this point...actually writing a letter to my daughter! I'm nervous and giddy, and have I mentioned I'm nervous?

I'll include all my contact information below. I truly hope to hear from you, Madison.

> *Be well,*
> *Farrah*

EPILOGUE

FARRAH

"YOU HAVE ARRIVED at your destination," the annoying, robotic voice boomed from the GPS system on the console of Farrah's rental car. She had flown into Columbus, Ohio, earlier that morning and then drove to her final destination…Marietta, a small town located on the banks of the Ohio River. She had done quite a bit of research on this little town in the weeks since she and Madison had begun conversing. It was the first permanent settlement of the Northwest Territory and the home of Marietta College, a private liberal arts school, which her daughter was currently attending.

She gazed at the large, blue-gray monstrosity sitting on the hill overlooking the valley—the home where her daughter had learned to walk; the home she'd left for her first day of kindergarten, where she'd weathered childhood illnesses, and dressed in preparation of the prom. Farrah was heartsick that she'd missed so much of her daughter's life, but she was reassured seeing that she'd grown up in such a lovely place. Madison's father was a general surgeon at Marietta Memorial Hospital, and her mother was an English professor at the same college Madison was attending. She'd obviously led a charmed life.

Stepping out of her car, Farrah reminded herself to savor every minute of this day—the day she'd once again hold her beautiful daughter within her arms. Her heart pounded in anticipation as she slowly made her way up the stairs to the imposing, candy-apple red front door. Before she could knock or ring the bell, the door was opened by a middle-aged man with kind eyes and of short stature.

He stared at Farrah, perhaps looking for similarities between her and his daughter.

"You must be Dr. De Biasi. I'm Jon Strand," he verified, motioning for her to come inside. "Welcome to our home."

"Thank you, Dr. Strand. I appreciate you allowing me to visit. I look forward to getting to know your family," Farrah replied, putting her best foot forward. She followed him throughout the cavernous house, warmly decorated in autumnal colors, until he finally stopped outside a mahogany door. He paused, stared at her for another moment, and then opened the door...but opted not to enter. "Make yourself comfortable. I'll gather everyone up, and we'll be with you shortly."

Pleased by the courteous welcome, Farrah smiled and walked into the room—which obviously served as a combined office and library. Her gaze immediately went to the photos lining the walls, dozens of pictures of her beautiful, blonde-haired, blue-eyed daughter...a daughter who could be her twin sister. She was so engrossed by these never-before-seen glimpses into Madison's life, she didn't notice the man standing in the far corner of the room.

"Hello, Farrah." His voice echoed throughout the sizeable room.

Farrah's spine stiffened, and goosebumps found their way onto every inch of her skin. *No. It's not possible. I'm surely mistaken.*

She turned slowly and came face-to-face with Detective Javier Perez.

Farrah could feel the blood draining from her head

and into her body's core as her sympathetic nervous system prepared her fight-or-flight response.

"You look surprised, Farrah," Javi murmured with a small grin, walking toward her with an obvious limp. "Why is that?"

Farrah stared at this ghost heading in her direction, at a loss for words.

"Cat got your tongue?" Javi asked.

Finally pulling herself together, Farrah managed to force her mouth into a garish smile. "Javi! I thought you'd died during the home invasion. I must have misunderstood Sergeant Reynolds' words," she gushed, striding eagerly toward him with her arms outstretched, waiting for a hug. "I'm so glad I was wrong. How are you, my friend?"

Javi casually pulled out his gun, pointed it at her chest, and ordered, "Stop, Farrah. Put your hands above your head and just stop. We both know it wasn't a home invasion."

Farrah heard a group of people entering the room behind her as she slowly raised her arms.

Looking pleased, Javi said forcefully, "Farrah De Biasi, you are under arrest for the attempted murder of Detective Javier Perez and the pre-meditated murders of LaRue Kingston, Ben Rodgers, Nancy Peet, and Dennis & Millie De Biasi."

As Sergeant Reynolds placed her wrists in cuffs, Farrah's head snapped upright after hearing her parents' names included in the list of people she'd murdered.

"Surprised we know about your parents too, Farrah? You shouldn't be. Following my emergency surgery, and as soon as I was physically able, I filled Sergeant Reynolds in on absolutely everything. We decided to let you believe I'd died. The sergeant and I figured you'd feel more comfortable that way, thinking the only person who knew your secrets was long gone. Melissa Goodwin, the nurse you had planned to kill, was taken into protective custody, along with her entire family. Instead of arresting you right away, we decided to stand back and watch, hoping to catch you in the act. At the same time, part of our team began digging into your past, and it became quite obvious to us you set fire to your parents' house shortly after you gave birth—that you waited until they were sound asleep and burned them to death. I have to admit, Farrah, I'm impressed by how very carefully you made it look like an accident." Javi grinned, flashing his perfect, white teeth. "Remember that diary you wrote in following your rape?" Farrah glared at Javi. "I remembered you mentioning it…and we found it, Farrah. Your house is being raided as we speak. It verifies everything. Dennis and Millie didn't willingly pay for your college education. It was the money you inherited—after callously murdering them—that covered your expenses." Javi sounded disgusted.

"We also tapped all your electronics. You can imagine our surprise when we realized you had begun conversing with your long-lost daughter and even agreed to bring Bart—or should I call him Jaxon?—to Marietta College for a private book reading event tonight. So where is he, Farrah? Did you drop him off at the hotel like you'd planned? Or did you kill him too?" Javi asked snidely.

Farrah refused to respond. Her thoughts flashed back to that very morning, as she and Bart had boarded their flight…

"*Have you heard anything more from the detectives? Do they have any leads?*" asked Bart, his worry evident.

"*No, I haven't heard a thing since I left the hospital. It appears the case has gone cold,*" Farrah replied, the warning in her tone clear. Neither of them said anything further until the plane was in the air, Chicago far behind, as they jetted eastwardly.

Bart recklessly began, "*I've always wondered, Farrah, why you wanted your name included in Scars—why you wanted to be a contest winner. For years, you've been adamant, downright obsessive even, about maintaining your privacy. So why now?*" He gazed at her expectantly, as her heart thudded in her chest. No, Jax...no! Don't do this. Hiding her emotions and choosing not to respond, Farrah turned toward the window, peered intently at the farmland miles below, and sighed. You should have kept your mouth shut, Jax. It didn't have to be this way.

Javi's voice brought her back to the present. "We were very concerned you'd try to kill Madison's adoptive parents. Honestly, Farrah, I couldn't think of a better place to arrest you. Now your precious daughter can see just what a monster her mother really is. No family reunion in the cards for you...*my friend.*" She ignored Javi's sarcasm, instead falling back into her thoughts.

"*I'm hungry. Want to stop and grab some snacks?*" Farrah questioned Bart.

"*That sounds good, actually. I could use some caffeine.*"

She pulled their rental car into a convenience store and opened her door. "*You wait here. We don't have time for autographs right now when people inevitably begin recognizing your face. Just tell me what you want and I'll grab it for you,"* she requested diplomatically.

"I'll splurge and have a Pepsi, and maybe a small bag of mixed nuts, please."

"You've got it. I'll be right back."

After making the purchases, she slid back into the car and handed Bart his goodies. "My bottle opened and a straw already added to my Pepsi? You know me well, don't you, Farrah?" He laughed.

"You know it!" *she answered with a serene smile.*

Sergeant Reynolds, obviously upset, stormed back into the library, his heavy tread against the hardwood floors pulling Farrah from her thoughts. Sweat trickled down the sides of his reddened face. "Get out here, Javi. You *need* to see this," his voice rumbled with tension. "And bring the good doctor."

As Javi led the disgraced Farrah through the well-appointed home, she finally laid eyes on her daughter…her Angelina…standing protected within her parents' arms. As mother and daughter locked eyes, Farrah felt pain stabbing throughout her gut. Madison was glaring at her, a look of contempt and disgust on her face.

In that moment, she looked just like Ben Rodgers, her rapist father.

Dear God, how did Farrah ever think that little bitch looked like her? Madison was clearly her father all over again. Revolted by that brief, repugnant glimpse of Ben, Farrah swallowed her pride and reluctantly admitted to herself that perhaps her parents, and LaRue Kingston, had been right all along.

Stepping outside, Farrah noticed the cops surrounding her rental car.

Well, fuck.

As Javi pushed her toward Reynolds, who was peering into the car's trunk, Farrah found herself wondering how far she could get if she attempted to run. "I'm guessing he was poisoned," Reynolds said, shaking his head. Both cops, and their disgraced perp, peered into the trunk.

Staring at them from the depths of the rear hatch was Jaxon Dufresne, known to the world at large as Bart Christensen, a gruesome white froth covering the lower half of his handsome face.

JUSTICE

Dominick Cancilla

"Injustice is relatively easy to bear; what stings is justice."
— *H.L. Mencken, Prejudices, Third Series*

JUSTICE STOOD FAR ENOUGH BACK THAT someone peeking out through the curtains beside the door would get a good look at her smiling, practicedly honest face in the porch light. The knives, in their sheaths at the hollow of her back, tucked into her jeans and hidden by her denim jacket, were a nice reminder to watch her posture. You only get one chance to make a first impression.

She reached for the doorbell and just after pressing it noticed a few flecks of work product on her hand, already dried in the summer heat. Justice hastily wiped the back of her hand on her jeans and was giving her other hand a quick once over when the door opened. So much for her planned perfect presentation.

"Hello?" the woman who opened the door said. It was the wife— white, early thirties, and plain in the "one movie makeover montage away from gorgeous" sense. She was maybe five three, almost a foot shorter than Justice, and not nearly as fit. Her long brown hair was tied back, and she wore loose exercise pants and a matching sweatshirt. Pretty much exactly what Justice had observed her changing into each evening since she'd moved in.

"Hi!" said Justice, brighter than she felt, friendlier than she'd ever been. This was a duty call she had to paint as a social visit, and she had to diffuse the automatic defensive reaction many women had when meeting a woman of her height. Justice held out her hand, worked her smile. "I'm April, from down the street." It wasn't her name, and she didn't live in the area, but Justice had long ago made her peace with lying.

The woman shook Justice's hand. She had a firm grip, which spoke well of her. "I'm Meghan," the woman said. "Nice to meet you. We've only been here a few days and haven't really had a chance to make the rounds."

The correct response, combined friendly caring and understanding, and Justice had that down. "Of course not! Moving dominates your life for weeks and is never really done for months, am I right? Anyhow, I just wanted to say hello and welcome you to the neighborhood."

"That's so sweet," Meghan said. "Would you like to come in for a minute? I could make some coffee."

"That would be lovely," Justice said. Meghan stood aside, and Justice walked in past her.

The house smelled like paint and cardboard. The entry fanned into a day room to the left, a living room ahead, and a hall to the right. In the two visible rooms were stacks of packing boxes in various states, from sealed to half-emptied to flattened. A slight draft came from the hall, which Justice made a mental note not to mention.

"I just put our girls to bed," Meghan said, closing the front door. "We'll want to be a little quiet."

"That won't be a problem," Justice said.

"Sorry about the moving mess," Meghan said. "Let's go in the living room. I think there's someplace in there that's at least minimally suitable for sitting."

The man was in the living room, moving books from a large box into a stack on the floor. He was Asian, about the same height as his wife but skinnier, and dressed in cargo pants and a T-shirt, which displayed a ridiculous picture of a caricatured duck. Probably from some TV show. Justice didn't get the reference. Or watch TV.

"Well now, who do we have here?" the man asked.

"This is—" Meghan, clearly having already forgotten, hesitated.

"April," Justice filled in.

"April—sorry. This is April from down the street. She came by to welcome us to the neighborhood."

"Cool! Nice to meet you!" the man said overenthusiastically. His greeting was nothing but insincere ego, begging to be liked. Justice took an automatic dislike to him. The man put the books he held—all pointless novels, Justice noticed—on the floor, wiped his right hand on his pants leg, and held it out in greeting, as he stepped toward Justice. "I'm Kim."

She accepted the offered hand.

The man was no more athletic than his wife, and neither of them moved like they'd had any kind of martial arts training. His handshake was unimpressive, they had hired professionals to unload the truck when they arrived at the house instead of doing it themselves, and there hadn't been any visible exercise equipment among the possessions unloaded. Neither jogged in the evenings or did daily workouts. It could be that they were tired from moving, but Justice got the distinct impression that watching their kids run around in the yard was the most exercise either of them got on a regular basis. All the better.

A dining room was adjacent to the living room, and on the counter, between it and the kitchen, two cell phones sat charging. That was the last bit of information Justice needed. It should be smooth sailing from here on in.

Instead of releasing Kim's hand, Justice clamped down and yanked it, pulling the small man toward her and throwing him off balance. With rote precision, she smashed her forehead into his nose, shattering it. As Kim fell to his knees, Justice shot a powerful side kick into Meghan's stomach, knocking the wind out of the woman and doubling her over.

Finally letting the smile unplaster itself from her face, Justice grabbed Kim's hands as he raised them to his nose and wrenched them behind his back until his shoulders threatened dislocation, blinding him with pain. A rough shove sent Kim faceplanting into the carpet, all of it happening too quickly for him to take a breath, let alone cry out for help.

Justice kneeled on Kim's back, whipped out one of her knives, and held it to the back of his neck. Glaring at Meghan, she said, "Either of you makes a noise and he's a dead man. Got it?"

Meghan—doubled over, straining for air, and looking as stunned mentally as she was physically—rapidly nodded.

"Got that, Kim?" she said to the man with a face full of bloodstained carpet.

"You broke my nose," he said in a nasal half whisper.

"That wasn't the question," Justice said. "Are you going to be quiet?" She pressed the knife into his flesh, not quite hard enough to draw blood. That would be later.

"Fine! Yes!"

She let the knife linger for a moment, making her point, before taking away a little of the pressure. "Good."

Her attention went back to Meghan. "Sit on the ground, cross-legged, with your hands under your ass."

Justice allowed the woman a moment to process that and awkwardly get into position. Kneeling on the guy made Justice less than perfectly stable should he get a clue and try to buck her off his back, so she remedied that situation next. Justice stood, putting weight on her knee to drive it into his back and give him something to think about, other than trying to run, while she adjusted her position. She then dropped down, straddling him like a log, hard enough to violently compress his diaphragm. The sudden exhalation made a little fan of blood in front of his face, its bottom end pointing right at his flattened nose.

"That's better," Justice said. "We're going to be here for a bit, so might as well be comfortable."

"I'm not comfortable," Kim, still struggling to get his air back, half whispered.

"Nobody cares, Chuck," Justice said.

"My name's not—"

"Nobody cares." She rested the point of the knife between his shoulder blades, its weight enough to stop it from being easily forgotten without her having to press.

They sat, saying nothing, for almost a minute, Justice in no hurry to carry out her joyless duty.

Meghan was the one who finally broke the silence. "What do you want?" she said, her voice strained.

"What we all want," Justice said. "Justice."

Then she let them stew.

Kim broke first this time. "For what? Justice for what?"

"You are shit at being quiet, Chuck. You know that?" Justice said. "But it's a good question. First, though, some ground rules." She tapped the flat of the knife a few times on Kim's head, like someone tapping a wine glass with a dinner knife to get attention, before returning the point to his back. "And no interruptions.

"This isn't my first rodeo," Justice continued, when no further protests came. "I put to peace a couple other folks not half an hour before I knocked on your door, so I am not at all squeamish when it comes to doing what has to be done."

"Who?" Meghan asked, then made a little jerk, like she would have reflexively slapped a hand over her mouth if her hands weren't currently going numb between her backside and the floor.

"Some people just as guilty as the two of you."

"We didn't—" Kim tried to protest.

Justice fell forward onto him, pressing his face deeper into the carpet. She brought the knife behind one ear and whispered into the other. "You in a hurry to die, Chuck?"

He tried to shake his head. "No."

Justice sat up again and put her knife back in its place on Kim's back. "Good. Like I was saying, I've got rules. Any more objections to listening?"

She paused, as if seriously entertaining the possibility that they might say something. "Good. Rule number one, be quiet, or this ends quick. Yelling, shouting, not using your inside voice because you think someone might notice—I hear any of that, and it's game over. The knife goes into Chuck and we're one down, one to go. Meghan, I'm not going to bother getting up, either. If you yell, Chuck gets the knife. Chuck, if you yell, you get the knife. It's not fair, but neither is life.

"You can speak when spoken to, but maybe you should avoid that as much as you can. Nod if we're clear."

They both nodded.

"Good. The same goes for doing what you're told. Disobey and Chuck gets the knife. Nod if we're clear."

They both nodded.

"Good. Last thing is, we're going to have a little conversation. I'm going to explain myself, I'm going to ask a few questions, and it's all going to be very civil. If you stick with the rules, nothing's going to happen until we're done talking. Nod if we're clear."

Kim nodded, but Meghan shook her head.

Justice gave her a look. "Meghan? Are we going to have a problem?"

"The girls," Meghan said. "What are you going to do with the girls?"

Mama-bear instincts were juicing up. Justice could see it in Meghan's eyes. If she thought her kids were in danger, all bets would be off real quick.

"Cool it down, honey," Justice said. "We can keep this out here. I have no reason to go to the kids' room unless you give me a reason. We clear?"

The fire in Meghan's eyes backed away a bit, and she gave several rapid nods.

"Good," Justice said. "Now I'll explain."

She gave a hard look down at Kim, tilting a little so his one visible eye could catch her, then shifted her gaze to Meghan. "Someone in this room has sinned," Justice said. "The Bible says that when someone has sinned, you should take an eye for an eye, a tooth for a tooth, and a life for a life. Sometimes, a sin is committed, and I have to extract the payment because nobody else will."

"What did I—" Kim started to ask.

Justice slapped his head with the knife. "Don't be in such a hurry, Chuck."

"Meghan," Justice asked, turning back to her. "Tell me what happened in Bakersfield the day before you moved."

Meghan thought for a second, clearly sensing there was a right answer. "Nothing," she said. "I mean, nothing important. Kim—my husband, Kim…" She nodded to the man under Justice.

"I know Chuck's name," Justice said. "I just don't respect it."

"Oh, okay," Meghan said, as if it was. "Kim had his

last day at work, then a few coworkers took him out for a drink, then he came home. I'd pretty much finished the packing, so we ordered pizza and ate off paper plates. We all slept in sleeping bags on our beds, and the girls pretended like they were camping. It was so we wouldn't have to pack dirty linens for the move. That's it. That's all that happened."

Justice shook her head. "No. Not what I was looking for."

She slapped Kim's head with the knife.

"Stop doing that," he said.

"Or?" Justice asked, letting the question trail.

"Kim!" Meghan stage whispered, glaring at him.

"Listen to the woman," Justice scolded. "She's got all the brains in this house." Another thwack with the side of the knife. "Now, tell me how you would answer that question. What happened the day before you moved?"

"What she said," Kim said. "That's all. Just what Meghan said."

Justice tsked. "Chuck, Chuck, Chuck. You cannot lie worth shit." She leaned forward on him and took the lobe of his upward-facing ear between the thumb and finger of her left hand. With her right, she slid the blade of her knife behind it. "Remember," she said, "loud noises from either of you and Chuck goes south."

With a quick motion, Justice sliced off the lobe of Kim's ear.

He gave a violent, palsied shake then buried his face in the carpet to muffle a yell.

From the corner of her eye, Justice saw Meghan roll forward, free her hands, and try to stand. Justice glared at her, leaned her forearm on Kim's head to drive him hard enough into the ground to crack teeth, and without even looking, brought the knife around to slice off fully half of the already mutilated ear.

Meghan froze. Kim was writhing, limbs flailing, blood running down the side of his head, Justice's weight preventing him from rising.

"Sit, or he suffocates," Justice barked at Meghan. "You come any closer, and I'll finish him."

With barely a pause, Meghan sat back down on her hands and crossed her legs. Justice also sat back, letting Kim turn his head and gasp for air.

"What the *fuck*," Kim said.

"Noise," Justice warned.

"What the fuck did you—"

She punched him in the back of the neck with the fist holding the knife. "I can shut you up if I need to," Justice said.

"I'm bleeding."

"No shit."

"Why'd you do that?"

"You lied. It's against the rules."

"You didn't say that."

"I have to say you shouldn't lie to your wife and to the woman with the knife? You are definitely not the smart one, Chuck."

"Fuck!" Kim exclaimed, keeping the volume low this time. "It hurts!"

"I can end the pain," Justice said.

Kim said, "Then do it," at the same time Meghan protested, "No!"

Justice gave a sharp laugh and smiled at Meghan. "You married an idiot." Then to Kim, "You think I was going to get you an aspirin?"

"He's a good man," Meghan said.

"Let's see if he can prove that," Justice said. "So, Chuck, I'll spell this out for you. Back in Bakersfield, on the day you moved, something important happened. What was it?"

"Okay, okay," Kim said. "Give me a second."

She gave him more than a minute, which was necessary if she wanted coherent responses, given how much pain he had to be in.

"Okay," said Chuck when he'd gotten himself a little together. "It wasn't exactly like Meghan said. I didn't go to work."

"What?" Meghan asked.

"I did meet some of the guys for kind of a brunch thing," he hastened to add, as if it made him less of a liar. "I just didn't go into the office. My last day at the Bakersfield office was Thursday. They wouldn't make me go into work on the day I moved, right?"

"And your wife was supposed to figure that out herself?" Justice asked.

"Well..." Kim just let the thought trail off.

Meghan, with a new focus, took over the questioning. "Where did you go? You were out until seven. I could tell you'd been drinking."

Kim sighed. "Here's the thing," he said. "We weren't ever going back to Bakersfield, right? I had people to say goodbye to."

"For five hours," Justice added.

Kim's eye, underscored by a thick mascara of blood, shot from Meghan to Justice. "Oh, fuck," he said. "That's what this is about, isn't it? You think that I—oh, no no no no, nothing happened. You've got to believe me." He started to squirm a bit. "Did Daryl send you? Because if he did, you can tell him—"

"You son of a bitch," Meghan said. "You were at Diette's, weren't you?"

"It's not like that!"

"Weren't you?"

"Well, yes, but—"

Meghan looked at Justice. "Stab him. Just fucking stab him right now. Do it!" Then back to Kim, "You son of a bitch, I—"

"Stop!" Justice said, vocally slapping them still. "You're getting out of hand.

"Chuck," she continued after a scolding moment of silence. "You're missing the point. I don't care where your dick has been."

"I didn't—"

A thwack of the knife on his half ear stopped the protest. "I don't care."

"She was his girlfriend before we met," Meghan said, sounding a little distant. "He said he didn't have feelings for her anymore, but they were still friends on Facebook and sometimes texted. I always suspected it had to be more than that. I just knew it."

"It wasn't—"

"Maybe it wasn't," Justice said, interrupting Kim to agree with him. "I have no idea. That's not the point."

"Then what *is* the point?" Meghan asked.

"The point is that you're both so involved with your own lives, you don't even consider that important things happen that have nothing to do with you. I don't care about your move, I don't care about your pizza and kids, I don't care if Chuck is getting some from a woman who, frankly, didn't age nearly as well as his wife."

"Thank you," Meghan said.

"Just saying. The point is that on the night before you moved, there was a murder in Bakersfield. A whole family was murdered. Right there in their home. Not two blocks from where you lived."

"What are you talking about?" Meghan asked.

"A man—a good man—had taken a day off work and gone out with his kids. They left early and spent the whole day at Knotts Berry Farm. It was a treat for everyone— kids got a day with Dad, and Mom got a rare day off from housework and homeschooling.

"When they got home, the kids ran into the house from the garage, and the man thought he heard something a little strange. Was it someone falling? A yelp? Had one of the kids hurt themselves? He called their names as he walked, more quickly than normal, to the door connecting the garage to the house. The man had just enough time to see his kids lying on the floor before the baseball bat caught him in the face. One strike, he was out.

"When the man came to, he was in his living room, gagged, hogtied. His wife, similarly tied, lay on the ground next to him, one lifeless eye staring at nothing and the other just gone. Hunks of hair, bits of unidentifiables, a finger, a toe, broken glass—she sat at the center of an island of shrapnel and her own gore, clearly better off now than she had been an hour before.

"His son, still unconscious, lay on the ground near him. His daughter was piled on the kitchen table, having had her head nearly taken off by the bat that caught her coming through the door.

"The man caught a glimpse of the person who did this. It was a large form all in black—boots, gloves, ski mask, all damp with what, he didn't want to know. He was still trying to get his bearings when the claw end of a hammer swung into view once, twice, and he rocked back, blinded, screaming into his gag."

Justice paused a moment, for effect. She was a natural storyteller.

"When the man's cries had trailed into a soft sobs, he thought he heard a small voice. It was cut short by three sharp whacks from the bat. He returned to incoherent screaming.

"It was almost an hour before he grew quiet again. The pain in his eyeless eyes must have been horrible, but the body can adjust to almost anything. He lay there, listening, hearing nothing. Then a voice whispered in his ear, with no hint of motion preceding it, like the person had been sitting at his side all the time.

"You know what the voice said?"

They clearly didn't.

"It said, 'We're going to start with your fingers.' And that's exactly what happened. Police estimate he lived for another hour and a half, and I bet they're pretty much on the nose. Now, what do you think of that?"

Neither spoke for the longest time. Then Kim said, "An eye for an eye."

"What was that, Chuck?" Justice asked.

"You said you're here for revenge."

"I said I'm here for justice."

Kim shook his head, just a little, like he barely had the energy. "You think I did it, don't you? You think I killed those people."

Justice laughed out loud at that, long and hard. "Hell no, Chuck!" she said. "You're a condescending asshole who lies to his wife and needs to learn to listen, but you haven't got the guts to kill someone. I'd believe you're into bloodsports as much as I'd believe a 'Gas, Grass, or Ass' sticker on a minivan."

"Who was it?" Meghan asked.

Justice pointed at her with the knife before putting it back between Kim's shoulders where it would soon be needed. "Assuming you mean who died and not who did the killing, that is the right question to ask. The two of you haven't even been watching TV news the past few days, have you?"

"It's been busy," Meghan said. "Unpacking, moving furniture—it's exhausting."

"And the world outside isn't as important as your world in here," Justice said. "I get it."

"I didn't say that," Meghan said.

"You didn't have to. With all the shit in the world, a family being murdered didn't dominate the news, but you sure would have noticed it if you'd been paying attention. There'd been four killings like that in four different states this year, so it got some decent play."

"Wait," Kim interrupted. "If you don't think it was me, you can't mean Meghan?"

Justice rolled her eyes. "Don't be stupid. Neither of you did it, Chuck, but you know who did."

She let him stew on that for a minute.

Finally he asked, "Who?"

"When you left Diette's house, after talking about old times or committing double adultery or whatever, there was a car parked across the street. It was a black Lincoln, and you took notice of it. I know you took notice of it, because you also noticed it when you went into the house. It had been parked in a different spot, but you remembered seeing it."

"I like cars," Kim said.

"Too bad for you," Justice said. Also, too bad for him that Justice had noticed him looking at her car when he went into the house. She'd duct taped a spare cell phone to his car's wheel well so she could track it with her "Find Your Phone" app if he turned out to be too nosy for his own good, which he did. She'd originally planned to dispose of him if he might be trouble, but after Justice saw his family—well, it was just too perfect.

"It was you?" Meghan asked.

"And I'm a witness," Kim added.

"Yes and no," Justice said. "I do have what society considers inappropriate impulses, and I've been told I should seek help at some point. In the meantime, though, I admit I took great pleasure in Diette and Daryl Bedford before they died. You have no idea what it's like— the smooth, wet feelings, the sounds, the smell." She seemed to drift off for a moment and then hastened to add, "I didn't do anything with the kids, of course. They were done with quick. I'm not like *that*."

Kim burst into sobs. He was being too loud, but Justice let it go. His friend was dead, and if he'd been fucking her—not that it was particularly likely—his DNA was all over her corpse. Justice wasn't a monster; he deserved a good cry.

"Are you going to torture us, too?" Meghan asked, over-calm by half, probably edging into shock. "Because Kim saw you?"

"No," Justice said definitively. "Killing those people was a sinful act, performed out of my weakness, in the face of temptation, to engage in the baser pleasures. I'm not here for gratification. Killing a witness would also be a sin—a sin to protect a sin. I'm not here for that, either. I'm here for justice."

"But you admitted that you did it," Meghan said. "How is this justice? Do you want us to call the police? Help you turn yourself in?"

"You haven't been paying attention," Justice said. "It's in the Bible. To pay for a sin, to wipe it clean as if it never happened, and leave no blemish on the soul, there has to be an exchange. An eye for an eye, a tooth for a tooth—"

"—and a life for a life," Meghan finished.

"Now you're getting it." Justice smiled. It was nice when it went this way, though it seldom did. Kim was a sobbing mess, so she concentrated on leading Meghan to the truth. "It's a life for a life, so if we want to make up for four murders, a man, a woman, and two children…" Justice let it trail off, prompting Meghan to finish the thought.

To her credit, the woman understood almost immediately, the mama-bear look flooding her eyes.

Meghan leapt to her feet more quickly than should be possible from her awkward position. Justice had been ready for the move and slammed her left fist down on the hilt of her knife, driving it between Kim's vertebrae, severing the whimpering man's spine. His scream was a starter pistol as Justice sprang after Meghan.

The woman ran down the hall, yelling for her daughters. "Get up! Run! Run!"

She reached the hall's T-shaped junction, a bathroom in front of her, and turned to the right where the girls' rooms stood, one on either side of the hall. Both doors were open, though they shouldn't have been. In her haste, Meghan slammed into the doorjamb of her eldest's room, still yelling for her daughters. Her barely sensate hand fumbled for the light switch, and she'd almost stumbled into the room, when a firm hand grabbed her forearm and yanked her back into the hall.

"You don't want to go in there," Justice said, slamming Meghan into the full-length mirror that covered the wall between the two rooms, cracking it.

Through the open door, in the now-lit room, Meghan could just see the open window where Justice had entered earlier in the evening, her daughter with a pillow over her head, and a nightgown gone red over the young girl's heart.

Meghan would have seen a similar scene if she'd looked into the other room, though this open window was an exit instead of an entrance. Justice spared her the sight.

With all her strength, Justice jabbed another of her

knives up under Meghan's ribs, its long blade finding the woman's heart. It was over in seconds. Brief. Merciful. Just.

After a moment for final twitches, Justice yanked out her knife and let the body fall to the ground. She wiped the blade on the corpse's sweatshirt and replaced it in the sheath at the base of her back.

Unhurried, Justice returned to the living room.

Kim was still there, moaning in pain, hands clawing at the ground to try and make up for functionless legs.

Justice took two quick steps, then field-goal-kicked the side of Kim's head with the steel toe of her boot. There was a brutal snap, then peace.

The house fell suddenly quiet. Justice could hear a gentle hum from the refrigerator, feel a touch of the draft coming down the hall from the open windows, but other than that, it was still.

She wrenched the knife from Kim's back, cleaned it, put it away. Leaving him behind, she went to the kitchen and washed her hands in the sink, letting the blood flow away with the water as her sin for taking the Bedfords' lives had been washed away by extracting justice from— whatever these people's surname had been. She'd not gotten around to checking that.

A little later, Justice loaded her black Lincoln with a few things she'd taken from the house—jewelry, cash, food, a gun that they probably wished they'd kept closer at hand. It was all ownerless property, justifiably taken, and Justice needed it to keep her on the road. She was headed up the coast to Oregon. It wouldn't do to be caught here. People wouldn't understand. They seldom had the stomach for justice.

MURDER, INC.

Steven Pajak

NOW

DAVINA HUDDLED IN THE DOORWAY of the shuttered bodega, hidden in the shadows. The stench of stale urine gave her a headache. The night was cold, damp. She shivered within the dark hoodie, crossed her arms over her breasts, and clutched her elbows for warmth. Light traffic, mostly taxis and ride shares, splashed through puddles on the boulevard, left in the wake of an earlier downpour. More than half an hour passed, and she waited patiently. She was good at waiting, biding her time.

Near midnight, they emerged from the brownstone. The man was tall, lean yet muscular. He had light brown hair and walked with a confident swagger. He wore charcoal gray sharkskin slacks and a pale blue fitted polo shirt that clung to him, flattering his well-built pecs. The woman—girl, really—followed behind him, dressed in a revealing black skirt that left little to the imagination; her blond hair contrasted against the garment and seemed to glow against her spray-on tan. She followed in his wake, mousy, obedient, shivering from the cold and fear.

Approaching the silver BMW, the man, Bobby Vaughn, paused and turned toward the woman—Davina knew her by the name Kataryna, though the name was likely an alias or stage name, to draw in men with a fetish for foreign girls from Eastern Europe. Bobby's movement was quick, agitated. Kataryna said something to him, though Davina could not hear what from the distant shadows across the boulevard. Whatever it was, Bobby didn't like it. He raised his hand as if to slap, and Kataryna flinched, her arms instinctively coming up to guard her face. Instead of slapping her—it was not good to bruise the girls—he grabbed her arm roughly, jerked her toward him, growling something into her ear. With her head down, Kataryna dutifully pulled open the car door and slid into the passenger seat. Bobby gripped the door and leaned in, spoke again—probably another threat—before slamming the door and walking around to get behind the wheel. The engine fired up, and in seconds, the Beemer was racing down the boulevard.

Davina remained in the shadows for a few minutes before finally leaving the rancid smell behind, crossing the street, and ascending the steps of the brownstone. At the door, she paused and looked around, making sure she was not being observed. Without hesitation, she punched the four-digit code into the security pad—she'd gotten the code from a contact at the security company, one of the many women Davina and Kim helped with their "problem" and who owed them a favor—and pulled the door open when the lock disengaged, then stepped inside.

Bobby liked flashy things—his clothes, his watch, his car, even his girl—and his apartment building was no exception. Davina chuckled, thinking about the urine-soaked entry of the trashy bodega right across the street. But the fact was, the two- and three-story condos, like Bobby's, were being resurrected at an alarming rate in this up-and-coming Northside Chicago neighborhood. This time next year, the bodega would likely be demolished and replaced by a series of residential buildings, with lower prices for those who were willing to get in on the ground floor before the neighborhood became desirable and prices skyrocketed.

The foyer was well-lit and gleaming. The floors were tiled marble, polished to a high sheen, and the stone carried up the walls, interrupted only by three brass mailboxes. There were three flats in the building: a garden apartment on the lower level, with separate access outside the building; one apartment on the first floor; and Bobby's on the second (which he probably thought of as the penthouse). Normally, this would have posed a problem for Davina, as neighbors were potential witnesses. But the garden apartment was vacant (the For Rent sign on the window listed Bobby's phone number, which meant he owned the building), and the tenants on the first floor were vacationing. She knew this because they'd informed the alarm company they would be away for two weeks.

Davina consulted her watch. Bobby and Kataryna wouldn't return from the club for at least two hours, maybe longer. She knew she had time, because she'd spent the last two weeks following Bobby Vaughn, clocking his movements and patterns. The time spent at the club would depend on Bobby's business, how many of the girls had "dates" for the evening. She ascended the stairs slowly.

Once given an assignment, Davina had autonomy to do the job in her own way and on her own time. The golden rule was whatever happened, the deed could not lead back to Murder, Inc. in any way. Davina knew this, and she also knew that scoping out the night club for an extended period on her own was dangerous. The risk of being seen at a place frequented (and co-owned) by the mark, on multiple occasions, could be very bad and arouse unwanted suspicion. But this wasn't an assignment, at least not one passed on to her by Kim. Davina had been working off-book for more than two years now, picking her own assignments.

On her first outing, after she'd selected Kataryna as her next job, Davina spotted the unmarked panel van parked in the alley behind the club and watched as four girls were brought out from the basement (obviously drugged) and manhandled into the back. Though she was here for Kat—her nickname for the girl—this new development nagged her gut something fierce. She called an audible in her surveillance of Bobby and Kat, and followed the van, keeping a safe distance so as not to be spotted. The two thugs (hired muscle? security?) took the girls deep within the inner city, to what appeared to be an abandoned warehouse on the southwest side of the city.

The warehouse that had once housed a booming textile factory until the mid-2000s had been repurposed as an underground brothel, where Bobby Vaughn and his associates pimped out these girls they lured here from Russia, Poland, and the Czech Republic. Davina didn't dare try to get inside. She watched from a distance, and over the next few hours, various men arrived at the side door and were frisked by two burly men with firearms before being allowed to enter. She would bet there were more men inside, making sure the girls weren't damaged by these horny dregs who exited the building several hours later, clothing disheveled and cheeks flushed with the heat of their passion. The rage Davina felt burned her gut like molten lava. That night, Davina made up her mind that the girl, Kataryna, was not the only girl that she needed to save. Kat was but one soul in grave danger of being lost to the sea of violence and corruption of the city. Those nameless girls in the white van were all Davina's mission now.

THEN

DAVINA STARED AT the ceiling. She'd been semi-awake for a while, listening to the sounds of nurses and doctors in the halls and the machines at her bedside. The intravenous catheter hooked to her arm just below her left elbow itched. Her left eye was swollen almost shut, but there was little pain there. Her nose and lower jaw throbbed fiercely, the pain moving up the side of her face and into her temple. Perhaps she even had a few broken ribs, she couldn't be sure. She just knew it hurt like hell to breathe deeply.

Time passed slowly, and she dozed; the heavy narcotics they'd pumped into her IV for pain made it easy to slip into the safety and bliss of undisturbed sleep. When she woke much later, a young black nurse was beside the bed, changing the IV bag. Davina feigned sleep, but she wasn't fooling the nurse.

"You're awake. How are you feeling?"

Davina didn't speak, because it hurt when she moved her jaw, but mostly because she didn't want to talk. There would be questions; there always were. She learned the hard way that keeping track of your lies, the details, so you wouldn't get tripped up, was a fucking chore. "The devil's in the details, babe, and you have to sell it," Reggie had said to her the first time he'd taken her to the emergency room. It was easy to screw shit up when there were too many questions, especially when your mind was clouded with drugs and your body throbbed with pain.

"Sorry, dumb question. Can you at least tell me your name?"

Davina wouldn't speak her name, and she sure as hell wouldn't tell the truth about why she was banged up— that was always the next question. She wouldn't ever make that mistake again. Never again, because things would be so much worse when she got back home if Reggie knew she'd snitched.

"Snitches get stitches, babe." More of Reggie's words of wisdom. He was full of helpful advice on how to deceive and keep his ass out of jail.

After a pause, the nurse said, "My name's Kim."

Kim waited a moment for a response, but Davina said nothing.

"That's okay, I'm sure the police will figure it out soon enough. For now, I'll call you Jane Doe. How's that?"

Davina groaned and turned her head away.

Kim looked at the poor girl with empathy. She took Davina's hand gently, cupping it in both of her rough, chapped ones. Healing hands.

"It's okay, honey. I know what you're going through," Kim said. She released Davina's hand and gently turned Davina's face toward her.

Davina felt Kim's gaze piercing her soul, as if she could see right through to her innermost hidden secrets. Davina saw absolute truth in Kim's eyes. Somehow, she did know, maybe not exactly, but enough. Davina looked away; she could not bear the shame of judgement.

"You can talk to me, honey."

Gently, Kim grasped Davina's chin, again slowly forcing Davina to look at her. Davina allowed her face to be turned but would not meet Kim's eyes.

"I know what you're going through because I *was* you, was in your...situation. For an awfully long time. Longer than I ever should have been, God knows."

There was a long pause before Kim glanced toward the door to confirm they were alone. She crossed the room and closed the door. When she returned to the bedside, she lifted her scrub top, revealing her stomach. Her skin was dark like maple syrup, but the puckered, twisted flesh of the scars—it looked like someone carved a hellish game of tic-tac-toe into her skin—were pale reminders of a horrible past. Davina's eyes were drawn to the grotesque map carved across the woman's abdomen.

Kim allowed the shirt to fall after a few seconds, like a curtain hiding a shameful part of her that few would ever see or know. "This was the last thing he ever did to me. The last thing I *let* him do to me."

Davina now looked into Kim's brown eyes—hard on the surface, but soft below—searching for answers. "How?"

Kim understood the question. "I finally had enough." She pulled the guest chair beside the bed and eased into it. She was silent a moment, choosing her words. She locked eyes with Davina and continued. "When you reach the end of your endurance, when you see there's only one thin thread of who you once were, holding the *real* you—the girl you were before that bastard corrupted and twisted you—from falling into the abyss *he* created, you realize there's only one way to save yourself. You realize it's either him or you because he's never going to stop, not unless you stop him. Do you understand?"

Tears rolled down Davina's cheeks, and slowly she nodded.

"I think you know in your heart that you're dangling precariously by that thin thread, honey." A brief pause, then, "You're going to have to make a choice, Jane Doe. Do you want to keep living that way and hope he doesn't kill you one day? Or do you want to live the life you deserve? Yes, that you *deserve*. I see a fire in you, girl. It's buried down deep, dampened but smoldering, and you don't even know it's there. But it is, and I see it. And I see you have a strong will, and I think you'll choose to live. At least I hope you do. So, what's it going to be?"

Davina was quiet for a long moment before she finally whispered, "I want to live."

Kim patted her hands and then squeezed firmly. "Good, Jane Doe. Then *live*."

NOW

SHE STOOD ON the second-floor landing, taking in the silence. Davina knew the building was empty, but caution was habit in this line of work. Two locks secured the apartment door, and Davina made quick work of the deadbolt and knob locks with the small electric lock-picking gun. The small, cylindrical device looked like a stainless-steel flashlight. It was portable and simple to use and was well worth the investment ten times over. The small motor made little noise as it worked against the pins and tumblers. She stowed the device in her hoodie pocket and again stood silent, this time listening for movement inside. Bobby and Kat did not have houseguests that she was aware of, but habit was a trusted ally. She learned to never underestimate a situation and to always expect the unexpected.

Satisfied she was alone and undetected, Davina entered the apartment. They'd left the living room light on, so they wouldn't come home to a dark apartment, but the rest of the rooms were in shadows. She moved from room to room, acquainting herself with the layout of the floor plan. The apartment was about two thousand square feet. The main living space was an open concept, with living room, dining room, and kitchen, all with clear sight lines from one end of the apartment to the other. The furnishings here were tasteful and fit the floor plan well. A lot of thought went into selection, and Davina had no doubt Bobby Vaughn had hired a staging consultant, which explained the obvious lack of Neanderthal-man-cave style.

Off the living room was a full bath done in tasteful stone tiles and dark walnut woods. A short hall led to the master bedroom, and a second bedroom that was furnished as an office with dark wood built-in shelves (though not lined with books, but instead with trophies and sports memorabilia), a gaudy marble-topped desk that dominated the room, over-sized leather chairs, and an extremely distasteful white fur carpet that looked like alpaca. The room smelled of stale cigars and booze. Behind a framed watercolor painting of Michael Jordan in mid-dunk, Davina located a wall safe. It was substantial and beyond her skillset to breach without Bobby providing the combination. Fortunately, Davina was good at extracting information from the likes of the Bobby Vaughns of the world. She'd have the combination before the night was over.

After careful consideration, Davina settled on the master bedroom as her workspace and set about the task of preparing for Bobby and Kat's return. She had nearly an hour before they were expected, so she took her time, making sure she missed nothing, and was prepared for any contingencies.

THEN

AFTER DISEMBARKING THE aging, filthy CTA bus, Davina walked three blocks west from her stop toward the address Kim had written on the back of a napkin after their domestic violence support group adjourned the previous evening. Kim said it would be an intimate gathering of her most inner circle, her closest friends, women who had shared similar traumatic experiences and dedicated their lives to helping others. Kim thought it would be a good healing experience for Davina, to be around these women, outside of the group setting where they could *really* talk. Davina tentatively accepted the invitation to be polite, though she hadn't made up her mind to show up until two hours prior.

She travelled by subway train and then two bus transfers to get from her sister's Northside home to the Southside location. The neighborhood was sketchy as fuck, and Davina kept looking over her shoulder, half expecting to be followed by some pervert or, worse, Reggie, who she could totally imagine tailing her, bent on putting her back into the hospital. He'd given Davina some space after she'd been released, mostly because while she recovered, she was staying with her sister who had absolutely no love for Reggie and had told him point-blank that she had a pump-action shotgun and would use it if he showed up at her house uninvited. Reggie bristled at the promise and glared at her but said nothing. With everyone but Davina, Reggie's bark was worse than his bite. He saved all his rage and frustration especially for her, then he gleefully unleashed it with his fists and feet.

Davina wasn't followed by Reggie or any other ne'er-do-well. She arrived at Streeter's Tavern a few minutes later, just several blocks from the bus stop. The place was a legit hole in the wall, with dimmed neon signs reflecting sickly against filthy windows. An unlit Old Style beer sign creaked above the door on a soft breeze, the lights long dead and the sign mostly yellowed with age. She wasn't sure this was the right place. In fact, she was almost positive Kim made a mistake when she'd written the location on the napkin. Hesitantly, Davina stepped inside and gave her eyes a moment to adjust to the dimly lit joint. A long, weathered bar spanned the length of the main room on the right. Two- and four-seater tables took up much of the rest of the main room. In the room beyond were two billiards tables flanked by two rows of booths, three on each side, the deep maroon upholstery cracked and filthy.

Davina scanned the mostly empty establishment before turning to leave but stopped when she heard her name. She spotted Kim waving at her from the last booth on the end, beside the joint's storage room and office, where she sat with two other women that Davina didn't recognize. The rest of the booths were empty, Davina noted, as she slid in beside Kim.

Kim introduced the ladies (to whom she referred as her inner circle and trusted advisors), Margo and Carrie (no last names offered), and Davina shook hands. Margo had a shock of curly red hair, and a plump, pale face with a smattering of freckles on her rosy cheeks. She appeared to be in her mid-thirties. Her soft green eyes were direct and seemed to devour every detail of Davina. Carrie was older than both Kim and Margo, probably in her mid-sixties. Her wispy silver hair was thinning—Davina could see her dry, pink scalp—and her face and neck were wrinkled like a pug, but her grip was like iron and her voice gritty from years of smoking. She eyed Davina with sharp, prying eyes.

After drinks were ordered, Kim got right to business and made her proposal. The trio referred to themselves as Murder, Inc., a tongue-in-cheek joke that ended up being all too appropriate. The idea surfaced after one of the support group meetings, while deep into a bottle of Jack Daniels and four sheets to the wind (or shitfaced and pissing the bed, according to Carrie) when the old woman suggested their problems would easily be solved if their husbands (or live-in boyfriend in Margo's case) ceased to exist. Which led to a candid discussion of ways they'd like to kill the men in their lives (some creative and others just downright diabolical). Kim, slightly less shitfaced than the rest of them, said if they were going to do it, they needed to be smart about it, plan it so they wouldn't be caught. Spending the rest of their lives behind bars for killing three abusive assholes would be marginally worse than their current situations.

The following day, hung-over and somber, the ladies met for coffee, thinking that in the light of day and without liquid courage they'd lose their nerve and have a good laugh over their wildly insane fantasy. Yet no one laughed, and they found that after years of abuse, both mental and physical (mostly physical), their nerves had steeled. That morning, Murder, Inc. was founded.

Davina couldn't take her eyes off Kim as she spun her yarn. She never said directly that they'd killed their husbands (or live-in boyfriend), or how, or who'd done it (Davina suspected they'd each killed one of the other lady's men, giving them each leverage over each other, in the event one of them later felt squeamish or guilty over their transgression), but Davina understood that the men who laid hands on these women were buried six feet under in some godforsaken place.

After a moment, Davina finished her beer in several long gulps and flicked away the foam mustache above her quivering lip. She looked at each woman, from left to right, then back again, until her eyes settled on Kim, the obvious leader of this group of femme fatales.

"Why are you telling me this?" Davina finally asked, holding the empty beer mug between tightly clamped fingers. "Why am I here?"

Kim folded her hands in front of her. "That night we met, you remember what I told you? About reaching the end of that thin rope and having to make a choice, to say you've had enough?"

Davina nodded. Her hand gripped the mug so tight, her fingers were beginning to stiffen.

"I showed you what Darius did to me, the last thing I allowed him to do to me, and you asked me how I made it stop."

Davina couldn't speak.

"And now you know the answer."

"I still don't know why I'm here. Or what you want from me."

Carrie said, "We want to help you."

Margo said, "We all lacked the courage to do…what needed to be done…to our own. I know I couldn't. My Harold had me so terrified of him I could barely look him in the eye."

Kim said, "We want to do what we know you can't. Or won't. We want to free you from your bonds, Jane Doe."

Davina started, surprised by the use of the moniker given to her by Kim the day they met in the hospital. With wide eyes, she looked at each woman, their faces somber yet serious.

These women are seriously offering to kill Reggie for me, she thought. *To kill him. What the fuck?*

NOW

WHEN SHE HEARD the key scratching around in the deadbolt, Davina rose from the sofa where she'd been waiting patiently in the dark. She slid the black-and-white bandanna that hung around her neck over her mouth and nose as she crossed the room, cinching the hoodie down tight as she went. She didn't care if Bobby saw her face, because come morning, he wouldn't be around to give a description of her to authorities. But she didn't want Kat to get a look at her, because she wasn't yet sure how this was going to play out. If things didn't go as planned, and Kat could identify her, she'd have to deal with the girl, which she didn't want to happen. She was here to help her, to help the rest of the girls. To do that, she needed Kat.

Davina was several steps away from the entrance when the door opened, and the hall light sliced a diagonal across the living room carpet. Bobby paused in the doorway and flipped the light switch, up, down, up, down, confused when the apartment remained dark. He flipped the switch up and down a few more times (duh, fucking get a clue already) and said, "What the fuck?" before Davina stepped out of the darkness and hit him with the stun gun.

Bobby made a gurgling sound and stumbled forward, reaching for Davina, who simply side-stepped and watched him fall to the carpeted floor face-first. She bent and zapped him again, planting the two electrodes of the stun gun into the side of his neck. He bucked like an angry bronco, his feet drummed against the carpet like a sick beat, and then he grew still.

Davina checked his pulse (still alive) and started to rise when Kataryna launched herself onto Davina's back, pushing her forward onto the carpet. The younger woman started throwing hands, ineffective slaps, and punches to the back of Davina's head. Calmly, Davina pushed to her knees (her head tucked down so that her shoulders took the brunt of the assault) and then shifted sharply to her right, tossing the flailing blonde off. In less than a few seconds, Davina was now on top of the struggling girl.

"Shh, it's okay, I'm not going to hurt you," Davina soothed as she reached into the pocket of her hoodie for the syringe of Midazolam. Deflecting slaps with her right arm, Davina somehow managed to get both of Kat's arms pinned against her chest, using her weight to hold them there while she slid the needle into her neck, releasing the fast-acting sedative into her carotid.

"I'm here to help, Kataryna. That's your name, right, honey?"

The girls eyelids drooped, the sedative already working. "How do you know my name?"

"Don't worry about that now. Just relax, rest. We'll

talk about more in a little while."

Davina stood and went to the sofa. She grabbed one of the throw pillows and returned, lifting Kat's head and sliding the pillow under.

"Who are you?" Kat slurred, and her eyes closed for a few seconds, then fluttered open. She was fighting the drug, but her efforts were futile.

"My name is Davina. It's probably a mistake telling you my real name, but I'm hoping when this is done, we'll be friends."

"I...have...friends..." Kat trailed off. Her eyes closed and stayed that way.

"You do, honey. And we're going to help them all soon enough."

With Kat sedated, Davina turned to Bobby Vaughn. He lay still where he'd fallen. She kicked him in the ribs, and he moaned, turned his head to the side. Blood spread down his mouth and chin from his busted nose. His eyes were open, and he stared at her but made no attempt to move when she knelt beside him. Using the same syringe (who the fuck cares if he gets hepatitis) she'd used on Kat, Davina dosed Bobby with the heavy remainder of the Midazolam.

She went about the task of dragging the asshole into the master bedroom. Bobby weighed about one hundred seventy-five pounds, but unconscious, he felt more like three hundred. She wasn't gentle with him as she tugged him across the carpet like a sack of oats, and the rash of carpet burn on the bastard's face gave her satisfaction. The armchair stood at the foot of the bed where she'd placed it earlier. The rear legs were secured to the headboard with several rounds of duct tape, making it easier (not really, he was heavy as shit) to hoist him into it without upending it. While slumped in the chair, his breath wheezing through his deviated septum, Davina secured his arms and legs to the thick wood frame using the industrial zip-ties.

Standing back to admire her work, she said, "That went better than expected."

Now it was time for the hard stuff.

THEN

THE DAY FOLLOWING her introduction to the holy trinity behind Murder, Inc., Davina woke with a horrible headache pushing her eyes out of her sockets, and her sister, Daniela, yelling at her to get out of bed as she rushed out the door on her way to work. Davina sat on the edge of the bed for about ten minutes, then shuffled to the bathroom and swallowed a couple extra strength Tylenol. In the kitchen, there was coffee (thank you, Daniela), which was exactly what she needed right now, maybe more than the pills, and she poured a large mug.

She called in sick for work—no fucking way she was going to be able to work with this rager of a headache—and took her mug of black coffee into the living room, plopping onto the sofa. The house felt too warm, but she was too lazy (hungover) to get up and switch on the A/C, even though the sweat pooling under her tits was annoying. She left the coffee untouched on the end table and dozed for about twenty minutes before the doorbell rang.

Davina reluctantly dragged herself off the sofa, went to the side door in the kitchen, and looked through the peephole.

"Fuck me."

She put her head against the door, considering her options. She was in no mood to deal with Reggie's shit right now. After three weeks at her sister's and away from Reggie, she felt like she'd won an all-expenses paid luxury vacation, except when Daniela hounded her about getting a restraining order on Reggie. The girls from the support group also suggested, at the very least, to start documenting the abuse, but she'd have to amend her previous statement to the police (she'd told them she'd fallen, or some other bullshit, she couldn't really keep her stories straight anymore). Also, it would only piss Reggie off and make her life worse. Davina always knew she'd go back to Reggie (she fucking *always* did and hated herself for it), but she thought she'd have more time.

She unlocked the deadbolt and opened the door. Her heart raced in her chest and her head still throbbed (though dampened somewhat by the Tylenol) at the sight of him. Reggie was average looking, with dark, shaggy-cut hair. His wiry arms were covered with tats that extended from wrist to shoulder. He favored rock T-shirts (Slayer and Misfits were his favorites and were so faded they'd become more gray than black) and ripped jeans. Reggie wanted to be a rock star, but his band sucked, though he was a decent guitarist, so he worked at a secondhand record store ("it pays the bills, babe, and I get shit on discount") that sold mostly vinyl and would likely be out of business within the year.

When they were out at bars or clubs, everyone stared at them, probably wondering what the fuck she was doing with him. Or maybe they were wondering the opposite. A pretty, well-dressed black woman on the arm of a grunge-emo-wannabe rock star did make for an odd couple, though. Lord knew there were plenty of fugly musicians dating hotties half their age.

"You look like hammered shit, babe," he said and stepped past her, into the kitchen. He stopped just inside and peered over Davina's shoulder, likely remembering a certain threat from Daniela of a shotgun. "Your sister home?"

She should have said yes, and he probably would have left (no, he wouldn't), but if he caught her in a lie, he'd slap her (if she was lucky) or punch her breasts (if she was less lucky).

"No."

"Good. That bitch hates my ass."

Davina said nothing as she closed the door.

"You shouldn't be here, Reg."

"I know," he said and sidled up to her. He put a hand on her hip and his voice was sweet. "But I missed you, babe. I mean it."

Reggie was in his sorry phase, when he would be overly sweet to her, revealing his most vulnerable and loving side, trying to win back her affection. Davina knew it was all bullshit, just another way Reggie manipulated her, controlled her, but inevitably, she would swallow the bait and he'd reel her back in. Things between them would be okay for a while, like when they first started dating and he was trying to get into her panties, but soon enough, the abuse would start all over again—he'd come home from a bad day at the store, and he'd home in on some little thing she did, and he'd unleash his shit on her. The vicious cycle she was doomed to repeat. She was tragically caught in a loop that she couldn't get out of until he fucking killed her.

"Aren't you supposed to be at work?"

Reggie scoffed. "I took the day off to come see you, and you're gonna nag me about it?"

"I just asked a question."

"Fucking interrogation is more like it."

Wow, that lasted for about ten seconds, Davina thought.

Reggie's patience over the past three weeks had obviously worn thin, and him coming here now and throwing the sorry phase out the window…he meant to take her back with him now, today.

"Jesus, Vina, you just can't help yourself, can you? I came here offering an olive branch and you slap me in the face with it."

Davina was quiet, knowing anything she said would set him farther down the path of anger. She needed to diffuse him, get him gone at all costs, before he beat the shit out of her in her sister's kitchen.

"You want some coffee?"

Reggie scowled at her. "No, I don't want coffee. I want a fucking apology."

"I'm sorry, Reg." Her response was automatic, and she hated the words leaving her mouth but was incapable of stopping them from rolling off her lips.

He stared at her for a beat. "That's a start. Now get your shit so we can get out of here."

"I'm not—I can't leave yet. I'm still healing. My sister—"

Reggie grabbed her arm. "Don't give me that shit. You've been holed up here too long, and that sister of yours is putting shit in your head, got you thinking you can milk me for sympathy. Fuck that. Get your shit *now*."

Davina jerked away. Her heart pounded in her chest and her hands trembled, but her voice did not betray her fear. "I'm not going."

"God damn it, Vina! Don't start your shit. I'm trying to be nice about this, and you're pushing me. You don't want to be pushing me. I'm going to tell you one more time. Get your stuff. Now."

Davina shook her head. "I'm not going with you. Not now. Maybe not ever."

"What?" Reggie blinked. "The fuck you say?"

"I said maybe I'm never going back with you."

She expected Reggie to respond to her back talk, and he didn't disappoint. Quick as lightning, his hand snatched across her face, his bony fingers smacking her cheek, and his ragged, chewed fingernails drawing blood from her lips and nose. The pain was immediate. She backpedaled, bumped her hip against the table. Before she could recover, he swung on her again with a whopping back hand that knocked her to the floor and rung her bell hard. Her eyes watered, and her sinuses flooded. Blood and snot ran down her nose.

Reggie stood over her, a blurred shadow figure viewed through tears. Before he could strike again, Davina swung an uppercut and punched him in the dick (she hoped with enough force to ram his balls all the way up into his stomach). He bent forward, grabbing his bruised jewels, presenting Davina with an opportunity to make a run for the door.

Whirling around, a potent mix of fear and adrenaline fueling her, she fumbled at the knob and tore open the door and almost made a horrible mistake before she realized she'd gotten turned around and was staring down the long flight of stairs leading to the basement rather than the side door that led to the driveway.

Fuck!

Fueled by anger, pain, and his hatred of his own inadequacies as a man, Reggie bolted up and seized Davina's wrist. He pulled and swung her, snapping her around like a clumsy ballerina, and she flailed across the kitchen until she crashed against the kitchen sink, smashing her hip sharply. He came at her quickly, Reggie-rage (a phrase she'd coined when describing the look to the girls in the support group) filling his eyes. Davina fought the innate instinct is to cover up, cower, absorb the punches, slaps, and kicks Reggie dealt out. But in her mind, Kim's voice repeated what she'd said to Davina at the hospital: *You're going to have to make a choice, Jane Doe. Do you want to keep living this way, and hope he doesn't kill you one day? Or do you want to live the life you deserve?*

And Davina had responded, *I want to live.*

Good, Jane Doe. Then live.

Davina screamed with years of pent-up rage and frustration. Reggie halted in his tracks, shocked (frightened?) by her sudden outburst. He faltered only a moment, then he came at her again, bent on dealing out pain. Davina knew at that moment, only one of them was going to make it out of this house alive.

Good, Jane Doe. Then live.

Only seconds before he'd be on her with fists pounding her, Davina pivoted and grabbed the coffee pot. Heat seared her hand as she fumbled for the carafe handle. She gripped the plastic handle so tightly she felt the beat of her heart throbbing through her fingertips. She swung the carafe with fury, and it connected with Reggie's face. The pot didn't break (fuck!) but Reggie's hands went to his face, his eyes rolled to whites, and he screamed. Davina saw red skin extend above his clutching hands, all the way up to his temple. Reggie screamed again, more anger now than pain. His eyes rolled back and settled on her, and he charged. Davina reacted, jumped one step back, and splashed hot coffee in his face.

Scalding hot coffee—Reggie's scream sounded like an opera soprano—didn't stop him, or maybe it was just his momentum that carried him forward, blindly swinging his arms like windmill blades. Two or three blows landed before Reggie's body pinned Davina against the sink. With closed eyes and a face that looked like an open wound, he slapped and clawed at her; his nails gouged her neck, tore streaks down her chest and her upper right breast before his hand snagged in her shirt and got caught.

Already bleeding, her face and nose throbbing from his first barrage, Davina squeezed her eyes shut and ignored the new pain inflicted. The carafe was still in hand, and she lifted it above her head before swinging it downward on the top of Reggie's head. The carafe still held, and she raised it again, but as she swung it down again, it careened off his flailing arm, and the second blow landed with much less force.

Abandoning the carafe, she let it fall from her grip (and damn, if she didn't hear it shatter when it hit the floor) and attacked Reggie's pulpy face with her nails. Fresh pain took the wind out of Reggie's sails, and he fell back, still flailing blindly, but he was off her now, creating space for her to bolt. But she wasn't running. Not this time. She'd made up her mind that only one of them was walking out alive. Instead of running, Davina stepped forward and swung her leg, like she was kicking a field goal, aiming for his nuts. Her aim was off, and instead of hitting him in the sack, she caught all thigh, but with enough force that Reggie went reeling back, his feet slapping hard against the tile and his arms flailing for balance. Davina inadvertently gasped when he suddenly disappeared through the open door, and then she cringed seconds later at the sound of his body booming down the long basement staircase.

MORE THAN TEN minutes passed before Davina finally descended the stairs to learn Reggie's fate. As she slowly made her way down, even from a distance, she could tell from the way his body had landed, and the way his neck was bent and twisted, that Reggie was dead. She needed to check, to know for sure. She knelt beside him, put the back of her hand in front of his nose and mouth. No breath. She couldn't bring herself to touch him, to check for a pulse. So she waited for nearly a half hour to see if he'd come around, move, or groan.

Later, in the living room, Davina found her purse on the coffee table. She sat on the sofa, set the purse on her lap, and fished out her cellphone and wallet before setting the purse beside her. She unsnapped her wallet and found the folded piece of paper in the billfold section. She smoothed the page open then used her cellphone to dial the number. It rang twice before the person on the other end picked up.

Davina said, "Kim, it's Davina. I need your help."

NOW

DAVINA SAT IN the armchair across from Kat, watching the slight rise and fall of the girl's chest with each breath. The skimpy black skirt rode up high on her thighs, exposing her vagina. Poor girl wasn't wearing panties. Davina went to her and adjusted the hem of the skirt, then covered her with a throw blanket.

Sitting on the floor in front of the sofa, watching the girl in her narcotic-induced sleep, Davina pulled her knees to her chest and hugged herself. For a moment, her breathing became labored and warm fear radiated through her veins and a minor panic attack settled over her. She'd had panic attacks many times in her life. Living under the reign of terror (known as Reggie the Great) constantly pushed her to her psychological limits, until her body became overwhelmed and unable to cope. The panic attacks were frightening and sometimes lasted for five or ten minutes.

One of the women Davina met in a domestic abuse support group years back shared her coping routine whenever a panic attack overwhelmed her, and Davina employed the technique now. She closed her eyes and focused on her breathing, taking deep and deliberate breaths, feeling the air slowly filling her chest, then holding for a second, before breathing out for a four-count. Next, she focused on her hands, flexing her fingers open and closed. Her fingers were all she thought about, picturing them in her mind; open, closed, open, closed. The final phase of the technique was the mantra, "This too shall pass." She repeated it, and by the tenth time, her calm was restored.

Davina opened her eyes and looked at the unconscious girl on the sofa. This was why she was here. Freeing the girl from her prison of rape and abuse was the mission. Feeding her own desire to inflict pain and suffering on Bobby Vaughn was the method (bonus), but she could not lose focus on the reason. The reason was how she coped (rationalized) with what she'd done. Within the hour, she would accomplish her mission. That would be the easy part. She could walk out of here with Kat. The other girls, though, not so easy. She couldn't do that part alone. She needed help, and she knew where to get it. But doing so would come at a high cost.

She dug her cellphone from her back pocket and dialed the number from memory (she didn't keep numbers in her phone in case she was taken into custody). The phone rang a third time before Kim answered. Her words slurred by sleep, she asked, "Do you know what time it is, girl?"

"Kim, I need your help."

"What's wrong? Where are you?" Her voice was alert, concerned.

Davina took a deep breath and then told Kim about Kat and Bobby. Told her as much as Kim needed to know about the current situation and the trafficked girls to solicit help, but she did not share more than that. The less Kim knew, the better, for both of their sakes. Davina was exposing her extracurricular activities (her murder therapy?), and she needed to be careful how much she shared with Kim. If Kim really knew what she'd been doing over the last couple of years, she'd be out of Murder, Inc., shut out from the sisterhood forever.

As expected, Kim was livid, and with good reason. "Wait, the vic is there with you?"

"Yes."

"What the fuck, Vina? What the hell were you thinking? You're making that girl a witness and a target. You're putting that girl at risk, and that's not what we do."

"I know, I know. But I need her. She has details about the operation from the inside that I could never get on my own."

"What you're doing is reckless and stupid. You need to stop now, before you get too deep and can't find your way out."

"Kim, I've been to the club, and I've seen the girls, what goes on. I can't walk away."

"Jesus, when? When were you at the club?"

Davina paused. "Two weeks ago. Well, pretty much every day for two weeks. Scoping it out from a distance."

"For fuck's sake. Didn't I teach you any goddamn

thing, girl? The fucking rule is you don't go around *any place* that is associated with the mark. It's too fucking dangerous. If you're filmed or photographed around the place, you become a person of interest, even if just to question you as a witness about what you might have seen."

Davina didn't respond. There wasn't much to say, because Kim was right. When you were assigned to a mark, your job was to do the deed and move on. The others—Carrie and Margo, or other women that owed Murder, Inc. favors—did the research, the surveillance, and staked out the mark. That was Murder, Inc. 101. Davina also stayed quiet because it was best to let Kim get the bitching out of her system. Then she could be reasoned with.

"You put the whole club—our whole fucking mission—at jeopardy, you know that? We've spent far too much time and made too many sacrifices to be brought down by your stupid bullshit extracurriculars. This is why we only work assignments we all agree on. Period."

"I was careful, Kim. I wore different disguises, changed my hair, used different cars, came around at different times of the day."

"That's not the point!" Kim took a deep breath, and Davina knew she was trying to get control, find her composure. "Why did you even do it? Why put us all at risk?"

Davina looked at Kat sleeping on the sofa. "Because she needed help. Because she had no one that cared."

"I mean why not come to us? Why go it alone?"

Because I'm a murder junkie. I'm addicted to killing, because after Reggie, it's the only thing that helps me get through the night, keeps the demons at bay. And I didn't want you to know because you would stop me, Davina thought.

"Because this isn't a job you'd normally get involved with. It's too big and too dangerous."

"You're damn right it's too big! Organized crime and trafficking? Vina, that is the kind of shit that puts us all in the crosshairs. You know what kind of heat that will put on us? And I don't mean cops. I mean the kind of people that will put us in the fucking ground."

"So, what was I supposed to do? Just leave her and those other girls to the wolves?"

"Call the cops with an anonymous tip—"

"These guys have cops in their pockets. I saw them out of uniform in the club, saw them escorting girls to clients."

"Fucking Christ! This is bad, Davina. This is *so* fucking bad."

"I know. That's why I'm calling you. I need help. I need to know what to do."

Davina realized in that moment, she was hoping Kim would talk her out of this. Subconsciously, did she possibly want to cut bait and run from this?

"You walk the fuck away. Right now. I mean it, Davina."

"You want me to just leave this girl now? Those other girls? Kim, they're being raped every day by sweaty pigs, and no one gives a fuck!"

"Maybe…maybe we can help them later. Just take the girl out of there for now. You both get out of there, get safe, and then we'll put our heads together and think on it, get Carrie and Margo's input on how we can help the rest."

"You said yourself, this will put too much heat on us. Especially if I just take the girl and walk away. And there's no way Carrie and Margo will agree to take this on, no matter what I say."

"You're exactly right. So why the fuck are we still talking about this? You know it's all kinds of wrong. *Walk away.*"

"I can't let this go."

Kim was quiet a moment, just soft breathing over the phone. "If you do this, you have to stay away from us. You know that, right?"

Now Davina was silent, considering what she was about to lose if she saw this through. She had a family in Kim, Carrie, and Margo, one built on a level of love and trust she'd never known before. She had an entire network of support and meaning in her life that she was going to throw away for strangers.

Strangers who have no one, who have lost all hope.

Davina had once been just like Kat, just like those other girls at the club. She'd once lost all hope, resigned herself to a nightmare fate. But Kim had given back hope, and now Davina needed to pay that hope forward, even if it meant losing Murder, Inc.

"I know. But I have to do this, and I know you understand. I love you, Kim."

Davina hung up. She closed her eyes and shook her head, feeling so stupid right now. She'd fucked this up so many ways she couldn't even count them. She just burned her bridge with Kim and Murder, Inc. for nothing. She stood, feeling hot bile rising in her throat, and she swallowed it down. There was no time for wallowing and self-pity. There was still work to be done.

It was time to wake the girl.

THEN

THERE WERE ALWAYS donuts and coffee after support group. Sometimes there were cookies, and occasionally one of the ladies would bake some other tasty treat like banana bread. Once there were even cheesecake bites, which lasted less than fifty seconds. Today was just the basic spread, and Davina nabbed up a chocolate glazed donut (lucky!) and carried it and the Styrofoam cup of black coffee and sat next to the redhead.

Her name was Donna Patterson. She attended some of the same domestic survivor groups—frequented by victims of rape and beatings (or worse) by boyfriends, husbands, relatives, strangers—as Davina. The support groups were an easy way to find women that needed her brand of justice (and to feed her dark need). Davina attended several meetings a week, targeting one or two women she suspected were near tragic endings, and worked her way toward getting to know the women better.

Trolling support groups was not sanctioned by Murder, Inc. Kim and the girls didn't make a practice of seeking out victims, but rather the victims came to them for help, through word of mouth from trusted, discreet women who were once also victims. Murder Inc. solved their problems, and they paid them back in other ways when Kim needed them. What Davina was doing was risky business, but she felt her actions were justified. There were so many battered and abused women who never sought help—or were too afraid or embarrassed to reach out. Women who weren't lucky enough to know the right people to help.

Someone had to help them, too, right?

So Davina stalked the support groups knowing the danger, and the risk of getting caught was high. But Davina was careful. She used the tactics Kim taught her and supplemented her own that she'd learned through trial and error. She used fake names, disguises, and only approached those women she was sure needed her most and would never suspect Davina to have a hand in the horrible accidents that might befall their abusers.

Donna Patterson caught Davina's attention, and for two weeks she'd been studying the woman, learning things about her husband through seemingly random questions and short conversations each meeting. Donna's husband, Charles, was not the same man she married thirteen years ago. He'd grown significantly more abusive the last few years, and his weight also continued to grow, with him ballooning up to four hundred fifty pounds after sustaining a knee injury.

Charles was morbidly obese, and although Donna didn't care so much about his appearance (she was not shallow or superficial), she couldn't bear his immense weight on top of her when they had sex. He was causing her physical pain, and she finally told Charles she would no longer have sex with him unless he lost weight and started taking care of himself (she even cried and told him she was concerned for his health and wanted him to live for a long time). That was the first time he beat her so severely that she called in sick to work for the entire week.

After that, Charles began to rape her, purposefully forcing her into positions he knew were painful and pinning her down with his massive girth. And the sex was rough, cruel. He started to pinch and choke her during their non-consensual intercourse. The more Donna fought or protested, the rougher and more sadistic Charles became. At one point, he'd choked her to the point she'd lost consciousness, and she came to moments later wishing she'd just died, so the nightmare would be over.

Charles, a former college football star, wore his college ring on his pinky finger (his sausage fingers were so fat, the ring no longer fit his ring finger anymore) and he liked to slap Donna around with his ring, like he was some wannabe mobster. Sometimes he'd punch her with it, leaving horrible bruises and indentations in her body where the ring dug into her flesh.

Donna said she thought about poisoning Charles' food one day (it was the only thing the fat bastard loved, and it would be poetic to watch him die while he stuffed his fat face), but she was frightened she'd be caught and sent to prison for murder. But mostly what kept her from spiking his food with rat poison was fear of losing their home and being destitute. Charles didn't allow her to work, and Donna had no income of her own. Chuck had a life insurance policy through his business, though she didn't know the details or even if she was the beneficiary. But she knew it wouldn't pay out if an autopsy revealed he'd been poisoned.

Each night, Donna prayed silently that Charles' enlarged, overworked heart would just give up—explode in his chest, *please, God*—and he would just fucking die already. Or if his heart wouldn't give up, she prayed for an accident when he was driving home from the bar. Either would do, and she'd be rid of him for good, and claim his insurance policy. A girl could hope, right? Hope was all women like Donna had.

Davina sat next to the pretty redhead with the obese, abusive husband and listened. She'd made up her mind days ago that Donna was the one who needed her most. As she listened to the woman, Davina already had the beginnings of a plan on how that fat fuck Chuck would meet his demise. All she could think about as Donna jawed on (once the woman started talking, it was hard to get her to stop) was that Charles would make a baker's dozen. Thirteen notches. That thought made her both excited and frightened at the same time. It was that moment that Davina realized that she might be doing this more for herself than for the women. And even more frightening was the fact that she like dishing out death.

NOW

DAVINA USED AMMONIA inhalants to wake Kataryna from the light, drug-induced sleep. Still groggy from the narcotic, she didn't thrash or fight to get away from Davina. To the contrary, she was docile and a bit confused, which was to be expected. Davina had a bottle of water ready because the drug caused severe dry mouth. Kat accepted the water and drank it down greedily. After a few minutes, Davina got the girl talking. It wasn't hard; she wanted someone to know her plight, and Davina was an excellent listener.

Kat was younger than Davina first thought. She was seventeen years old and had arrived from the Czech Republic a little over a year ago, lured here with the promise of becoming a model, meeting a wealthy older gentleman, and living the American Dream. Instead, she was picked up from the airport by scary men in suits, driven to an abandoned warehouse, and locked in a room with a dirty mattress. Shortly after, they started to give her drugs, kept her high all the time, so she wouldn't fight or scream (she mostly slept). Then they started to bring in the men.

That went on for nearly six months before Bobby Vaughn showed up. The girls were all made to shower and were then lined up for inspection. The handsome man with the dark hair looked them over like a drill sergeant inspecting his recruits. He had them turn and pose, and then he put his hands on them, sampling the goods. After a few minutes, he pointed to three of the girls and then left. The following morning, the three girls, Kat among them, were given nice clothes, and an older woman with tattoos all over came in and styled their hair and did their makeup. That evening, they were driven to the club, where they were instructed to give private dances for VIPs. They were never to perform sexual acts in the club, but if the men wanted certain...favors, they were to tell one of the burly men who stood outside the rooms. They would then escort the girls back to the warehouse, where they would host the VIP in one of eight remodeled rooms that were nothing like the dank, smelly one she was kept in previously.

The girls were treated well enough (if you ignored the rape and terror), given nice clothes and good food. The men who stood outside the doors kept the Johns in line and never let any of them get abusive, though sometimes the men wanted kinky shit. Some of the girls wanted the drugs while they "entertained" the clients. Kat understood the need but had worked to wean herself off because she wanted to be clean. She still had hope she'd leave this life sometime, that they couldn't keep her forever. It was likely her going clean—and the fact that she was gorgeous with a tight body—that made Bobby pick her for his personal plaything.

Rumor was, Bobby selected the prettiest girls among them to be his private partner. They would live with him, travel with him, live the good life, like a real girlfriend. This was considered an honor among the girls because this meant they could "earn" freedom. Rumor had it, eventually Bobby would grow bored with his live-in girl, and they'd be given $20,000 and their passport and be sent on their way to start their life. That was just bullshit, of course.

Living with Bobby was better than working in the club (now she only got fucked by one guy, instead of many), but it was worse in other ways. Bobby liked to hit when he was pissed or frustrated. He had a short temper and flew off the handle at even small infractions. He also got in Kat's head, using psychological terror to manipulate and control her. Kat said that was worse than getting fucked against her will.

Kat broke down, tears smearing her makeup. Davina

hugged her, soothed her.

"I'm going to help you. I'm going to take you away from all of this. And we're going to help the other girls too."

Kat sat back and stared at Davina. "You mean that? You'll help me? Help them all?"

"I do."

"How? How can you?"

Davina stood and extended her hand.

"Come with me," she said and took Kat to see Bobby.

THEN

DAVINA WATCHED CHARLES Patterson—the self-absorbed fat tub of shit with poor impulse control and a penchant for smacking and choking his wife while he raped her—from the comfort of her cozy booth. She'd been nursing a Diet Coke and plucking at cold chili fries for nearly an hour while the heart-attack-waiting-to-happen downed his sixth rum and Coke. The suit he wore appeared expensive and custom tailored. Though he'd outgrown it some twenty pounds ago, he still squeezed himself into it. The fabric strained against his enormous girth, and Davina fully expected the seam of the jacket to burst each time he leaned forward across the bar, and his love handles (spare tires, more accurately) to spill out through the gash. His sandy brown hair appeared much darker now that it was greasy with sweat. She couldn't stand the way his jowls quivered when he laughed. The stool supporting his enormous ass almost completely disappeared into his rotund crack; the poor furniture creaked dangerously each time he shifted his weight. Davina hoped it would give and spill him onto the concrete floor so she could have a good laugh watching him try to get up.

When Chuck was finally ready to settle his tab, Davina left the bar and jogged to the car she'd rented under one of her three elaborately backstopped aliases, none of which could be traced back to her. The car was an economy job, with barely enough legroom for her five-foot-five frame, but the hatchback was roomy enough to store away what she needed for this job. She started the car, and when she exited the parking lot and turned left—following the route she knew Chuck would take on his way home—he hadn't yet waddled out to the parking lot. She had a good enough head start to get set up. So far, everything was going exactly as planned.

About half a mile down the road, Davina slowed down and pulled onto the sloping embankment, roughly twenty feet before the two-lane road transitioned to an overpass above a thin vein of the Chicago River. The road was flanked on either side by forest preserve. At this time of night (morning, really, it was almost three a.m.), traffic was rare, and though there was always a risk that another motorist could be injured by her actions, the odds were in her favor, and she was determined to see this through and give the wide-load bastard what he had coming to him.

Leaving the engine running, Davina turned off the headlights, then exited the vehicle. Around back, she lifted the tailgate and retrieved the Spike Devil standard spike strip, an accordion design that folded and rolled into a compact package. The spike strip itself deployed up to sixteen feet, plenty long enough for the job. Securing the strip had been a bit of a challenge, but using Kim's connections with several branches of law enforcement (without Kim's knowledge, of course, because this was off-book), with a little bit of flirting (men were so easy when you knew what buttons to push) she had what she needed.

After stowing the strip in her garage for safekeeping, she spent nearly an hour watching over a dozen YouTube videos learning how to deploy the damn thing without injuring herself. She'd found one presenter whose tutorial presented the material in a simple and detailed format, though, and she felt confident she'd be able to do it right. Davina's intention had been to practice deploying the device a few times before using it, but she worried someone might spot her and ruin her plan before it was underway. This shit was going to be trial by fire.

Mindful of the time, knowing fatty wouldn't be far behind, she removed the spike set from the plastic holster. She firmly gripped the service reel in her left hand and the rolled spikes in her right. She placed her left foot on the cord that extended from the reel and anchored it firmly to the pavement with her weight. She cocked her right hand back behind her butt, like she saw demonstrated in the tutorial. Holding her position, she only had to wait forty-five seconds before she saw the headlights sweep up the road in the direction from the bar.

Her mouth was suddenly dry, and her hand trembled, though not from the weight of the spike strip. She worried about timing. To minimize risk of harming someone other than the fat slime ball behind the wheel, she wanted to confirm the car coming up the road was his. To do so would mean she'd have to wait for it to get closer, which significantly diminished the time to accurately deploy the spike strip. If she botched this, she didn't have a plan B, and three weeks of surveillance and planning would be wasted.

So don't fuck this up, she thought.

She heaved the spike strip into the street as hard as she could. The strip slid easily across the two lanes of blacktop with the strip ending up on the opposite lane and the forty-foot black cord that attached to the service reel across the lane immediately in front of her. Her fingers gripped the reel tightly, and her heart raced as the headlights bore down. Now Davina heard the whine of the car's engine. The bastard was driving far too fast for this road, let alone for his inebriated condition. What came next would be of no surprise to authorities after the autopsy revealed his blood alcohol levels.

Fatty's car was nearly twenty feet away. Davina's grip on the reel tightened, and she backpedaled, pulling the cord sharply, deploying the spikes onto this side of the road. A moment of panic washed over her when she thought she'd mistimed her pull. The front tires were already beyond the spikes, but they caught both rear tires. The left rear tire popped, though it did not explode as she expected (fucking movies never got shit right). The result, though, was better than she'd hoped. The car started into a 180-degree spin, and tons-of-fun slammed on his brakes in response, which was a mistake. The rear-end fishtailed completely around, carrying the car into the opposite lane as it entered the overpass. The high speed he'd been traveling created enough momentum and force so that when the car struck the retaining rail, it tore through the concrete lip and rebounded into the air, ass over teakettle.

Davina frantically gathered up the spike strip (stabbing her hands and arms, but she didn't give a fuck right now) and heaved it through the open driver's door where it landed on the passenger seat before rebounding to the floor. She slammed into the driver's seat when she heard the horrible sound of the car smashing into the shallow river below. Her hands shook as she shifted into drive, made a U-turn, and sped away in the opposite direction.

It was past three a.m. when she got home. She was exhausted and tried to sleep, but she lay awake for nearly an hour, trying unsuccessfully to turn her mind off. Not knowing whether the fat bastard was dead or alive was frustrating. Eventually she slept. She woke four hours later and rushed into the living room to turn on the news, hoping for an answer. She watched for half an hour, but evidently the story wasn't big enough for the morning news.

Later that afternoon, Davina logged into her online subscription to the *Chicago Tribune*. She entered an advanced search and immediately found what she was looking for. Charles Patterson (aka fatty aka tons-of-fun aka fat bastard) was pronounced dead at the scene of an unfortunate accident. Charles, the article speculated, lost control of his vehicle. He was driving while intoxicated and possibly swerved to avoid a deer or other nocturnal animal that were notorious for crossing the road at night. His vehicle, traveling above the speed limit, too fast for the small two-lane road, smashed through the overpass retaining rail and plunged twenty-five feet into the shallow branch of the river below, the impact killing him instantly (she hoped that part of the article was speculation and that he'd suffered before his enormous belly heaved one final time as he took his last breath). Davina closed the article. She didn't need to read the rest.

In her bedroom, she stood on a plastic stool and pushed aside several pairs of folded jeans from the closet shelf, revealing a four-inch-by-four-inch cedar roofing shingle. The pungent aroma immediately filled her nostrils as she took it down and carried it with her to the kitchen. She set the shingle on the island and retrieved an icepick from the utensil drawer. She paused a moment, her eyes focusing on the dark corner of the wood; her blood absorbed and dried into the wood over five years ago now. The shingle was a reminder (souvenir) of Reggie's violence, the first time he drew blood by pushing her savagely into a tiki bar at the beach when she'd politely told him he'd had enough to drink and they should return to their hotel. The corner of the shingle lacerated the back of her head. As the hotel medic bandaged her head, she spotted the shingle in the sand, dislodged from the violent encounter, and snatched it up. She didn't know why, at the time, she wanted the macabre souvenir. But now she understood.

Ignoring the dark stain, Davina used the pick to scratch a tick mark into the soft wood. There were thirteen slashes now (two groups of five and one group of three), each representing not the men she'd killed, but the women she'd freed. None of the thirteen tick marks represented assignments for Murder, Inc. (Davina did not keep track of those, though, that number was far smaller, and easily counted on one hand), but rather her own campaign of service. At least that's how she rationalized her lust for kill-ing. It made it easier to look at herself in the mirror.

NOW

KAT STOPPED COLD at the threshold when she saw Bobby in the chair at the foot of the bed. His head was slumped forward, chin resting on his chest. She was not expecting to see him incapacitated and with blood run-ning from his busted nose.

"Is he dead?"

"No, not yet."

Davina looked at Kat, trying to read the girl. Her eyes were wide, but she looked more curious than frightened as she took in the scene. Thick gauge plastic on the carpet beneath the chair. Zip-ties secured his arms and legs to the seat. The blinds on the windows drawn tight and only the lamp on the nightstand illuminating the room.

Kat's gazed shifted to Davina. "What is this?"

"Your path to freedom."

Davina didn't wait for the girl to respond. She went to Bobby. She took the stick of ammonia inhalant from her hip pocket, tore the top half of the package open, and shoved it under Bobby's nose. His reaction to the inhalant wasn't as immediate, given the increased dosage of the sed-ative Davina hit him with earlier. He moaned, and his head moved slowly from side to side for a few seconds be-fore his eyes popped open and his head snapped back.

After a moment of confusion, Bobby locked eyes with Davina.

"Who are you? What the fuck is this?"

"Your atonement."

Bobby's face furrowed in anger, and he started rocking his body frantically, his arms and legs struggled against the bonds holding him to the chair. He grunted in exertion and frustration and then stopped struggling when he realized he could not free himself.

"You cut me loose right now. You have no idea who the fuck you're messing with."

"I know exactly who I'm messing with. Bobby Vaughn."

"Who sent you? And who the fuck—" He stopped when he saw Kat in the doorway. "You little bitch! Did you do this? After all I've done for you? Cut me loose now or I'm going to kill you, you fucking whore!"

Davina didn't look at the girl but instead moved to stand in front of Bobby. Slowly, she unzipped the hoodie, shrugged out of it, and laid it on the edge of the bed.

"What are you doing?" Bobby asked, his attention back on Davina.

Now, she pulled off her t-shirt. Beneath, she wore a spaghetti strap tank that didn't cover much of her upper body, but that was the point. She was scarred, her upper arms and back, her chest (most of the twisted and puckered scars were inflicted by Reggie, but some from the other men who she'd dealt with over the years), and Davina wanted Bobby to see (and Kat, especially Kat), to know she had suffered, and that she'd survived. She wanted Bobby to feel fear.

"I don't know what this is," Bobby said, the anger in his voice waning. "Whatever it is, you better stop now before you do something you regret."

From her back pocket, Davina retrieved a pair of weighted knuckle sap gloves and pulled them on. She looked down at the gloves as she flexed her fingers open, then closed them into tightly balled fists.

"Don't do nothing stupid—"

Before he could finish his sentence, Davina hit him with a right cross. The sound of the gloves striking his jaw brought pleasure, but not as much as feeling the impact of the blow travel up her wrist and forearm.

"That's just a taste of what's coming," Davina said. She pulled off her gloves and turned to offer them to Kat.

"Don't you fucking dare!" Bobby shouted.

Kat was trained by fear and violence, and a mere glare from Bobby made her hesitate to accept the gloves.

"Don't look at him," Davina said. "Look at me, honey."

Kat's eyes remained on Bobby, as if pinned there, then slowly slid to Davina.

"Cemeteries all over the world are full of women, girls—children—who didn't stand up for themselves or couldn't. They just kept taking the abuse until they were put into the ground by pieces of shit like him." Davina jerked a thumb over her shoulder in Bobby's direction. Pushing the gloves into Kat's hands, she said, "You have a chance they didn't. Honey, you are young and beautiful and *alive*. You have a chance to take your life back. This is your chance right now. Right here. In this moment."

Kat held the gloves in her hand but didn't put them on. Her eyes were glassy, but she remained silent, a battle of conscience raging within the young girl.

Undeterred, Davina continued. "You have to want

your freedom. Do you want your freedom?"

Tears streamed down her cheeks. Kat was silent, indecisive.

"Don't listen to her bullshit. You hear me, girl? Don't you fucking listen to her. I treat you well, don't I? You want to be free, just let me loose, I'll deal with this cunt, and then you can go on your way, if that's what you want."

Davina took the sap gloves from Kat. With her free hand, she reached into her back pocket and pulled out a knife. She held both items in front of her. Behind her, Bobby started to struggle with his bonds, straining to see what she held in her hands.

"If you can't do it for yourself, Kat, think about the other girls. You do this now, and then we can help the other girls, you and me. Together. You want that, right? You want to help them?"

Kat nodded. "Yes." Her voice was but a whisper. "But you don't know what his people will do to the girls if they find out about this."

"That's right! Anything happens to me, my boys will hunt you to the end of the Earth and cut your fucking tongues out! They'll do worse, you hear me?"

"I'll protect you. He won't hurt you. No one will hurt you."

"Oh, I'll do more than hurt you," Bobby said. He seemed to get his balls back, but that was just desperate bravado. He knew his time in this life was short.

Davina held the gloves and the knife in front of the girl. "Take your life back. Help the girls."

"I can't..." Kat said, then turned and ran from the room.

"That's my girl!" Bobby shouted. "Call the club, tell Vlad to get down here. We'll get this all settled. You hear me, Kataryna?"

Davina was not discouraged by Kat's inability to do the deed. She wasn't ready, and Davina wasn't going to push the issue. The girl had been through traumas that would haunt her for years to come, but she would likely get over those with enough time and maybe therapy. Taking a man's life, even a disgusting piece of shit like Bobby Vaughn, was something that could break the girl, something she might never recover from. To be honest, Davina was pleased that she would be left to deal with Bobby. She had certain dark urges that she needed to satiate.

Davina closed the door. She faced Bobby and tucked the sap gloves into her back pocket. She flicked the automatic knife open and smiled when Bobby flinched.

"Looks like it's just you and me, Bobby McGee."

"You're not going to touch me," Bobby said, but there was no confidence in his voice.

"Oh, but I am. I'm going to touch you plenty. And before I'm done, you're going to beg me to kill you. But first, you're going to give me the combination to the safe in your office."

DAVINA FOUND KAT in Bobby's office, sitting behind the desk. Her head was down on the blotter, and when she looked up, her eyes were red from crying.

"I'm so sorry."

Davina shook her head. "Don't apologize, honey. You made the right choice."

"Is he…?" Kat's voice trailed off.

Davina saw Kat's eyes shift to her bloody hands. "Yes."

At the wall safe, Davina punched in the six-digit code and pulled open the hinged door. She reached in and pulled out the large, zippered pouch and set it down on the desk and then sat down in one of the chairs opposite the girl.

"Go ahead, open it."

Kat hesitated a moment, then reached across the desk for the pouch. She unzipped it and spilled the contents onto the desk. A stack of passports, nearly twenty, piled out. Kat's eyes grew wide for a moment, then she went to work looking through each. She set several passports aside—the girls that were currently captive at the warehouse—and continued leafing through them desperately until she found her own. She held it to her chest, her eyes closed.

After a moment, Kat opened her eyes and collected the six passports, placing them into the pouch. She looked at Davina. "What about the others?"

"Take them all."

"I mean the other girls. You will help them?"

Davina nodded. She was tired, and her eyes burned. But she smiled reassuringly.

"I will."

There was still plenty of room on that blood-stained shingle tucked away at the back of her closet, and she had the urge to fill it with hash marks.

IT'S ALL FUN AND GAMES UNTIL

Rebecca Rowland

"**D**O YOU SMOKE CIGARETTES, ER..." THE pretty nurse looked down at her clipboard. "Kristin?"

The patient smiled. "It's Kristina, and no, not for a long time." She remained pleasant, still smiling. The clinic wasn't one she'd used before, but it was nearly identical to all of the others she'd visited: urban, mobbed, and under-staffed. She wouldn't be remembered, and that was her goal. This nurse had forgotten her already.

The distracted woman's eyes remained glued to her clipboard. "Drink alcohol?"

Kristina pretended to check her watch. "Is it after twelve yet?"

There was no response, not even a wince. Kristina

could see by her tag that the nurse's name was Deenie. Her scrubs were covered with tiny cartoon animals: dogs, cats, bunnies. She thought she might even have spied a snake among the menagerie. She was an attractive woman and might even be someone Kristina would approach in a bar, if the situation were different. When the patient said nothing more, Deenie looked up. "I'm sorry, I didn't catch that," she said.

Kristina smiled again. "Just kidding. Very rarely." Kristina was lying. She meant *rarely* in the sense that rarely a day went by that she didn't have a vodka tonic in her hand before sundown. It was always five o'clock somewhere. She limited her drinking to one, however. Any more than that, and things got sloppy. One was just enough to take the edge off, give her a bit of liquid courage to continue her hobby.

Deenie didn't ask her if she used street drugs. She didn't look the type, she supposed, and Kristina wondered if that was a compliment.

"How long have you been diabetic?" Deenie asked.

"I was diagnosed when I was twelve, so almost twenty-one years," the patient told her. She had her responses committed to memory, down to the subtlest detail of facial expression. In a pinch, she could always visit a needle exchange program, pick up a handful of syringes that way, but the staff would be more likely to commit her image to memory in those types of places. Junkies, it seemed, were less likely to be believed than those with broken pancreases.

"Do you test your sugar regularly?" Deenie finally

looked up from her chart, her eyes skimming the young woman, for just a moment, before busying herself with fumbling with a lancet and test strip.

"Of course," Kristina lied.

Deenie held her hand out. "What's your most recent A1C number?"

"Four-point-seven," Kristina said. Confident, proud. She didn't respond to the hand yet. Sometimes, just saying this number allowed her to avoid the needle.

Deenie waved her palm toward the patient. "Let's have a finger."

Kristina was not so lucky today. She offered her left hand, and the nurse wiped a white wet pad over the top of her middle finger. The alcohol smell was crisp, anxious. Deenie held the lancet to the disinfected digit and pressed the button. It snapped, and a tiny bead of bright red appeared. Deenie scooped it onto the test strip and the two women waited for the countdown on the test machine to beep.

"Are you sexually active?" Deenie asked, returning to her clipboard. She was wasting no time. Minutes were at a premium.

"No," Kristina said.

"Are you interested in being tested for sexually transmitted infections today?"

Does chlamydia pass by osmosis these days? Kristina wanted to ask. "No, I don't think that's necessary. I just need a refill." The patient was batting a thousand in the bullshit department this visit, bowling a perfect game. "Anything special on your request list for Santa this year?"

she added, only recognizing afterward how creepy the attempt at small talk sounded.

If Deenie was repulsed, she didn't show it. The machine beeped, and the nurse recorded the number on the chart. "Four-point-nine," she said. "Good work."

Kristina smiled, hiding her irritation at this patronizing statement.

Deenie dumped the needle and used test strip in the sharps container. "The doctor will be in shortly. Have a good holiday." She did not look at the woman again before leaving.

Kristina removed her refuse from the bright orange bin marked with a *Caution!* warning, wrapped the pieces in a tissue, and shoved them in her purse. She was obsessive about keeping her DNA inside of her body; even one stray hair could be the end of her fun. She never knew what hypochondriac might be lurking at her family reunions, sending their saliva to 23andme. *It's all fun and games until someone gets handsy and scratches themselves a fat genetic sample for the police to test,* she thought.

A half hour later, Kristina was on her way to the nearest pharmacy. On the rental car's radio, Bing Crosby crooned about silver bells. Kristina sang loudly along as she tossed the prescription onto the seat next to her and turned on the wipers to clear the softly falling snow. She would be restocked and back on the road by nightfall.

Though in truth, it began years before, the game truly took shape in the spring of 2006. Kristina was a freshman in her second semester at Hofstra University, her big adventure to Long Island, the strip of land abutting the Big

Apple. Her only friends on campus, three boys who shared a room at the other end of her dorm hall, invited her to join them on Spring Break. Edward, the oldest of the boys, borrowed his parents' Ford Taurus sedan, and the four took turns driving the long haul down Interstate 95, the landscape changing from browns and grays to sunny greens as they approached Florida.

Kristina hadn't minded sharing a room with the other three—they knew she favored women and didn't bother trying to convince her otherwise—but after two nights, she was bored, antsy. There were only so many drunken pool gatherings and beach fires to keep her interest. On the third evening of their stay, she bowed out from the festivities. Edward lent her the car, and she cruised the boardwalk before heading north, finally turning into the parking lot of an ancient IHOP when her stomach began to growl.

A middle-aged woman with reddish-brown hair, the kind that used to be fiery but had dinged and darkened after years of hard drugs, hot sun, and cheap motel shampoo, approached the passenger window, just as Kristina turned off the motor. She motioned to the driver to roll down the window, but Kristina climbed out of the car instead.

"Hey," she called over the car roof to the woman who remained bent, staring inside at the cloth front seat. "Can I help you with something?"

The redhead straightened up, but her shoulders slumped. "I was just wondering if you could help me out. I ran outta gas." The woman's lip twitched a bit, a nervous tic.

IT'S ALL FUN AND GAMES UNTIL | *Rebecca Rowland*

Kristina raised her eyebrow. "Where's your car?" she asked. "I have a can in the trunk. I can drive you to the station to fill it up." She didn't, and she wouldn't, but Kristina never missed an opportunity to call out a con game.

The woman hesitated, thinking. Then, "You need any company tonight?" she asked but looked slightly apprehensive. It was the South, after all, and while prostitution might be casually tolerated, lesbianism very often was not.

Kristina glanced at the woman's clothes. It was clear she hadn't showered in days. Her hair hadn't been brushed in quite some time, and her orange blouse billowed around a skeletal frame. "You got a place?" Kristina asked. "I was just going to get some food here, but I'd be up for some pizza delivery." She'd eaten pizza for the past four days and couldn't fathom smelling the sweet tang of tomato sauce and grease again, but it was clear this woman was desperate for a way to make quick cash. Kristina mentally counted the stack of bills in her back pocket.

The redhead looked around nervously. "Yeah...yeah," she stammered. "I got a place not far from here. It ain't on the beach or nothing, though."

Kristina laughed. "That's okay. I've had my fill of sand for the day." She climbed back into the car and unlatched the lock. "Get in," she said, loudly enough for the woman to hear her through the glass. When the woman obliged, Kristina stuck out her hand before turning the key again. "My name's Kristina," she said.

"Julie," the redhead offered, avoiding Kristina's eyes.

She shook her hand limply. Her fingers were long and soft, her fingernails bitten down to the quick.

They drove a mile down the road until Julie pointed to an abandoned-looking motel abutting a tattoo parlor. "Right there," she said. Her hand shook a little, and she replaced it on her lap.

As the two women approached one of the room doors, Julie glanced sideways at her companion. "Wasn't expecting company. Sorry about the mess."

Kristina smiled, taking great care to show Julie all of her teeth. "I'm not a neat freak myself."

The room was dark. Heavy curtains were drawn across the picture window where a small, round table stood with two rickety chairs. Nearby, a queen-sized bed, its sheets and coverlet a tangled mess, and its two bed pillows pushed together against the headboard, appeared slightly damp, the mattress dented with shadows. The red-head raised her arm and turned on a hanging light above the table. An empty jar of peanut butter, a handful of dirty, wrinkled t-shirts, and two well-worn fashion magazines, their covers slightly frayed, jumbled themselves into a tall heap a few feet below the bulb.

Julie held her arm out. "You can sit anywhere," she said, and Kristina rested herself in one of the chairs abutting the pile.

They were both silent for a moment as Kristina surveyed the room. Julie remained standing and began to tap her foot slightly. "So, what were you looking for?" she asked. Business-like, impatient.

Kristina stretched her arms and folded them behind her head. "I thought we were getting pizza. I mean, if you have other plans, I don't want to keep you…" She reached one hand back down behind her jeans and pulled out her folded money. "But I'd like to buy you dinner and maybe pay for a bit of your time." She unfolded the bills and spread them out into a fan. She had close to three hundred dollars, more than half of her money left for the week.

Julie's eyes widened, and she sat down on the edge of the bed. "You really want pizza?"

Kristina shoved the money into her front pants pocket. "What I'd like is for both of us to relax. Not worry about the time for once. Catch my drift?" She smiled again, making her mouth as wide as she could manage. "Why don't you call and order, then hop in the shower while we wait? Put on some comfy clothes, some pajamas maybe. And I'll take off my shoes—if that's okay with you—and wait for the delivery guy."

Julie bit her lip and glanced at the pile of debris next to Kristina. "You sure?" she asked, hesitant, her eyes still on the pile.

Kristina nodded. "Yep." She crossed her legs.

The redhead picked up the beige telephone beside the bed and dialed, already knowing the number by heart. As she replaced the receiver on the base, she stood up. "About thirty minutes, the guy said. Probably closer to forty-five, knowing them."

Kristina kicked off her shoes. "Great. I'll just hang out while you shower." When Julie looked around nervously at this, she added, "I promise: I'm not going to rob you. If it makes you feel better, I'll hang out in the bathroom."

Julie looked at the floor. "You really just want to hang around? Nothing else?"

Kristina cleared her throat. "Well, Julie, to be honest, I am hoping for a little more. But I'm also not a fan of making women do anything they don't want to do. I know you sleep with men for money. I have enough to pay you, too. But just kicking back and watching some tube is cool, if that's all you're comfortable with."

At this, Julie crossed her arms across her chest and peeled her blouse over her head. A carpet of orange freckles was splattered between the edges of her light green bra. "Come join me in the shower," she said, and Kristina followed her into the bathroom without another word.

Forty minutes later, she was wiping the handles of the faucet with a corner of the wet bath towel and checking the drain for remnants of her hair when she heard Julie chatting with the pizza delivery person. When the outside door shut again, Kristina emerged from the bathroom. She hadn't bothered to redress, and Julie paused to stare at her naked body as she walked uninhibited across the room.

Julie sat cross-legged on the bed in a ragged pink bathrobe, the unopened box of pizza in front of her. She reached her hand forward, pointed the remote control at the ancient television, and clicked a few of the buttons. The sound screamed to life, a newscaster covering a race at the local speedway. "They never give me napkins," Julie yelled over the cacophony. "But I keep a stash of them over there, on the table." She nodded toward the pile of debris, then stopped, suddenly remembering something. "I'll get 'em," she said, starting to unfold herself.

Kristina held her hand up. "I got it." She walked toward the table and began to rifle through the mess until an unusual item revealed itself. "What's this?" Kristina asked, holding up the large black gun using a corner of one of the t-shirts.

Julie slid to the edge of the bed. Her eyes were wide. "I got it for protection. Two of my friends, they went...they disappeared over Christmas, you know." She swallowed, staring at the gun. "One turned up dead. Just thought this would maybe help."

Kristina turned the gun carefully so that the t-shirt fabric covered her finger as she aligned it against the trigger. "You're a regular Annie Oakley, huh?" she asked, closing one eye dramatically and pretending to aim the muzzle at the lamp. Smiling. Nothing to fear here.

Julie laughed nervously. "Annie Oakley used a shotgun," she said.

Kristina lowered her arm. "You wanna play cops and robbers?" she asked playfully. She smiled again, and Julie had to admit, the sight of the starkly nude woman holding the big gun seemed slightly comical. Kristina winked at her. "Well, ma'am, I'm gonna have to take you in," she said in a mock drawl. "You're too darn purty to be eatin' that here pizza all alone." She walked slowly toward the bed, then gestured gently with the gun. "Turn over and lie on your stomach so I can cuff ya."

Julie smiled nervously but didn't move. Surely, this woman was joking. She had expected the woman to get dressed, eat a slice of pizza or two, and be on her way. Perhaps she could be persuaded to stay longer, pay more money. She hadn't expected to be horsing around with a gun. The woman was close enough to touch her.

Kristina nudged Julie's knee with her own. "Go ahead. Turn over and lie down," she whispered.

Julie hesitated for a moment, then did as she was told. Immediately, she felt Kristina's weight shift onto the bed behind her, the visitor's knees on the back of her arms.

Kristina had never been a fan of strangling her prey. Though satisfying in its own right, the act was too time-consuming. She knew other killers confessed to wanting to savor the moment, to take their time watching the life drain from their victims' eyes, but Kristina knew the truth. Strangling caused a woman's vagina muscles to clench up, and most of her male brethren stuck their undersized cocks in their prey, as they killed them, because it gave them a sense of not being the woefully ineffectual lovers they actually were. For Kristina, being gratefully absent of this problematic appendage meant strangling was nothing but a nuisance. She was working on crafting a signature, injecting air into a target's vein—clean yet satisfying—but she hadn't quite perfected the move.

"Don't take this personally," she said softly, then held the tip of the gun up to the back of Julie's head and fired. Blood, skull, and gray matter blew everywhere, including onto Kristina's stomach, but she did not flinch. Where the muzzle had been, a deep red hole, almost black, wet and gooey, appeared in its place. A faint trail of smoke drifted up from between Julie's wet locks. Kristina rolled off of the limp body, rested the gun and t-shirt on Julie's terry-clothed back, and pushed the pizza box open with her knuckle.

IT'S ALL FUN AND GAMES UNTIL | *Rebecca Rowland*

On the television, a lacquered-hair reporter squinted seriously at the camera as she walked sideways alongside a wooded area. "*This is the third body to turn up along LPGA Boulevard,*" the woman stated robotically. "*Police say the victim suffered a gunshot wound to the head and…*"

Kristina picked up a slice of pizza and took a generous bite. The pie had cooled significantly, but the chef had been generous with the tomato sauce, and a glob of it spilled from the side and dropped onto her thigh.

"*…There appears to be no connection between this recent murder and the string of bodies being discovered along…*"

Kristina shoved the rest of the piece into her mouth and chewed. She looked down at Julie's body, completely still. "Well, I'll be darned," she said to it, her voice muffled through the mouthful of masticated cheese and dough. "You just gave me the best idea."

No one expects a woman to attack them. Unsurprisingly, men are statistically more likely than women to commit violent crimes, sexual crimes, even low-level, petty assaults. Even in innocuous social situations, men are more likely to trigger anxiety in others. Because of this, women are more likely to be on guard when in the presence of a strange man than with a strange woman. Gynophobia, the specific fear of women, is a rare disorder and only develops years after the person suffers chronic abuse by women, and even then, the sufferers tend to be male. Not female. Not Kristina's victim of choice.

Kristina knew these facts. Christ, the college had financed her education with a full-ride scholarship for her to study them. After her graduation with a degree in criminal justice, Kristina stayed in Long Island, working as a process server. The pay was dismal, but the position allowed her little restriction on her travel and time consumption. She was good at her job, able to blend in nonchalantly with just about any crowd. She was also harmless looking, so no one hesitated to open their doors when she rang a doorbell. She saved up her vacation time, and each December, she traveled to a new part of the country, one she'd researched weeks in advance. One with a recent history of unresolved crime.

She perfected her syringe technique, but she was careful, even meticulous, to stage her bodies to match the victims of area predators. In the Information Age, the internet, especially with its histrionically headlined news-zines, was nothing but a geyser of details in which copycats could freely bathe.

December 2009. *Remains of a twelfth victim appear near the Mouth Pleasant neighborhood of Cleveland.*

December 2010. *Suffolk Police report four bodies along the north side of Ocean Parkway.*

December 2011. *Discovery of a fourth body in the Matanuska Lake region, north of Anchorage.*

December 2012. *Bodies unearthed in lot next to Kentucky homeless shelter.*

December 2013. *Santa Clara authorities track the culprit behind fourth shooting in Sunnyvale.*

December 2014. *Dismembered remains of four victims uncovered near Paris, Maine, bed and breakfast.*

IT'S ALL FUN AND GAMES UNTIL | *Rebecca Rowland*

December 2015. *Skeletons of four people found behind a Connecticut strip mall.*

December 2016. *Seventh woman bound, gagged, and stabbed in Detroit neighborhood.*

December 2017. *Dallas police "baffled" after nine residents found dead at same apartment complex.*

December 2019. *The bodies of five sex workers located in field near Oklahoma City drug house.*

December 2020. *New Orleans officials "disturbed" over missing women dragged from nearby swamp.*

From the clinic, Kristina stopped at a chain pharmacy in northern Connecticut to refresh her supplies before heading toward Boston. Revere Beach, its shoreline mostly vacant in the brutal winter months of New England, was the recent recipient of three unidentified corpses, the flesh so water-logged that cause of death had yet to be determined, though initial reports theorized the victims had been injected with something. A predator after her own heart.

As she pulled onto the interstate, the snow intensified. Bing Crosby became Elvis Presley, crying about a blue Christmas. As the sign for the Massachusetts Turnpike came into view, the white flakes doubled, then tripled in size and intensity. Just beyond the green placard, bright lights of consumerism illuminated the sky. Target. Bed, Bath & Beyond. Barnes & Noble. Kristina glanced at the digital numbers on the dashboard. She had plenty of time to wait out the squall.

The mall's three-story garage was packed, and it took a bit of circling to secure the only open parking spot, one hidden from view inside a dark corner. As she slipped through the glass doors leading directly into the Christmas Tree Shops, Kristina stuffed a twenty-dollar bill into a bell ringer's red kettle. The store was oppressively warm, and she wandered slowly along the aisles, maneuvering around over-flowing shopping carts and screaming baby carriages. Her hands remained clenched in frustration at the traffic and storm.

She entered a nearly empty aisle full of housewares and table settings and pretended to scan the dinner plates in interest. A young woman wearing a gray winter hat, the only other shopper in sight, turned to look at her. Kristina felt her gaze and shifted her body away in discomfort.

The woman pointed a woolen gloved finger at her. "Kristin, no, Kristina, right?"

Kristina swallowed and turned slightly. The nurse from the clinic. "Yes, how did you—" she began, feigning confusion.

"Doctor's office," she said, smiling. "Earlier today." She glanced at the rows of unboxed glassware lining the shelves in front of them. "Holiday shopping?"

Kristina smiled but kept her lips tight. "Yes, just a few last-minute things. More so seeing what they have, so I know what I'll be back to buy later. I tend to work best as a last-minute shopper." She pretended to evaluate a frosted blue beer stein. "You?"

The nurse laughed, then, inexplicably, leaned close to Kristina and whispered conspiratorially. "To be honest. I'm just wasting some time before I jump on the Pike." She leaned back and smiled warmly. In the air between them lingered a flowery musk scent, a perfume Kristina recognized but could not quite identify. "I've been helping to care for my great-aunt over the past few months. She lives on the shore, so I stay there on weekends to give my cousin a break. The snow kind of grounded me for a bit, but I'm glad for the postponement." Her eyes stared directly into Kristina's. "My name's Denise. Deenie, for short."

Kristina nodded. The piercing of her bubble of anonymity made her uncomfortable. She thought of her car in the parking garage, the clumps of snow already melted by the time she got out and began walking to the mall door.

"Hey," the nurse continued. "This is going to sound weird, but are you hungry? I was thinking of getting a drink and some dinner at one of the places inside. You feel like a bite?"

Kristina frowned but said nothing. An elderly woman in a pastel pink coat and hair scarf walked obliviously down the aisle and pushed past them, knocking Deenie forward again. Kristina felt the nurse's knee graze hers and smelled the subtle perfume again. The feeling, the smell, was pleasant. Comforting, somehow. She felt her hands relax.

Deenie waved her hand in front of Kristina's face. "Hello? Some food? What do you think?"

Kristina snapped back to attention. "Sure," she said. "That sounds good, actually. Lead the way."

Despite the mob of shoppers clogging the hallways, the pizzeria chain was relatively empty and sat the women right away. As she slid into the booth, Kristina pulled her jacket from her shoulders. A member of the young wait staff materialized beside their table with a pad and pen. "Can I start you off with something to drink?" she asked brightly, handing each woman a thick, heavy menu.

Kristina laid hers on the table. "Vodka tonic. Tito's, if you have it," she said. "With lime."

The server looked at Deenie. "For you?"

Deenie glanced over the menu at Kristina, then turned to the girl. "I'll have the same. Thank you." When they were alone again, Deenie balanced the menu on the edge of the table and began to flip through the plastic-covered pages. "Do you need to test?" she asked, still looking down.

"What's that?" Kristina asked, folding her hands on top of her menu.

Deenie jutted her chin toward her companion's menu. "Test your blood sugar. Before you eat."

Kristina paused. The comment felt like a trap. "No, no," she said, keeping her voice even. "I'm fine. I'm not hungry. My machine's in the car."

"I'm sorry," Deenie said, looking up and resting her menu on the table. "That was unintentional. Everyone says I need to learn to shut off the 'nurse voice.' My mom was the same way. Always offering unsolicited medical advice on diet and lifestyle."

Kristina smiled. "Your mom's a nurse, too?"

"Yeah," Deenie said. "Was. Pediatric, though." She pushed off her coat and unwrapped her scarf from her neck, revealing a plain white blouse unbuttoned down past her cleavage. Kristina wondered what had happened to the animal-print scrubs. "Up in Maine. Small town near the Canadian border no one's heard of." The server reappeared and placed their drinks in front of them. "Sucked being a kid," Deenie continued. "I practically had to be bleeding out my eyes to stay home sick from school." She laughed and took a sip. "This is good," she said, then to the server, "I think we'll just stick with drinks for now, if you don't mind."

The waitress forced a smile and retreated without a word, leaving the menus on the table.

Kristina swallowed a small mouthful of her drink. "So, *Deenie*. That's unusual. What made you choose it for a nickname?"

The nurse gulped her drink quickly. When she finally rested her glass on the table again, it was half gone. "My mom named me Denise just so she could call me Deenie. You know, like the Judy Blume book."

Kristina ran her finger along the condensation on the edge of her glass. "I think I remember reading it as a kid. Doesn't the girl have scoliosis or something?" She eyed Deenie's collarbone. The skin there was unblemished, smooth and soft-looking. When she looked up to Deenie's face, she realized the nurse had been watching her.

"Well, that makes sense," Deenie said, laughing. "Named after a character with a medical issue. Of course." She looked over toward the bar and made a soft gesture with her hand, to wave down their server, before bringing the glass to her lips and hurriedly swallowing the rest.

She ordered a refill, and, as if on cue, the restaurant was silent for a moment, then resumed with its holiday soundtrack. Annie Lennox purred about a winter wonder-land.

"Eurythmics," Deenie said when the server disap-peared again. "One of the few holiday songs I'm not sick of hearing."

Kristina laughed. "I think that's the point: to play the shit out of Christmas songs until we can't stand the sound of them anymore. That way, come January, we won't feel so depressed that the holidays are over."

Deenie smiled. "You're probably right. It's all a ruse to try to psyche us out." She reached over and squeezed Kristina's hand suddenly, then pulled it back. Her cheeks flushed slightly.

An hour later, as the two women walked out into the bustle of the mall thoroughfare, Deenie stumbled a bit, then put her hand over her face in embarrassment. "I know, I know," she said. "Don't worry: I'm not planning on driving for a while. I still have some things to do here before I head towards Boston." She wrapped her arm around Kristina's and leaned in closer. "Where are you parked? I'll walk you to your car."

Kristina felt her stomach jump. She thought of the nurse's collarbone, how soft the skin looked. The unbut-toned placket of her blouse. "I'm way over in a dark cor-ner," she said. "And it's freezing. I appreciate the offer, but you're not walking me all the way over there."

Deenie hugged her arm tighter, then leaned closer to whisper in Kristina's ear. "Tell you what. I'll walk you, and you can drive me over to the other end of the mall." Her breath was hot on Kristina's skin, making it feel as if a cur-rent had run through it. "I have to walk over there anyway.

This way, I have some company." She leaned her head on Kristina's shoulder. "Besides, it's safer if there are two of us."

The two hurried, still clutching each other, across the parking garage to the furthest corner until Kristina unwrapped her arm to fish inside her jacket for her keys. She pressed the button on the fob twice to unlock both doors, and the car's lights blinked softly in the dim light.

"Wow," said Deenie, giggling. "You weren't kidding. This *is* a dark corner." She opened the passenger door and slid inside.

Kristina shut her door and put her key in the ignition. The radio sprang to life, Bruce Springsteen screaming that Santa Claus was coming to town. She turned to grab the seatbelt when she felt Deenie's hand on her shoulder. "Hey," the nurse's voice whispered. "Before you do that…"

Kristina turned her head, preparing to kiss the woman sitting beside her, when she felt a sharp sting on the side of her neck. Instinctively, she reached her hand up to touch it, and her fingers met Deenie's gloved hands. They were holding a syringe firm against her vein, the nurse's thumb pressing forward the plunger until the barrel's contents emptied themselves into Kristina's bloodstream.

Deenie leaned closer and whispered into her ear, her voice completely absent of any slur or joviality. "Don't take this personally," she said, her tone measured. Businesslike. Patient. "But you were the easiest one yet."

ABOUT THE AUTHORS

LP HERNANDEZ is a writer of horror and speculative fiction. His work is featured in many anthologies and collections, including *Lockdown Horror* from Black Hare Press, *A Monster Told me Bedtime Stories* from Soteira Press, *Forgotten Ones* from Eerie River Press, and *If I Die Before I Wake* from Sinister Smile Press. Several of his stories have been adapted as audio dramas by The NoSleep Podcast, and he was awarded second place in the 2019 *Writer's Digest* Annual Writing Competition for genre fiction. When not writing he serves as a medical administrative officer in the Air Force. He also loves his family, heavy metal, and a crisp high five. Find out more about LP at www.lphernandez.com.

SARAH JANE HUNTINGTON is a writer and lover of horror and strange tales. She works as a psychiatric nurse when she is not writing. She has two rescue cats and one rescue dog, and a fascination with serial killers.

R.E. SARGENT is the author of several novels, as well as a handful of novelettes. R.E.'s novels include *Relative Terror* and The Fury-Scorned series. At a young age, R.E. fell in love with books. While many of the other kids were playing sports, he was reading as many books as he could. He quickly got hooked on mysteries and suspense. It was his love of books and storytelling that led to his passion for writing. One of his biggest inspirations is Dean Koontz. R.E. currently lives in Oregon with his wife and their two fur-children, Riley and Mason. Riley is a Chocolate Lab and Mason is a Bernese Mountain Dog. Find out more about R.E. at www.resargent.com.

ROBB T. WHITE is the author of two hardboiled detective series: Thomas Haftmann and Raimo Jarvi. White has been nominated for a Deringer award and "Inside Man," published in *Down and Out Magazine*, was selected for the *Best American Mystery Stories 2019*. "The Girl from the Sweater Factory," a horror tale, was a finalist in *The Dark Sire* magazine's 2020 awards. *When You Run With Wolves* and *Perfect Killer* were named finalists by *Murder, Meyhem & More* for its Top Ten Crime Books of 2018 & 2019. "If I Let You Get Me," a crime story, was selected for the Bouchercon 2019 anthology. Find out more about Robb at www.tomhaftmann.wixsite.com/robbtwhite.

RICKI WHATLEY is a horror writer whose work has appeared in HellBound's recent anthology, *Satan Rides Your Daughter*. A veteran, a wife, and a mother of three, she lives in Texas with her family and rescued Great Danes.

BEN GAMBLIN is a crime, mystery, and horror writer who currently lives in Tacoma with his wonderful partner and comically large dog. His work has also appeared in print and online publications such as *Déraciné*, *Ink Stains Anthology*, and *The Dark City Mystery Magazine*, as well as anthologies from Forty-Two Books, Underland Press, and Writers Co-op. Find out more about Ben on Instagram @bengamblinofficial.

NIKKI R. LEIGH is a forever-90s-kid wallowing in all things horror. When not writing horror fiction, she can be found creating custom horror-inspired toys, making comics, and hunting for vintage paperbacks. She reads her stories to her partner and her cat, one of which gets scared very easily.

PETER MOLNAR is an author, singer-songwriter, educator, and editor. His short stories have appeared in *City Slab: Urban Tales of the Grotesque*, *Necrotic Shorts*, *Hydrophobia: A Charity An-*

thology to Benefit Hurricane Harvey Victims, and Tenebrous Tales Anthology. His blog, "As the Shadow Stirs," is a mashup of music, movies, horror, and superheroes and can be found on his home webpage. He is the author of *Broken Birds* and *Rhapsody in Red: Two Novellas of the Damned.* He is also a staff writer for *House of Stitched Magazine.* He lives and works in Southeastern Pennsylvania with his wife, daughter, and two cats. Currently, he is at work on his next novel. Find out more about Peter at www.petermolnarauthor.wordpress.com.

BRIDGETT NELSON is a registered nurse turned horror author. Her stories have appeared in numerous anthologies, including the 2021 Splatterpunk Award–nominated *If I Die Before I Wake: Tales of Deadly Women and Retribution.*

She lives in West Virginia with her husband, Doug; teenagers, Parker & Autumn; three pugs—Bodhi, Harlow, and Dexter Morgan, and her frequently aroused, 180-pound St. Bernard, Sal—who has WAY more followers on Instagram than she does. She also likes tarantulas. A lot. Find out more about Bridgett at www.bridgettnelson.com.

DOMINICK CANCILLA lives in Santa Monica, California, just a couple blocks from where part of *Pee-wee's Big Adventure* was filmed, which honestly makes him happier than it has any right to. His horror writing has appeared in dozens of publications over the years. A limited-edition hardcover of his most recent novel, *Tomorrow's Journal,* is scheduled to be published in 2021.

STEVEN PAJAK is the author of novels such as the U.S. Marshal Jack Monroe series and the Mad Swine trilogy, as well as short stories and novellas. When not writing, Steven works as an administrator at a university. He continues to be an avid reader of Stephen King and Dean Koontz, John Saul, Richard Matheson, and many other favorite authors in the horror, suspense, thriller, and general fiction genres. Steven lives in the Chicagoland area with his wife and two teens. Find out more about Steven at www.stevenpajak.com.

REBECCA ROWLAND is the dark fiction author of the short story collection *The Horrors Hiding in Plain Sight* and the novel *Pieces*. She is also curator of the horror anthologies *Ghosts, Goblins, Murder, and Madness: Twenty Tales of Halloween; Shadowy Natures: Stories of Psychological Horror; The Half That You See, Unburied: A Collection of Queer Dark Fiction;* and the upcoming *Generation X-ed.* Her work has appeared in venues such as Bloody Disgusting's *Creepy* podcast, *The Sirens Call, Coffin Bell, Curiouser,* and *Waxing & Waning* and has been anthologized in collections by an assortment of independent presses. Find out more about Rebecca at www.rowlandbooks.com.

MORE FROM SINISTER SMILE PRESS

BETTER OFF DEAD SERIES

Do you love IF I DIE BEFORE I WAKE – The Better Off Dead Series? The Better Off Dead Series delves into the farthest corners of your mind, where your deepest, darkest fears lurk. These masters of horror will haunt your dreams and stalk your nightmares, taking you to the edge of sanity before pushing you to the brink of madness! Read the series now!

If I Die Before I Wake Volume 1: Tales of Karma and Fear
If I Die Before I Wake Volume 2: Tales of Supernatural Horror
If I Die Before I Wake Volume 3: Tales of Deadly Women and Retribution
If I Die Before I Wake Volume 4: Tales of Nightmare Creatures
If I Die Before I Wake Volume 5: Tales of the Otherworldly and Undead .
If I Die Before I Wake Volume 6: Tales of the Dark Deep (12/6/2021)
If I Die Before I Wake Volume 7: Tales of Savagery and Slaughter (6/6/2022)

LET THE BODIES HIT THE FLOOR SERIES

Let the Bodies Hit the Floor is the latest series from Sinister Smile Press, the creators of The Better Off Dead series. These volumes bring you the very best in horror/slasher/stalker/serial killer crime fiction. The more vicious and bloodier, the better. So, put on your pee-pee pants, because you're in for one hell of a dark, sinister journey.

A Pile of Bodies, A Pile of Heads Volume 1
A Pile of Bodies, A Pile of Heads Volume 2

SINISTER SUPERNATURAL STORIES SERIES

The Sinister Supernatural Stories series brings you delicious horror that focuses on elements of the supernatural. Pull up a chair and dig in, but never after dark— everyone knows bad things always happen after dark.

Screaming in the Night: Sinister Supernatural Stories Volume 1 (3/7/2022)

NOVELS

Devil's Gulch: A Collaborative Horror Experience

Made in the USA
Columbia, SC
07 December 2024